CITY OF MASKS
A WAR OF BANES AND DEMONS
BOOK TWO

KEVIN HARKNESS

SHOUTING ROOM BOOKS

CITY OF MASKS

Cover design by Design for Writers

Editing and typesetting by Liminal Pages

Chapter opening illustrations by Galen Dara

https://kevinharkness.ca/

To my family, my friends, and above all, my students, who blessed me with a portion of their lives. It was an honour to watch you grow.

Also by Kevin Harkness

A War of Banes and Demons Series:

City of Demons (Book 1)

City of Sand (Book 3)

City of Shadows (Book 4)

City of Blood and Fire (Book 5)

CONTENTS

CHAPTER 1
DEMON AND MASK

There was a pinch of frost in the air. Spring had arrived to warm the days, but the nights still belonged to winter, and the three men waiting on the hill felt it.

Or maybe they felt something else.

"Are you sure we are safe up here?" asked a young man who shivered in his fine, warm clothes. It was not the first time that night he had asked the question.

The man beside him shrugged, and the third man, a match in age and fine cloth for the first, laughed.

"Really, Lord Kirel, stiffen your spine! Your uncle Gost is just as frightened as you are. So am I, for that matter, but at least we hide it better."

"Proper respect please, Tarock," the oldest of them said. "As an actual lord and not merely the son of one, my nephew outranks us both."

Tarock gave a mock bow. When he straightened, the moonlight showed the strain in his face as he attempted to keep smiling.

"It's close, isn't it, Uncle?" Lord Kirel said. "Can't you both feel it?"

No one answered him.

They didn't need to. The fear had crept in with the cold and laid its fingers under their thick cloaks. It stroked their skin and dug into the muscles and bone beneath until they were almost paralyzed.

Almost.

"The distance tubes," Gost said through clamped teeth.

Three tripods stood before them. On each was fixed a long brass tube with glass lenses set within each end. All three pointed down the hill into a high-walled pocket of stone and brush. Peering through the tubes, they could see torches fixed along each side from the narrow entrance to the blocked end. A solitary figure stood in the light of those torches – a woman, it seemed, though she stood with her back to the watchers.

"Why is she alone?" Tarock asked. "Where are Adrix and his people?"

Without taking his eye from the tube's lens, Gost answered. "Calm yourself. Adrix and the others are leading it towards that defile. To its death, we hope."

"Or to its dinner," Tarock replied, though under his breath. He looked again.

"Can she really do it?" Lord Kirel asked. "I mean, I know she's a Duellist..."

"Ex-Duellist," Tarock said. "She's a labourer now in our friend Chirat's trading house."

"Quiet," said Gost, and it became evident who was in charge from the silence that followed.

Below them, the figure leaned down and picked up a long pole. Torchlight glinted off a narrow blade and thick cross hilt fixed to its end. The woman held the spear in front of her, towards the defile's entrance, ready. She did not have to wait long.

There was movement, a trick of light perhaps, as one shadow seemed to separate from the others. It became more than shadow. The flickering light illuminated a long, beak-like mouth that split open to display rows of sharp teeth and a questing tongue.

"Heaven shield her," Lord Kirel said.

"And us!" Tarock added. The tube shook in his hands.

Gost said nothing.

Two ropy arms appeared in their lenses, tipped with nightmare claws. The creature walked on thin legs, oddly jointed things that carried it into the stone cut. Lord Kirel could see that its small black eyes never left the figure standing at the other end of the defile.

"What-what is it?" he asked and straightened to wipe his mouth and cough.

"What do you mean?" Tarock demanded, perhaps glad of the distraction. "It's a demon, you idiot. If you mean what kind, I don't know."

"Silence!" Gost said. "And watch. It doesn't matter what kind. If she can withstand the fear it casts and kill it, she can kill any kind of beast we bid her to."

There was a hiss that reached up to where they stood arguing, and the three men returned quickly to the distance tubes. The demon snapped its mouth, twice, and charged the woman facing it. She stood, spear outstretched, still as the rocks around her.

"Move, you fool," Gost whispered, "or this is all for nothing."

The creature tore up great patches of the winter-killed sod as it sped forward. The watching men held their breath and willed the woman to break the demon's spell and move.

She did. As the demon made its final leap, she thrust her spear cross-hilt deep into its chest. It struggled for a moment, though whether it was trying to pull itself off the spear or run through it to claw at the woman was unclear, even with the tubes.

The beak snapped once more and was still. The winner tipped the spear so that the horror slid off of it. Then she stabbed it again and again until the shaft cracked, and she cast the spear aside to kick at the corpse with a sustained fury.

Gost and his nephew looked at each other.

Tarock chuckled. "A toast," the young man said and produced a wine skin from under his cloak. "The best wine the Twelfth Ward can offer!"

Lord Kirel accepted the skin and replied, "That must make it the best in the South, since you trade all along the river." He drank and passed it on to his uncle before taking one last look through the distance tube.

Two men, one large and limping and the other thin as rope, came into the defile and pulled the corpse away from the woman's continued attack. The big man did something to the demon's carcass, and the thrill of fear vanished. He stood up and loomed over the spear-woman. There were words, indistinct, and then she turned abruptly to look up the slope.

Lord Kirel had an impression of blond hair, so common in the South, and amazingly dark eyes, but all else was covered in a mask made out of thin stone slices weaved together with gold wire.

He blinked and turned back to his companions.

"The material for the masks, Uncle. You never told me how we acquired it."

Tarock took back the wine skin and answered when it became obvious Gost would not. "Through much wealth and a little bit of blood, Lord Kirel. My mother provided the wealth, but you'll have to ask your uncle about the blood."

Gost saw his nephew's look and shrugged. "The chief of our ward guards is a resourceful man, and he only spilled the least amount of blood necessary to – how did you put it, Nephew? Oh yes, acquire the material."

"To a change, both in profit and power," Tarock said and drank. He passed the skin to Lord Kirel.

"Change is a hard horse to ride," the young lord said. "And we don't know if this will change a single thing."

Gost took a long swallow of wine. It was good. He looked at the others and finally smiled. "You saw what Shirin did just now. Everything has changed, and the bane-hall is finished."

Below them the torches were extinguished, one by one.

CHAPTER 2

THE DUTIES OF A GREEN

"No, no, no! At the first sense of the demon's jewel, you were supposed to get off the horse."

Garet looked up at his master, Tarix, from where he lay on the grass, still smarting from the fall.

"I thought that's what I just did," he said.

Master Tarix laughed and reached out a hand. The dust of grey in her short blond hair and the metal brace on one leg didn't keep her from hauling Garet straight to his feet. She raised one eyebrow, causing the long scar on her cheek to twitch.

"It was supposed to be your decision, not the horse's."

The horse in question was running off towards the distant city walls, Garet's rope-hammer still coiled around the saddle horn. The two banes started walking after it across the fields. It was hard going, for the fields were freshly plowed, but Tarix's leg had improved so much over the last few months that Garet found he no longer had to slow his pace to accommodate her.

She turned her head towards him as they walked. "Why did you hesitate?" she asked.

6

Garet thought for a moment. He had been riding around in a questing circle, trying to sense the fear broadcast by the demon's jewel placed by his fellow bane, Marick, somewhere beyond sight. In truth, there was little to actually fear, since the small, stone-like organ was no longer attached to the rest of the demon, but the horse didn't know that. This particular jewel had come from a Shrieker killed two days ago in the Third Ward.

"Nice and fresh," Marick had told him, before riding off to find a proper hiding place.

A tiny trickle of dread had passed up Garet's backbone, and the hairs on his neck had trembled. He reined in the horse, a usually placid bay, and tried to determine if the sensation came from a particular direction or was just his usual unease at riding a horse. Then he had found himself on the ground with Tarix looking down at him.

"I . . . was trying to make sure," he told her. "In case I was wrong."

Tarix laughed and clapped him on a sore shoulder. "The horse was sure, and I think you might be smarter than a horse, so trust yourself next time and avoid the bruises. Ah, here's Marick with your mount."

A younger bane rode up on a pony, pulling Garet's protesting horse along with him. He looked down at his friend and laughed.

"Here's your horse, Garet. He promises to behave himself if you become a better rider!" The young man threw the reins to Garet, who remounted, calming the animal when it shied away. Set once more in the saddle, he grinned ruefully at Marick.

"It's easy for you to mock me, but please remember that my experiences with horses have been painful ones."

Marick laughed again, perhaps remembering their first

meeting. Marick had been one of a small party led by Master Mandarack, a bane of great skill and kindness, who brought Garet back to the Southern city of Shirath to train as a demonbane.

Though that journey had been both wonderful and terrifying in turns, Garet's worst memories were of the saddle sores he got from travelling on a horse for the first time in his life.

Sadly, Mandarack had perished months ago, dying to save the city from a terrible new demon which could control others of its kind. The chaos caused by that creature, now known as the Caller demon, had torn the city apart, putting the banes, the Duellists, the king, and the ward lords at each other's throats. Those had been desperate times. Garet still bore the scar of a sword thrust through his thigh. Salick, the Gold Sash he felt so strongly about, had a similar scar on one cheek. He did not think it lessened her beauty.

How was she doing with her own new master, Bandat, he wondered, and was she thinking of him as well?

"Garet," Tarix called out, "if you're finished daydreaming, run the circle again!"

He reddened and started off, spurred on by Marick's hoots and this time successfully getting off the horse before it threw him. Tarix only made him repeat the exercise sixteen more times before dismissing him for the day. As the former training master of the banehall, she could be annoyingly thorough.

After closing the jewel up in its silkstone box to block its horror, Marick walked with him through the outer gates of the First Ward. Garet had felt a blessed relief as the lid closed and the box disappeared into one of Marick's many hidden pockets. Silkstone was the only thing known to block out the demon fear, and it was a great shame that there was so little of it in the city.

They left the horses in the care of the stable workers just within the gates. While the younger bane joked with the farrier, Garet paused to look up and appreciate the height and width of the city wall. It had protected Shirath for six hundred years, not by keeping demons out, but by working with all the inner walls, ward walls, gates, and barricades to trap the vicious beasts within so that the banes could corner and kill them. Managing that before the creatures attacked any of Shirath's citizens was the hard part. It was why a bane spent most of his time either training or patrolling.

Garet's eyes traced the curve of the wall. On both the north and south side of the River Ar, the white stone barrier ran in an arc then cut across to close off each half of the city. These half circles were joined by three graceful bridges, and the whole of it was the most beautiful thing Garet had ever seen.

"If you're quite finished daydreaming?" Marick said, in a skilled imitation of Tarix.

Garet smiled and pushed him forward. He knew the little bane meant no disrespect towards his master; Marick worshipped Tarix's skill and generous nature. Mockery was how Marick met the world, and had been his sword and shield since he was left as a child on the streets of the city of Old Torrick, years before he was brought to Shirath to be a bane. Since then, he had gained a well-deserved reputation for insults, practical jokes, and creative acts of revenge.

Now he led Garet through the narrow lanes of the First Ward, threading a path between the four-storey tenements and other, smaller buildings. Each structure was white-washed and bright as new paper in the spring sun. Most buildings in the city were as plain as these, for the citizens of Shirath feared to live in a dwelling that was set apart by colour or decoration, believing it could attract a night-hunting demon to their door. They were braver in their choice of clothing, for they arrayed themselves in a myriad of hues. Burning reds, bright yellows, vivid greens, and every other cheerful shade swirled around him. Moving through these midday crowds, Garet always felt like he was fording a rainbow.

His own clothes were less colourful, but he wouldn't have traded them for gold cloth and jewels. A bane's purple vest might stand out a bit, as did the colour of the sash – Garet's was green, one level above Marick's blue and two levels below a master's red – but they were worn over a black tunic and grey pants tucked into black calf-high boots. Add to this his black hair and a skin darker than anyone else's in the city, and it was a wonder he didn't disappear in the sharp shadows cast between buildings. No, he could not match the fantastic garments of even the poorest citizen edging around him, but it was for this sombre uniform that people made way, smiling and nodding.

Turning to pass through the funnel of an inside gate, Garet caught a glimpse of a figure even more muted than himself, but the person disappeared before he could get a proper look. Who would wear a heavy grey cloak on a fine day like this? Then there came a flash of memory, or at least familiarity. Hadn't he seen this cloaked figure before, always in a crowded street or square, always disappearing when he turned to look? The thought bit at him, but he let it go when they reached the inner gate and passed into the Palace Plaza.

Marick had been sniffing at the many scents of the city

as they walked, shaking his head at some and licking his lips at others. Garet was sure the boy could find his way from ward to ward blindfolded and guided by the smell of pastries or privies, but he suspected Marick might have a particular scent, and plan, in mind.

Garet laid a firm hand on his young friend's shoulder and steered him past the temptations of the market stalls and towards the nearest bridge gate.

"But Garet, aren't you hungry after all those tumbles?" Marick asked. His nose seemed to pull him towards a meat pie cart.

Garet steered harder. "No, I'm not, but I will be if I have to wait and watch you wheedle a bellyful of free food and drink. You know how Master Tarix feels about using our position to beg for such things. Besides, she expects me to be about my duties, and I believe you have a training session after lunch, don't you?"

Marick twisted a bit, but Garet held firm.

"All right, all right! Let's get back to the banehall then, but you know it will be water and cheese and bread – poor fare compared to what I could get us here."

Whether or not I believe him is beside the point, Garet told his gurgling stomach, and marched the younger bane across the East Bridge and into the Banehall Plaza. There was less bustle here, save for on the playing fields, where teams of young men and women hit and kicked a ball back and forth according to rules Garet had yet to understand. Surrounding these fields were low gardens. The trees and bushes were trimmed close to the ground so that a demon would find it difficult to hide. Beyond those gardens stood the banehall.

Not as imposing as the palace with its multitude of glass windows and gilded pillars, the banehall was more practical, a machine built for housing and training banes. Its centre block was four storeys tall, its east and west wings a floor shorter. Over two hundred banes lived here, and Garet could see a constant stream of them coming and going, some Reds and Golds to patrol, some others to communicate with the palace or the ward lords, and a few Greens like Garet going out to train in the fields beyond the wall.

The entrance hall was even more crowded than the streets, but everyone was going in the same direction, called by the luncheon bell. Marick took the lead and found a path through the other banes, pausing occasionally to jump up and search for his friend Dorict.

"Over there!" he shouted to Garet, and the Green pushed after him to grab a seat at a bench in the rear of the dining hall. The bowl of bread was half gone, but Dorict had his hand over it, guarding against the depredations of the ever-hungry young Blues sharing the table.

"You've had firsts already," he said to them. "You have to wait for seconds."

"You didn't!" one accused.

Marick laughed and told the indignant bane, "Three things are sure in this world, my fellow Blue: demons will attack, banes will defend, and Dorict will eat."

His friend scowled but managed to grab another piece of bread before the rest vanished. Dorict was a heavy lad, though he trained as hard as any other bane, and muscles were beginning to replace the softer bulges in his uniform.

"Did you hear, Garet?" he said around a mouthful of bread. "Another demon this morning. Came as far as the orchards to the southwest. Banes at the logging camp nearby tracked and killed it."

"Any injuries?" Garet asked. He took advantage of his

height to poach a wedge of cheese off the plate the harried servers carried table to table.

"No," was all Dorict said, eyeing the cheese and calculating his chances.

Marick thumped the table to get his friend's attention. "That's three in three days, isn't it?"

Dorict nodded and left to follow the server.

Marick leaned back in his chair, looking uncharacteristically thoughtful. "And that's the third week we've had three or more demons attack."

Garet bit into the wedge of cheese and grimaced at the sharp taste. Banehall cheese was rarely the best, coming as it did through the generosity of the ward lords and the king. Swallowing, he looked at the small bane.

"Hasn't this happened before?" he asked.

Marick shook his head. "Not since I've been here, and from the worried look on the masters' faces, I bet it hasn't happened to them either."

Garet looked to the dais at the front of the hall where the thirty or so masters ate. Not all were there, of course. The Reds did many of the city patrols and all of the administrative duties of the hall. There were only twelve present today, and he saw that their faces were drawn and tired. Branet, the hallmaster and so marked by a red sash trimmed with a black stripe, came stalking in and fixed Garet with a less than friendly eye before moving on to take his place at the centre of the masters' table.

"What have you done now?" said a voice behind him, and Garet turned to see Vinir standing there, plate in hand and smiling down at him.

Vinir was Salick's friend, a year older than Garet and the object of Marick's undying affection. That much younger bane straightened up in his chair and brushed a collection of crumbs off his vest.

She shook her head, blond braids swishing back and forth, and laughed. Marick blushed and smiled when she sat down beside him.

"So Garet, what did you do to anger our stormy hallmaster?"

Garet shrugged. "Nothing that I know of, but I'm sure to find out. Hallmaster Branet isn't one to let a fault lie forgotten."

"Those are the truest words ever spoken," Vinir said. "Yesterday he yelled at me in front of the other Golds for laughing at something Bandat said."

"If you want, I could . . ." Marick said, leaving open the suggestion of whatever devious prank he had in mind for the hallmaster.

Vinir rubbed his hair, and Marick wiggled like a puppy.

"Don't you dare, you imp. We've enough trouble with all these attacks without you causing an uproar."

"Is it that bad?" Dorict asked. He had returned with a wedge of cheese in each hand.

"It's not the number so much as that they've happened so close together," Vinir said. "It doesn't feel normal, and if it weren't for the fact that we can still feel the fear they cast, I'd think, you know, the Caller demon had returned."

Garet shivered. The Caller was a unique breed of demon, one who could hide its own and other demons' projections of fear so they could attack without the emotion providing a warning. It even had some control over other demons, or so many thought. Such a creature had not been seen in six hundred years, and its return had almost destroyed the city. Master Mandarack had killed it at the cost of his own life. The thought that another might attack kept Garet from sleep many nights.

After their meal, Garet walked the reluctant Marick right to the door of the largest training room and made sure the slippery bane joined the others. As he left, he shook his head. There was no guarantee Marick wouldn't slip off again, but he had done his duty and now had other tasks to complete. As he arrived at the door to the smaller training room, Garet heard the dull slap of wooden poles on sand-bags. Looking in, he saw a line of young banes, children really, striking the bags with long poles while a master supervised.

"Turn those hips, Corfin! Snap your shoulders into the strike, Sata! On the count: one, two, three . . ."

The count went on while Garet hung his sash and vest on a hook. He took up a pole from where it stood in the rack and joined Master Forlinect in watching the young Black Sashes hit the bags with less and less force.

"Do what you can with them, Garet," the Red said when most had collapsed onto the floor, breathing in great gulps of air. "This lot is claw bait or I'm a Trader!"

He turned and walked to the small office and equip-ment room to fuss with the paperwork, or perhaps just fuss.

Garet watched him go. He had some sympathy for the Red. He knew Forlinect wanted Tarix's approval. His devo-tion to the former training master was strong, proven by the fact that he had changed sides in the bitter civil war within the banehall last year just to protect her, and Tarix had pushed Hallmaster Branet to name Forlinect training master while her leg healed. Garet knew the newly made master was grateful, and he truly wanted him to succeed, but still, working these children to exhaustion would not make them banes any faster.

He looked them over, trying to think of a better method. What could eight-to-twelve-year-olds do that was useful? His own experience was not helpful. He had been older, sixteen, when he first wore the Black Sash. At that time, they didn't use weapons at all. They just ran around the banehall every morning and did exercises with weighted clubs and such until they passed the physical and knowledge tests and became Blues. Then the training changed, and the poles and hooked ropes came out. After the banehall's conflicts had ended, Tarix altered the training routines. Garet thought this new way was much better. It might make Black Sashes feel more like proper banes if they started off using weapons in training.

"All right, get up now. On your feet. Slow your breathing. That's right, one breath at a time. Pick up your poles and get your wind back."

The Black Sashes stood in an unsteady line and looked at him, apprehensive but ready. That was the look of a bane, Garet thought. The people in this hall did not have the ability to fight demons because they were born heroes, but because they had learned to live with some kind of fear. At the centre of each was a wound. Garet's was caused by an abusive father and brothers, as well as the prospect of a wasted life on a backwater farm. Each of these children had also suffered some kind of dread and, like him, had learned to fight against it – or at least live in spite of it. So, if they did not seem ready to charge forth with their staffs, neither did they seem likely to flee.

No, we are not shining heroes, but scarred children training for an endless war.

"We'll do walking exercises first," Garet told them. He

demonstrated the crossover step, eyes fixed on the far wall and pole held out in a guard position. He moved among them, making gentle corrections and praising those who improved.

"Now back to the bags," he told them, to general groans. "Come now, you won't mind the practice when you've got a Shrieker in front of you. Then it will be your weapon against its claws, and the winner gets to live! Quick now, in position."

He again demonstrated the proper form, hips rotating and upper body snapping into the strike. He set them to it slowly, only allowing speed when the form was correct. He walked down the line and saw a girl wedged in behind the sandbags, head down and arms crossed over her chest.

She must have been hiding there the entire time. At first he was irritated at such deception, but he pushed it away with a deep breath and approached her. The banehall could be a frightening place for newcomers.

"Hello there. I didn't see you before. Come out now and show me how you hit the bag. Come on, you're a bane, aren't you? Here, take this pole. It's about your size."

He handed her one of the smaller staffs, and she took it after a long hesitation.

"Grip it with both hands," he said, tugging on the sleeve of her left arm, which had slipped behind her when she took the pole. He tugged again, and the arm came out. The end of the sleeve was empty, the cuff tucked in over the wrist.

The girl stood still as stone, though the pole trembled in her single hand. Somebody tugged his own sleeve, and he looked down to see a small boy staring up at him.

"She can't be a bane, can she, if she only has one hand?" he asked.

Garet considered his answer before speaking. What he said would be heard by this boy, his fellows, and especially the girl. She stood waiting, her hair swept forward. Garet had yet to see her face.

"Well, Corfin, isn't it?" he said to the boy. "Do you know a master called Tarix? She needs a big iron brace just to walk around, and she's the best bane in this hall. And the master who brought me here had only one good arm. That was Master Mandarack, who became hallmaster and was famous in the city."

"Could he fight demons with one arm?" Corfin asked, doubtful.

Garet smiled and put a hand on his shoulder. "I'd known him for only a few days when I saw him kill a great big Basher demon with that sharpened shield he used, the one hanging up in the dining hall. You know he was the one who killed the Caller demon, don't you?"

The boy paled. He and several others half raised a hand to the sides of their heads before self-consciously lowering them again. Ordinary people in Shirath would touch a finger to their ears to flick away the word "demon" upon hearing it, lest their luck turn and they meet one. New banes were taught to think this foolish, but it took much repetition to set it firmly in their minds.

Garet slapped the boy on the back. "You see? One arm is no trouble! Now, what's your friend's name?"

Corfin frowned. "My friend? Her name's Allifur. She's from the Tenth Ward, but she doesn't talk."

Garet waved them back to striking bags and took Allifur over to a bench set against the wall. Sitting beside her, he held out both his hands, palms up.

"Put your hand and your arm on top of my hands and push down as strongly as you can," he told her.

18

It took a while for her to obey, and his arms were beginning to ache from holding them out when she shifted around and did as he asked. He let her push until the tension began to ease from her neck and shoulders. Her head came up a bit, and he caught sight of green eyes peering through the fringe of blond hair.

"Did Master Mandarack really have only one arm?" she whispered.

"Yes, he did. His left arm was withered from when he was a child. He couldn't use it at all. You, on the other hand – if you will excuse the expression – have a lot of strength in that arm of yours. You must use it a lot."

The whisper came again. "I use it to hold things."

Garet smiled and stood up. "That's good. It means it can help you."

"How?" She spoke louder now, demanding, perhaps begging for an answer she couldn't find herself.

Garet smiled. "People say I think too much," he said. "They say, 'Garet's thinking again, so watch out!' So I'm going to think about how you can use that arm as a bane, and you are going to help me think."

They tried the pole again and found a way to brace her arm against the shaft to aid in the swing. After a few slips and false starts, Allifur started hitting the bag with a satisfying thud. She would curl her arm around the staff to retrieve it, then push it with her forearm to strike. The others paused to watch her.

"Good one, Allifur," Corfin told her. "Do it again!"

She did it again, and again, until Garet set them back to cross-stepping up and down the floor. This time Allifur joined in.

"How did you do it?" Forlinect said behind him. "I

couldn't get a word out of her. I thought we would have to send her back to her ward. My first failure."

Garet shrugged. It wasn't his place to tell a master his business, but then again, it wouldn't be the first time he had done so.

"I just remembered how it was when I came here. It was so strange, and my welcome was . . . well." He didn't finish. Forlinect coughed and looked away, perhaps remembering how badly the hallmaster of that time, Adrix, had treated the first bane come from the Midlands.

"It was hard," Garet said, "harder than anything I've ever done. Many times, I wanted to run back to the Midlands, or anywhere else, really, but one thing stopped me. There were people here, a few, who were on my side. Masters like Mandarack and Tarix. Good banes like Salick and Vinir, and even odd ones like Marick and Dorict."

Forlinect chuckled at this. Marick's reputation as a troublemaker was legendary in the hall.

"And that was enough?" he asked.

"It was for me, and I think it will be for these Blacks as well."

There, that was meddling enough, but he hoped the training master knew that Garet wished him well.

The Red rubbed his chin. "Well, that's better advice than I've been giving myself. Off you go to your studies now. Come early next time, and we'll cut some of the poles into sticks and let them have at the bags one-handed with those. It will even things out for her, at least a bit, and after all, some might be mad enough to choose axe and club over something sensible like a spear."

Garet smiled. That was a great compromise on Forlinect's part. He was a spear bane through and through, the best Tarix had ever trained, or so she claimed.

According to her, Forlinect could put the point of his weapon through a demon's eye at a dead run.

Garet retrieved his vest and sash and left Forlinect contemplating which poles were to be sacrificed. When he arrived at the room he shared with Marick and Dorict, he took down a coil of wire-reinforced rope from its hook. He wondered what Forlinect thought about Garet's own weapon, the rope-hammer, as he stretched out its length, checking for tears or fraying. Luckily he was alone, for extended it ran from one corner of the room diagonally to the other.

It was no spear, though it would obviously outreach one. Neither did it have the heft of an axe or club, though it could be made to strike like one. Tarix had offered him this weapon when she heard of his accuracy in throwing stones, a talent picked up herding the stubborn sheep on his family's farm. One end of the line was fixed to a heavy spiked ball, and the other to a short-hafted tool that was half pick and half hammer. He had suffered many bruises learning how to fling it out or wrap it around a target, but this weapon had protected him against both demon and human adversaries many times.

Reluctantly, he coiled it again and replaced it on the hook. Much as he might want to practise with it, his duties were not over for the day. He had set himself a task, and in the space of time he had before the dinner bell, he toiled at it.

Beside a desk claimed for his own, partly due to his rank and mostly due to his obvious need for workspace, stood a wooden box of records. The old scrolls and tattered logbooks were on loan from Master Arict, the ancient Red who kept the hall's history. Garet was going through them, a box at a time, and making notes as he did so. His intention was to discover why the Caller demon suddenly appeared last year, and what else might follow if, as he feared, a six-hundred-year-old fixed pattern of demon attacks was changing. He tapped his brush's wooden handle against his chin. He should record the increased attacks mentioned at the midday meal, for in his research so far he could recall no mention of a sudden jump in the number of demons.

He was soon lost in the work, for it was much suited to his nature. He had told Allifur the truth; people did believe he thought too much. That only added to his oddness for some citizens of Shirath, but, as an outsider from the Midlands, Garet would always be an oddity, for few people travelled to see other places or peoples. Indeed, no one could, without the protection of banes. So his dark hair and skin, inherited from his mother, kept him from fading into the background. Once seen, he was known, and once known, he was judged.

Despite his resentment of this treatment, he had worked long and hard to improve people's opinion of him, though Branet's glare at lunch told him he still had some way to go in that regard. That was one reason he liked reading. A book might give horrible opinions of a battle, or a treaty, or some great person long dead, but it never criticized the reader. A book always told you things as if it was your dearest and most accepting friend.

Comforting as the process was, however, he had come no closer to an understanding of the Caller or these new attacks when Salick burst into the room, trident in hand.

Before he could say a word, she barked, "You can't wear that vest! What have you been doing to get it so stained?"

Garet took a deep breath. He was becoming very familiar with Salick's moods.

"I've been training Black Sashes, spilling some ink, but

mainly falling off a horse, if you really need to know," he said as calmly as he could manage. It was no use trying to match outrage to outrage with Salick; she always seemed to have more in reserve.

She swelled up once more and opened her mouth. Abruptly, she closed it and left the room.

Garet waited. After ten breaths, there was a knock on the door.

"Come in," he said.

The door opened, and Salick walked in, blank-faced. She carefully propped her weapon against the wall.

"Garet, we are called upon by Hallmaster Branet to accompany him to a formal dinner at the palace. Every ward lord and the king, of course, will be in attendance. Is there some way you can make yourself presentable for such an occasion?"

Garet jumped out of his chair, spilling more ink.

"The palace? Why didn't you say so? I have to get a new vest and tunic. Claws, these pants are muddy too. Wait here while I go down to the stores and see what they have."

Salick stomped her foot. "I did say so, or I was about to. Come on, hurry! We only have a bit until the first bell, and that's when we leave."

Garet almost ran over Dorict, who was coming into the room with a pile of clothing in his arms.

"Claws! Sorry, Dorict. Wait, are those for me?"

He grabbed at a clean tunic obviously too big for the Blue. A green sash lay under it.

"Of course it's for you," the younger bane grumbled. "Salick told me about the dinner, well, yelled it at me really, when we met on the stairs, and I remembered how you looked at lunch. Did you manage to stay on that horse at all?"

"Briefly," Garet replied. He stripped off his tunic and undershirt while Salick studied the corner of the room. Luckily, his boots only needed buffing, and there was a bit of water in the basin to wash his face and hands.

The dinner bell sounded from the floor below.

"Claws!" said Garet, struggling with the buttons of his new tunic.

"Finished?" Salick asked. By her tone it was clear the corner had lost whatever interest it might have held for her.

"Yes. I owe you, Dorict. You are a treasure as a friend!"

Dorict smiled. "You can repay me by asking Lord Andarack when he will call me again to work on the silk-stone suit of armour. It's been weeks since I was last summoned, and we still have much testing to do. Now here, take your rope-thing and go!"

Garet fastened the last of his tunic buttons on the stairs. Halfway down, he paused so that Salick could adjust his sash. Her own was perfectly draped over one shoulder. She leaned her trident against the wall and pulled his sign of rank straight, bright green slashing across the deep purple of his tunic. When she was done, she checked to make sure the stairs were empty of others and kissed him quickly on the lips.

"There, that's for being so savage when I burst through your door. You were so shocked. You looked at me like I was a demon!"

Garet wished there was time for a longer kiss.

"No demon I've faced could match you for creating pure terror. But I can understand why you were upset at a summons from the palace."

Salick grimaced in reply.

Last winter when the two banes were commanded to arrange a perilous meeting with King Trax, Salick had told

Garet of her history with Shirath's ruler. Before Trax came to the throne, he had tried to force marriage on her, the daughter of a ward lord but already a bane. There had been harsh words and perhaps blows in that confrontation, and Salick had never forgiven Trax. So despite the king's agreement to support the banehall, Garet had little trust in the man, and Salick had none.

She brushed at Garet's collar but didn't speak. If she had, she might have betrayed some weakness in her voice, and that was something the Gold could never bear to do.

When they reached the bottom of the stairs, they saw Hallmaster Branet standing by the open doors of the hall. He was having words, and not pleasant ones, with Relict, a Red and husband to Garet's own master, Tarix.

"No," the hallmaster said in a voice just a touch below the level of a shout. "We won't make any more attempts to convince them. Let Solantor and the other cities mind their own halls, and I will mind ours. Am I making myself clear?"

He tapped the spikes of his iron-bound club against one boot.

Relict flushed. He had known Branet for a long time, and the change in their relationship from equality to subservience appeared to be wearing on the smaller man's good humour.

"Branet – forgive me, *Hallmaster Branet* – there are rumours that this increase in attacks is taking place all over the South. Hallmaster Corix from Old Torrick Banehall has sent letters . . ."

"I know what she sent," growled Branet, "and that is my concern, not yours. Now, don't you have patrols to organize?"

"Yes, Hallmaster," Relict said in a voice so cold it belied the arrival of spring. He turned on his heel and left.

The hallmaster switched his glare to Salick and Garet where they waited at the bottom of the stairs pretending they were deaf.

"You two, come along. Banes should be punctual," Branet shouted.

As they ran to catch up with the hallmaster's long strides, Garet said to Salick in a voice just a touch above the level of a whisper, "Well, the company may be sour, but at least the food should be good."

CHAPTER 3

THE HEIGHTS AND THE DEPTHS

T he food was very, very good, but they had to endure much before they could enjoy it.

The banes arrived as the light in the west was changing from red to silver. Salick, always concerned with the hall's reputation, had insisted they both wear winter cloaks, which gave them a certain dark dignity but were over-warm when one was running after an angry hallmaster. Once they were out of the plaza and onto the bridge, the cool breeze coming off the river was a blessing. They were not alone in enjoying it. Many still made their way from one half of the city to the other, and Garet had to step out of the path of a wagon loaded with bags of grain. He waved away the driver's apology and caught up with Branet and Salick just as they stepped through the palace-side gates.

He wished he had time to pause and enjoy the scene. The colourful crowds, now muted in the fading light, passed back and forth across the expanse of stone pavement. Thousands could fit inside the plaza – and often did. Tonight there were only hundreds, and most of those were making their way back to their wards. A few merchants still called out hopefully from the forest of market stalls that occupied the eastern end of the plaza, but their cries were going unanswered. But all this Garet had to take in at a brisk walk, as Branet showed no signs of slowing down or stopping his grumbling.

"You two remember that the dignity of the hall is on display tonight. Do not speak until you are spoken to and keep hall business to yourselves!" he told them.

Salick nodded. "Of course, Hallmaster, but may I ask why Garet and I are attending this . . . event?"

The hallmaster ignored the question and climbed the steps leading to the palace doors. He was all energy and anger tonight, Garet thought.

Like most nights lately.

The door guards surveyed them with little interest or approval and let them enter. A more respectful servant took their weapons and cloaks and led them into an anteroom already full of the decorated elite of the city. Amid all this glory of jewels and lace, Garet felt for a moment as he had when he first came to the city, less than a year ago. Seeing his black hair and darker skin, some of the pale, blond people of the town had called him "the Midland crow."

Here, he felt like the crow again until Salick pinched his arm and whispered in his ear, "What are you staring at? You've seen all these ward lords before."

"But not in such fine dress," Garet whispered back. "And some I've never met – or seen – at all. Who is that one, the one with the pregnant woman?"

"That's Lord Kirel of the Thirteenth Ward, very young to be a ward lord, if you ask me. His uncle is there beside them, Gost, I think his name is. Supposedly he's the real power in that ward. And," she said, taking his arm and leading him over to a small alcove, "if you want to attend such dinners, you don't refer to the wife of a lord as 'pregnant.' Pregnancy is for mares, cows, and common people. Lord Kirel's wife, Kaela is her name, is 'guarding within her the future hope and luck of her ward.' Understand?"

"I think so," Garet said, rubbing his upper arm. "Speak nicely about my betters or you'll pinch me again."

Salick was spared the necessity of further answer or punishment by Branet's peremptory summons.

"Come here, now! They are about to call the lots."

"Is this a meal or a game?" Garet asked, and found the question smothered under Branet's glare.

A steward resplendent in a green coat and silver pants came to the door of the anteroom. All fell silent. She looked the guests over, found them wanting, yet graciously allowed them to enter the dining room. Once inside, Branet pushed Garet and Salick to a space against the wall. The others found their own spaces until all four walls were lined with aristocratic splendour. No one attempted to sit at the long tables arranged in a square around the centre of the room.

Garet looked around. There was a sense of anticipation, as if their luck – a very important thing in the city of Shirath – was about to be tested. The steward announced, "Honoured guests, the Calling of the Places begins," and another steward, a man this time, appeared with two bowls, each full of small wooden plaques. He held one while the chief steward took the other around the room, allowing each guest to remove a single token.

The bowl was held too high to see within, and Garet grabbed the first one his questing hand touched. He looked at it. It was a simple wooden tile that bore nothing but a number in gilt, a twenty-six. He looked at Salick's. It had the number sixteen.

The chief steward took the other bowl and reached in a long-fingered hand. "To the king's right, number ten."

The pregnant, or rather hope-guarding woman clapped her hands together and was escorted to the table at the other end of the room from where Garet stood. She was seated in a cushioned chair beside an even more magnificent central seat that must belong to the king. Many congratulated her as she passed by, but only some of the smiles seemed genuine.

As the steward prepared to draw again, a hand knocked Garet's and he dropped his token. Salick and Branet both frowned, and he hurriedly bent to pick it up. He paused in mid-movement when he saw that there were two tokens on the ground.

"I'm so sorry," said a woman's voice near his ear.

He turned his head and saw a pair of very beautiful green eyes regarding him. They were the most enchanting eyes he had ever seen, and the rest of her face was just as lovely. Later, when he was remembering what happened, he decided that was why he lost the power of speech.

When it became obvious he wasn't going to reply, the young woman laughed a little, not cruelly, and scooped both tokens up – a feat in itself, considering the copious folds of her gown – and handed one to Garet.

He nodded his thanks and tried to smile back. Salick's pinch was barely noticeable.

"Forgive his clumsiness, my Lady Lysere," Salick said, and Garet recovered enough to add a stammering apology of his own.

"Not at all, Salick, isn't it? I remember you from those endless meetings after the troubles of the winter. You were so polished then, I hoped you might be a master now."

Garet took refuge in Salick's obvious embarrassment to compose himself.

The hallmaster turned to the young woman and frowned.

"Masters are not so easily made, Lysere, or has the king been telling you differently?" he growled.

Salick looked shocked, but Lysere merely smiled up at the large bane.

"It seems manners are made even less easily than masters in the hall. Ah, your number has been called, Green. I wish you a happy supper."

The steward was standing in front of Garet, expectant and displeased. Garet could not remember doing anything except dropping his token, and that wasn't really his fault, but it seemed his sin wasn't clumsiness, but good luck. He was taken to the head table and placed at the left side of the king's chair.

No one except Lysere smiled as he passed.

The rest of the places were soon called, and the guests seated. Salick was at one side, far to his left. She sat beside a ward lord Garet knew very well, Lord Andarack of the Eighth Ward, brother of the late Hallmaster Mandarack. Branet was placed across from Garet and looked unhappy with his seatmate, a hatchet-faced woman who seemed just as dissatisfied with him. Besides Lysere and Kaela, there were a few others scattered around the table who were neither ward lords nor banes. Four temple priests sat silent in their blue robes, perhaps waiting for Heaven's guidance before starting a conversation. Garet also noted a physician and an elderly steward and guessed they would be the heads of their respective schools. At the side table to his right, and every bit as uncommunicative as the priest beside her, was Dasanat, the newly named head of the Mechanicals School. It was she who had made Tarix's brace, and could perhaps fit the child Allifur with some weapon capable of killing a demon. Garet was glad to see her. She had been of great assistance in the hall's fight against the Caller demon, and he counted her as a friend, though an unusually distracted one. He nodded at her, and she scowled in reply.

Garet shook his head. Dasanat was never happy in company, unless that company was made of gears, glass, and spark containers.

"Stand for the king," intoned the chief steward, her voice making much of each syllable in her announcement, and the company rose as King Trax entered the room. His dress was subdued; he wore a white tunic over black pants and boots, with a purple cape over all. The jewels on his collar and sleeves were equally understated. The steward removed the cape, and Trax sat down. After a long breath of time, and at some signal Garet failed to catch, the rest did as well. His was the last bottom to hit a cushion.

Unsure of what to do next, his nerves were quieted by a miracle taking place in the empty centre of the table square. Parts of the floor were disappearing.

With a muted grinding sound, five sections of the tiled surface descended into darkness. A marvel, he thought, though none of his neighbours or anyone else in the room seemed to take notice. After some time, the grinding started up again and the sections reappeared, but not unburdened. The four corner sections now bore tables laden with plates, and these plates were piled high with food. The centre section had an even greater cargo, for it held men and women, eight in all, dressed in palace livery. Eight expressionless faces appeared first, then eight sets of stiff shoulders, then the whole, elegant length of them until they could step off the platform and busy themselves with distributing the feast.

"One of Andarack's toys," a voice to his right said, and Garet turned in his chair to face the king.

"It is amazing," Garet said, and added hastily, "Your Majesty."

"Lord Andarack is simply full of amazing, isn't he? These trapdoors and their gears, automatic gate closers, and of course, those very interesting spark containers."

"And the silkstone suit," Garet added. He had meant to ask Andarack about the suit, as Dorict had requested, but he would have to wait until after dinner since the distance between them was beyond mannerly speech.

"Ah yes," the king replied, "the suit was indeed amazing," and turned to speak to the lady of the Thirteenth Ward, Kaela, on his right.

Garet smiled at the server who brought his plate. In return, he received no indication of his existence. Frowning, he examined his food. It was pickled vegetable and fish, though for some reason it had been arranged to look like a bird flapping its wings. Mis-decorated or not, it was delicious, and he finished it with a speed that probably broke all the rules of decorum.

"Don't they feed you in the hall, bane?" asked the older man to his left.

Garet swallowed quickly and said, "They do, but not so well as this." He remembered that Salick said this man was from the Thirteenth Ward, but not a lord, so he added, "sir."

"Gost," the man said and extended a hand.

Garet took it. "Garet," he said, and the man smiled.

"I know who you are, bane. Your heroics during the

recent . . . troubles were relayed to us by Mandarack before he died. Yes, many sang your praises then, but I wonder why you are here now."

Garet wasn't quite sure what to say. Branet had been very clear about not discussing banehall business, but he had also said he should speak when spoken to. Gost had spoken to him and now waited for an answer to his almost-question.

"As a lowly Green Sash, I merely follow orders; I don't question them, sir."

Gost laughed. "Well said, well said! Forgive my intrusion, Green. Perhaps I should not have pried since I am here only by 'orders' as well."

"How so, sir?"

Gost took a drink of the wine a server placed in front of him. "Ah, good stuff this. Ninth Ward, I think. They'll soon take over the Eighth Ward's primacy in the vineyards. Now, why am I here? This dinner is to celebrate my nephew's production of an heir, to put it bluntly. I am here by courtesy, as is Kaela."

Garet said the safest thing he could think of. "Congratulations, sir, to your family and your ward."

"Thank you, bane. Heaven has blessed our ward in many ways recently."

Gost then turned to speak to the woman on his left, a ward lord named Braxa, signalling their conversation was at an end.

Garet was then allowed to eat in peace through three more plates. Each dish was more delicious and more ornate than the last, and he slowed at each course until his pace more closely matched the others. The moving platforms groaned again, and he groaned with them. All this rich food was gurgling in his stomach, but he dared not refuse anything. Looking over to where Salick sat, he saw her shared discomfort. Of all the guests, only Dasanat the Chief of the Mechanicals ignored the growing piles of delicacies before her, picking at whatever plate was nearest while she stared off into the distance. Servers hovered around her, but she was impervious to their distress.

Garet sighed and forced down another mouthful. Dorict would have been a better choice, he thought. At least he had more capacity.

At last the final plate of sweet pastries from the Tenth Ward had been consumed and hot drinks distributed. The king turned back to Garet and chuckled.

"A serious test of one's stomach, eh bane? Don't worry if you are overwhelmed. Most of us at this table train for it, just as you train in the hall. It's true! We start off in childhood with large breakfasts and move on to enormous lunches until we are old enough and fit enough to handle a formal dinner!"

"Your Majesty is in high spirits tonight," the woman on his right, Kaela, said. "Is this the Midland boy I have heard so much about?"

She extended a hand, and Garet rushed to stand and bow before taking it. Trax leaned back to allow the contact.

"And who has been telling you about him, fair Kaela?" he asked when Garet resumed his seat. "Your devoted husband, Kirel, or your most able uncle-in-law, Gost?"

"Probably both, Your Majesty. After all, the lad is famous in the storytellers' tales, though I expected him to be older and perhaps not so small."

Garet smiled, feeling the burden of his reputation squeeze him smaller still.

Trax laughed.

"Oh, size is not an issue with this one! He's a young man

who fights with his head as well as – what was it you used to attack Draneck that night in my chambers? A fire poker?"

"Yes, Your Majesty, though it was your butler who was the hero that night," Garet said, wishing one of Andarack's amazing machines would open beneath his feet and carry him to the banehall.

"Didn't you also injure that horrible banemaster, oh, what was he called?" Kaela said. Her delicate condition took none of the malice from her tone.

"Adrix," Garet replied. He had lamed the ex-hallmaster with one throw of a stone that shattered his knee. If he hadn't, Adrix would have killed Mandarack, so Garet had made the choice to cripple one to save another.

"Old stories now, my dear Kaela," Trax said, and pointedly turned back to Garet.

"Speaking of old stories, I read a funny one the other day. It was in an ancient scroll of palace proceedings. What was it now? Ah, I remember! You must know, bane, that the people of the wards once lived in different areas of the Ar Valley, until the beasts came and drove them all together. Along with their cows and cots, they brought different ways of measuring things. It was very confusing! What would be a yard in the Sixth Ward would be three-quarters of a yard in the Eighth. A pound to the king would be three ounces to the Traders, and so on around the whole circle of the new city. And of course none could agree as to whose weights and measures would be the standard in Shirath. Trade within the city was chaotic, but no ward would give way to another on the matter. When harangued about this in court one time too many, our first king, Shirat, yelled at his chief of guards to close his eyes and walk out fifty paces into the Palace Plaza, which was just a dirt field then, I suppose, and bring back the first person he saw when he opened them again."

At a wave from Trax, a server hurried over and refilled his wine glass. The king took a sip before continuing.

"Well the guard did as he was told and returned with a cursing, spitting woman of the Tenth Ward who wanted nothing more than to get back to her vegetable stall. At Shirat's command, every part of her was measured and weighed. The distance from her heel to hip became the standard yard. The length of her little finger became the inch. Her weight divided by a hundred, for Shirat claimed she struck the chief of guards a hundred times during the process, became the pound, and all other measures followed."

Garet pondered this. "What about the gallon and quart?"

Trax smiled. A handsome man, still young, he knew how to be charming.

And he expected his charms to work, Garet knew.

Trax stroked his chin in apparent thought. "Those came from the weight of different volumes of water in pounds, I believe."

Garet shook his head. "Then what about the league? Surely she wasn't long enough to measure that?"

Trax took another sip. A buzz of conversation surrounded them, but to Garet, it seemed Trax was focused only on him.

"Some say it was a multiplication of the yard, but the version I read says that King Shirat so liked the woman's spirit he offered to marry her then and there, his own wife having been claw-killed. The terrified woman bolted from the court, and the league was measured from the king's throne to the point where the guards finally caught up with her."

Garet laughed, almost against his will, then caught Hallmaster Branet's disapproving look. He covered up his coughing with a gulp of wine.

"Your Majesty is well read in the history of the city," Garet said, when he could speak again.

He wondered why Trax was being such a delightful host. In Salick's oft-stated opinion, Trax was first and foremost a manipulator of others, getting what he wanted with a mix of flattery and threat, but what could he possibly want from Garet? His usefulness to the king should have ended months ago when the Caller demon was killed and harmony restored between the hall and the palace.

"Well read? Oh, that's Barick's doing. I'm afraid he found the duties of palace butler too stressful, having to kill Duellist assassins and such, so I created a new position: City Historian. He's writing a complete history of Shirath – a huge undertaking, he claims, as I'm sure you would agree. As a matter of fact, you might be able to aid him in this important task."

Ah, Garet thought, *here comes the hook to catch the unwary fish*. He must swim carefully if he didn't want to get caught up in a dangerous game of politics. The last one had almost killed both him and Salick.

"The banehall is always happy to assist the palace, Your Majesty, but in what way?"

"Oh, researching bane history, I believe. The palace keeps its own records; the wards maintain theirs separately, and of course the banehall does as well. Can't have a complete history without all of them, can we?"

Faced with such logic, Garet decided the only thing he could do was squirm out of a definite answer.

"I'm afraid Hallmaster Branet will have to agree to sharing the hall's records, and to my own participation."

Trax waved Garet's concerns away with one manicured hand. "Oh, he has already agreed. That's why I asked him to bring you here tonight, so that I could propose it to you. I take it, then, that you will do this, for the city?"

Garet felt the hook digging in and saw no way to shake it out. He took another sip of wine and glanced over at Salick. The look she was giving Trax should have set him on fire.

"Salick looks well tonight," Trax said. "If you can look well while so obviously wishing others ill. Hmm, on second thought I'm not sure that's possible. Poor Salick, we will never be friends, I fear. Well, bane. What do you say?"

He slapped Garet on the back.

It was to Garet's credit that neither his dinner nor a heartfelt sigh escaped him.

"I am at Your Majesty's – and your ex-butler's – service."

"Excellent!" said Trax. "I'm sure Barick will soon be in touch with you."

He pushed back his chair and stood. The rest of the group hastily, and in some cases unsteadily, joined him. The temple priest on Dasanat's right shook the mechanical to get her attention. She jumped up and frowned at her surroundings, clearly not quite remembering where she was.

Trax waved his hands.

"I thank you for coming to celebrate the future heir of the Thirteenth Ward, warmly and maternally protected by the fair Kaela, who was so fortunately seated beside me," he said.

He paused while the company made polite applause in

the Shirath way of slapping the back of one hand with the fingers of the other.

"Thankfully there is no need for a council meeting this night, though perhaps the hallmaster might linger for a few words. Goodnight, and may Heaven shield you all!"

The stewards led the other guests out with great efficiency, leaving Garet and Salick waiting in the antechamber for Branet. Garet frowned. He had found no chance to talk to Lord Andarack about the silkstone suit.

"What did he want?" Salick asked when they were alone. Her eyes pinned Garet as if they were the tines of her trident.

"Trax? How do you know he wanted anything?"

"That trick Lysere did with the tokens. You were manoeuvred into sitting beside him. Didn't you see? That was her own place she gave you!"

"No, I didn't see that," Garet admitted. He went over the event and found nothing to support her accusation. Lysere had seemed perfectly honest and friendly.

"Well," Salick said, folding her arms across her chest. "Perhaps you were thinking of something else at the time."

Garet frowned. It was true. He had found Lysere . . . distracting. Had the young woman used that against him so that she could switch the tokens?

He reddened at the thought.

"If I did, I apologize, but what difference would it have made? The seats were called out by chance."

Salick's long blond braids swung as she shook her head.

"The Calling of the Places is a very old tradition, and one that is often manipulated. That chief steward had more than lace up her sleeves! What do you think they teach them in the Stewards School?"

"To serve their masters, I suppose," Garet said. He

hoped Branet would make a quick return so that this conversation could end. It was too reminiscent of his first days with Salick, when he was the ignorant stranger and she was his very superior teacher.

"Yes," Salick said, in that familiar lecturing tone. "And Lysere – who will be married to Trax soon, if the city gossip is any guide – would be miraculously chosen by those 'random' lots to sit by his side. A sign from Heaven, one could say, or the manipulation of a clever steward serving her master. But Lysere had other ideas! She wanted you to take her seat so that Trax could get something from you. What was it?"

Blushing deeper, he told her.

Salick ran a finger along the scar that marked one of her cheeks.

"Helping with research? Well, I can't see any plot in this . . . yet. And we do owe Barick something, I suppose."

"Salick, why do they draw lots anyway? Why can't Trax just decide who sits where?" Garet asked, hoping to change the subject. "He is the king, after all!"

Salick shrugged. "Because people would complain. The king's table is the highest honour, and besides, there is always one ward lord feuding with another – you must have seen how Lords Sacourat and Birsal glared at each other. There's a reason they were at different tables. No king wants a duel fought with fish forks at his feast!"

She glanced at the door to the dining hall, but it was still closed. It may have been Garet's imagination, but he thought he heard raised voices beyond it. Salick tapped the butt of her trident lightly against the tiles and continued her explanation.

"Supposedly it was the first king, Shirat, who decided

on the lots. The story goes he just had enough of arguing one night and declared it law, if you can believe it."

Garet smiled. "Oddly enough, I can."

He began to tell her Trax's story about the vegetable seller, but at that moment the door to the dining hall swung open and Hallmaster Branet stormed out.

"Give me my club! You two, come along. Garet, why did you say yes to this history nonsense? It was not your place to agree, and we can hardly spare banes now when attacks . . . Well, we shouldn't forget our duties."

Garet looked at Salick, then back to Branet. "But Hall-master, the king told me you had already agreed, so I—"

Branet snarled and glared at the door he had just exited. "Did he? Well, never mind. But you will report to me all that he asks you! Is that clear?"

Garet nodded at Branet's retreating back. It seemed no agreement on his part was really necessary. Branet expected it as his due.

The two younger banes left the palace as they had entered it, running to keep up with their hallmaster.

CHAPTER 4

BENEATH THE PLAZA

The palace guards saw them off with an air of satisfaction and returned to their duties of standing and looking fierce. Since Garet knew such courage would collapse at the first touch of a demon's fear, he ignored their splendour.

He couldn't ignore this latest tongue-lashing from the hallmaster. He fumed as he walked.

"I thought him fair when he was just a master," Garet said to Salick. They trailed Branet at a safe distance, or at least safe enough for quiet conversation in the empty plaza.

"*Just* a master?" Salick said and rolled her eyes. As a Gold, her efforts were almost wholly directed to proving she could one day be "just" a master.

"You know what I mean! He fought beside Master Mandarack against Adrix, and he was a popular choice to follow him as hallmaster. So why is he so . . . angry all the time?"

Salick didn't answer for several steps. She was never one to criticize the banehall if it could be avoided. It had been her life and salvation, and her instinct was to defend it like a mother bear defends her cubs.

"He has near three hundred banes to worry about, Garet! And remember, he was never . . . an easy man to begin with, though he is one of the bravest banes of his generation, or so others say, even Tarix."

If she hoped to quiet him by conjuring his master to support her point, Salick was disappointed.

"What does that matter?" Garet asked. "Even that tyrant Adrix patrolled and killed demons, which made him brave enough, I suppose, but it didn't make him a good hallmaster. No, there's a worry or a hatred eating at him. Is something else going on, something that so bothers him that he must take it out on us?"

He looked closely at Salick. Though they had a deep affection for each other, Garet knew that she would not hesitate to keep secrets from him for the good of the banehall.

"Nothing that I know of. Stop staring at me! It's the truth. But you're right that something may be amiss. Master Relict has just returned from Solantor. He's obviously downcast, yet says nothing of the journey nor what happened in the overking's city. Even my own master is as closed-mouth as a wood-turner's clamp," Salick said. "Which is a big change for her!"

Garet smiled. He knew Salick missed the taciturn Mandarack, a man she had regarded as both a mentor and a substitute father. Her new master, Bandat, was as skilled as she was talkative, but she was no Mandarack.

Salick raised her eyes to the moon skimming the top of the city wall. That and the torches near the bridge were the only illumination on this side of the plaza.

"I had hoped we were done with shadows and plots," she said.

Turning suddenly, she put a hand on his shoulder.

"Do you know what's going on? What are you thinking in that wise head of yours?"

"I'm thinking something is wrong," Garet replied, stretching up to look past the hallmaster towards the bridge gates.

"Yes," Salick snapped. "We both agree on that, but what?"

"We'll know in a moment," Garet said. He pointed towards the bridges, directing Salick's attention to a Gold Sash bane running towards them, lantern in hand and a trident similar to Salick's bouncing on his shoulder. The two banes started running to catch up with Branet.

"Hallmaster! Hallmaster!" the Gold shouted. The ring of light around him bounced and quivered as he ran.

They reached the hallmaster the same moment the Gold skidded to a stop in front of him.

"Snake demon, Hallmaster. It got away from us . . . and went into the sewers!" he gasped out.

Branet grabbed the young man by the shoulder.

"Kitoroth, you let it get into the sewers? Fool! It could go anywhere. Where did it go in?"

The bane struggled for breath but answered, "River end . . . beneath the Centre Bridge."

Branet let him go. He turned to the two banes standing close behind him. "Salick, we have to block off this end of the sewers as quickly as possible. Find the nearest grate and open it."

Garet went with her. In the poor light it took a little time to find the iron grating set flush in the stone of the plaza. Garet knew these grates were to be found in several parts of the plazas, and also throughout the wards. This was where the excess water went when it rained. His nose wrinkled when he remembered that the sewers emptied all the privies of the city as well.

They used the pick end of his rope-hammer to pry it open, then Salick inserted the butt of her trident in the gap. With both of them struggling, they levered the grate far enough aside for entry into the deeper darkness below.

The hallmaster was behind them now. Kitoroth was gone, but he had left his lantern. Branet handed it to Salick.

"Go down into the tunnel and make your way towards the bridge outlet. Check each side pipe for any sign of the beast. I don't have to tell you how dangerous they are, do I?"

"No, Hallmaster," Salick replied. She took the lantern and lowered it into the hole. The drop would be a good ten feet.

"Your weapon," Salick said, and took one end of the rope-hammer while Garet eased her down. After he handed down her trident, the hallmaster helped Garet down and dropped the end of his rope-hammer to clatter beside them.

No going back that way. At least he didn't replace the grate.

He looked around. The lantern illuminated several yards of a stone-lined tunnel, arched at the top and flat at the bottom. Luckily for them, the days had been dry of late, so there was only a thin layer of scum and mud covering the floor.

He desperately hoped it was mud, but his nose disagreed.

The ceiling was high, but the walls were close enough to touch with extended arms. Garet realized he had no room to swing his weapon effectively. After a moment's thought, he wrapped the loose coils around his chest, layering them over his new sash.

So much for these clothes. I hope the stores bane won't blame me for the state of them when we get back.

If we get back, he added to himself, for there was a demon somewhere under the plaza, and that never meant a sure homecoming.

They heard Branet move off, calling to Kitoroth. Salick looked at how Garet was arranging his weapon: the spiked weight with a bit of slack in one hand, and the short-handled hammer and pick in the other.

"Have you invented a new sash?" Salick asked. Her voice sounded odd, a high-pitched echo in the confined space. He felt twitchy himself, a dependable sign that a demon was about.

"I suppose I have," he said. "What rank would this be? Green sewerbane?"

"Red at least," she said, and chuckled nervously. "I'll go first, Master Sewerbane. You keep the light high and behind us so that we're not blinded. If we meet the beast, watch my trident, so mind me if I say get down!"

Garet nodded. He had to admit that Salick's weapon would be more effective than his own. He just hoped that he could be of some use if the Snake demon came their way.

As they walked down the narrow tunnel, splashing in puddles of water and filth, Garet tried to ignore his nose and remember what he could about this particular type of demon. The beasts came in many forms, and each had their own dangers, from the tiny Rat demons to the massive Bashers.

He considered what he already knew. Snake demons were rare, thankfully. No other had appeared in Shirath in the many months Garet had been in the hall. From his studies, he knew they had tiny legs and arms, and a long body befitting their name. *The Demonary of Moret* said they could grow to the length of a tall tree, but Garet hoped this was one of those times when the old book was more fanciful than accurate. He stopped to hold the light near a side tunnel, but saw nothing within. Hadn't Moret said something about their bite as well?

"Listen," Salick commanded.

Fear jumped in Garet's chest. The demon's effect was growing.

From a far distance, if the number of echoes were any guide, voices came, quick shouts back and forth, and over all a dry rasping sound, as if someone dragged an uncured hide over rough stone.

The rasping sounded closer than the shouts.

"Claws!" Salick said. "I can see a light far off. They're driving it this way. Set the lantern as high as you can and get ready."

Garet propped it just within a head-high opening and prepared his sadly hobbled weapon. He would use the pick-hammer end on the demon if Salick could pin it down with her trident.

The rasping grew louder. So did the shouts. Splashing feet followed, then a scream. The confines of the tunnel echoed the cry terribly, then the rasping was everywhere and the demon appeared in the light of their lantern.

It was a thick cable of muscle and malice. Its head looked large in proportion to the rest of its body, the usual horn-like ridges of the skull sweeping back into serrated blades. Its beak gaped and the split tongue waved from a fringe of needle-sharp teeth. Two of the teeth were proper fangs and longer than Garet had ever seen in a demon's mouth.

It swayed for a moment, regarding them with small black eyes.

"Watch out for the teeth!" Salick shouted, and stabbed at the thing with her trident.

The Snake demon clamped its jaws down on the tines of her weapon and shook it – and her – like a toy. The Gold was thrashed repeatedly against the tunnel walls, but she held on to the shaft.

"Salick!" Garet cried and rushed forward, only to be battered to one side by a flick of the demon's beak. He bounced off a mossy wall and fell directly below the creature's head.

Luckily, the other banes, lanterns and weapons in hand, ran up behind the beast. The Gold in the lead brought down a spiked club upon the demon's tail.

Unluckily, this caused the demon to release the trident – sending Salick flying up the tunnel – and brought its attention to the morsel lying at its underdeveloped feet.

That was Garet.

With no time to recover the ends of his weapon dangling in the mud, the bane scrambled up and wrapped his arms around the Snake demon's long neck, just below the head, hugging it tightly so that its beak could not twist around and set its fangs in him. In snatches, he could see the Gold still pummelling its tail and back, to little effect except to make the beast angrier, it seemed. At last, unable to devour Garet, and perhaps beginning to resent the continuous attack on its rear parts, the demon slithered away, knocking aside the lantern and sliding its head into the side pipe.

"Don't let it get in there," the Gold yelled. "Heaven knows where that pipe goes!"

To a very large privy, Garet guessed, for he was in an

excellent position to smell where it might lead. He still hung from the demon's neck, more from desperation than strategy. Now the Snake demon could not move forward and escape unless it dislodged him. The tail thrashed, knocking over the Gold with the club and sending Garet swinging like one of Lord Andarack's pendulums.

"Get down!"

Garet let go, dropping to the slimy floor. Salick's trident pierced the Snake demon just behind its head. This was both a demonstration of her strength, for demon hide was notoriously thick, and her cleverness, for the beast could go no farther and had not the wit to pull back.

She held it there while Garet and another bane wrestled with its body, avoiding the small, sharp claws while the Gold with the club set himself and proceeded to kill it with blunt force.

After twenty or so blows, he stopped and wiped his brow.

"Thank you, Salick. That's so much easier when it isn't moving!"

Salick pulled the trident free, bracing one booted foot against the demon's head.

"Don't mention it," she said, rubbing her back where she had hit the floor of the tunnel. She took her hand away and looked in dismay at the filth on it. "Yes, please don't mention it ever again!"

Garet laughed, as did the others. It came out a bit hysterically, but that was to be expected when a demon's jewel was so near.

He leaned against the slick wall and caught his breath while the other banes stretched the creature out to its full length. Not for the first time he wondered why the fear cast by a jewel outlasted the demon that bore it. After six hundred years, there was still much they didn't know about these terrors.

Another Gold and a Green stood behind the demon's killer, a young man named Salar, if Garet remembered correctly.

"Look at that! Seven yards or I'm a Black Sash," Salick said. "But honestly, Salar, how did you let this get by you and into the sewers?"

Salar held out a hand just as filthy as Salick's. His face was also caked with slime, as if he had fallen at least once in his pursuit of the beast. Garet's dinner threatened to reappear.

All of us will need an hour in the washing rooms before we get any sleep tonight.

"Not our fault, really. We were coming across the bridge to relieve the Palace Plaza patrol when we heard splashing in the river. We tied our sashes together and lowered a lantern to see the tail of this misbegotten thing disappearing into the outlet pipe. The grate was rusted – something the palace should look to – and besides, who ever heard of a Snake demon swimming anyway? Nobody, that's who!"

Salick nodded. "Branet will have to hear of this right away. He's in the Palace Plaza. Garet and I will return that way if you would take care of . . ."

She didn't have to finish the request. Salar nodded. He would cut out the demon's jewel from where it sat above the small black eyes and take it to the depository in the hills north of the city. There it would be cast into a deep pit, where its penetrating fear would be a danger to no one. The body would be cast there as well, unless Lord Andarack wanted it for his investigations into the nature of demons.

Salar borrowed the Green's axe and told them to go back up the tunnel.

"Find Chetorth and bring him directly to the physician. Tell Banerict he was cut in the sewers so he knows how dirty the wound could be."

"Is he badly hurt?" Salick asked.

Salar laughed. "More scared than hurt. The clawed beast came out of a side tunnel where it had been waiting to ambush us. It raked Chetorth with these ridges," he said, and tapped the sawtoothed skull protrusions with his borrowed axe. "Gave him a good cut, and a good scar to brag about when it heals, that's all."

Garet smiled. He had enough scars now that he had stopped bragging months ago.

Salick touched the sword scar she bore on one cheek.

"Tell him not to boast too much. It's bad luck."

They bade the others farewell and walked back the way they had come. The echo of axe blows followed them as Salar chopped out the demon's jewel. This put Garet in mind of Dorict's request that he speak to Lord Andarack, something he had failed to do as the other guests had left so quickly. He looked at Salick.

"Has Lord Andarack called for any more jewels or dead demons?" Garet asked.

Salick shrugged. "Not that I have heard. Perhaps he's onto some other project now," the Gold said and smiled. They both knew the ward lord's scientific investigations were at times erratic.

"You sat beside him. Did he speak to you at dinner?"

Salick was busy wiping her hands over and over again on her ruined tunic.

"A few polite words," she said. "I tried to ask him about

the silkstone experiments for Dorict's sake, but he seemed deaf to such questions."

Garet wondered why. In his opinion, those experiments were incredibly important, not just to Dorict and the rest of the banes but to the entire city. So far Andarack had found that silkstone was the only substance that blocked the fear radiating from a demon's jewel. The lord had discovered this last winter, and the suit of silkstone armour he fashioned had saved both Garet and Salick in the final battle with the Caller demon. Unfortunately, the stone was rare in the city, and by now Garet had expected to hear of some trading mission to get more. Such stone suits might be clumsy, but they were also the first real chance to end the six-hundred-year curse of the demons, not just here in Shirath but throughout the South and the Midlands.

Branet was nowhere in sight when they came to the space below the open grate. Calling brought no answer or help, so Garet hoisted Salick onto his shoulders, staining the last clear patch of his vest. Once up, she caught one end of the rope-hammer and hauled him up after her. It took both their efforts to push the grate into place.

"Perhaps we should swim across the river rather than use the bridge," Garet said. He stripped off his ruined sash and vest, balling them up and tucking them under one arm.

Salick shook her head. "You forget that's where the outlet pipes are. We'd have to go upstream to get clean water."

Garet sighed and followed her towards the bridge gates. She was right. Shirath's drinking water came in by clean tunnels from the east. The sewers emptied here and flowed west towards the distant sea. At the bridge gates, the two guards stood back as they passed, both holding a hand over their noses.

"Claws, banes," said one, a young man in gleaming cuirass and helmet. "What have you been doing?"

"Hunting in the sewers," Garet said. "I won't say for what."

The man nodded, glad the evil word had been left unsaid. His companion, a middle-aged woman, bravely lowered her hand and stepped forward to open the gate wider for the banes.

"Thank you for your service to the city, banes. We felt what you hunted."

While such praise did not lessen the smell that followed them to the hall, it made the endless scrubbing and re-scrubbing easier to bear.

CHAPTER 5

THE OTHER DEMON

L
ong after Garet was scrubbed and asleep, another demon came to the city. From the north it crawled, single-minded in its hunger. Unlike the Snake demon, this one went on all fours, long-limbed and muscular. Its skull-ridges were not serrated, but swept back and around like many-pronged ram's horns. At each step, hooked claws tore up the ground, laying gashes across the furrows plowed just that day. Some scent in the night made it pause and open its short beak. The split tongue tasted the air, found nothing human nearby, and withdrew into the forest of teeth. The demon rattled in its throat like a raven, snapped shut its mouth, and continued its stalking journey to the outer wall of the Seventh Ward.

This demon needed no hole through which to slither; it set claws in the rough stone and mortar and climbed quickly for all its bulk, gaining the top in but a few breaths. The entire ward now lay below it. The cows and sheep in their barns began to moan in their sleep and wake in fear of what they could not see. The youths who watched the livestock shivered and began to run towards the lanes and alleys leading to their homes. The gate guards came out, dropped their spears, then fell trembling upon the ground.

The beast scraped and skittered down to its business.

Save for the demon, only one other figure in the stockyards still moved. A young cowherd sprinted towards the first of the gates separating the stockyards from the ward proper. She was but a step ahead of the full strength of the demon's fear, and it clutched at her heels as she sobbed and ran. Her fingers fumbled at the latch, but too late. Terror caught up with her and ran along her bones, stroking each white length and twisting the attached muscles, binding them, and dropping her to her knees.

In falling, she turned and saw the demon approach. Even her eyes would not obey her chattering mind to shut and close off the sight. The monster's beak was painted with the blood of her friends, others of her age that worked nights in the barns that season. One thick arm dragged the body of a guard by its armour. Seeing her, the demon flung the body away. The corpse crashed through a paddock fence and off the haunches of a downed horse. The stallion's eyes rolled, but it didn't stir from the ground.

The girl by the gate whimpered. She had run the nightmare race every child of Shirath dreaded, and she had lost. Now, her mind could not turn from this terrible image. Red claws and teeth filled her unwilling sight, and she knew the last thing she saw would be her own blood spraying out and painting those weapons anew.

The beast came nearer, and in her locked perception, she didn't hear the latch open behind her. A hand grabbed her collar and dragged her through the gate. Figures in black rushed by, towards the demon. Lying stricken on the ground, she had no voice to warn them. If she had, she would have screamed, "What are you doing? You're not banes! You'll all be killed!"

She could only watch them die. But they didn't.

The first thrust a spear at the demon's reaching hand. There was a bellow of pain, and the creature swiped at its attacker, only to be cheated when the spear-wielder jumped out of range. A second dashed forward, slicing down with a broad-bladed sword on the demon's heel. When the beast rounded on him, he leaped back as well.

"Turn, run," whispered the girl, but the attackers, four of them in all, kept their faces towards the demon.

The spear-wielder attacked again, barely missing one of the beast's small black eyes. By form and size, she was a woman, while the others seemed to be men. One of them, a giant of a man, chopped down with an axe as the demon reached for the spear-woman. There was a cracking sound and a spray of blood. The fourth drew his bow and put an arrow in the creature's back, then another in its good leg. Now they all came at it, shooting, chopping, and thrusting until the demon collapsed under their assault and howled out its pain on the stone-paved ground. The braying call was cut short by a spear that pierced its throat and an axe that split open the massive skull right between the horned ridges.

The attackers backed away. The axe man reached behind him without turning his head and took a small object from the woman. One-handed, he chopped at the massive head again and again. Leaning his axe against the carcass, he reached into the hole he had made. The watching girl was suddenly sick, her stomach's contents spilling out on the ground beside her head. Before she had stopped retching, she felt a blessed relief from the fear, as if the demon's power had been shut behind a door.

The girl stood unsteadily, wiping her mouth and grabbing onto the open gate for support.

"Thank you, thank you," she said and reached out a hand to the four in black. At last they turned their backs on the demon to face her, and the girl dropped her hand.

"Your faces!" she said. "You're not banes! What are you?"

The woman shifted her bloody spear and raised a finger to stone lips. She nodded at the others and slipped away. Within ten heartbeats, all passed into the shadows of the stockyards and disappeared.

CHAPTER 6
RUMOUR AND RESEARCH

"**B**etter you than me," Tarix said, and grunted as Garet pushed her leg farther into the stretch. He had been telling her about the fight with the Snake demon and the trouble he had cleaning up afterwards. He had not expected much sympathy, considering the injuries Tarix had suffered at the claws of demons.

The Red was on her back in the small training room, the same room where Garet had first met her. Back then, Tarix had been limited to a rolling chair – or, on good days, crutches – due to a crooked leg broken by a Basher demon and badly set. A new banehall physician, Banerict, and the mechanical Dasanat had worked together to reset the leg and brace it with an intricate iron support.

This stretching was part of Tarix's daily routine, suggested by Banerict to keep the leg flexible so that she might return to her full duties as a bane.

"A bit more," she grunted, and Garet added another inch of pain.

When she was done, it was Garet's turn, for Tarix found

the leg-stretching invigorating and wished her apprentice to enjoy it as well.

"Not so far!" Garet said. "I'm not jointed that way."

Tarix relented, a bit.

"Stink or not, it was good work with that Snake demon last night," she said, and switched to the other leg. "Salar was singing your praises to his master this morning. He claimed you tried to strangle it with your bare hands before Salick pinned it. I wanted to ask you about that odd strategy, but you weren't at breakfast. Too much wine at the palace again?"

"No, too much food, but that wasn't the problem this morning. Partly it was because I was getting another new uniform," Garet said through gritted teeth. "And Marick told me that the odour kept him awake all night and would put a pig off its feed, so I stayed upstairs and scrubbed some more."

Tarix laughed and extended a hand. After more stretching of back and arm muscles, they moved to sparring with staff and stick. Tarix claimed it sped up his reflexes, and she never hit him hard. Well, not very hard.

"Just as a matter of interest" – *smack* – "did you or any of your adventurous friends go out hunting more demons last night?"

Smack, smack, swish.

Garet dodged and countered with a backhand that drove Tarix back a step.

"More demons? No, Master, I found the one quite enough for my taste." *Swish.* "And smell."

Now it was he who was driven back as Tarix's staff tested his guard. Each strike was as precise and swift as a bird's wing.

"Stiffen your wrist or you'll lose your weapon," she said, and quickly demonstrated how that might be done.

Garet held up a hand for truce and picked up his stick.

"Was there another demon, Master?"

Instead of answering, Tarix feinted high and then swept his feet out from under him. At least he landed well, stick out to guard against further attack. The Red smiled and motioned him up. She leaned her staff against the wall and dipped a ladle into the water jar standing in the corner.

"Ah, that is good! Yes, in the Seventh Ward, a Catcher demon. Think of a Basher with longer arms and hooked claws."

Garet would have preferred not to think of such a thing. A Basher was one of the most dangerous demons, large enough and strong enough to batter down a small house or punch a hole through a courtyard wall. He had never met a Catcher demon, and was not upset to have missed the opportunity.

"Who got it? Master Forlinect?" Garet asked. He remembered the Red had been listed for patrols on the board lining one wall of the dining hall.

"That is the hitch in the rope, as we used to say in the Sixteenth Ward. No one knows who killed it or will admit it if they did. All the hall knows is that the carcass of the beast is still there, or was there, if my dear husband has moved himself smartly to shoo away the gawkers and dispose of it."

Garet stared at her. Every master kept track of their kills – and the kills of their apprentices. It meant praise in the hall and was a sign that you were worthy of your sash.

"Gawkers? If people are nearby, that means the jewel is gone!"

Tarix nodded and handed him the ladle. She stretched her arms above her head as he drank.

"Ahhh, nothing like a morning training session to set you up for the day! Yes, the jewel was gone, chopped out of the demon's head and spirited away."

"But Master, you know you can't just 'spirit' a jewel away. They must have had . . ."

" . . . a silkstone box, yes? Here, give me that ladle and let's get back to it. It seems the banes, or whoever they were, had a box to hide the jewel away. Otherwise we'd feel it still, or some patrolling bane would have found it."

She picked up her trident. Once she had favoured the shield spear, but this weapon gave her extra stability when her leg tired.

"Garet, where's your rope-hammer?"

The younger bane blushed. "I'm afraid it still hasn't . . . recovered from its trip into the sewers. I washed and soaked it last night, but now it must dry and then be stretched again."

Tarix laughed, a sound of pure delight in the gloom of the training hall. A pair of Golds who had just come in turned to look at her before smiling and picking up weighted clubs to lift and roll about their shoulders. There were few masters in the hall as well liked as Tarix.

"Well, I'm glad you left it behind. Poor Garet, sent down into that stench to defend the city! Take one of those claw-ended batons and try to rush me."

That Garet managed to touch Tarix once with the training weapon, leaving a small scratch on the back of her hand, was a sign of his improvement since becoming a Green. The Red trained him relentlessly, but Garet doubted he would have survived wrestling the Snake demon the night before without the increase in speed and strength Tarix had brought about.

Marick was waiting for him in the front hall after lunch.

"Come on," he said, looking left and right to see if anyone in authority could hear him.

Garet resisted the pull on his sleeve.

"Marick, I've got Black Sashes to train with Forlinect in a few minutes. Can't this wait until evening?"

Since they shared a room with Dorict, any secrets – or more likely plots, if Marick was involved – could be shared then.

By wiry strength and determination, Marick manoeuvred him down the hall and into a cubbyhole under the stairs. He shooed out two youngsters hiding there and settled himself on a wooden box.

"I see you've furnished the place since I was last dragged in here," Garet said. He chose a box for himself, dusting it off to avoid dirtying his new uniform, the second in two days, as the stores bane had reminded him.

"I hold meetings here for Black Sashes who show promise," Marick said.

"Promise in what? Thievery? Pranks and rebellion?"

The boy grinned. "Good friends know each other so well, don't they? And I know that you'll want to hear this. I talked with someone who talked with someone else, who heard something someone had passed on in the palace market this morning."

Garet rolled his eyes but signalled the Blue to continue.

"It seems that Catcher demon – and Heaven's shield, what a great monster it was! I went out early to see it for myself after I heard this. But anyway, it seems the beast was not killed by banes at all, but by a dozen strangers covered in black and wearing ferocious masks. According to my source . . ."

"You mean your source's source's source's source – if I count it right."

"Yes, yes! You'll be as picky as Salick soon. According to my source, the masks shot out tongues of fire, and Heaven struck the beast with lightning and fierce winds before they killed it." He spread his hands out. "Now, what do you think of that?"

"I think I'll be late, and Forlinect won't be happy. Tell me the rest tonight, Marick, when I have a moment of my own time to listen!"

He left his friend fuming in the dusty alcove and ran off to reach his duties in time. Once, he would have happily helped Marick follow whatever wild rumour he was chasing, but that was before he had so many duties as a Green. Now he wondered when his immature friend intended to grow up. Garet sighed as he came into the empty training room. If only Marick could be more like Dorict, then he could worry about one less thing.

He was sorting the last of the old and splintered staffs when the Black Sashes came dribbling in. It was a better session than the day before. The initiate banes were working harder, swinging their staffs with a will and shouting things like "Take that, Basher demon" and "There, got you Rat!" Even Allifur yelped as her weapon struck the bag. Corfin was the most enthusiastic, and Garet had to restrain that energy lest he reduce the number of his classmates and increase the number of patients in Banerict's infirmary.

"Less waving and more attention to your stance, bane," Garet told him, and the title softened the criticism enough for it to take hold. The Black Sashes nearest Corfin looked happier.

Forlinect brought out the new short sticks and handed them out. Allifur took one and looked at it with obvious relief.

"Now, a bane may choose from any of a number of weapons when they become Blues," Forlinect lectured and, for once, he had their full attention.

"Some are long, like the spear – which is a very effective weapon against most demons – and some are short, like the axe, the hammer, the shield, and the short club."

He laid out each of the weapons he had mentioned and picked up the spear first to demonstrate its use. He was the best Garet had ever seen. When he thrust out at full strength, the point never wavered, but stopped precisely where he aimed it. He swung the butt end around like a staff to trip an imaginary demon, then leaped up and brought the head down in a swishing strike that would have stunned a Basher.

The Blacks applauded, fingers of one hand on the back of another, except for Allifur, who had tried to shrink behind the others. Corfin stopped her by reaching over and using his hand to strike the back of hers. She actually smiled at him.

"Now Garet will demonstrate these others," Forlinect said, and stepped away to give the Green room.

"Oh, of course," Garet said, though his thoughts were less enthusiastic. Tarix had made him practise with every weapon the banes used, but he was no expert with them. He had even questioned the necessity of practising with weapons he never intended to use.

Tarix had been firm.

"Sometimes in a big fight, banes get knocked down,

lose their weapons, and must grab what they can. If you lose that rope-hammer of yours – say a Horned demon goes running off with it wrapped around its neck – and you find a dropped axe, what will you do?" she had asked him.

Since then he had spent part of every training session using the unfamiliar weapons. The only one he liked working with was the sharpened shield, since it had been Master Mandarack's weapon of choice.

Garet picked up the axe and began to strike out at an imaginary creature. He let the memory of Tarix's voice guide him.

"Let the weight of the head do the work. You're just the pivot point. Start at your feet, good stance, and twist the hips with the swing."

He stopped as soon as he could and picked up the club, showing the strikes and thrusts, and finishing with a daring jump and twist that he barely pulled off.

The hammer was a much larger version of the one on the end of his own weapon, and he acquitted himself better with that than with the first two.

The shield was last. He put his arm through the double straps and gripped the metal handle bolted on the inner side. An oval of steel, sharpened along the sides and drawing to a point, covered his arm from elbow to a foot below his knuckles. Taking a guarding stance he had learned from Tarix, he swept and thrust the shield with some confidence, earning almost as much applause as Forlinect had received.

Corfin had his hand up as soon as the noise died down.

"Why don't you, I mean we, use swords like the ones the guards have?"

Garet smiled. "Because an axe blade or a spear point

gets through a demon's hide much more easily. Their skin is very thick, and a sword might just bounce off."

Forlinect spoke up. "I went to Solantor once with the Traders. Lots of banes there use a type of sword, well, more like a long meat cleaver to chop with. The handle is very long too, so I suppose it is more like an axe than a sword."

Allifur's one hand was raised. A good sign, thought Garet.

"Why don't we use bows and arrows?" she whispered.

Forlinect shook his head. "It takes a steady aim, Allifur, and if the fear is running over your arms, you'll likely miss and hit another bane, like Corfin almost did with his staff!"

The others laughed, and Corfin joined them.

Forlinect waited for them to stop before continuing.

"When the demons first attacked the South, the soldiers with their swords and armour were killed right away, except for those who ran, of course. That left only the common people, ones like you and me. Remember that our first hallmaster, Banfreat, was a baker! And he killed his first demon with his baker's paddle, and that turned in to the long club you see on the wall there. The flat end is smaller now and bound in iron, but it's still Banfreat's paddle, passed down to us like so many other common tools that became weapons. Can you think of any?"

A boy put up his hand. "That hammer? My mom's a blacksmith, and she uses one too."

His neighbour chimed in, "The tridents, aren't they used for the fish ponds?"

"Both right!" Forlinect said. "So, you see, the weapons we used were the weapons we had then, and since they worked, we've kept them ever since, though different cities might use different weapons."

"Garet," Corfin said, "what do they use in the Midlands banehall?"

Garet did not quite know how to answer. "I left before there was a banehall in Bangt, so I don't really know."

"Well, what did you use to kill demons there?"

"Hmm. Well, if you really have to know, I killed my first demon with a copper pot and a fireplace poker!"

Even Forlinect joined in the laughter then. "We won't ask you to demonstrate those weapons," he said, then pointed at the newly dried rope-hammer coiled from its hook at Garet's waist, "but maybe you could show them something of that?"

He cleared the others back, and Garet took the loops of wire-reinforced leather rope in his hands. Holding it so the line would play out without tangling, he flipped the spiked end out and hit the nearest sandbag dead centre. A bit of sand flowed out when he jerked the rope back and caught it nearer the incoming metal ball, letting it swing harmlessly past his head. Then he showed them the strikes one could make with both sides of the pick-hammer end.

When he was done, Allifur put a finger in the hole torn in the bag. "I wish I could use that," she said.

Corfin nodded.

"You wouldn't if you knew the number of bruises I got learning it," Garet said. He put a hand on her shoulder. "Don't worry, we'll find you a way to kill demons. I've promised, haven't I?"

She nodded, and Forlinect dismissed the class. Before Garet left, the Red asked him an odd question.

"After the Snake demon – and good job on that, well killed, bane – you didn't see anything strange on your way back to the hall, did you?"

Garet shook his head, and Forlinect smiled and waved him away.

After dinner, Garet retreated to his room to rest, forgetting that Marick would be waiting for him with his wild story of masked demon killers wandering the streets.

"Can't this wait until tomorrow? I have patrols tonight with Tarix's Golds, Ratal and Kesla."

"But this is important, Garet!" Marick said. The small bane was almost dancing in his irritation.

"Leave him be with your rumours and foolishness," Dorict said from where he was curled up on his bed with a book angled to catch the last light of the day coming in through the window. "Why don't you try practising your reading for a change!"

There was a knock on the door, and Garet opened it to find Salick waiting outside.

She came in and sat on the edge of Garet's bed. That something was bothering her was clear from the way she fiddled with the end of one braid.

"Garet, did you hear anything about a second demon last night?" she said.

Before he could answer, Marick exploded. "That's what I've been trying to tell him, Salick! There's something strange going on, and nobody is admitting it."

Salick stared at the little bane and raised one eyebrow, a trick all Golds seemed to practise in hopes of becoming masters.

"Oh, and I suppose you know all about it, as usual," she said.

Marick smirked. "Of course. No one steals secrets better than I. Remember, I knew you two were in love before either one of you did!"

He dodged a slap from Salick, a kick from an equally

mortified Garet, and ended up beside Dorict, who hit him with his book.

"Ouch! Stop playing around and I'll tell you. The girl who survived the attack said men and women in black clothing slew the demon with sword, spear, and bow."

"Bow?" Garet scoffed. "No one, not even a bane, could send an arrow straight when a demon is near! The girl is too upset to remember clearly."

Salick held up her hand. "Perhaps not. I saw Master Relict come back in some haste last night when Master Bandat and I were returning from patrols. He said nothing to us, which was strange, and even stranger were the arrows he carried in his hand, their points still bloody."

"And it was his Golds who borrowed a cart and dragged the beast, a big Catcher demon, to the depository. Salar was one of them, and he let slip that the jewel was already cut out," Marick added.

Garet thought this over. "Perhaps the banes who did it haven't recorded the kill yet. Or old Arict forgot to write it down."

"*Master* Arict might be old," Salick said, "but she is scrupulous about the daily entries. That means, and I can't believe I'm saying this, that it is possible the demon slayers were not banes, or at least not banes of this hall."

"But that's *not* possible, Salick," Dorict said. He closed the book carefully on a strip of cloth to mark the page. "Any bane that travelled from another city would be known in the hall and would not patrol on their own. And what non-bane could do this? It all seems like mist and moonshine to me."

"Marick," Garet said, looking to where the small boy pouted beside his friend, "didn't you tell me earlier that the slayers wore fiery masks and were aided by Heaven's lightning or some such froth?"

Marick waved his sarcasm away with one hand while the other covered his heart.

"That last part was just for dramatic effect. What's a good story without it? But I swear by Heaven and all the stars that the mask part is right. They weren't children's masks either, but made of stone, or so the girl said."

"How would you really know what she said?" Garet demanded. "You heard this from a chain of people that stretched across the city!"

"Well, I had business – hall business, that is – in the Seventh Ward after lunch and happened to run across this girl in one of the south-side tenements. Out of courtesy, I asked after her health. I was invited into their room, and we had tea together. It was quite nice. Her parents might have thought my visit was on the orders of the hallmaster, though I have no idea how they got that impression. But the story stayed the same, more or less: four in black, three men and a woman, all wearing stone masks and fighting like banes against the beast. Save for the bow, of course."

"Stone masks?" Salick asked. She looked to where Garet sat at his table.

He was studying Marick, but it was to Dorict that he spoke. "When was the last time you saw the silkstone suit of armour at Lord Andarack's house?"

There was a shocked silence as the others wrestled with the implications of the question.

"Weeks," Dorict said. "Perhaps a month now."

"We need to find out more," Garet began, but Salick held up a hand to stop him.

"Do we? Do we really need to? We aren't in charge of the banehall, Garet. I know we did much last winter that fell beyond our . . . duties, but that was a thing of life and death for the city, and it was Master Mandarack's lead we followed. I think we should not . . . overstep our bounds this time."

Marick gaped at her open-mouthed, and even Dorict seemed surprised. Garet was not as shocked. He had seen many banes cling to the traditions and authority of the hall since the Caller demon had been killed and peace restored with the palace and the wards. It was as if they tried to forget the horror of that time by pretending that no great upheaval had occurred.

Salick, who loved the hall more than her life, displayed this feeling to a greater degree than most.

Marick stuck out his chin, a sure sign of volcanic disagreement.

"Let's leave this for now," Garet said, hoping to forestall an argument and restore calm between them for the time being. "I'll ask Tarix about this tonight if she comes on patrol with us, and she can choose to enlighten us or not. We can all trust her, can't we?"

Marick stopped in mid-swell and nodded. He worshipped Tarix and would not say anything that might jeopardize his future chances of apprenticing to the Red. Dorict nodded because it was sensible, and Salick smiled because Garet had suggested it. Garet turned to talk to her of more pleasant things. At least he still had a few hours until the late patrol.

CHAPTER 7

MASKS AND THEIR MASTER

The warehouse was a cavernous structure, filled with stacked crates and barrels. There was little light, perhaps by design. What light there was shone on a space left open in the centre where a group of men and women, all dressed in black and bearing weapons, stood in rough lines. Their conversations were held in whispers and ended completely when a man came out of the shadows. He was not dressed in black, but in colourful silks that blazed in that gloomy company like a bird displaying its feathers in a dark forest. He stepped up on a box before speaking.

"Last night went well, very well. The city already speaks of your bravery, despite the banehall's attempts to deny it. Let them whine! The time of their supremacy is over. For centuries they have ruled, standing behind the palace to keep us imprisoned within these walls. No more! Chirat, bring them now."

A middle-aged man of portly shape and wearing even finer cloth than the speaker came bustling into the group.

He pushed a small cart upon which was set a tray. What the tray held was hidden by a black veil.

"Yes, Gost, I have them right here."

Gost stepped down and laid a hand on the covering cloth. "You have all earned the right to wear these. You earned that by enduring what you did last winter. When the banehall and the king triumphed, you were cursed and hunted through the streets. It was Heaven's will that you came to me, and that my friend Chirat could find refuge for you here in the Twelfth Ward. I know it must chafe at you to disguise yourselves as workers and warehouse labour during the day, but at night you can assume a truer, higher identity."

He pulled away the cloth and revealed stone masks, bound and twined in gold threads, and each arranged so that they looked up into the eager and more expressive faces surrounding them. Carefully, Chirat handed them out and watched as the men and women tied them on with black ribbons. Soon, all save Gost and Chirat were masked.

"Go now," Gost told them. "Show Shirath that even if the Duellists are no more, something greater has risen from their ruin."

The masked figures edged into the shadows and were gone. The last to go was a woman bearing a spear, and she looked long at Gost before she too vanished. Whether she looked upon him in respect, fear, or even contempt was unknown – for a stone mask shows nothing of the wearer's heart.

CHAPTER 8
DEADLY REUNION

"It's an insult," Ratal declared in a voice loud enough to turn the heads of other banes passing by. They were standing outside the banehall doors, waiting for Tarix. The Gold was incensed, his large moustache quivering as he spoke. "Sweep duty? Why should we follow other patrols while they make all the kills? We're the best team in the hall!"

"Are we?" Garet asked. He was coiling his re-stretched rope-hammer so that it would feed smoothly off its hook. He still worried about its flexibility, for the leather felt different after its foul soaking, but he had no wish to break in another if he didn't have to. His cloak was in the way, and he threw it off his right arm to keep his movements free. The spring night was cold enough to show breath, but better a cold arm then a fouled rope if a demon attacked.

Kesla smiled at Garet and shrugged. She was the senior Gold, and Ratal's superior, but it was a distinction he often forgot.

The big man continued. "I've made three kills since mid-winter, haven't I, and Kesla's made two . . ."

"Four," said Kesla.

" . . . and even little Garet here killed a Snake demon last night . . ."

"I just held on to it while Salar killed it," said Garet.

" . . . so why are we put to such insulting duties?" Ratal demanded.

"That would be because of me," said Tarix. She had come up behind them unnoticed. She leaned on her trident and looked up at the tall Gold.

"Ratal, I'm so sorry that a bane's duties leave you dissatisfied, but we are on sweep because Hallmaster Branet is unsure of the condition of my leg and wishes to test me out on lighter duties. Does that meet with your approval?"

Ratal hung his head, abashed. In Garet's experience of the young man's attitude, this would be a temporary condition.

They listened while Tarix explained their patrol.

"Since there have been so many demons lately, one a day and two last night, more sweeps have been added. Most of the attacks have been on the palace side of the city, so we are going to cross the bridge, sweep the plaza, and then take the Sixth, Fifth, and Fourth Wards, in that order. We will wait for the main patrol to leave each ward before entering, and then make a quick sweep. Any questions?"

Garet spoke up. "Master, has this happened before?"

"This increase in attacks, you mean?"

"Yes. It seems to be a lot. From my limited experience, I mean."

Kesla laughed and punched him lightly on the shoulder. Garet stumbled forward. The Gold was a strong woman. She pushed herself harder than most and cut her hair scandalously short so that it wouldn't interfere with her duties.

"From mine too," she told him.

"And mine," Ratal added, unnecessarily, since he had become a bane a few years after Kesla.

"I would have to add my own experience to that impressive total," Tarix said. "I've seen records that show greater and lesser numbers of demons over time, but nothing like this. Lately the beasts have been very . . . enthusiastic."

"I wonder why," Garet said, mostly to himself.

Kesla rubbed his head. "When you find out, let us know."

"Is there reason in such horrors?" Ratal mused, and the others looked at him.

"Wondering is contagious, it seems," Kesla said.

They arrived at the bridge gates, greeted the guards, and passed over. Garet looked down, trying to see the sewer outlets where the Snake demon had entered, but it was all darkness.

The Palace Plaza was even quieter than the night before. At first no lights showed save the lamps from the palace and the bridge gates. The banes had brought their own lanterns and lit them now. Then they spotted small lights moving in the distance, passing between the temple and the palace.

"That would be Forlinect's patrol just starting in the Sixth Ward. Well, let's make our plaza sweep and then get over there," Tarix said. She tapped the end of her trident against the brace strengthening her leg. "We'll see if this mix of iron and flesh can last the night."

"We'll do the plaza," Ratal said. "You meet us by the ward gate."

"Respectful, isn't he," Kesla said. "Giving orders to a master!"

Ratal got a punch from her, one that looked a lot harder than the one she had bestowed upon Garet. She glared at the Gold and then turned to Tarix.

"Fool as he is, Master, it might be the best for this first night. There's nothing here or we would have sensed it already, so if you don't mind, the three of us will do this and meet you at the gate."

Tarix stopped laughing long enough to nod. She put a hand on Ratal's shoulder, the unbruised one.

"Ratal, Heaven has willed that you learn manners the hard way, under your senior's gentle instruction. Go. Sweep the plaza, and I will meet you at the ward gate."

Kesla sent Garet and Ratal to the right, for patrolling the warren of market stalls was a two-person job at the very least. She trotted left towards the three domes of the temple, her flail rocking on one shoulder.

Ratal shouldered his own weapon: a long iron-bound staff, the squared head studded with short spikes. It looked like a slow thing to wield, but Garet had seen the young man catch a Shrieker in mid-leap and smash it against a wall. Manners or not, Ratal was a good bane to have on patrol.

They divided the market into halves and wound their way, alley by alley, through the tents and stalls. They found nothing amiss, save a loose flap on a tent covered with drawings of the sun and moon. The sign proclaimed the owner was a seer. He smiled, for this was Mistress Alanick's fortune-telling stall. He had met the old woman on his first day in the city, and she had been of great help in securing a certain meeting with the king. He tied the flap tight and moved on.

Kesla was right, there's nothing here or we'd have sensed the fear already.

If he felt any unease, it was that Tarix would be unable to complete tonight's sweep, even though her leg was much improved from when he first had seen her, sitting in a wheeled chair. If she couldn't patrol, Branet might demand that she give up her Golds and Greens to another master. Garet sent a prayer up into the star-sprayed sky above that his life would not be upended yet again.

Ratal whistled to get his attention, and Garet brought his concentration back to the duties of the night. The market finished, Ratal sent him around the front of the palace while he took the rear. There were guards standing in front of the doors, one under each light, but they didn't move as Garet passed by. Alarmed at first, Garet paused to study them. After a moment, he realized that they had mastered the skill of sleeping while standing up, or rather leaning against the wall. He coughed and walked on while they woke and looked blearily around.

"Anything?" Kesla asked when they met again at the west end of the palace.

"Two sleepy guards," Garet said.

"And two assistant cooks kissing in the shadows," Ratal added. He grinned, leaving the others in no doubt that he had frightened them out of their embrace.

"Nothing by the temple, save priests preparing for the funerals of those kids and guards from the Seventh Ward," Kesla said. "It will be a sad day tomorrow. Come on, let us make sure they don't get any busier."

They met Tarix at the ward gate. She was sitting on a stool, drinking tea and chatting with a ward guard.

"I never knew patrols could be so relaxing," she told him, and stood up. "But it's back to work. Goodnight, Hoster."

After months of patrols, Garet knew the ways of each

ward as well as he knew the path to his own room in the banehall. This one had long tenements stretching almost across the ward for some distance in. The gates were all on the north-east side, and although they slowed their progress, the banes didn't mind. The barriers divided each ward into spaces small enough to trap and kill demons before they could run wild through the entire population. They checked each gate as they passed, finding it closed and latched as it should be. Either Garet or Ratal then ran down between the three-storey tenements to the end of the row and back.

When they were halfway through the ward, the buildings became smaller and the passages between them multiplied. Tarix sent each of them off to check a lane while she took the main path between the lord's house and a squat block of rooms reserved for the wealthy. Garet found all these gates secured as well – unsurprising, since Forlinect's patrol had just passed. The Red would have noted any open gates, and the ward lord would receive a stern message from the hall the next day. It would be deserved. Some demons were incredibly fast, and many could kill on the run. Trapping them was the only way to limit their destruction.

They finished their sweep of the ward by the outer gate in an area used for warehouses and stockyards. Now they must walk back to the inner gate to get to the next ward. For a moment, they stood huddled by the outer gate. The cold prickled at them, and Garet shivered for a moment before raising his head to stare at the others.

"Do you feel that?" he asked.

"Yes," Ratal said. He shifted his staff to grip it with both hands.

"Form a circle and face outwards," Tarix commanded. "Try to locate it."

They did so, Garet facing the wall separating the Sixth Ward from the Fifth.

There it was, the little scratch along the nerves, the tightening of his muscles for no reason at all. He closed his eyes as Master Mandarack had taught him, swinging his head slowly back and forth, closing out everything but that slight touch of terror.

"Not this side," Kesla said.

"Not from where we came either," Ratal added.

"Nor from the north," Tarix said. "Garet?"

"The Fifth Ward, on the other side of the wall."

"We're in the wrong ward!" Kesla said. "Do you think Forlinect is nearer?"

Tarix grimaced. "At our speed, by which I mean mine, Forlinect might already be in the same situation we are, on the other side of a wall in the Fourth Ward. But he'd have sensed it too, so maybe we can pin it between us. Come, let's go through the outer gate and come in the same way to the Fifth."

Bad leg or no, she ran with the others, out past the trembling guards at the outer gate and towards the entrance to the neighbouring ward. They pounded on wooden doors that, when opened, would be wide enough for wagons of grain and sledges of timber to pass together. There was no response.

"Claws!" Tarix said. "The fear has likely frozen them. Garet, keep trying. The rest of you look for something to slide between the doors and open the bar."

Garet pounded the gate with the hammer end of his weapon. He realized that Tarix was right. The slit between the doors was paper thin: too narrow for the pick end of his rope-hammer, or any other weapon they bore. A knife might do it, but he carried none.

He kept hammering until Ratal shouted out, "Here! Over here! A hole in the wall!"

The rest joined him. Something had dug into the stone and mortar to make a tunnel through the great thickness at the base of the wall. The mouth was high enough and wide enough to make Garet swallow. What demon could leave such a trail?

"A Basher demon?" Kesla asked. She sounded unsure.

Tarix said nothing. She was the first through the tunnel. The rest followed. It was many paces before they were through, for the rubble created in its making slowed them down.

The fear was jumping higher now. As soon as he got through, Garet let out a loop of rope on the missile end of his weapon, wondering if even this heavy spiked ball could slow the demon that made such a hole.

"Fan out. Check for wounded and dead," Tarix said.

"No guards?" Ratal asked Kesla when they met again. His voice sounded unnaturally high, and he stroked his bushy moustache over and over.

"No guardhouse," Kesla said through gritted teeth. "And a barn has been destroyed as well. Over there, by the Maze."

Garet looked to where she pointed. A short wall cut off a corner of the Fifth Ward. Within was a warren of small buildings, shacks, and hovels. It was said that every part of the ward looked like this once, but a great fire destroyed all but the Maze two hundred years ago.

"Let us hope it hasn't gotten into that pest hole," Tarix said. She told Kesla to lead them to the destroyed buildings.

The small guardhouse was flattened, but the barn had only been rent in the middle, split from roof to foundation by something pushing through. Garet had seen a Basher demon do worse, but he had never heard of one tunnelling though a wall. A Basher would have knocked down the gate or, for all its size, used its claws to climb over anything it couldn't break down.

The trail of wreckage led through the stockyards. Parts of cows lay scattered, and the fences were now kindling.

"So," said Ratal, "it doesn't just eat stone."

"Maybe not, but look how the paving is torn up," Kesla said, pointing to huge gouges in the lane leading between the Maze and rows of ward housing.

They must have been close, as the fear was enough to send trembling along their arms and legs. Ratal swung his staff vigorously. Kesla was more restrained, but she kept shifting her grip on the flail and darting glances into the darkness between the buildings.

Tarix turned her head back and forth. At last she put her lamp on the ground and ran along the Maze wall, ignoring the buildings to her left, though they were full of helpless families. The others followed her. Before them rose an imposing house, pillared and fraught with carvings of wealth: fat cows and sheep, pools of swimming fish, stacks of cloth and raw wool, even a forest of trees being cut down. This was the house of Sacourat, lord of the Fifth Ward, and every light in it was now burning – and probably had been since the first light touch of fear woke the inhabitants from their sleep a short time before.

"There!" Tarix cried.

The creature was half in darkness and half in light, but no mere shadow could have hidden this demon. It was big, larger than a Basher but squatter, its wide belly almost dragging on the ground. At the sound of running feet, it turned its head towards them.

"Claws!" Kesla said, and Garet murmured profane agreement. The head ridges of the demon, usually raised as horns of some kind, were here spread out into flattened plates that protected it from beak to shoulders.

Garet had never seen anything like it.

Adding to his wonder, he realized that the demon's eyes, hidden in twin hollows of the faceplates, were white instead of black.

The banes stopped twenty feet from the creature. It paused, then turned its back on them. Lunging forward, it pushed its beak into a narrow passage it was trying to enter. The lane was too small, but instead of turning around and seeking another way, the demon reared up on its hind legs and scraped at the corner of the lord's house with its claws. There was a screeching as those heavy hooks cut into the building.

Garet looked on in awe.

Those claws are longer than my forearms – and thicker. That's how it got through the wall!

The demon continued its attack on the lord's house, tearing down avalanches of brick and plaster at each swipe.

Ratal ran up and swung his staff at the thing's hindquarters. The iron head of the weapon made solid contact, but the demon showed no sign of feeling it. "What now, Master?" the Gold shouted at Tarix.

The creature stopped its demolition and swivelled towards Ratal. The bane stood, open-mouthed and for a moment too long.

The demon charged.

Kesla pushed Ratal out of the way and scooped up Tarix with her other arm to go rolling away with her in a tangle of limbs, bruised but safe. There was a crack as Ratal's staff snapped in two under the demon's feet. Garet was farther away and ready to jump, but the beast stopped short, twisting its head back and forth, searching for what it wanted to crush.

At this range, even with the beast's head moving, Garet could not miss. Three whirls of the missile end above his head to build up speed, then a whipping throw. The studded metal ball hit the left eye of the demon . . . and got no more reaction than Ratal's staff.

That eye isn't just white – it's covered with the same armour as the rest of its head!

After a moment's pause, the thing shook itself and returned to its task of tearing down Lord Sacourat's house. Tarix pushed herself up and ran at it with her trident. She bounced off, again with no reaction. A scream sounded from a tenement somewhere down the passageway, and the demon redoubled its efforts to widen the entrance.

Tarix waved the others over and spoke softly to them as they huddled near.

"Well, this is something new! I've never met a demon with such a thick hide. It seems to be blind and noises attract it, so we'll use that until Forlinect gets here. Ratal, you run off to the left there and yell at it. I'll do the same on the right. Kesla, you and Garet have the worst part of this plan. You have to get Garet's rope-hammer around its back legs. Then we'll all pull. If we're lucky, the thing will topple and give us a chance to find a softer spot. Go on, you two. Don't worry about being seen, just make sure you're not heard!"

She limped off to the wall surrounding the Maze and waited for Ratal to start distracting the demon.

"Hey! You! You big ugly beast! Over here!" Ratal yelled.

In a burst of uncommon resourcefulness, he picked up two fallen bricks and drummed them together until the beast paused and turned its head.

At that point, Tarix struck the wall with the head of her trident, and the two alternated in distracting the demon, forcing it to face one way and then the other, while Kesla and Garet crept up on it from behind.

The Gold motioned to Garet, and he gave her the hammer end, but it was obvious that it would have to be he who slipped under the hanging belly to make a loop around the legs. Shivering at his closeness to the demon, for the fear it cast was made worse by its touch, he crawled on his belly until he could hand off the missile end of the rope to Kesla. She, however, was not satisfied with a single loop, and had Garet do it all again while the big, blunt head swung back and forth, confused about whom to kill first.

Kesla tied a quick knot in one end, threaded the other end through, and waved at Tarix and Ratal. The two stopped their noise and came over as quietly as possible. The demon shook itself and turned back to the passageway. It was almost large enough to admit the monstrous beast.

Holding up her fingers, Tarix counted down from three and when the last finger folded into her fist, they all pulled on the rope. At first, there was no reaction, just as with the other attacks. Then the beast moved forward, and Kesla's knot tightened, drawing the back legs together. The banes redoubled their efforts, and with a surprised grunt, the demon fell upon its belly.

It pushed up on its front legs and turned to sniff at the rope. The door lamps of the house shone full upon it from this angle and gave the banes their first clear look at the entirety of their foe.

The face and beak were indeed covered in thick, curled

plates, encrusting its head and shoulders. Beside the hollows of the useless eyes, two holes were visible, cupped in ringed ridges. It was these it pointed at the rope, then at where the banes stood. Unsatisfied, it raised its head and sniffed, the air whistling in and out of its beak. The light showed that, from needle-toothed mouth to broad chest, its skin was splashed with blood.

Finished with its investigation, it opened its beak and bit down upon the line. Garet's rope-hammer, despite the wire woven into the leather strands, parted like a piece of string, sending the banes falling in an unfortunate clatter.

Garet saw the abomination bearing down on them, but could not disentangle himself from Ratal's flailing limbs. Kesla rose first and struck at the demon with her flail, a terrible weapon with a five-foot hardwood handle ending in a short chain and spiked iron ball, but she was shouldered aside to land ten feet away.

Garet pushed Ratal off him and looked up at his doom. A foot as broad as a tree stump and armed with sword-like claws hung above him, blocking out the stars. The creature bellowed, shaking the dust from its shoulders, and the foot came down, onto the points of Tarix's trident.

The shaft bent like a bow, but held, and the creature fell away, its hoarse call transforming into a hooting, spiralling shriek.

Tarix pulled him up. Garet swept up Kesla's flail and stood shoulder to shoulder with his master. Ratal got groggily to his feet, looked at his empty hands, and stumbled over to help Kesla. The demon bit at its foot, then reared again, throwing its head back and forth as if it would batter the night senseless.

Garet raised his borrowed weapon with little hope it would save him. They were beaten, and if help did not come soon, half the ward would be torn down, and their own bodies, not the demon's, would lie beneath the growing piles of rubble.

There was a cry behind the demon, not one of fear, but of rage.

"Is it help at last?" Ratal asked stumbling over to them. Kesla hung over one of his shoulders, though the Gold looked like he could barely stand. "Has Forlinect come?"

Tarix peered into the shadows and shook her head. "It's help, I think. But it's not Forlinect – or any other bane."

Black figures appeared atop the low walls of the Maze bearing lanterns and torches which they set down before descending. More came through alleys and lanes all around the beast, bearing more light until the demon was bathed in it.

A bowstring twanged, and an arrow with a needle point buried itself to the fletching in the demon's back. The demon roared and snapped, but more arrows followed. Several of the attackers chopped at its back legs with axes and great swords. A slim figure danced before it with a spear, as fast as firelight, darting in again and again to pierce the monster's throat just below its armoured beak.

The demon bit at them, charged, and swept out its long claws but hit nothing. A last desperate rush brought down one man, rolling him over and over until he lay unmoving in the street. One of his comrades went to help him and froze as soon as his masked face turned from the demon. Two of the other attackers forced the man back around, their own eye slits always facing the weakening beast.

It could not charge now, as its back legs were cut to bits. Its throat and chest were painted with its own blood, and its bellows faded until it sank to the ground to suffer the final blows of its attackers. The black figures gathered in a circle around it while the large man with the axe chopped its head open, needing many blows to cut through the plate armour. At last he knelt over it, and the fear vanished.

All this time Garet, Tarix, and Ratal had stayed where they were, guarding Kesla and watching the battle.

They have a silkstone box. Those masks must be silkstone as well, but who are they?

The black-clad slayers turned to the banes: Tarix with her trident, Garet with a flail, and Ratal with no weapons at all, only Kesla in his arms. They came closer, forming a semicircle around the four. Each masked figure bore a weapon, and those weapons were not lowered.

Tarix eyed them. She stepped forward and held her arms wide.

"Well killed . . . my friends, and I thank you on behalf of the people of this ward. May I ask who you are?"

The big man laughed. He tapped the flat blade of his axe against his leg.

The woman with the spear still stood by the dead demon, stabbing it again and again. She stopped her attack and whistled. The others swiftly retreated, some going over the Maze wall and others disappearing down the ward's alleys and lanes. They took the wounded man with them.

The spear-woman stayed and came nearer. Her mask was expressionless: two rectangular slits for the eyes, a slightly downturned mouth, and an oval under the nose for breathing. The gold thread that held the pieces of silkstone together glinted in the flicker of lamps and torches. There was something in the way she moved that was familiar to Garet. The gliding of her feet, the animation of her arms, but he could not remember where he had seen this before.

The black figure stopped in front of Garet and pointed the spear directly at his heart. There was a tension in the figure now, as if she were consumed by a desire held barely in check. The spear point trembled and Garet tensed, ready to jump aside if she attacked.

Tarix caught the spear point between her trident's tines and twisted, locking both weapons in place.

"I thank you for your help tonight," the Red said, "but I will not allow you to hurt this bane." Her tone was as cold as the night, and her face as much a mask as that which confronted them.

Ratal stood, mouth open, looking from one to the other.

The woman laughed, a strange sound amid all the blood and destruction surrounding them.

"And will you stop me, cripple?" she asked. "Do you think any bane can stop us? We are the future of this city. You, master of a dying hall, you are the past, and one that shall soon be buried."

The two women faced each other for a moment, wills as well as weapons locked against each other. With a quick twist, the woman in black freed her spear and backed away from them, pausing only to stab the corpse of the demon once more before following her companions into the shadows.

Now that the jewel had been blocked by silkstone and taken away, the people of the ward came out to see what had happened. The door of the lord's house opened and Sacourat stood there, blinking at what used to be the corner of her magnificent house.

"Banes?" she called out to Tarix and the others. "How could you let this happen?" She walked towards them, shaking her tiny fist and berating them until she came upon the demon, which she had perhaps mistaken in the torchlight for another pile of rubble. When she saw it for what it was, she turned and ran back into the remnants of her home.

"Here's Forlinect," Ratal said.

The Red came running with three Golds behind him and stopped short at the sight of the huge demon lying across the road.

Tarix harrumphed. "I'd say better late than never, but I don't think it's true this time. Garet, tell him what occurred and then report to the hall. Forlinect can have this monster moved, though he might have to do it in sections! Ratal, fetch a cart for Kesla. We'll take her to the infirmary, and perhaps I'll ride with her."

She walked forward a bit, using her trident as a support.

"Maybe Branet was right; perhaps I'm not ready, even for something as easy as a sweep!"

CHAPTER 9

BETWEEN HALLMASTER AND HISTORIAN

"Tell me this story again, from the beginning," Hallmaster Branet said. He folded his arms across his chest and looked down at where Garet sat on a chair in the records room.

Tarix rolled her eyes but nodded for Garet to go ahead.

In this third telling, the near fatal adventures of the night were beginning to seem boring even to Garet, but he went through it again. The hallmaster stared down at him the entire time.

"His story isn't going to change, Hallmaster," Tarix said. "Nor is Kesla's nor Ratal's . . . nor mine, for that matter. What happened happened, no matter how distasteful you find it."

"Distasteful? You were attacked by these . . . amateurs. Men and women in black playing at being banes and endangering the lives of real ones! I hope you find that 'distasteful' as well, Tarix."

He turned back at Garet.

"Why did the woman with the spear attack you? She did attack you, didn't she?"

"So it seemed to me," Tarix replied. She was sitting as well, her bad leg propped up on a stool.

"But you don't know why," Branet said, and threw up his hands. "You don't know anything. Go on, get out, both of you!"

Garet stood and helped Tarix to her feet. Her irritation was evident in her trembling. He assisted her to the door, but turned back before opening it.

"I think, Hallmaster, that I might know why she hates me, because I might know who she is."

"Well," roared Branet, "speak then! Who is she?"

Garet kept his face blank and his voice neutral.

"Tarix is my master, sir. I will tell her, and I'm sure she will inform you."

He helped Tarix into the corridor, not daring to look behind him to see Branet's reaction.

When they had travelled a safe distance down the corridor, Tarix signalled him to stop.

"Garet! That was very . . . undiplomatic of you, and perhaps foolish to prod him so. What were you thinking?"

Garet smiled ruefully. "I was thinking that you are my master, and he insulted you, if you must know. Let him wait on your pleasure for a change."

The arm around his shoulders tightened for a moment.

"Hah! My students are always teaching me something. Well, at least you didn't take Kesla's approach and punch him for his rudeness. Take me to the infirmary, if you will, and I'll let Banerict fuss over this knee while you tell me what you know."

Garet changed course and helped her towards the infirmary. He noticed banes watching them pass and talking to each other in whispers. The story of a new and incredibly dangerous demon – and the aid of the mysterious masked figures – was spreading through the hall. When they entered the room with its row of beds – one occupied by a sleeping Kesla – Tarix groaned with relief.

"Is it very bad?" Garet asked. He waved at Banerict, and the physician frowned when he saw whom he was supporting.

"Well, Kesla here might have saved my life, but she didn't do this brace any favours. I'm afraid Dasanat will have to make a trip to hammer it back into shape."

"Master, let me know when she is here, I have another project for her," Garet said.

Tarix nodded, her face now drawn and pale.

After he had lowered her onto a bed, and Banerict had clucked and fussed over her injured leg, she pulled Garet down to a stool beside her.

"Now tell me what in Heaven's name is going on."

Later that evening, Garet repeated to Salick and his two roommates what he told Master Tarix.

"Claws," Salick said. "The Duellist who came to the hall with my late and unlamented cousin Draneck, she was the masked woman with the spear? But I thought they were all captured!"

Garet nodded. He had thought the Duellists safely imprisoned as well. The woman's voice had tickled his memory, but something else made it all clear. In telling the events of the attack to Forlinect, he had suddenly remembered that the masked figures had moved just like the Duellists, gliding and keeping their weapons in motion as if they were alive. Then he knew who the woman with the spear must be.

"She almost cut my throat!" Marick said. His fingers traced a thin scar along his right shoulder.

"Almost doesn't help anyone," Dorict observed. "But

Salick's right, weren't the Duellists rounded up and put under palace guard?"

Salick nodded. "I remember when they made that decision in the Ward Council. Trax was there and Master Mandarack . . ."

She fell silent. Her lips made a thin line as if it were her last defence against weeping.

Garet put an arm around her shoulders. The night the two Duellists attacked the hall was the same night Master Mandarack sacrificed himself to kill the Caller demon.

"I've seen some on chain gangs in the fields," Marick said, oblivious to the emotion in the room. "I always stop to chat with them, but I never saw her. I'd remember!"

"Chat or mock?" Dorict asked. He shook his head. "Well, do we know if their masks are made of silkstone?"

Garet reached into his vest pocket and drew out a sliver of stone and handed it to the younger bane.

"This came off the mask of the one that got knocked down," Garet said.

It had an oily sheen, and Dorict nodded as soon as he held it.

"Yes," the Blue said, "dark with green veins. It's silkstone, the only thing that stops demon fear. But how can such a small mask protect them? It took a whole suit to do it before."

"That was against the Caller demon," Garet reminded them. "And that monster cast a fear much more powerful than any other demon, even the one last night for all its size. These people have at least two jewels to play with now. Maybe they have a way of training non-banes to withstand part of the fear, and then the mask takes care of the rest."

"Some kind of half-banes, you mean?" Salick asked.

She seemed disgusted by the notion. "You know enough about the history of the hall to realize that was tried centuries ago. In the beginning they were so desperate they would do anything to increase the number of banes: children terrorized on purpose, torture, and threats. Nothing worked. It can't be done."

Garet shrugged.

"Perhaps, but they didn't know about silkstone. These people do. I don't think they really are banes. Not like us. After all, the masks make the difference. I saw one frozen in place when he turned his head away from the demon last night. His companions had to rescue him by turning him back around!"

"So we're still better," Marick said and grinned. "Which I already knew!" He took the piece of stone from Dorict and stared at it. "Why are they doing this?"

"They were not generous with their explanations," Garet said. "The masked woman only said that they were the future of the city, and we were the past."

Salick struck the mattress with her fist. "What a clawed lie!"

Garet sympathized. He had worked hard and sacrificed much to become a bane. And now, according to this masked Duellist, it had all been for nothing. Like Salick, he would not believe it.

"Well, whatever she means by that, it is not the question I want answered first. What I want to know is where did they get enough silkstone for at least ten masks and a box to hold demon jewels?"

They brooded on that particular question for some time before Dorict spoke up.

"Lord Andarack has not responded to any of my

messages. Is there any way you two can approach him and ask about it?"

"Walk up to the lord's house in the Eighth Ward and demand answers, all without an official banehall reason to be there?" Salick asked. From the height her eyebrows reached, it was obvious she didn't require an answer.

"So what do we do then?" Marick asked.

Salick raised a hand in protest, but Garet intervened. "Salick, it will be a great help to the hall if we can find out something about these . . . Masks, for lack of a better word. Anything we discover will of course be passed along to our masters immediately."

Salick considered this for a moment and then nodded. "All right, as long as this is on your own time and doesn't interfere with your regular duties."

"Of course. I'll pass on everything to Tarix, and she can inform the hallmaster."

"And I'll do the same with Master Bandat," Salick said. She eyed the two Blues sitting on the bed opposite. "These two don't have a master yet. To whom are they supposed to report?"

Marick hopped off the bed and curtsied. "Why, to you, of course, Master Salick," he said in a cloyingly sweet voice.

With a short goodbye to Dorict and Garet, and none at all to Marick, Salick took her leave. It was late, and Bandat's team was on day patrol, alternating between roving the fields and the wards.

As soon as she was gone, Marick curtsied again, this time to Garet.

"Don't worry, we'll report to you as well," he simpered.

"Imagine my joy," Garet replied, "though you may find nothing at all."

"Oh, I'll find something. I already know where to look."

Dorict had stripped off his tunic and was preparing to blow out the room's single candle. He paused and looked at his friend.

"Would it make any difference if I told you not to do anything stupid?" he asked his fellow Blue.

Marick looked wounded, but did not answer.

Two days later, a kitchen boy brought a message up to Garet's room. It was from Barick, the new historian, asking if Garet would please bring to the Stewards School any records concerning the founding of Shirath Banehall after the midday meal. The paper was soft and the writing elegant. On the envelope was the broken seal of the palace.

Someone had obviously read this request before it reached Garet, and he guessed who it might have been. A little later, another messenger, this one a harried-looking Green, found Garet in the infirmary. He was sitting with Tarix and discussing the strategies of the fight with the "Tunneller demon," as it was being called by many in the hall.

"I think we hit upon the best method," Tarix said around a mouthful of buttered bread. "Distract it and then attack with as many banes as possible."

Her leg was much better, and Garet thought she might be staying in the infirmary just to annoy the hallmaster.

"But with what?" Garet asked. "They used big swords to chop at its back legs. Do we even have swords in the hall? As for our other weapons, axes might work, but clubs and flails were useless, and even your trident couldn't pierce the beast's hide." He saw the Green waiting at the door and looked at Tarix.

She waved her over and held up a hand to stop her from launching into the message so she could finish her conversation with Garet. "We'll just have to use sharper points. That friend of yours with the spear did some damage." She turned to the messenger. "What is it, Dalesta?"

The Green sketched a quick bow. "Garet's wanted, Master Tarix. The hallmaster wants him right away in the records office," she said, and wiped her nose with a handkerchief.

"Another cold? You have to train more to build up your lungs, Green. All right, take him away, and I'll have a word with your master – that's Taron, isn't it? Maybe he'll let you train with me a bit."

Dalesta managed to express both gratitude and terrified anticipation in her farewell bow, and led Garet to the front of the banehall.

The records room, where Branet had interrogated Garet the day before, was a rat's nest of leaning bookcases, untidy stacks of scrolls, record books, and mismatched chairs that each had its own hill of paper growing out of the seat. Anyone entering for the first time would doubt that a single needed piece of information could be retrieved from such chaos, but if one gave the ancient records master, Arict, a request and time enough for her to shuffle through the narrow alleys of the room muttering to herself, she would bring back anything required.

"The earliest records of the hall," Branet was roaring at the old woman, not in anger but in necessity, for she was more than half deaf.

Garet lingered by the door while she wandered off, scratching the wisps of grey hair falling loose over her wrinkled vest. Two Blues followed her, ready to assist if needed.

"You, Garet, come here," Branet said, at a slightly reduced volume. "You are to take these records . . ." And here one of the Blues dropped a pile of scrolls on the desk in front of the hallmaster. " . . . and deliver them to this Barick person. You will then . . ." He moved back as another stack of paper joined the first. " . . . come back and report directly to me what happened. Do you . . ." Now Arict herself appeared with a third load of papers, and Branet had to grab the pile before it tumbled on to the floor. " . . . understand?" he finished through gritted teeth.

Garet rushed over to help him. As Arict kept sending out more scrolls and mouldy ledgers, it became obvious that one person could not carry them all. Branet told him to find someone to assist him, and that he should return to the hall as soon as possible so as not to neglect his "more fitting" duties.

"Tarix is still unable to patrol," he added, "so you will have to patrol with other masters for now."

Dorict was quite happy to be pulled out of a physical training class to help Garet. Marick was nowhere to be found, so he knocked on Salick's door, hoping to turn this job into a chance to spend some time with her. Lately, their separated duties had limited their meetings to a few minutes in the evening, or a word of greeting on the stairs. Far too little contact, in Garet's opinion.

Salick's roommate Vinir answered the door. The young woman, Salick's friend since she became a bane, looked him over and smiled.

"I suppose it's not me you want to see, is it?"

Garet shook his head, reddening. Vinir had been kind to him, and loyal to Master Mandarack. She did, however, know exactly how to tease him.

"Vinir!" a voice called from within the room. "Don't you have something less annoying to do?"

Salick came to the door, wearing her tunic but not the vest or sash, and elbowed Vinir out of the opening. Her friend retreated, chuckling.

The two faced each other, both flushed. Garet spoke first.

"The hallmaster has allowed me and Dorict to take some records over to Barick. I was wondering if you would have time to help me . . . us."

"If the hallmaster has permitted it . . ." Salick abruptly turned and went back into the room. In a moment she returned, in full uniform, with her trident held tightly in one hand.

They walked to the front hall and waited while Salick found Bandat and asked permission to leave her duties for the day. When she returned, Dorict and Garet had secured the pile of records in three separate baskets with shoulder straps that were normally used to bring firewood into the hall's kitchens. Salick took up the first without speaking, and they left the hall.

"Bandat wasn't angry with you, was she?" Garet asked after much time passed in silence.

"No," Salick said. "It's just that she . . . well, she laughed and thought I was asking just so I could spend some time with you!"

Is that such a bad thing? he wanted to ask her, but kept silent. He knew that Salick's whole life, at least before she had met him and they had fallen in love, revolved around the banehall. Whether he liked it or not, she sometimes saw him as a distraction to her duties, a distraction that must be contained, controlled, and kept at an unfortunate distance.

She saw his sombre look and shoved him with her shoulder, both hands occupied with a basket full of scrolls.

"Don't frown so!" she said. "I want to be with you. I just wish the entire banehall didn't find who I . . . love so interesting."

She smiled at him, and he would have kissed her despite the daylight and the people passing, but the baskets and their burden of ancient knowledge were barriers too unwieldy for passion to overcome. They satisfied themselves with soulful looks into each other's eyes and occasionally stepping on the ever-patient Dorict's heels.

The banes passed the palace, going around the west side of the imposing building to reach the small Palace Ward behind it. This was not a regular ward crowded with people and livestock, humming with the work of the city, but a quieter place. Here, the king allowed some of his servants to live in relative luxury. There were small parks with greenery and ponds, wider streets, bigger rooms, and special warehouses for the taxes and treasures of the Royal House. Even Salick seemed impressed, though she must have patrolled here many times.

"Maybe people lived like this before we were crowded into the walls six hundred years ago," Dorict said. He shifted his basket of scrolls to one hand and pointed with his iron-bound staff. "I think the Stewards School is over there."

He indicated an imposing three-storey building near the east wall. Men and women dressed in conservative clothes of muted greens, reds, and blues were coming in and out of the three entrances. Above the central door, a circular carving showed a pair of hands holding up a model of the city and a crown over all. The meaning seemed clear enough: the king may rule and the people may go about their business, but it was the stewards who made all this possible.

"Where are we in this carving?" Garet asked, speaking to no one in particular, but he got an answer.

"In the circle that surrounds it, bane," a deep voice said behind him.

They turned and saw Barick, the new City Historian and previous butler to the king, standing behind them. He wore a striped robe of blue in different shades wrapped around his prodigious belly and chest. His great soft face smiled down on them, and he waved a fleshy hand.

"I sought to greet you at the gates but was too late, I'm afraid. It is so hot to be walking. Aha! These records are most welcome. Perhaps Garet can bring them in? I wouldn't want to hold these others from their important duties at the hall."

Salick's smile disappeared and she looked as if she might protest, but in the end she handed her basket to an already overburdened Garet, gave him a look he couldn't interpret as anything pleasant, and left with Dorict.

"There now," Barick said, looking to where Garet juggled three baskets full of paper. "That's, er . . . better, isn't it? Come along, bane. We have much to do."

The large man led him up the stairs at a stately pace, which was just as well, for Garet had to stop every three steps to pick up a fallen scroll.

CHAPTER 10
SECRET MEETINGS

B arick led Garet to a set of rooms on the third floor. He indicated a table, and Garet placed baskets at each end and stacked the slippery scrolls between them. When he was done, he turned to find the historian waiting by an inner door, one ear pressed against the wooden panels.

"Excuse me, Barick," Garet said. "Did you need me for anything else?"

Barick waved him over, and Garet went to him, wondering what was going on. Thinking about the apologies he must make to Salick, he had no wish to linger.

After a moment, Barick lifted his head from the door and turned the handle.

"Would you mind stepping in here for a moment, bane?" he asked. He said it so courteously that Garet could hardly refuse, though he wondered why he had been asked here just to be ushered away.

The door closed softly behind him before he realized the inner room was already occupied. Two men, one older and the other still young, were playing Surround, a board game

Garet had often seen. Dorict was fond of it and had explained the rules to him many times in the hope that Garet would agree to a challenge. So far Garet's duties had not given him the necessary time, for it could be a very long game, and he valued his own studies – and his sleep – too much.

The board was divided into two halves by a blue stripe called "the river," rather like the city itself. On each side, pieces representing hounds, harriers, and huntsmen tried to trap a single piece, the prey. Each player controlled the hunters on their own side and the prey on the side opposite. To win, one had to both catch the opponent's prey and destroy the hunters chasing their prey. Draws were quite common, and a decisive victory meant you were good at both chasing and escaping.

One of the two men, the younger, looked up and smiled. "Ah, Garet, how surprising to meet you here."

"Your Majesty!" Garet said, for it was indeed King Trax sitting there, pushing a hound after the prey controlled by Lord Andarack, who sat opposite him.

The king continued smiling – genuinely, for once, Garet thought.

"Since this meeting is not actually taking place, why don't we drop all titles for a while like we did in our first – very violent – meeting. I won't call you bane, and you won't call me Majesty, all right? Now since we aren't here, you should know where we really are. Andarack and I are in another part of this building, checking with the chief steward about preparations for the festivities to come. Go ahead! Tell him, Andarack."

The ward lord blushed and put down the game piece he had been turning in his hand. "Well, Garet, it seems I'm getting married."

Garet stared at the man. He liked and respected Andarack, but he must have been in his fifties at least, and though Garet supposed love could strike at any age, it just seemed . . . odd.

"Who is the lady . . . Andarack?" he asked. Perhaps she was the daughter or sister of a neighbouring ward lord. He might even have met her on his patrols.

"Well, it's Dasanat, actually," Andarack said, and his cheeks reddened until he resembled one of his furnaces.

If Garet was surprised before, he was stunned now. The chief of the mechanicals thought of nothing but the machines she so expertly made. To believe she was in love was more than just odd. It was unbelievable.

Courtesy forced him to say something. Anything.

"I had no idea she was of a . . . marrying mind," he said.

The king gave an ignoble snort.

"Well," Andarack replied, "there was much wooing involved before she agreed. In the end, I think she decided to take me on as a sort of experiment."

He was now flushed from chin to hairline.

Trax laughed. He reached across the board to put a hand on Andarack's shoulder and give it a friendly shake.

"Nonsense. She suits you down to the boots, man! And you're the only one who knows how to talk to her, since even her king can't get a word out of her most days. So let us say it was a match ordained by Heaven but much delayed."

Andarack smiled. He turned to Garet, who awkwardly extended a hand.

"Congratulations, Andarack!" he said.

The ward lord stood and took Garet's hand in his own, pumping it vigorously.

"Thank you, Garet. You have been a friend to both me

and Dasanat since you came to Shirath, and I honour that friendship. I hope you will attend the ceremony with Salick and those two youngsters, but I'm afraid this is all the time we have to talk of such pleasant matters."

He released Garet's hand and pointed to a third chair.

"As you have no doubt guessed, we are here to discuss matters of import to both the hall and the city."

There it is again, that split between the two where there should be none.

Garet sat down in the place the ward lord indicated. The older man remained standing and began to pace as he talked, a habit Garet had seen before.

"I'm sure Salick told you that I avoided answering the questions she put to me at that dinner. She wanted to know about the silkstone armour suit, probably for Dorict's sake. That young man has been very helpful in testing and refining it. Why, he found ways to cut its weight by four and a half pounds! I'd say the mechanicals lost a fine prospect when he joined the banehall."

"Andarack?" Trax said. He made a running motion with two fingers along the board.

"Ah, yes. Well, the reason I haven't asked him to help me with the suit is because I no longer have it."

Garet stared at the ward lord, then at Trax. The king shook his head.

"No, I don't have it either. I have enough suits of armour lining the palace halls, and I have no use for that particular one without Andarack's expertise."

The ward lord nodded. "Nor would you have taken it in such a criminal fashion! Three guards wounded, one badly. Gonect – I think you remember him, Garet – Gonect was nearly killed by an axe blow. Luckily he had his plate on or I'd have lost a friend and a good chief of guards. They came upon a group of black-clad men and women breaking into my house. The armour was in the great room, set up for testing. They took it and all the silkstone boxes not already at the banehall."

"But why, Andarack?" Garet asked. "What good would it do any but you?"

"What good indeed?" Trax said. He tossed a folded piece of paper to the bane, and when he opened it, Garet found a sketch of one of the masks he had seen two nights ago.

"My agents saw a man wearing this and sneaking out of the Seventh Ward just after a demon was killed there, and not by banes."

"Your . . . Trax, these are made of silkstone. I found a chip of it after the Masks attacked that big demon in the Fifth Ward."

The king nodded. "The Masks, hmm? My guards say that's what they're being called in the streets now. Regarding the silkstone, we thought as much, for what else would allow a man or woman not of your hall to fight such a creature?"

Andarack stopped his pacing and faced Garet. "What can you tell us of them?"

Garet paused for a moment to think. Branet would not approve of this meeting. He would say this was hall business, that anything to do with demons fell under his control, not the king's. Garet guessed that anyone born in this city might well agree, but Garet was from the Midlands. He could see the city from the outside, see how each part helped or hindered in a way those raised inside its walls could not. Master Mandarack had valued that in him. Like Garet, the old master's loyalty had been to the city as a whole, rather than just the part of it that was the banehall.

"At least one of them was a Duellist. She is the one who survived that night when the Caller was killed by your brother."

King and lord looked at each other.

"Shirin, I think her name is," Trax said. "Officially the Duellists are extinct, and many of them now work on chain gangs in the fields and woods, but I can tell you that some escaped, or rather hid with the help of others. We think we know who, but without certain proof, I cannot accuse a ward lord of treason!"

"Treason?" Garet asked. The word had an unpleasant taste in his mouth, especially since some would consider him a traitor to the banehall for telling even this much to the king.

Trax said nothing but looked to where his prey stood menaced on the board in front of him.

"He's right, Garet," Andarack said. "That charge might set the wards against each other in a brutal conflict, the like of which hasn't been seen for two hundred years. Then, it was a plague and a bad king who started it. Now it might come out of a war between the banehall and these Masks, with everyone else taking sides."

"Well, at least we don't have a bad king this time," Trax said, "unless you'd like to disagree, Garet? I know what Salick's opinion would be."

Garet looked at the king a long time before replying. He was surprised to see the man was actually waiting for a response.

"I think, Trax, that you care more for the city than yourself, which is saying something indeed. I also think you are a manipulative man, and not to be trusted in personal matters, but that you would lay down your life for Shirath."

Andarack looked mortified at such honesty, but Trax laughed.

"You sound like my father! Heaven's shield, you two would have made a pair. But you're right. I was given this city's care, and for my pride's sake, I intend to see it kept safe until I rise up in the smoke of my funeral pyre – if Heaven will take me, that is."

Even Andarack laughed at that. The king wiped his eyes and waved Garet to sit back down when he made to stand, thinking that the interview was over.

"One more thing, oh honest man! I've come to respect your view of things since our first meeting in the winter. If it breaks no vows, can you tell us what the hall is doing about the increase in demon attacks? Branet is close-mouthed on the topic, and although people want to believe in the renewed power of the hall, you and I have both seen it slip at times."

Garet bristled at this last bit, but answered. "Anyone can see that the patrols have been increased – to the limits of our numbers, as you must have guessed. One patrol comes soon after another, and then the next, and so on. The same strategy, just more of it, you might say."

"Would you change the strategy?" Andarack asked.

"Yes, what would you do if you were hallmaster?" Trax asked.

"I'm not," Garet said. His tone could have chipped ice.

"Nor likely to be, so don't fret," Trax said. "I won't repeat your criticisms, but I would like to know what you think should be done."

Garet took a deep breath. He *had* been thinking about this, if only because it was his nature. Years spent sitting on rocks in the sheep pastures of his father's farm, throwing stones to frighten any ewe that tried to leave the flock had left nothing *but* time for thinking. On those endless days, he had examined all the "what ifs" and "what nows" of his life over and over. He had planned escapes from his abusive father and brothers a thousand, no, a hundred thousand times. He had dreamed of Shirath and the other cities of the South, populating them with people both ordinary and bizarre, building their walls and homes in his mind, only to tear them down and build them higher, better. Coming to the real city had not cured this habit. He guessed that nothing ever would.

"I would split up the hall, Andarack," Garet said.

He was pleased with the effect. Trax's mouth actually dropped open before he remembered himself and tried to regain his façade of genial superiority.

"Break up the hall?" Andarack said, looking at Garet as if he had spouted steam.

"Yes," said Garet, plowing ahead. "The patrols are hit and miss. Why not have small banehalls at the outer and inner ends of each ward, like the guardhouses? Keep the main building for training and records, but rotate Reds and their teams through the smaller halls. Let them live there, for days or seasons if you wish. They can patrol in their ward and the near plazas but always be within their ward when they sense a demon approaching, rather than a ward away, as we were two nights ago."

He stood up and started to pace in an unconscious imitation of Andarack.

"And if we could devise a system of quick communication, something I think you should turn your mind to, Andarack, then we could call up more banes as needed, swarm the beast and cut down on our own injuries and deaths."

He stopped pacing to look at his audience. Andarack was smiling, and Trax was shaking his head.

"I take it back," he said. "I think you will be hallmaster one day, if there's any sense in that pile of bricks and mouldy traditions!"

Garet bristled again. "Mouldy traditions? Like the Calling of the Places, and all the other ceremonies of the palace, you mean?"

"Point taken!" Trax said, holding up one hand. With the other he tossed his prey piece to the bane. "And the game to you. Come, Lord Andarack, I believe we stumbled into the wrong room. The chief steward's office is not even on this floor. Goodbye, bane. Good to see you so soon after our last meeting."

"Your Majesty, my lord," Garet said, making the necessary bows. He looked at the sketch of the mask he still held in his hand. Wrapping the prey in the drawing, he shoved both in his vest pocket.

There was a knock on the inner door, and Barick stuck his head in.

"If you're done, there's a great mess to sort out," he said, sounding rather aggrieved.

"Yes," Garet said. "So it seems."

CHAPTER II
SECRETS SHARED

It was late in the evening when Garet returned to the hall. He knew he had missed dinner, so he walked through the palace market, looking at the stalls and trying to convince himself to ask for something to eat. His conscience argued with his stomach as he walked past the last displays of steamed buns, skewered bits of meat, and cooked vegetables. His conscience may have won, but his stomach still gurgled in complaint.

Marick would not have hesitated, and he had seen even Salick ask for food when on extended patrol and unable to return to the hall to eat. No bane went without a meal in Shirath. Those of the hall worked hard, but they never knew hunger, and what they didn't eat, they gave back to the poor of the wards.

Garet shook his head at the thought. He had grown up on a farm, a poor ramshackle place that always seemed one bad patch of weather away from failure. That memory seemed closer at this time of year. Spring was when hunger always pinched the worst, for the stores of grain and salt meat would be gone by now, and the fresh vegetables and newborn animals were not yet ready to harvest.

That his mother and baby sister were gone from that poor place and safe in Bangt was a great relief to him, for they were the only good memories of his childhood. His mother had taught him to read, to track animals, and to wait patiently, hungrily, for his share, as she must for hers. He remembered many days when she went hungry so that he and his sister could eat.

Such waiting had bred a certain stubbornness in her son. It shamed him to ask for another's food, because to take it for yourself meant that someone else must go hungry.

"Hey, bane!" a voice called from behind him.

He turned and saw an older man waving at him from the last row of stalls. Garet went over to see what he wanted and was presented with a piece of cloth tied into a bag. Within was a collection of buns: sweet ones, savoury ones filled with meat, even plain steamed buns. There had to be at least half a dozen.

"Saw you looking them over, but too shy to ask, eh?" the man said, and laughed when Garet protested and tried to hand back the food.

"Eat! Keep your strength up, and Heaven protect us all! You're the bane from the Midlands, aren't you? Well, lad, if you're ever hungry, you come and see old Torfor. Best buns in the market, you'll see!"

With that he turned to pack up his stall, and Garet took his treasure away to the banehall, reducing it by two buns as he walked. A gift given freely, rather than demanded as a right, didn't seem to offend his conscience, which stayed silent while his stomach rejoiced. The buns were delicious, and soon the air seemed fresher and the light reflecting off the city walls brighter. The hall felt like home again when he came through the east wing doors and took the remaining buns up to his room, reduced once more by Vinir, whom he met on the stairs. In return for a sweet pastry, she promised to tell Salick he needed to see her.

Dorict was grunting through a movement exercise Forlinect had set him some weeks ago to improve his strength and agility. He bore no weapon, but had iron weights strapped to his wrists and ankles. Even with that burden, his arms and legs moved like the snapping of a pennant in the wind, and Garet waited until the exercise was over before he felt it was safe to enter the room.

"You are getting better," he told the Blue. "I bet you could beat a Basher to death!"

"If I were wearing these weights, I'd give it a try," Dorict said, untying them and dropping them to the floor, "but claws, that's hungry work!"

Garet showed him the bag and smiled. So did Dorict when he saw what was inside. They sat on their respective beds and ate.

"I'm sorry that Barick turned you away today," Garet said. He limited himself to just one more bun then took his new rope-hammer down off the wall hook. He ran his hands over its length, checking for flaws in the leather strapping.

Dorict shrugged. "After such a wonderful meal, I'm not sure I could criticize you for anything, but it was not me who was angry."

"Salick?"

"Like a Shrieker in a fish pond! She stomped off to see her uncle rather than return to the hall and tell Bandat she was turned away."

"Did she tell you that?" Garet asked. He began to regret sending Salick a message to meet if she was so put out.

"No," Dorict said. He got off the bed and began the movement exercise again, slower and without the weights. "You could see it though. What happened with Barick, anyway?"

"I'd rather tell it when Salick and Marick are here. Where is he? Don't tell me someone let him go on patrol?"

After last winter, when in the depths of the crisis even Blues had been pressed into patrol duties, Marick had whined about being left out of all the fun. The masters, even Tarix, had so far ignored his pleas to join a team, though Garet guessed that would change if the increase in demon attacks continued.

"No, or not that I know of, but he's been out of the hall all day. He didn't show up for training, so Forlinect's got claws out for him."

Garet felt very little sympathy for Marick. He liked the boy and considered him a good friend, but he knew the little bane worked only as hard as he was forced, relying instead on his skills of trickery and charm to get through each day in the hall.

There was a sharp knock on the door, and Dorict gave Garet a meaningful look before opening it and inviting Salick in. She walked over to the desk, sat in the one chair, and regarded Garet.

"First," he said before she could speak, "I want to apologize for how you were treated. It wasn't my idea, and I should have argued for you to stay, though I think Barick had orders to let only me in."

There was an easing in the tension of her shoulders. She lifted an eyebrow. "Fine, but I expect you to knock him out with your hammer next time he treats me like your servant. Or any other bane for that matter . . . What's this?"

"A bun I was saving for Marick, but he's still out," Dorict said. "And you deserve it more."

"Apologies and presents," Salick said and bit into the bun. "Mmmm, I should get angry more often."

"Please don't," Garet said, "and especially when you hear who was waiting to meet me."

He told them of the meeting with the king and Andarack. Salick and Dorict listened, at first in surprise, but increasingly thereafter in confusion and shock.

"Why weren't they saying all this to the hallmaster?" Salick demanded. Half the bun lay uneaten in the palm of one hand. The sketch of the mask was crumpled in the other.

Dorict nodded agreement. He turned the game piece in his hand and looked to Garet for an answer.

"I got the impression they had tried and been turned away, perhaps for 'interfering' in banehall business."

"Would the hallmaster deny Master Mandarack's brother?" Dorict asked.

"Garet," Salick said. She came over to the bed and sat beside him, taking his hands in hers. The remnant of the bun lay trapped between their fingers. "You can't keep this to yourself. None of us can."

He gingerly removed the bun from her hand and put it in her mouth. Dorict was kind enough to control his reaction, though his nose wrinkled.

"Salick, I know that. You talk to Master Bandat, and I'll talk to Tarix. They can bring all this to Branet – Hallmaster Branet – themselves. All I ask is that you tell your master that the meeting with the king and Andarack took place by chance, or else Branet will chain me to a pillar in the training room until I'm old enough to be a Red."

After much chewing and swallowing, Salick nodded and kissed him. This was too much for Dorict, and he retreated to his bed and made a great business of opening his book and reading.

"I miss this," Garet said, when air became necessary. "It seems we have no time for each other these days."

He could not keep regret from entering his voice.

"I told you this months ago." Salick rested her cheek against his. "Remember, while we travelled across the Midlands, and you wanted to learn everything about Shirath and being a bane in a single day? I told you that one cannot be a bane and any other thing at the same time. Not a baker, a farmer, or in love; at least, not easily."

"I miss it."

Salick drew back. "What, things going easily?"

Garet laughed. "No, I've never known that, not as a bane or before! But I miss believing that things *could* go easily, that all the world would change for the better because I was in love."

"My world changed, and so did yours, I think," she said.

He pulled her closer again and touched his forehead to hers before answering, "But two people make a very small world."

"And a very annoying one," Dorict said. He turned to the wall and put the open book over his head. He was forced to stay that way until Salick left for patrol. She promised to talk to Bandat sometime during the night. Garet told her he would do the same with Tarix tomorrow, for the Red had promised to drop by the training hall to check on the Black Sashes Forlinect was instructing.

When she was gone, Garet went over to tell Dorict he

could stop pretending to sleep, but found the Blue had stopped pretending some time ago and was gently snoring under the open book. Garet lifted it off him and placed it on the thin mattress beside Dorict, then lay down on his own bed to find his rest. He fell to dreaming of a giant playing board and pieces that moved of their own accord. Across from him towered some shadowed opponent, countering his every move. The sun woke him just before his prey piece was captured by huntsmen and hound pieces that shrieked like demons. He lay for a while, watching the square of light creeping into the room and thinking that if dreams were Heaven's messages, they should speak more clearly.

THE NEXT MORNING, Garet was pleased to see Dasanat accompany Tarix into the training room. The Red was moving easily now, her repaired and improved brace letting her work through several exercises with Garet using both the trident and the sharpened shield. Dasanat glared at the offending leg the entire time and stopped its owner once to adjust the tension on the brace with a tool pulled from one of the many pockets of her tunic.

The Black Sashes had all stopped to watch Tarix practise, and Allifur had pressed forward for a better view when the Red picked up the shield again and flashed it through several deadly thrusts. Garet took the opportunity to pull the girl forward and introduce her to the mechanical.

"This is Allifur. Dasanat, I thought you might come up with a weapon for her that favours one hand."

Dasanat looked down at the child and abruptly squatted so that their eyes were on a level.

"You have only one hand?" she asked. There was no mockery or judgment in her voice.

Corfin came up behind his friend and stuck out his chin, clearly ready to defend or attack, if need be.

"Yes," whispered Allifur, and then she stuck out both arms.

If there was a trembling in her little voice, Dasanat paid it no mind. She examined both arms the way Garet had, testing their strength and flexibility until she was satisfied. Then she took out a small roll of paper and a stick of charcoal. With a marked string, she measured the one hand and the length of both arms, and noted down all. Garet was careful to suppress a smile as he remembered King Trax's story of measuring the vegetable seller.

"What weapon do you require?" Dasanat asked.

"A shield," Allifur said, no longer whispering. There was a determined set to her mouth.

Corfin nodded in agreement. "You'd be dangerous with a shield," he said.

Tarix laughed, and squatted beside Dasanat. "Allifur, a shield is heavy and hard to manage, though Master Forlinect and Garet can teach you how to use it. Still, it will be a few years before you're strong enough to wield one, so perhaps we'd better start you on something else first. Forlinect, what were you thinking of for Allifur here?"

The Red hurried forward. "A braced dagger, Master Tarix."

Tarix nodded. "Could you get us one, Garet?" She looked back to Allifur, who was nearly in tears. "Ahh, don't worry. You'll get your shield when you're ready, and until then, you can be dangerous with something else."

Corfin put a hand on her shoulder, and the girl took a deep breath and nodded.

Garet came back from the office and storage room with three practice daggers of different lengths. All had been reinforced with flanges running up the broad sides of the blade to allow them to punch through a demon's hide without bending, though Garet would have bet that none of these could have pierced the skin of the Tunneller that nearly killed him. Only the Masks had managed that, Shirin with her needle-pointed spear and the bowman with his arrows.

Tarix looked them over and gave the shortest to Allifur, kept the longest for herself, and after a moment's thought, handed the third to Corfin.

"Now follow me."

She took them through an elementary set of movements, repeating each one, and then the whole set again until they had it right. Garet could see Forlinect was memorizing it too, and even Dasanat seemed to approve.

"Efficient," the mechanical said. "I will consult with Lord Andarack on the shield. You believe it is not possible, but one of appropriate size and weight is not beyond reason."

She looked down to where Allifur stood, dagger tucked under one arm and tugging the mechanical's sleeve with the other.

"Thank you," she whispered. Then she ran off with Corfin to the corner of the training hall to practise the movements again.

The other Black Sashes looked at them enviously until Garet waved them back to bag practice.

"Now you've done it," Forlinect said, and shook his head. "I'll have to let all of them train with daggers now, and our poor physician will have no end of stitching to do."

"Don't fret so much, training master!" Tarix told him.

"Those are blunt practice daggers, and you can use wooden ones if you think bruises are better than scratches." She looked at the line of children striking the bags with their single sticks.

"It's time to move them on to real weapons, Forlinect. With these attacks increasing, we might need every bane to fight for the city."

Garet looked up to see how Forlinect would react to this joke, but seeing the faces of the two Reds, he realized Tarix had not meant it to be amusing.

"Is it really so bad?" he asked Tarix after Dasanat had taken her leave and Forlinect had resumed the supervision of his students.

They stood in Tarix's old office, the place where she had once quizzed him on a basic knowledge of demons. Back then, he was still an unhappy Black Sash wondering if he should run away from the banehall just as he had fled his father's farm. She had asked him about his knowledge of Moret's *Demonary*, a confusing text he had actually rewritten to make clearer. Garet had answered all her questions not knowing what the result would be, and had been shocked to find himself promoted to the rank of Blue Sash.

She had been the first master besides Mandarack to treat him with kindness and respect. He trusted her and was relieved to unburden himself of the information he carried. He told her everything that had happened with King Trax and Lord Andarack at the palace.

"Garet, what have you gotten yourself into?" were the first words out of her mouth – when she recovered the power of speech.

"Nothing of my own choosing, Master," he said. "I was dragged into this by King Trax and Branet!"

"Careful," Tarix warned. "Branet is master of this hall and deserves our respect."

Garet reddened. "Yes, Master Tarix."

Tarix took him by the shoulder and gave him a shake. "Don't 'Master Tarix' me. If I'm upset, it's because I see you running towards your own funeral pyre. You are being used, Garet, used to spy for the king and to spy for the hallmaster, and maybe even for Lord Andarack, though I'd rather not suspect him of such things. What happens when you're no longer useful? Do you think anybody will care what happens to you?"

Garet smiled. "I hope you will, Master."

The thud of staffs against bags was the only sound for a long time.

"Well," Tarix said. "Let me think on this. I'll tell Branet, of course, and I'll add that bit of fluff about you meeting them by chance, as if he'll believe it! Go on and help Forlinect. We'll talk further about this on patrol tonight, now that Dasanat has given me my leg back."

"Yes, Master," Garet said. "Please believe me, I really didn't seek this out!" He was worried that Tarix might think he was meddling for some selfish reason.

Tarix raised an eyebrow. "But you didn't flee from it as you should have. I know you have a taste for plots and conspiracies, Garet. You used it for our benefit when the Caller demon and the Duellists threatened us. We, and by that I really mean you, were very lucky that time. You got out with your skin. We all did; well, except for poor Mandarack, of course. I wish he were here to talk some sense into you!"

Garet hung his head. He too wished Mandarack were still here to listen to him in his quiet way. More than once, he had poured out his heart to the old bane and come away the better for it.

Tarix put an arm around his shoulders.

"Enough of all that. Do you promise to tell me before you do anything else?"

Garet nodded.

"Good, then we will speak again tonight. The theft of the silkstone is a serious matter, and you can be assured I will find out if the hallmaster knew of it, and if he did, why he didn't inform the rest of the masters. Go on now. Help Forlinect with that lot. I like the girl, she's a brave little thing."

The Red left the small room and waved at Forlinect as she exited the training hall. Garet stayed and worked with the Black Sashes the rest of the morning, saving time at the end for Allifur and Corfin to practise with the blunt daggers while the others again watched their every move.

At lunch he saw Dorict sitting without the company of their capricious roommate.

"Where's Marick?" Garet demanded. He took some pickled onions and pushed the plate towards the younger bane, but Dorict ignored it.

"No idea! I woke up after you left the room this morning and found a badly written note from that idiot on top of the book I was reading. It said he was chasing information on those Masks, and that he'd be back before dark. What has that fool gotten himself into now?"

Garet could see Dorict was worried, but both knew Marick's moods. The boy would sometimes roam the city for days, sustaining himself by begging food from an astonishing collection of friends and acquaintances. That he would do it now, when the hall was so stretched, was unfortunate but not surprising.

"Eat," he told the Blue. "Right now, Marick is probably feasting like the king in some back alley while he tells his tales."

Dorict smiled and spooned up some of the onion. "Oh, Andarack sent a note today. He apologized for not sending for me all this time and promised the work would go ahead as soon as 'certain obstacles' were overcome. I guess we know what that obstacle is."

"Yes, the theft of all the silkstone," Garet replied in a lowered voice. He needn't have worried. The other Blues and Greens at the table were entirely occupied with eating.

Dorict spoke around a mouthful of onions. "So then, are these Masks our enemies or allies?"

"Both? Neither?" Garet said. "They kill demons, but one of them, that Shirin, looked like she wanted to kill me too."

"You weren't very kind to her when she came into the hall with Draneck," Dorict reminded him.

"They attacked Marick and me! She tried to kill me. Both of them did. I was only saved by a demon's attack. And then it almost killed me too!"

Dorict laughed. "After all this time, that's still funny! Well, at least this Shirin is consistent. I've been told that's a virtue. Pass the butter, please, before those greedy pigs over there finish it all."

CHAPTER 12

WHAT SHALL BE DONE?

That afternoon, Garet worked with Forlinect one-on-one. He had asked for this session precisely because of Shirin's "consistency," as Dorict had put it. Although he had a new rope-hammer, it would be of little use against her spear at close quarters. Garet had first asked Forlinect to train him in spear against spear, but the Red had refused.

"It won't work. From Tarix's description, that woman is an expert, taking on that monster the other night! And if she is a Duellist as you suspect, she'll be very good at thrusting and parrying, even with a spear. No, you have no great skill with that weapon, I'm afraid, and she'd soon best you, but why not try a shield? You're quite adequate with it, and it should be effective at close quarters."

"What about at a distance?" Garet asked.

"That's what your rope-hammer's for, idiot," Forlinect replied, grinning.

They tried that combination, Garet with the shield and Forlinect with his long spear. It went awkwardly at first, as Garet had never used a shield to fight any weapon save for the baton that mimicked a demon's claws. He soon got the hang of it though, and worked on using the shield to parry the spear point then dash inside its range to attack.

"Good," Forlinect said, after finding the shield point at his neck. "Now let's speed it up a bit."

At that pace, Garet could barely defend himself, let alone attack. He could only hope Shirin was not as good as the Red. They stopped when the Blues came in, and Garet was released to study on his own. Forlinect promised to continue the training as time allowed. Leaving the room, Garet caught Dorict's eye, but the Blue shook his head. Marick had not returned.

Garet took some writing materials and two of the books Greens were meant to study up to the central wing's roof in the mid-afternoon. He was in the middle of making clear notes on the strategies for fighting Water demons, something he had never seen, when Salick popped her head up through the open trapdoor.

"Hah! I found you. Marick said you used to hide up here. Is he back yet?"

"No," Garet said, and moved over to give her room to sit on the folded tarp he was using as a cushion. "He's still gone, and Dorict's worried. So am I, given how those Masks treat banes."

Salick sat down. She pulled a handful of nuts out of her tunic pocket and shared them with him.

"From what you've told me, you're the only one they seem to dislike. Why does that woman hate you so? Ratal thinks she's an old girlfriend of yours and you broke her heart."

Garet groaned. If Salick had heard this, then Ratal must have spread the rumour through the entire hall.

"I was angry with her and cruel in what I said, I

127

suppose. When that Digger demon attacked us both in the dining hall that night, she was injured and confused. She had just killed a demon, after all, a feat that should have been praised, but I saw her only as an enemy and mocked her. Maybe that's why she's with the Masks, to prove she's worthy of our respect."

Salick snorted. "Then why didn't she come to us and offer service to the hall?"

"Would we have accepted her?" Garet asked, and to this Salick had no answer.

After a long silence she said, "Bandat told me I'm to patrol with your team for a while because Kesla is still recovering from the beating she took the other night, though I suspect a different motive from our scheming masters. Here, have some more of these. When was the last time we patrolled together?"

"Just after Branet became hallmaster and before you apprenticed to Bandat," Garet said, and shelled another nut before popping the kernel in his mouth. "We went out with Relict once or twice."

Salick stood and looked out over the city. The wards packed into this side of the city were noisy, busy places today. At this height, the thousand and more voices below merged into a bee-hum that would only quiet as night fell.

Salick tilted her head and let her eyes follow a flock of birds racing across the southern sky.

"I thought of choosing Relict. Vinir would have been happy to have me on their team. She can always put up with my moods, but Bandat asked first, and I suppose I was flattered. Anyway, after Master Mandarack died, it didn't seem to matter much whom I chose," she said, eyes still tracing the fliers in the distance.

Garet nodded, understanding her feelings. Salick's love

for her old master, the love of a daughter whose own father had been a drunk and bully, had been clear from the first day he met her in the cabin of his family's farm. She had been accompanying Master Mandarack and had bristled at any challenge to the old bane, and it still hurt her terribly that she had not protected him in his final battle. Garet had tried to help her in the grey season after Mandarack's death, but she had resisted comfort and thrown herself into training and fighting. This was the first time they had talked of it since the end of winter.

He rose from the tarp and stood beside her.

"Do you miss your family?" she asked, turning her gaze from the sky to the people hurrying back and forth in the Banehall Plaza. They were moving streams of colour, swirling in momentary eddies around a dropped basket or a friendly greeting.

"Not my father and the twins," Garet said with a sincerity that made her laugh. "But my mother and sister, yes. It helps to know they are in the banehall at Bangt. My mother is a cook there, or so Master Boronict said in a letter that took half the winter to find me. She wrote a short note too, telling me if I found my heart in Shirath to stay here and she would be happy."

He took her hand and pulled her into his arms, leaving no doubt as to what he had found in Shirath. Reluctantly, Salick pulled free.

"I should really return to my room and rest. I was out in the western fields all morning with Bandat, and now I have a night patrol as well, thanks to you, I'm sure."

"Rest here," Garet suggested, unwilling to end so soon the pleasure of seeing her. "We can sleep right here. It's warm enough, and then we can go down to dinner together."

It did not take much more persuasion, and they both sat down and leaned against the parapet, the tarp giving them some comfort and their closeness giving them much more.

GARET WAS SHAKEN out of another desperate dream. He had been facing his hidden opponent again, but when he opened his eyes, the sky was stone-grey and the first stars were out. Dorict stood over them, alternatively shaking Garet and Salick. Salick realized what was happening first. She jumped up and stared at the sky.

"Claws! We'll be late for patrol. Come on! I'll meet you at the front door after I get my trident."

She was off then and down the trapdoor stairs before Garet was fully awake.

Dorict pulled him upright. "You heard her, come on! You have no time at all, so let's get your weapon and splash some water on your face. Tarix sent me to look for you!"

Garet was running down the front stairs to the door when he heard a clattering behind him and saw Salick a few steps behind. Tarix and Ratal were waiting for them by the door, along with the other two Greens who looked to Tarix – Aralon and Riga, both of whom grinned when they saw Garet sprinting up to his master.

"Well," Tarix said, breaking off her conversation with Ratal, "both late and both arriving together? What shall we make of this?"

Ratal shook his head. He still bore Kesla's flail, as if he wanted to maintain her presence on the team even though she was still in the infirmary.

"You're late," he said, unnecessarily.

"Yes, we know, Ratal," Tarix said. She waved the others out the door.

"Sorry, Master," Garet said, trying to catch his breath after a number of minutes entirely taken up with running. Salick stood beside him, equally flustered.

"I'm sorry as well, Master Tarix. And as for both of us arriving together, that's just a—"

"Coincidence?" Tarix asked. "Lots of those around these days."

"The truth is we both fell asleep," Garet said, then reddened.

"Separately," Salick was quick to add.

"Ah, to be young and doze while the world burns," Tarix replied, raising her eyes to Heaven. "Come on then. Let's hope this new brace can stand whatever is out there waiting for us."

"Have there been more attacks, Master?" Garet asked. He pulled his tunic and sash into some kind of order as he walked after her. Behind him, Salick was doing the same thing.

"Two this afternoon," Tarix said, all playfulness gone from her tone. "Different times, different wards. A Rat and a Shrieker, so they were easily dealt with. But we were lucky patrols were nearby in both cases or there would have been deaths."

They caught up with Ratal and the Greens. Aralon was arguing with Ratal. The squat bane was holding up his axe and making chopping motions.

"Look, I'm just saying that if we get a big one tonight, let me get behind it and hack its legs like the Masks did. That's what worked, wasn't it?"

Ratal rolled his eyes and looked at Tarix. The Red replied for him.

"The Masks were lucky that the demon was distracted by us first so they could launch a surprise attack on it. As I've told you before – many times, now that I think of it – everything depends on the circumstances of an encounter. Your idea might work one night, but what happens on the next when the demon charges before you're ready or stands inconveniently with its backside to a wall?"

Riga pushed Aralon into motion with the butt end of her spear. "Listen and learn," she told him. "Or at least listen."

Like Kesla, whom she idolized, Riga kept her hair short and practised with the single-mindedness of a demon herself. Even better, she was cool in a battle, and followed orders like she was already a Gold.

"Good advice," Ratal proclaimed, stroking his moustache, and Salick hid a smile under one hand.

Tarix held up a hand. "The Sixth, Seventh, and Eighth Wards tonight, and on primary patrol, not a sweep, so check every gate and note any left unsecured."

They left the Banehall Plaza and were soon in the Sixth Ward. Between the smell of horses from the barns near the outer wall and the pungent aroma of ointments and medicines from the Physicians School near the inner wall, many called this the smelliest ward in the city.

"I'll be glad to get out of here," Aralon said as they prepared to leave the ward. "Have you ever smelled anything worse?"

"Yes," Garet and Salick said together.

The Seventh Ward was less fragrant but just as quiet as the Sixth. Candles and lanterns showed in windows, but the noise of the city was fading into the drowsiness of evening. As summer approached, many of Shirath's citizens would linger outside while the light lasted longer, crowding the plazas and the rooftops to enjoy the weather and each other's company. For now, Garet was happy to walk the near-empty streets and feel no touch of unnatural fear.

The Seventh Ward completed, they passed through the inner gate of the Eighth Ward and soon neared Lord Andarack's house. Tarix summoned Ratal to her side.

"Take Aralon and Riga and make the patrol on the west side of the ward. Garet, Salick, and I will patrol in this area."

Ratal puffed out his chest and called his inferiors to follow him and "Look lively!" Riga cast a look of obvious appeal to her master, but Tarix had already turned to the remaining two.

"Let's check inside the lord's house, shall we?" she said, and walked up to the courtyard gate and rang the bell. Andarack himself answered with no guard in sight. Wordlessly, he led them into the great hall, which was much cleaner and more orderly than the last time Garet had seen it. The tables and chairs were actually free of spark containers, model engines, and stacks of plans and books, and even the anvil on the lord's dais had two rather elegant chairs placed in front of it.

"Congratulations on your coming wedding, Lord Andarack," Salick said. "I take it the wedding feast will be held here?"

"Yes," Andarack replied. "Much to my bride's dismay, I might add. She has chosen the earliest date the astrologers could give us so that she might get her workspace back!"

"I'll add my best wishes to the ones I gave Dasanat earlier," Tarix said. She looked around the room. They were alone.

"Lord Andarack, I need to have a conversation with these two, and I want you present, as long as you promise to keep this secret, even from any higher power who might want you to speak."

"I can do that, Tarix. I'll say nothing, though I have no love of conspiracies. Indeed, I think all this should be out in the open so people may see the danger we're in, but that is not my decision."

"No sweet words in your love's ear, either," Tarix added, smiling at the embarrassed man.

"Please, Tarix. No more teasing! Besides, our conversations are much more . . . practical than that."

Garet could hardly keep from laughing at this, but he liked the older man too much to prod him further.

Tarix must have thought so too, for she said, "Thank you for your discretion, Lord Andarack. I think we had better start, since Ratal will not be long in returning."

She signalled them all to sit and turned to Garet.

"I've already heard too much for my nerves, but much of it has been second-hand or worse. It's time to get it all straight. Garet, tell us all what you told me this morning and add anything you might have left out."

Garet did so, outlining the meeting with the king and Andarack and the attack on their team the other night. At the end of his tale, he hesitated.

Tarix was quick to notice. "What else? Clearly you have something more to say."

"Perhaps it's nothing, Master, but two or three times before the Tunneller demon's attack, I felt I was being watched, maybe followed, by a stranger hidden under a grey cloak."

"Was it that Mask, the one who seems to hate you so?"

Garet nodded. "I think it must have been, though I don't know why she is so . . . obsessed with me?"

"An admirer?" Andarack inquired innocently, getting some of his own back. "Perhaps she's just attracted to you."

"Hard to understand," Tarix said, "how she could be in love and still want to kill him."

"That part's easy to understand," Salick said under her breath, then aloud, "Master Tarix, with both this and the increase in demons, the hall is in a riot already. If these Masks continue to . . . interfere, there will be blood, and not just demon blood, on the streets!"

"True," Tarix said, "which means the king must find and stop these Masks as soon as possible. Lord Andarack, does Garet's account agree with what you know?"

Andarack stood. "Yes, Tarix, it does, and adds to it! As for the king, he will act. You have my word on that. Trax knows how delicate the balance of the city is. How could he not after the events of last winter? But what of these demon attacks? Are they a natural fluctuation or an aberration?"

Tarix scratched her head. "If I take your meaning right, they are the second one of those. No record in our hall talks of a similar increase. I can tell you the masters think it is the work of another Caller demon, one who stays hidden this time and works from the shadows."

"The other Caller could control only two other demons at a time," Salick said. She reached out to where she had placed her trident on the table beside her, as if the very mention of that beast would conjure it in the room.

"And we have felt these more recent demons' approach," she added. "A Caller would be able to mask their fear until they were upon us."

"These attacks come singly, though close together," Garet reminded her, "and perhaps not all demons of that type are able to hide their fear. So it could be a Caller demon, except . . ."

"What?" Salick said, turning to him. Her face was drawn, and he knew that she was envisioning the death of Mandarack at the Caller's claws, the old bane's shield piercing the thing's throat as his own chest was cut to bits.

He was seeing the same thing in his mind.

"I think we don't see the demons as they really are," he said.

There was a puzzled silence in the room. Andarack looked at him, head cocked to one side. Tarix leaned over and tapped his knee.

"Well then, how should we see these murderous fiends?" she asked. There was no humour in her voice, and Garet remembered that she had spent a life longer than his fighting the creatures and still endured the pain of that struggle.

Garet steeled himself and answered, "As a weapon, Master."

Silence again.

He pushed on, ready at last to say what had been building in him in all the months he had been in Shirath. Beginning as mere intuition, the dreams he had had the last two days had turned that into a definite belief.

"I've talked to many people in the city, both in the hall and outside it, and everyone accepts the demons as something as natural as bad weather and broken hearts. Nobody wonders what caused them to attack the South and now the Midlands. I've studied many of the ancient records, the writings of such early hallmasters as Moret and Sharict – even they didn't know! All their energies were used in fighting them, not understanding them."

"So it still is now," Andarack said. He poured four glasses of wine from a bottle on the table and handed the drinks around. "It is to King Trax's credit – I'm sorry, Salick, but it is – that he supports me in my study of the creatures. Because of that, we know something of the nature of the demons' jewels and perhaps how to counter them. But tell me, Garet, how would knowing the cause of them help us?"

Garet sipped before answering. It gave him time to order his thoughts.

"We might see what hand is behind these attacks and be able to strike at their source. I think that source must be a person. The Caller was clever, but not clever enough to coordinate every demon attack in Shirath, let alone the other four cities of the South and the entire Midlands! It acted on the basest of instincts, nesting, as it did in the banehall at the end, and attacking those that harmed it, which is why it followed me to Shirath after I blinded it in one eye on my way here."

Tarix stared at him and indicated he should continue. Salick's face was still as a stone mask, but at least she was listening.

Andarack scratched his cheek. "So this Caller demon was no king? Someone else was. But why? That demons are a Heaven-sent curse is easy to understand, but as a weapon in a war? Wars have a reason, though they may be idiotic ones. How can we be in a six-hundred-years war and not know it?"

"And are we winning?" Tarix asked.

Garet shrugged. "I think the reasons for it are lost in the past for now. Many records were destroyed when the demons came. We may never know why, but I fear we are not winning. In fact, I think we have been losing all this time, if only because our adversaries have what they want: our imprisonment."

Tarix looked at him in surprise. "How are we imprisoned? We have no jailers, no bars across our windows."

Garet waved an arm at the city beyond Andarack's hall.

"We've built our own cells, though we call them wards, and we dare go only a few leagues beyond them, and even then not without a bane guarding us. Fear is better than bars. As for jailers, that's what the demons are, attacking us just enough to keep us cowering in our cells. Because these attacks have continued for so long, they must be achieving their intent, and our confinement is the only thing that they have managed."

Salick stood suddenly, tipping the wine glass over on the table.

"So why have the attacks changed now? First the Midlands, then the Caller, now the increase – how do you explain that?" Salick demanded. She was flushed, and her hands were tightened into fists. Tarix put a warning hand on her arm.

"Let him speak, Salick. I know it rankles to think ourselves pieces in someone else's game, but there is at least some sense in what he says."

"Sense?" said Salick. "Heaven has decreed this curse for Shirath. Who are we to question it? Questions do nothing but ruin things. Our hall is under attack from both demons and the Masks while we sit here and debate a question that can't be answered!"

Garet stood up and deliberately placed his half full wine glass on the table beside him.

"Salick, I know things are bad right now, but give it some time and things will get better. We just have to think this through."

Perhaps he was talking about demons, perhaps he was talking about something else.

"But it does matter that the attacks have changed. It might mean that whoever is in control of the demons has tired of this war and wants to finish it, but I think they now act out of fear."

Tarix finished her wine, and Andarack poured another glass for her.

"Fear of what?" the Red asked.

"Us," Garet said. "They fear our increasing ability to fight back. Deaths from demon attacks have been falling for centuries for both banes and citizens, or so Records Master Arict tells me. The city's population has also been growing, especially since the plague of two hundred years ago. And one more thing: after the king and Lord Andarack left, Barick talked me half to death while we sorted those scrolls. He's a terrible gossip, but maybe that makes him a good historian. He told me that the ward lords and king are already planning to extend the city or even build a new town to the north-east. We're bursting out of the walls of our prison, and we are getting very good at killing our jailers. Maybe that's why this war is changing: first with the Caller and now with increased attacks."

"Enough!" Tarix said. "You'll make my head burst if you keep stuffing it like this. Let me think on this first and then you can fill it up again. What made you invent this grand conspiracy?"

Garet looked down at his master. Her face was troubled, but as long as he told her the truth, he knew that she would listen.

"I've wondered about this for a long time, but it was seeing Lord Andarack and the king play Surround. I dreamed of the game later and realized that we in Shirath were both hunters and prey. We hunt the demons, and they hunt us, just like on the board. Why are the Midlands being menaced now instead of six hundred years ago, and why the new demon forms and increased attacks? It might be our planned expansion, but I'm not really sure. What I am sure of is that there has to be a mind behind this change in tactics, and we know the demons have little in the way of thought."

Tarix nodded. "There is a logic in what you say, but I'll tell you this: your demon-wielding jailers have allies on the inside of this cell, for if Masks and banes fight, then the city will fall while we are distracted. That is why the hallmaster has demanded the king catch and imprison all these 'amateurs,' and he will not back down."

"Nor should he!" Salick said. She turned to Garet. "Don't you agree?"

"It is not my place to say," Garet said. He had no wish to make her even angrier.

Silence fell as they all took a moment to absorb what had been discussed. Then the banes took their leave of Andarack and rejoined Ratal and the others.

"We didn't see you, so we finished the rest of the ward and came back here," he told Tarix.

"You're beginning to improve, Ratal," his master told him. "Kesla's absence is bringing out the best in you, though I'll let you tell her that particular piece of news."

Ratal grinned and swung the flail up onto his shoulder, causing the two Greens to duck.

"Right then, to the hall!"

Salick did not walk beside Garet but took the lead, as if she wished to arrive at the banehall first and make sure it was still standing. Tarix dropped back beside him and put a comforting hand on his shoulder.

"Give her time, Garet. She worries about the hall more than most, maybe more than anyone except Branet. And like most of us, she cannot understand how to look beyond the hall, take it out of the centre of things, and put something else there. This war you speak of does that, and it frightens her. Claws, it frightens me! I'd think it all moonshine and mist except for the Caller's attack last year. That shook me to my bones, and nothing since has seemed sure again."

Garet was surprised she would speak so openly and gave only a nod as a response.

The Red smiled at his reserve and continued. "Mandarack once told me that Heaven sent you to us because we needed your eyes, needed to see what you saw before we all walked blindly off a cliff. We listened to you then and I'll listen now, though your words trouble me even more than before."

"You think I'm right?" Garet asked.

Tarix slapped him on the back. "I think you are right, but the hallmaster, the king, and the Masks all think they are right. You, however, have an eye for what serves the city, not what serves yourself. That, my young Green, can be a weapon as powerful as a demon."

The hall was still standing when they returned, but there was a beehive's swarm of banes in the courtyard and before the main doors. Pairs ran off towards the bridges and the hall-side wards as others came running back.

Tarix waved down one such pair, a Gold and a Blue, as they passed.

"Hey there! Kitoroth, what in Heaven's name is going on?"

Kitoroth slowed but waved his companion on. "I'll catch up. You go ahead and warn the palace-side patrols! Sorry, Master, we've not much time. A bane was attacked by the Masks. They chased him through the fields and city, they say. He's hiding at an astrologer's house. She sent word and the hallmaster's going there himself with twenty others to bring the lad back."

At that, he sped off again.

Salick and Garet looked at each other.

"Could it be . . ." Salick began. She started after the running banes but Tarix held her back.

"What do you two know of this?" she demanded.

Garet replied for them both. "It might be Marick. He's been away from the hall for two days."

"And he is the most likely of banes to find trouble!" Tarix said and raised her eyes to the sky. "I love that boy like he was my own, but I swear that I will kill him myself if he's hurt."

She pointed to the hall, and the others turned to see a column of banes jogging towards them. Red sashes graced their uniforms, and their weapons – from Relict's axe to Forlinect's spear – were all held ready.

Branet was in the lead and signalled them all to stop as they approached Tarix. "Tarix, I'm glad you're back. Have you heard of this outrage?"

"I have. Where are we going?"

Branet stared and shook his head. "I need you to guard the hall. We must travel fast and maybe fight our way through to the Fifth Ward!"

Tarix glared and turned to Ratal. "Take these others back and get all the Golds to guard each entrance to the hall. Lock it tight until we return." She shouldered her trident. "Set the pace, Hallmaster, we have a bane to rescue."

The Reds set off. Garet was glad to see Tarix keeping up with the rest of them, running beside her husband, Relict. At that speed, he guessed she might pay a price for it tomorrow, but he doubted she would fall behind. Ratal called them to follow and they returned to the hall. Dorict was sitting on the steps. He jumped up when he saw them approach.

"I knew it would be Marick. Who else would have a pack of Masks chasing him? Oh, what trouble has that fool gotten himself into now?"

The poor boy was fairly bouncing in his worry and irritation. Garet put an arm around his shoulders and turned his head to see the last of the Reds going through the central bridge gate.

What trouble indeed?

CHAPTER 13

MARICK'S ADVENTURE

O n the first day of his investigation, Marick was in no trouble at all. He had walked out into the wards, going from one to another looking for friendly ears in which to whisper his questions. Who are the Masks? Where can I find them? Do you know of any Duellists still free?

Despite his charms, which he knew to be many, and his guile, those questions went unanswered, and those he thought to be friends and admirers turned cold and bid him be off.

One, an old woman of foul temper and fouler language, threw a cabbage at him.

"Go on, you beast-born fool! Heaven smite you! Stop bothering a poor, defenceless woman and go away. Try the Twelfth, if you want your throat cut, and good luck to them."

Marick made an elaborate bow and ran off. Old Reebat might be unpleasant, but there wasn't a rumour in the city that didn't find its way into her hairy ears. He had no idea why she suggested the Twelfth Ward – it was the Traders' ward, one set aside to hold the many related families of the great trading houses that existed long before Shirath was built. They had a hand, or at least a few fingers, in every trade that went on within the walls, with the other Southern cities, and to even more distant places. Marick knew little about them, for they had always seemed too dull to attract his attention.

It was too late now to repeat his questions in the Twelfth Ward. Yawning, he went to find a place to sleep – anywhere but the banehall. He had several nooks and corners set in his memory, each one convenient to some kind of scam or plot, and sneaking away to one gave Marick a feeling of freedom that was as precious to him as air.

Lately, he had begun to question his life as a bane. They made little use of his talents, the hallmaster thought him a pest, and even Garet and Salick were beginning to sound like the others in their criticisms. Late last night, as he had snuck out the side gate, he had smiled. Let them snore, pressed down by tradition and stupidity!

The sun in his eyes woke him the next morning. He rolled off the bench set in the corner of a courtyard in the First Ward. A small girl with a large bucket of water stood nearby, staring at him. He smiled and waved, and she ran away, water sloshing out onto the stones. A neck-cracking stretch, a yawn and a scratch, then he was on his way. He hoped the day would be a busy one.

First, he snuck back into the banehall and left a note for the still-sleeping Dorict. He looked down at the Blue as he slept and wondered at their friendship. They had nothing in common except their shared experiences. Dorict hated adventures. He scolded Marick whenever he tried to have some fun, and worse, he loved reading and studying.

Marick shivered. Their friendship must be Heaven's

fate, for there could be no other reason. Sneaking out of the building again, he dropped into a stall in the Palace Plaza market and traded the cabbage he had kept from yesterday's investigations for the loan of a set of patched clothing: pants, tunic, and a faded green cloak that were never likely to sell. The merchant, a one-eyed occasional thief from the Fifth Ward, accepted the trade wordlessly. He and Marick had done business before. The bane's shield and uniform were stuffed under the shop's counter and covered with a basket.

So disguised, Marick went back across the bridge, avoiding the patrols of his hallmates and skirting the bane-hall by following the inner wall. At the Twelfth Ward gate, he slipped in between ox carts piled high with bolts of cloth.

He loped along, past Lord Tiralsh's house and up the main avenue dividing the houses of the rich from the tenements of the poor. Marick had never liked this ward. It was too ordered, each building placed as carefully as a piece on a game board. On his left were the square towers of the Trader families, with warehouses on the first floor and luxurious rooms above. Each was a uniform size and four storeys tall, and each had an elaborate clan crest carved over the door. Unlike buildings in the rest of the city, there were no windows on the first floor, only massive iron-studded doors, as if each family suspected their neighbours of plotting theft and murder.

Not an unlikely prospect, Marick decided. In the early days of the city, or so Garet had droned on about, there had been feuds over many issues: trading rights in certain wards; the chance to lead lucrative caravans to the south, east, and west; and even how much a pound weighed, if one could believe it. Knowing the stupidity of his fellow citizens all too well, Marick had decided he could.

Across from these commercial fortresses, three-storey tenements were lined up along the east wall. Here lived the workers who laboured for those Trader houses. These men and women lived in cramped conditions and ate poor food, but they lived. Some had been born in the ward and expected no better, though many had come because of bad luck in their home wards. A debt that couldn't be repaid, a brawl that left another badly injured, even a broken heart could send one here to work in a warehouse or scrub as a servant for a rich Trader family.

Marick shuddered. It was too much like the city of his birth, Old Torrick, situated at the top of the Falls on the River Ar. The ward lords there had grown wealthy by squeezing the trade moving from the rich Midlands to the other cities of the South. They had treated the whole population as their servants, and only now, with demons in the Midlands and an iron-willed hallmaster named Corix as their conscience, had the lords of Old Torrick reformed themselves.

He paused to let a pack of thin children run from the corner of one tenement to another as they chased a ball made of scraps of cloth. Before killing his first demon and being scooped up by Old Torrick Banehall, Marick had been a thief and beggar, living on the streets after his mother died. He knew first-hand how gnawing hunger could be when you saw the rich eat like pigs.

No, Marick did not like this ward.

"Make way! Move, you brat!"

Marick jumped aside as a cart's wheel missed him by inches. There was a snap, and pain crackled across his back.

He looked up to see a driver with a cart full of men and women turn his whip back to the horses. Fire danced in the bane's mind, and he was beginning to devise a suitable revenge when he caught sight of someone he recognized. One of the men in the cart was a Duellist, or an ex-Duellist, for all knew that group no longer existed. The man had a long face and a scar across his prominent nose, making him easy to place.

Marick followed the cart, careful to keep himself hidden in the shadow of buildings or behind taller workers carrying goods back and forth. The cart soon came to the outer edge of the ward. Here, large warehouses lay in the same irritating order. These held the goods meant to travel outside the city in bane-protected caravans, and the cart should have stopped there, but it didn't.

This was interesting. The Twelfth Ward had little in the way of fields and orchards outside the wall, preferring to make their profit from trade and buy their food with coin. Marick wondered where the bully with the whip intended to take these people, who might all be ex-Duellists and, perhaps, the mysterious mask wearers he wanted to find.

There was, of course, only one way to find out.

The cart went through the gates and out into the fields surrounding Shirath. When Marick tried to follow, the guards stopped him. The oldest, a woman with thin lips and cold eyes blocked his way with the butt of her spear.

"Where do you think you're going, beggar?"

In another ward, Marick might have played that part and tried to whine his way through, but the Twelfth Ward outlawed all forms of begging, and those who tried ended up in the warehouses, working for bread and water.

He straightened and pulled out a piece of paper from deep within his tunic.

"Trader Fairlock sent me to take this note to the Thirteenth Ward. It's a long walk to the other gate, so I want to go through here," he told the guard.

Drawn to his full height, he barely made her shoulder, but confidence made the lie believable. She took a cursory look at the note and tossed it back to him.

"Go on then, and stop bothering us," she said.

Marick strode out, ostentatiously placing the paper in his tunic – well, actually in a vest of many pockets he wore next to his skin. The paper had been torn from one of Dorict's books, something he hadn't discovered yet, and Marick trusted to the fact that guards were rarely literate. He stuffed it back in its pocket and checked to see if his other tools were still there. Thin knife for windows, lock-picks for the rare locked door in Shirath, cloth mask, coil of rope, ah, and there, a piece of bread and a crumb of cheese he had filched from the kitchens that morning.

Chewing as he walked, he found a drainage ditch, bone dry, that he could use to keep parallel to the cart. There were many workers in the fields today, using the dry weather to prepare the quiltwork of plots for planting or cleaning up after winter storms. Marick pulled up the hood of his cloak, lest someone call out to him and reveal his presence to those in the cart.

After much walking and occasionally jumping up to make sure he hadn't lost them, they came to the edge of the orchards. The newly leafed trees made it easier to escape detection, save that he still had to bend down to catch sight of the wheels.

The groves were not as wide as the fields, so Marick was only breathing moderately hard when they came to the wood lots that were the last sign of habitation surrounding Shirath, save for the river road. He expected the cart to stop for some secret meeting, but it continued on, deep into the woods. Now Marick had to make sure he didn't just lose the cart but himself as well, for the trees were set in identical rows in all directions, leaving no landmark save the road he needed to avoid. At last, he was forced to let the cart pass out of sight and then follow it on the track as it rumbled deeper into the woods.

He was footsore and thirsty when he heard voices calling ahead. He slipped into the trees, just beside the road, and made his way forward as quietly as possible. Being Marick, that was very quiet indeed.

There were wooden walls ahead, thick poles fixed upright to protect a logging station, one of many that lay scattered through these woods. This was a small one, and should have been deserted at this time of year while all turned their attentions to the fields. Winter was the time for cutting and trimming, or so Dorict had told him, and he should know, since his family were all loggers save him.

This station was humming with activity. The cart was emptied of its human cargo plus bags and casks of supplies that must have lain at their feet during the trip. None wore masks, and there was no taste of demon fear, which meant the stolen jewels were not there, unless they were safely locked in silkstone boxes somewhere nearby.

The cart started back to town. From behind a stout tree, Marick glared at the driver as he passed. He would leave that man, and his whip, for a more appropriate time. The gates of the station closed, and Marick creeped closer. Scaling the wall was a possibility, but there was a bane's tower in the centre of the station, built up above the level of the walls. If it was occupied by a watcher, any attempt to get over the wall in daylight would lead to capture, or worse. If Shirin was there, she might try cutting his throat again, and she would have plenty of help this time.

He found a crack between the timbers of the gate and looked within. The tower stood in the middle of the square. Barracks for the logging crews lined the inner walls but left a space open at each corner. The gate Marick peeked through stood in one such corner, and he could see that the corner directly across from him held a well. The people from the cart, and others, stood nearer the corner to his right, though that space was hidden from view at this angle by one of the long, low barracks. In all, about thirty people stood in the square, all of them looking towards that right-hand corner, save for one person inconveniently still in the tower, looking everywhere. They had tossed aside the clothes they wore from the city to reveal close-fitting black garments. A path of sorts had been laid out with white-washed rocks. Marick could not see where it led, but every person in the station was facing in that direction, and now they all put on stone masks.

Marick smiled at his luck then flinched. Something had tweaked his muscles, invisible claws that entered his body to pluck and pull at them. When he got his eye back to the crack, he saw a masked woman backing out of the hidden corner, spear in one hand and a small open box in the other. She kept going until she stood behind the first three of the other Masks. When she spoke, Marick heard her voice quite clearly.

"You feel it still, don't you? Well, the silkstone doesn't block it all out, just enough so that we can stand it, as long as you face towards the demon."

One of the three raised a finger to her ear to flick the unlucky word away, but Shirin, for Marick thought it must be her, slapped the hand down.

"Don't do that! We make our own luck here. Now, advance, just as if you were duelling. The trick is to keep in mind what you want to do. You want to kill demons, right? You want those clawed banes to eat dust, don't you? Hold those thoughts like a fire between you and the fear. Build that fire, stoke it with hate, and you'll get close enough to put a spear in some demon's throat."

Marick frowned. He didn't care to admit it, but Shirin was right. Most banes held a counter-thought to the fear. His own was imagining the anger of the demon when it realized Marick had tricked it. He held that image of them choking on their frustration in front of him now, and this allowed the fear he felt in his bones to loosen enough that he could act. That was how he had killed the Rat demon that made him a bane and how he had dealt with his enemies forever after.

This was interesting, he decided. If Shirin had discovered a way to help these clawed Duellists actually kill demons, maybe they should make a pact with them. He fingered the scar below his neck. It came from the knife Shirin once held against his throat. Well, maybe not allies, he thought. And who knew if the city would be big enough for both banes and Masks?

The first three advanced and backed up several times before Shirin released them. Now archers stepped up. Keeping their faces pointing directly forward, they loosed arrows towards the source of the fear, though some went wide of the mark and hit the nearby buildings.

Shirin stepped forward and took a bow, nocking an arrow and pulling the string back to her stone-covered cheek.

"Here's where breathing is most important," she told them. "Don't try to see everything, just the centre of the target, the spot on the demon you're aiming at. Then breathe normally, in and out as if you were walking down a street with not a care in the world. Focus on one spot and breathe. When you're ready, hold the in-breath and release."

The string twanged, and there was a solid thunk as the arrow hit the hidden target. The others took up their bows again and improved under her guidance. Then three more took the bows, then another group, until all had tried, and Marick began to suffer from boredom. He considered his next move.

Well, if it's all archery practice from now on, I'll learn nothing new, but I'm sure Branet and Andarack want to recover the silkstone, so telling them about this will get me into their good graces, even the king's, and wipe away a multitude of present and future sins!

Perhaps he should have been thinking of his retreat rather than imagining his triumph, for he failed to notice Shirin walk out of sight with the box in her hand. The thrill of fear vanished, and all the trainees took off their masks, including the man in the tower, who began to scan his surroundings in a depressingly thorough way.

Claws! Better to run than think, so remember that next time. Claws and jaws both! Some are coming to the gate. Time to find a hole to hide in!

Running around the wall would get him no closer to safety with that man in the tower, but a drying shed was nearby. He jumped across a saw-pit and managed to squeeze between the stacks of green lumber before the gate opened and disgorged a group of unmasked Masks.

"That was tough," a woman said. She was answered by a deep-voiced man.

"It gets easier. I nearly wet myself the first time, now it's nothing to split open a demon's skull with this axe!"

The voices paused near the entrance to the drying shed.

"That was closed when we arrived in the cart," the woman said.

"Get the others," said the man.

The door Marick had squeezed through, and not quite closed, creaked wide. A huge figure stood there, a man of prodigious proportions who held a large axe in one hand. His face was as blunt as stone, with heavy brows, a chin like a ship's prow, and small eyes that raked the stacks of boards and drying beams.

Marick eased back, trying to find a gap in the piles to slip into when disaster struck. His foot came down on something that snapped, and an avalanche of laths slid down the stack to come to rest at the feet of the searcher. Others came running up behind him, the first bearing a bow.

"Something or someone's in here," the giant said. "It's no demon, so find it and kill it."

Marick tried stepping backwards again, but the pile shifted alarmingly. He took a deep breath and kicked out. The boards flew towards the door, sending his pursuers scuttling to safety. Marick climbed spider-like up the next pile, then the next, trying to reach the rear of the shed. Something cut the air next to his ear and an arrow slapped between the roof supports to knock down a shingle. The light shone right upon Marick as he crouched, trying to pull slivers out of his hands. He gave up and returned to climbing and cursing as quickly as he could. More arrows followed, but the lumber that had given him away now protected him. The big man picked up the archer nearest him and threw him up onto the stacks.

"Get him. If he talks we're all dead!"

No further incentive was needed, and soon the piled lumber was crawling with black-clothed figures.

Shouts coming from ahead alerted him that some had run around the shed to enter from the other side – a problem, since that was the way Marick had intended to escape. Pausing for breath, he crouched low to avoid another arrow that, like the first, merely killed a few shingles. He looked up and grinned, for his enemies had shown him the best way out. With a dangerous leap across the gap, Marick reached the tallest pile of lumber. In moments, he was lying on his back and kicking at the roof. When he'd made a big enough hole, he reversed his efforts and kicked downward, shifting the top of the pile over and onto at least one of his pursuers, whose cry of dismay was cut off by an avalanche of oak.

Marick ran along the roofline of the shed, teetering until he got to the middle and slid down the slope. He swung over the edge of the roof, held onto the jutting eaves until he could will himself to let go. The drop was bad enough, but he knew to roll when he hit the ground, and came up more or less functional.

He whirled around. They had not found him yet, but soon would. He had no wish to meet that monster with the axe face-to-face, since the meeting would likely be a short one and end with him in two parts: a bodiless head and a headless body, neither of which would suit him. Where could he go that they wouldn't look? After a moment that seemed as long as a season, he slapped his forehead, yelped when the newest slivers were driven deeper, and ran into the station. If what he needed was still there, he might make it back to the banehall to prove his story. He found the place deserted. From the shouts outside, they were still searching around and inside the shed.

He ran past the bane's tower and stopped. There, the corner he couldn't see into before. He skidded into it. The space held an archery target with the arrows already pulled out and a stack of weapons pushed to one side. His eyes searched for the thing that might save him. Yes! Near the wall was a tree stump cut low for a seat and on it was a small stone box. He picked it up and hugged it to his chest, just as he heard running feet announcing the return of his murderous hosts.

He peeked around the corner and dodged back as an arrow zipped by. Unhospitable, he decided, but like a good guest he now had a gift to bring to the festivities. Marick opened the box he held, revealing the rough, pebble-shaped demon jewel within. The cries of anger turned to groans, and he stepped out of his hiding place, protected by the circle of fear that now surrounded him. With the box held high and the lid raised, Marick felt the effect the same as the others, but he was a bane after all, and demon jewels were nothing new to him.

"A shame you all took off your masks," he squeaked, though none appeared to hear him. "I must be going now. You know a bane is always busy, but I hope we meet again someday, Shirin. Perhaps if I ever pass the king's prison I'll stop by and say hello!"

Stiff-legged, he walked past all the crouched and writhing figures on the ground until he came to the gate. One figure stood there, not the axe man, for he was as blasted as the rest, but a woman, one Marick recognized.

"You," Shirin said. She was gripping her spear so hard the wood squeaked, yet she stayed, standing, in his path.

"Me," replied Marick. He waved the box at her.

The point of her weapon trembled like a leaf in the wind, but if she didn't attack, neither did she fall down.

Marick was forced to edge around her, feeling the heat of her gaze track him like shooting stars. He knew she would be the first after him and backed away, trying to keep them frozen with the jewel for as long as possible, for the moment they were free, they would put on their masks and run him down.

When Shirin shook herself and started running, so did he.

Marick kept to the road, depending on speed to make it to the fields and maybe lose himself in the work crews. He briefly debated dropping the jewel on the road and hoping it would delay them but realized that they would probably be wearing their masks by now and would be able to bypass that particular obstacle, especially if they had another silkstone box. He closed the one in his arms and ran all the faster. He needed no demon fear to spur him on. Human fear was enough. The oaks and ash trees turned to apples before he heard any sound of pursuit. Now was the time to dodge into the fruit trees. He swerved between cherries and pears and hoped that they would hide him well enough for him to reach the fields unseen.

They didn't. An arrow cut the leaves off a branch next to him, and a shout went up from the frustrated archer.

"He's here! I almost got him."

Almost doesn't help anyone, my friend, Marick thought, and laughed as he remembered Dorict's jibe. His own life had revolved around "almosts" since he was a child running on the rooftops of Old Torrick and stealing his suppers. He had been the best thief in the city, uncatchable, save by the Old Torrick banehall, and he had escaped even that prison within a year to come to Shirath.

He would not be caught again.

He changed the pattern of his weaving to confound the next arrow, and the next, until he broke out into the fields and groaned. No one was nearby.

He took a breath and sprinted for the nearest crew, a group of weeding women, half a league away. He hoped he was as fleet as the vegetable seller in Garet's story, for the noise of the pursuing Masks was getting louder.

He was nearly there when the first arrow hit the ground ten feet in front of him. He swerved, the wrong way as it turned out, for his leg spouted fire, and he looked down to see a black arrow, the needle point dripping blood, sticking through the fabric of his tattered pants.

Keep running, Marick told himself, *or you'll be caught. It's painful but not crippling, not yet.* The women in the work party were shouting and pointing, and one went running off towards a bane riding a horse several fields away.

"Leave the boy alone!" a stout woman shouted, and picked up a stone from a pile on the edge of the furrows and threw it at the Masks.

It fell woefully short, but Marick appreciated the impulse, especially when the rest of the women copied her. A cry from behind him told the bane that somebody found their target.

"Keep running, lad," the first woman shouted at him as he passed. "We'll hold them back!"

She picked up her hoe and swung it at the nearest pursuer, who raised his bow, arrow nocked.

"No!" Shirin cried out. She batted the bow aside, and the arrow wobbled harmlessly into the air.

"They aren't our enemies. Circle around, get the boy!"

The Masks tried to disengage from the fieldworkers but found it difficult as stones and hoes rained down on them. Bruised and pursued, at least until the women stopped, they took after Marick again, trying to cut the lead the bane had achieved.

The pain in Marick's leg grew from a burning to little

lightning shocks at each step. He made for the Fourteenth Ward's outer gate, for he had come out of the orchards to the east of where he had entered. The gate was open, and he ran through under the startled gaze of the guards.

"Bandits, robbers, murderers!" Marick shouted, but he had little hope the two could keep out the mob chasing him.

He found an alley to hide in and examined his leg. The arrow had pierced through the outer edge of his thigh. Marick tore off a strip of his tunic, wishing he was wearing something cleaner. With the small knife hidden in his vest, he cut his trousers between the two holes and pulled out the arrow.

That he didn't faint was proof of Heaven's regard, for the pain was worse than anything he had ever felt before. He tied the strip of tunic around his leg and tossed the arrow under a doorstep. After a moment's appreciation of his agony, he considered his next move.

The problem was that there were enough people wanting to kill him to sweep every alley in this ward. He looked up at the rooftops and then down at his leg. He would have to try. His youth had been spent above the city of his birth, looking down on the fools and villains who thought themselves better than a little thief and beggar. He had proved them wrong often enough, and now he had to do it again or die.

The courtyard provided stairs, and he climbed as fast as he could. The bandage helped, as did the cries of the Masks when they found his blood in the alley. On the rooftop, he looked towards the inner wall. It was at least ten buildings away. He would never make it.

This made him grin, then laugh, then start running. He cleared the narrow space between the first two buildings, landing in a painful roll but getting up again and running faster. So he went, from building to building, while some of the Masks ran below and two tried to copy his rooftop progress.

A long cry and painful thump sounded behind him, and he turned to see only one Mask left, and he was clinging to the edge of the roof, legs dangling in the air. Marick bowed and kept going, jumping the next building and avoiding the arrow that was shot up from below. The next gap was impossible to jump, as the facing building was a storey higher than the one he was on, so he looked at the distance across the street instead. After a moment, he grabbed a plank from a half-built summer shelter, a rough construction of poles, plank flooring, and colourful awnings. It bounced on his shoulder as he ran to the edge. Sticking the end of it under a water tower, he waved at his pursuers and ran out to the end, using the spring in the wood to bounce up and out. He cleared the wide street and fell onto a rooftop to the west. Shaken, he staggered to his feet and looked back. The remaining Mask on the rooftop was waving and shouting, trying to signal his change of direction to his friends below. Marick grinned. If it wasn't for the pain in his leg, he might actually have enjoyed this chase.

A deep breath and then running again. There was a gap ahead that was narrow enough to take him to his goal. After the jump, he climbed the ladder of a water tower, then pulled the ladder up and set it again. In a moment, he stood on the wall between the two wards.

Now he had to rest for a moment. He retied the bandage and was shocked to see it soaked with blood. Another torn strip served to reinforce it, but he wished he was in the banehall, being tended to by Banerict and fussed over by Vinir. Cheered by that thought, he looked over the wall into the Fifteenth Ward below. He had been there but a day ago, getting a cabbage thrown at his head by old Reebat. He balanced on the wall and pulled up the ladder, then stopped.

Tottering on the top of the wall, death by Masks on one side and death by gravity on the other, he began to dance, despite his leg, capering about in an ecstatic vision of how he was going to fool them all.

He hopped along the top of the wall until he found a place he could let down the ladder and slip into the nearest lane. Now was the difficult part. He twisted his torn pants around until his bandage was covered, and concentrated on walking as normally as possible. This slow pace grated on his nerves, for he knew the Masks would be searching for a way to follow him, even if it meant going all the way around to the Fifteenth Ward's inner gate.

At last he came to Reebat's hole-in-the-wall shop. Besides vegetables and dubious meats, she sold used clothing and small articles, providing a useful enough service that the ward ignored her horrible personality.

"You again!" the old woman cried when Marick entered the shop. She rose off her stool and looked about for another missile.

By the time she had settled on a chipped flowerpot, Marick had taken out the silkstone box and held it up in front of her watery eyes.

"Easy there, Grandmother! I need your help. I've got to hide this, and you're the only one I trust."

Reebat looked at the box suspiciously, weighing the pot in one hand.

"What is it?" she asked.

Marick made an exaggerated shushing motion of a finger across his lips.

"Shhh, I can't tell you, though you'd faint if you knew how valuable it was. Now, I need you to keep this for me, and I need a cart to get me away from here, something I can hide in. When I sell what's inside that box, I can pay you very well indeed."

The old woman put down the flowerpot and rubbed the hairs of her chin. The light in her eyes was not kindled by generosity or simple human kindness.

Marick smothered a grin. The hook was set. Now to pull in the line.

"Listen, Mistress, there's some after me that want this back. If you can get your son to take me across the bridge and away from them, I'll cut you in for, say, five percent."

"Fifty percent!" Reebat screeched. She looked around for where she had set the pot.

"Ten, no more!" Marick shouted, and so it went until thirty percent was agreed upon, and Reebat called her son to come out from the back room.

"Get the cart and pile some clothes on this wretch. Take him to, where are you going, scamp?"

Her son, whose name Marick didn't know, nor even if he had a name, nodded. He was a florid, middle-aged man who rarely came out of the back room where he sorted the flotsam and jetsam that came into the shop. Now that Marick thought upon it, he probably didn't need a name.

The bane presented Reebat the box. "The Fifth Ward, Grandmother. Now, I must warn you not to open this while I'm gone. If there's any trouble on the way, I'll come right back and retrieve it, at the agreed-upon split. Otherwise, I'll get it tomorrow, and we'll divvy up the profits then. On your life, don't open it. Agreed?"

The old lady attempted a smile. It did not suit her face, and even her son shuddered, sending ripples of fat dancing over his jowls. He led Marick to his cart, dumped a smelly assortment of clothing and trash over him, and set off, pulling it himself like a draft horse.

Marick held his nose and tried to calculate several timelines, any one of which could spoil his wonderful plan. The Masks might find him too soon, and his two-legged horse wouldn't say a word against them searching his cart, of that Marick was sure. If that particular disaster did not fall, then he might not make the bridge gates before the alarm went up, and that depended on a third interval, that of Reebat's volcanic greed. The bump accompanying each cobblestone was like the ticking of one of Lord Andarack's clocks. To quiet the pain in his leg, Marick plucked slivers from his hands with his teeth and counted the wheel's bumps, trying to guess how far they had come.

He felt a new smoothness to the road and decided they must be in the Banehall Plaza. He almost jumped from his hiding place to make a run for the hall, but restrained himself. He feared there would be an archer or two in the surrounding gardens, waiting for him to try so they could finish him off and then disappear into the midday crowds.

The distance between the hall and the bridge gates seemed to stretch into forever. Finally, they slowed down and stopped.

Marick pulled apart a peephole in the pile of smelly clothes and looked out. Ten or more Masks were ranged in front of the gates, including Shirin with her spear and the giant with his axe. The guards had been disarmed and were glaring at their captors.

The hall was sounding like the better plan now, though it would be a dangerous dodge, and he couldn't count on any help against such odds. Now he wished he had found a way to disguise his shield instead of leaving it at the shop in the market. That might have given him a chance against the arrows.

He was coiling himself up for a sudden springing escape when cries went up on the far side of the plaza. A thrill went up his spine, half fear and half exultation. Reebat had done it! She had opened the box, unable to keep her greedy fingers off whatever treasure she imagined was inside. At this distance, the effect was only apparent to a bane and, it seemed, to a Mask.

Shirin ran back from the gate, past the line of carts and waiting people, to stand and search, turning her head back and forth.

"It's a demon, probably in a ward behind the banehall. Let's go!"

The big man grabbed her shoulder. He towered over her, shouting. "You're mad! We have to find that brat. If he tells what he knows, we're done!"

Shirin whipped around, and the other felt the point of her spear at his throat, just under the stone chin of the mask.

"Listen very carefully," Shirin said. She walked forward, forcing the big man back. "We fight demons. That's why we exist, whatever your master thinks. If you want to leave, do so, but first give me your mask."

The man stumbled away from the point, a trickle of red running down his neck.

The other Masks ranged themselves behind Shirin. Nine Masks looked at one, and the one gave in.

"All right," the axeman said. "But you heard that bane. He knows who you are. Soon, the hall and palace will too. After this, you should hide out on your own for a while, lest you draw attention to the rest of us."

"Don't worry. Tell your master that I'll stay with a relative I trust until things calm down," Shirin said. "Now follow me. It's time to kill a monster."

They turned and ran off towards the southern wards, the big man still grumbling and taking up the rear.

The guards took some time to recover their weapons and pride before allowing anyone through. One ran off towards the palace while Marick followed at his cart's leisurely pace.

He had actually fallen asleep by the time they stopped. Light hit his eyes as Reebat's son pulled off the pile of clothing.

"Fifth Ward," the man said, and turned the cart around when Marick got out.

"Thank you, my friend!" Marick said. "Tell me your name, so that I might ask Heaven to guard you."

The man just shrugged and pulled the cart away with all the calm resignation of a nameless beast.

Marick made it to his goal step by agonizing step. He had treated his leg very badly today, and now it was returning the favour. At the steps leading up to his hopeful refuge, he paused and looked down at the bandage. Soaked again. He hoped Alanick wouldn't mind him bleeding all over her expensive carpets. With a smile on his face and that thought in his head, he fainted, and the great astrologer came down the stairs herself to order him carried up to her couch.

CHAPTER 14
THE MASKS REVEALED

Garet and Dorict were still waiting on the steps when Marick returned.

"They're coming back," Ratal said, using two higher steps and his own height to an advantage. The Gold had been there for hours, following his master's orders to guard the doors of the banehall.

"Who are all those with them?" Dorict asked. He needed neither Ratal's height nor his elevated position to see that the group was much larger than the one that had set out.

Garet strained his eyes to make something out in the bobbing light of the torches the arrivals carried. He caught glints of light reflecting off steel breastplates and the heads of pikes.

"I think the king's guard comes with them," he said.

"And some ward guards too, or I'm still seeing double," Kesla said. The Gold had come out of her sickbed to stand watch with her teammates. She still had a bandage wrapped around her head and leaned on her flail to keep from falling. Ratal's most passionate pleas had not persuaded her to return to the infirmary. She had snatched the weapon he had borrowed and snapped, "Get your own, oaf!" and then glared at Garet to smother any further argument against her presence.

The group was close enough now to prove her right. The masters clustered around a handcart, the palace guards surrounded them, and the Fifth Ward guards trailed behind, looking like they wished they were somewhere else.

The hallmaster was easily located by his raised voice.

"No, Captain. You will not ask questions of the lad. This is bane business. I shall inform the king when I find the time appropriate! You there, at the gates! Stand ready to close them and secure the hall."

Ratal rushed down to do so, and Garet followed reluctantly, leaving Dorict with the injured Gold. The palace guard came no further than the iron fence, and the ward guards had already turned eagerly towards the bridge gates. Together, he and Ratal pushed the heavy ironwork shut and threw the bar across to lock it.

The big Gold set himself there as if he meant to stay all night and repel the squadron of armed guards with just the superior look on his face. The captain stood and returned his stare for a moment, then signalled her squad to about-face and march back to the palace.

Ratal preened and turned to Garet. "The nerve of those arrogant fools to come against the banehall!" he said.

"Were they coming against us?" Garet asked. "It looked to me like they were guarding the masters. Can I leave? I have to go and see how Marick is."

Ratal nodded nobly and turned to face the darkened plaza. "I will remain here."

With Dorict's help, they got Kesla through the crowds

of confused banes in the hallways and back to the infirmary. By the time they laid her on her cot, she was sweating and green in the face.

"Claws! Next time I might just take Banerict's advice and stay in bed."

The physician came up and took her pulse. He made the appropriate disapproving noises and moved on to where Marick lay amid a circle of onlookers. Among the Red Sashes, Garet spotted a Gold one. He slipped through to stand beside Salick. Dorict appeared at his elbow, and they all looked down at the wounded bane.

"He's never been happier," Dorict growled. "All this fuss over him? It's all he's ever wanted."

"Dorict?" came a weak voice from the bed. "Is that you, friend Dorict?"

The stout Blue relented at the pitiful sound of his friend's voice and came close to take his hand.

"Are you all right? Were you badly hurt?" he asked.

Everyone surrounding the bed leaned in closer to hear the answer.

The all-too innocent face nestled among the pillows and blankets whispered, "Banerict said I might have died."

Dorict sniffed.

"Actually," the physician shouted, "I said I might kill you myself, if I recall." The usually compassionate man glared at his patient and then the other banes.

"Sometimes you are all too foolish for words! I have set more broken bones than all the other physicians in the city combined. I have stitched up tears from claws, punctures from teeth, slashes from demon skull-ridges, and Heaven knows what else. I have healed an uncountable number of training injuries, including broken toes and fingers, wrenched shoulders, twisted knees and ankles, and torn muscles I had no idea existed until I came here. Now add to that all the other ills of a bane: nightmares, nervous collapse, loss of appetite, broken hearts, and so on. I have even had the misfortune" – and here he glared at Garet and Salick – "of tending banes punctured by swords. But that isn't enough for you suicidal idiots! Now you bring me arrow wounds!"

He threw up his hands. "What is this city coming to?" he asked, and his audience wisely chose silence and retreat as their only answer.

The others left until only Dorict, Salick, and Garet remained, along with Tarix, who sat on the sleeping Kesla's bed and watched the physician boil.

"Easy, Banerict. I'm sure Marick didn't go looking for that wound," she said. "How bad is it?"

The stooped man huffed and then answered, "Not too bad. Luckily it just pierced the outside of his thigh. A bit to the left and it would have been but a scratch. As it is, he's lost enough blood to make him weak for a day or so. You can all stay for just a moment, then let the boy rest."

And with that, he was off to his room at the end of the infirmary, his progress marked by muttering.

Tarix left Kesla to sit on a stool beside Marick's bed.

"Oh, that's good to rest the leg. I daren't tell Banerict I overdid it by running all the way to the Fifth Ward. He'd burst like overripe fruit!"

She looked at Marick, who moaned at her. The Red frowned.

"I told Banerict I didn't think you went looking for that arrow, but we both know that is exactly what you did. Idiot! No, don't try your tricks on me. Moaning won't help you now. Marick, I swear by Heaven's shield that I will feed you to a demon myself if you don't immediately tell me all that went on and what clawed reason you had to do it!"

Marick sat up, looking less at death's door and more on his best behaviour. He avoided the glares of his friends, especially one from Dorict that might have set him on fire.

"Master, I really didn't try to get hurt! It just turned out that way. I was helping the hall, and I just got into a little trouble, that's all."

"A little trouble?" Salick said. "*Little trouble* doesn't need the protection of bane, king, and ward, or come back with a hole in its leg!"

Garet bit his tongue. He had tried to make the boy more responsible, but Marick would always be Marick. There was no doubt he would lead an interesting life, no matter how short it was.

"Talk," said Tarix.

An hour later, Banerict shooed them out of the infirmary, and Tarix took the others to the room she shared with Relict. Her husband was sitting at a table mending a tear in his sash when they came in.

"What's this? Company at such a late, no, I suppose *early* hour? My dear, how is your leg? I saw how hard you worked to keep up."

Tarix shrugged. "Painful, but if that is what it costs, that is what I'll pay. Now listen to what Marick told us."

She repeated the story of the Blue's spying on the Masks and his narrow escape. Relict's eyes widened at the young bane's near-capture at the bridge gate.

"Well, luck is better than wisdom, it seems. Though it was a clever trick with the jewel."

Salick shook her head. "One that might have gone badly wrong had that old woman opened the box too early or too late, Master. But what surprises me is that the Mask, Shirin, gave up the chase to go fight what she thought was a demon."

Relict nodded. "Branet would hate to hear me say this, but it was a very bane-like decision. He has sent a demand to the king that 'all false banes' must be captured at once. The wording of that letter was insulting enough that I doubt the king will even reply. And King Trax is on his side, if our hallmaster would just notice. The fortune teller who sheltered Marick sent word to both the hall and the palace, and the king ordered out his guards right away to protect us on the way back."

"There were some ward guards too," Garet said.

Tarix sat on the bed and raised her leg. She took off the brace, and Relict put a cushion under her knee.

"Those were from the Fifth Ward," she said. "Lord Sacourat wished to be seen as helpful and loyal, I would guess."

"There are only thirty or so Masks, according to Marick. They would never have dared attack a party that large," Relict added.

"Then what do they want?" Garet said.

"To replace us," Dorict said. There were shadows under the boy's eyes, and Garet remembered that none of them had slept that night, and now the dawn was almost upon them.

"That's what Shirin told you," Salick said.

Tarix nodded, but Garet shook his head.

"She may have said that, but really, how could they? Thirty Masks and sixteen wards to patrol? They can't believe it would work! I think she, and maybe all of them, just want to fight demons."

"An odd wish," Dorict said. "Maybe they should talk to

Banerict, and he can list all our common injuries for them. It might put them off."

Relict laughed. "It almost put me off. We'd better ask him to keep quiet, or some banes will be looking for a less dangerous job."

"Would they?" Garet asked. "Do you know of any bane who would stop fighting demons?"

The others looked at him. Salick bit her lip. Tarix shook her head.

Leaning back against the pillows, the Red said, "No bane I ever met would stop protecting the city. Even Adrix's threat to do so was a bluff, for the masters would never have agreed."

"Why?" Garet asked.

Salick answered, "Because you just can't stand by if . . . if . . ."

"If you can make a difference," Dorict said, and the room fell silent for a time.

Relict poured water for his wife, then his guests. "Maybe every man and woman in Shirath would do the same if they could," he said. "And maybe I've judged these Masks too harshly."

Salick bristled. "They tried to kill Marick, and that woman threatened Garet. Doesn't that matter?"

Garet put an arm around her shoulder. She was shaking with fatigue and anger.

"I'm all right," he said, "and so is Marick for all his moaning. Something is still hidden from us. I think that the Masks are being used. The big man, the one with the axe we saw, Marick said he tried to order Shirin around, as if he spoke for someone else. He even forced her to hide until things calmed down, so I don't think she's really in charge."

"If only we knew where she was hiding, we could go ask

her," Dorict said. His head drooped, and he jerked it back up again.

"I'm too tired to think now, Masters. I must get some sleep."

"Go, all of you," Relict said. "And keep out of trouble."

Dorict could barely climb the stairs and fell down on his bed still dressed. Garet yawned and pulled off the boy's boots and then his own. Salick watched him from the doorway, her eyes half closed.

"Garet, I can't believe you're defending Shirin, after all she's done to the hall," she said, and slid away when he tried to embrace her.

"My love, I'm not defending her. I'm trying to understand her! If we want to end this foolishness, we'll have to do it by talking, like we did last winter. The palace, the hall, you and me: we've always been stronger when we work together."

This time she did not evade his arms, nor his mouth as he kissed her goodnight, but there was no smile on her face as she broke away and went off to her own room.

CHAPTER 15
TWISTS, TURNS, AND TALK

To say that the banehall was in an uproar when the sun rose would be putting it mildly indeed. A pack of Shrieker demons skittering through the hallways could not have made more noise and confusion. The Black and Blue Sashes, as well as any Greens that had slept through the events of the evening, now woke and added their shouts to the loud calls for answers, for reassurance, and most of all, for revenge.

Garet had laid down his head for an hour or so in his room. He woke to the sounds of argument and lay for a moment, listening and remembering. His body protested as he got to his feet, but it was light, and there was washing up, breakfast, and training to do before Forlinect would need him to help with the Black Sashes. He yawned his way to the washrooms, trying to ignore the knots of banes discussing the Masks in very loud voices.

"We should find them and kill them all!" said a Gold, one of Taron's team, Garet thought.

His fellow disagreed. "Are we no better than them? They should be put on the chain gangs like the other Duellists!"

A third spoke up. "What about the king? Can't he protect us?"

The first shouted back, "And what if the king is behind it, like last time? What should we do then?"

And so it went down the hallway with variations of this conversation repeated over and over. After scrubbing himself slightly more awake, Garet went back to the room and got dressed. He decided that training would be quieter than breakfast, so he went to the training rooms first, only to find the larger one crowded with Red Sashes, one of whom shooed him away with one hand while shaking a fist in the face of Bandat with the other.

The other room was almost empty. Tarix was there working with Dalesta, the Green who was so often sick. They were doing the same exercise Dorict practised, though a longer version and without the weights.

"Breathe in and out with the movements," Tarix was saying as Garet walked into the room. "This is a good routine for building up your lungs. Big movements now. Breathe in . . . and out! Ah, Garet. Could you help me do my stretches? My leg is playing up today and needs the punishment."

While Dalesta moved through the sequences of punches and kicks, Garet helped Tarix regain some flexibility in her injured leg. She put the brace back on when they were done and sat with him on a bench watching Dalesta move.

"She'll breathe more easily if she keeps up the exercises, and Banerict has a salve for her chest that will help as well."

"She's not very strong, is she?" Garet said. He did not mean it as an insult. He was thinking of how unprepared most banes were to take up arms against their enemy. He knew he had been so and still felt overwhelmed at times by the responsibility on his shoulders.

"Yet she still wants to fight," Tarix said, reminding Garet of their conversation a few hours ago.

"I've been thinking of what you said, last night and in Lord Andarack's house," she continued. "If you are right about someone controlling demons, and if that player has now changed their tactics in hopes of destroying us – there are many 'ifs' in your arguments, aren't there – then we must change our tactics too, and quickly. The problem is I don't see how that can be done."

"The masters are meeting now," Garet said. He wondered why Tarix was here instead of with the others. "Aren't you . . . ?"

"Thirty people won't make any more sense than twenty-nine," she said, and fiddled with the brace for a moment, tightening one of the straps. "One thing I've found is that most people have to shout before they're ready to talk. Don't expect that talking to happen for a while, not while the Masks are attacking banes."

Dalesta stopped, wheezing heavily, and Tarix told her to walk once around the banehall and then go to get her breakfast. The Green smiled at them and shuffled out, one hand on her side.

"Not very strong, but not very weak either," Tarix said, and Garet nodded.

"Master, you said to tell you before I did anything. I'd like to tell you now."

Tarix raised an eyebrow. "It's nothing as reckless as what Marick did, is it?"

Garet grimaced and shook his head. "It's probably worse, but I don't see how it can be avoided."

Tarix raised her eyes, ran a hand through her short, sweaty hair, and sent up a silent prayer for patience.

"WAKE UP! We have somewhere to go."

Dorict opened one eye, and that only a crack. Garet stood over him, holding out a set of very non-bane clothes. The Blue's vision widened, focused, and the other eye appeared.

"What are those?" he mumbled. Dorict reached for the covers and found none. They lay in a heap on the floor, and he soon joined them when Garet rolled him over and over until he fell.

"Ow! Garet, what are you doing?"

He sat up and rubbed a smarting elbow. He opened his mouth to complain, and Garet stuffed a fruit-filled bun in it.

"That's compliments of Torfor in the palace market. He also got us these clothes while you've been abed. Come on, we'll change in one of the first-floor washrooms and sneak out through the kitchen yard gate."

Dorict was dragged down the stairs, his tunic and vest askew and his sash wrapped around his neck. Every time he tried to demand an explanation, Garet stuffed another bun in his mouth.

"Here, put these on. Take off your boots too. They're too shiny for where we are going. Here are some shoes; I had to guess your size."

Dorict chewed and put on the shoes. Garet had guessed a little too small, but he could still walk in them due to the sprung stitching. They stashed their uniforms and boots in a cupboard behind a stack of towels and slipped out of the banehall. They were halfway across the cropped gardens of the plaza when Dorict pulled on Garet's arm, stopping him short.

"No! No more buns, at least not now. Garet, will you please tell me what is going on. Where are we going, and why are we dressed like this?"

He planted his feet on the paving stones and refused to move. The crowds of midday swirled around them in currents of colour, ignoring this temporary obstacle on the garden path. Garet relented and smiled at his friend.

"Dorict, I need your help. We are going to try to track down Shirin and talk some sense into her," Garet said, leaning in so his words would go unheard by any other.

Dorict stared at him, mouth open. He looked back towards the banehall as if it were the last refuge of sanity in the world.

"First we have to get someone to talk sense into you!" he said, not lowering his voice at all. "Do you remember that she wants to kill you? And have you forgotten what happened when Marick found them?"

"Marick was spying on them, and I'm not entirely sure she would have attacked me that night. Let me finish! Someone has to open negotiations with the Masks. We can't stumble into another civil war, can we? They need to see that they'd be better off under the hall's command, or the king's, rather than whoever is controlling them now."

Dorict scratched his head, but stopped when he found a shapeless hat in the way of his fingernails. He took it off and looked at it in some confusion.

"I know you think there is some dark force behind the Masks, Garet, but maybe Marick got it wrong, or added that part just to make his story more fanciful. How can we tell?"

"By going to the source. That's why we have to find her,

and Tarix agreed with me . . . reluctantly. She also made me promise to run like the north wind if Shirin still wants to kill me. Now put that hat back on. If I have to wear one, so do you!" And with that he pulled the edges of his wool cap farther down so the last strand of his black hair was hidden.

"All right, all right, but how do we find her?" Dorict asked. He set the hat back on his head and pulled the brim low.

They started walking towards the bridges again, and Garet told him, "We are going to talk to one of the king's agents. He'll meet us in a tea shop just inside the Fifth Ward."

"You want me to hang my life on the words of a spy?" Dorict asked. He began to lag, but Garet pulled him along.

"Please don't call him a spy. He prefers the term 'historian.'"

When they got to the tea shop, Barick was in the back, occupying most of a corner table. He ignored them even when they sat in the little room left over.

"Barick . . . Historian?" Garet asked.

Their informant replied in a whisper out of one side of his mouth. "Should we be speaking? I thought we might pass notes under the table."

Garet stared at Dorict, and the Blue shook his head.

"Ahh, that is a very clever idea," Garet said, "but we are short on time, and neither Dorict nor I have pen and paper with us."

"Unfortunate," Barick whispered, then resumed in a normal voice, "I received your note this morning and began my research at once. You were right to enlist my help, Garet, for I dare say no one else could have managed this. Now, I asked to meet you here because this ward is where the only living relative of . . . you-know-who lives. Her family was mostly claw-killed when she was a child. An uncle, then married, took her in, but his wife died, again from the beasts, just before she joined the Duellists. This was an unlucky ward in those days! Perhaps the Duellists became a new family for her, for she was high in their ranks, and so was high on His Majesty's list to capture."

Dorict started to scratch his head again but stopped.

"Do you know how she evaded the king's guard?" he asked the historian.

Barick shrugged, an impressive trembling of the flesh. "We believe that a certain ward lord hid many, perhaps in league with rogue Traders from the Twelfth Ward."

Garet tapped the table in front of him. "That would explain why Marick saw that cart full of Masks leaving the Twelfth Ward to go to the logging station. Do you know why we need this information?"

Barick looked at the bane through hooded eyes. He put a piece of paper on the table and slid it across to him.

"Yes, and so does the king. He thinks it is a worthy risk. I think it is pure foolishness. You could become an adequate historian someday, Garet, and it would be a shame to end such promise by a knife-thrust in your back in some dark alley of the Maze."

Garet smiled at his concern. "Don't worry. We'll stay out of dark alleys if it makes you feel better."

"Impossible," Barick replied. "The Maze is all dark alleys."

The two banes stood back to let Barick leave before them. After he was gone, they ordered tea and sipped it while examining the piece of paper he had left them.

"Is this a map or an accident with the ink?" Garet asked. There was no order to the lines traced upon the scrap of paper, save for a broad stroke labelled as the ward wall and a thinner line marked as the Maze enclosure.

"They call it the Maze for a reason," Dorict said. He studied the map carefully and pointed to a small "X" inked near the middle. A line of symbols beside it read "Shinock, uncle of Shirin."

"How did Barick find this out?" Dorict asked. He slid the map to Garet, who folded it and placed it in the pocket of his borrowed coat.

"One of the things I saw when I took those records over was a census – a listing – of all the citizens in Shirath. Barick said such lists were necessary to balance the wards in the beginning, and the kings had kept them up to make sure no section was overpopulated or under-taxed."

They left a coin Tarix had supplied to pay for the tea and exited the shop. Outside, the sky was overcast. Garet shouldered the pack he had brought from the banehall, and they made their way towards the outer wall.

"What is in that pack?" Dorict asked. "A rope to tie up Shirin?"

Garet smiled. "Well, yes actually, though I hope we won't need it! I also have a shield in here and a short, spiked club for you. Let's hope we won't need those either."

The people of this ward were the least friendly in the city to Garet's mind. Suspicious glances were cast at them as they passed matrons in their doorways and merchants in their small shops. People hurried past, avoiding their eyes.

Garet shivered. It wasn't his imagination: there was a nervous tension running under the ordinary life of the ward.

"Of course everyone's nervous," Dorict said when Garet mentioned this. "Think what they've been through lately: a giant demon killing the city's children and trying to tear down a lord's house, not to mention the invasion of a pack of masters and palace guard in this ward last night to take away a wounded idiot."

Garet laughed, which earned him even more disapproving looks from those they passed.

"I thought you sympathized with Marick? You seemed worried enough in the infirmary." He stopped to help an old man pick up some spilled radishes and received no thanks for his efforts.

Dorict shook his head. "When I thought he was dying, I felt a momentary urge to forgive him. Now that I know how reckless he was, I wish he had been stuck with more arrows!"

He took the map from Garet and looked at the complex drawing. After turning it several times, he found the right orientation.

"The far gate is nearest to this Shinock's house. Do you really think her uncle would shield her if she's hunted by both the palace and the hall?"

Garet took the map back and put it in his pocket. "From what I've seen, she's a natural leader. I don't doubt she can be very persuasive – especially when she's armed."

"Don't lose that pack," Dorict cautioned.

The Maze was a fossil of the original city of Shirath, built hastily and with little regard for order or beauty. Most of the buildings were small and of one or two storeys. They were set here and there, walls jutting against each other, second floors sometimes stretching over lanes to make dark tunnels, and those lanes then twisting out of sight or ending suddenly in a blank wall.

"Another dead end," Garet said. He stepped out from under a second-storey overhang and examined the map in the grey light.

"Ah! We went left, left, right, left instead of left, left, left, right. Two corners back then."

They found themselves in a long, covered gallery where every second door opened on a tavern.

"Give me that club," Dorict said, after resisting a third attempt by a tout to drag him into a darkened door. Garet shook off his own persistent arm-grabber, ignoring promises of "the best wine in Shirath" and "food fit for Heaven's tables."

"Not yet. Just ignore them!"

At the fourth attempt, this time by a large thug who tried to pick the Blue up off the ground to get him into a dirty one-room drinking hole, Dorict exploded. He kicked his heel back into the man's belly and, when dropped, swept the man's legs out from under him in a move straight from his training exercise.

After that, they were left alone.

"Still need the club?" Garet asked.

Dorict shook his head. "No, just some air that doesn't smell like spoiled wine and vomit."

At the end of the gallery, they turned left and saw a blocky one-storey house at the end of the alley.

"That's it, or I give up," Garet said, and put the map away. He slid the shield out of the bag and fixed it on his arm. Dorict fished out the club and tapped the blunt spikes into the palm of one hand.

"All right, let's go talk some reason into her."

CHAPTER 16

TALK AT THE POINT OF A SPEAR

The reasoning had to wait because the door was locked and no one answered their persistent knocking. Dorict searched under his jacket for a moment, reaching this way and that until he produced a remarkable set of tools.

"What under Heaven's shield are those?" Garet asked.

Dorict smiled and shook his head. "Marick begged me to carry this thieves' vest of his until he got better. I think he was afraid Banerict would confiscate it."

Garet leaned over to look at the small blades and picks in Dorict's hands.

"He might have, just to use some of those tools on injured banes! Can they open this door?"

The Blue slipped the thin knife into the gap between the door and the jamb. He wiggled it back and forth until it stopped.

"If this is a simple bar, I might be able to raise it," he said, and tried to force the blade up. It refused to move. He withdrew it and reached again into his clothes until he pulled out a long key-like tool. It was thin enough to slip through the gap, and its teeth were as long and sharp as a comb's.

"The bar might be one that slides rather than lifts," Dorict explained. "So this might move it back."

"You seem very educated in this," Garet said. "And yet I always thought you were an honest bane!"

"I suppose a long friendship with Marick has ruined me," Dorict said, and twisted the shaft of the tool. There was a grating sound, then another, and the door swung in a bit.

"Corruption be praised," Garet said. "Here, put those back in your pocket and ready your club."

He pushed the door wide and jumped in and to the side, but no attack came. Dorict followed. They edged inside, each taking a different direction and waiting for their eyesight to adjust to the dimmer light. Garet swung the door shut behind them and threw the bar across it. When they could see, they found themselves in a storehouse of sorts, with boxes and bales stacked against the walls and in the middle of the floor.

"Nobody here," Dorict said. He moved further inside the room, checking behind each pile of goods. "Wait, these carpets are meant for the Third Ward, or so the tag says. And this cask of wine has the palace symbols on it!"

"There's a cot here, and a bit of bread," Garet said. He looked at all the stuff around them and shook his head. A gallery above them, reached by a ladder in the corner, had even more barrels and boxes.

"Perhaps the uncle is a thief."

"Who says so?"

Garet and Dorict both turned to see a bearded, middle-aged man standing in the doorway, a tool remarkably like the one they had used still in his hand. In his other hand was a skin of wine.

He waved the wine skin at them, and a few droplets sprayed out. "You two clear out or I'll call the guard!" he slurred.

"Do you have that rope handy?" Dorict asked Garet.

Shinock turned out to be hard to tie down. He twisted, bit, scratched, cursed, and assaulted them with breath that had been soured by wine for half a century. They finally had him fastened to a large rolled carpet and could stand far enough away to breathe without retching.

"Where is Shirin?" Garet asked.

"Claws take you!" was the only answer, aside from a prodigious burp.

Dorict tried his luck. "We only want to talk to her. We mean her no harm."

Shinock gave them a half-toothed smile. "A child lies better than you two. I know what you want. You want to banish her! The talks all around the Maze, how the banehall believes the Masks should be banished, and the king agrees. You two just want spies' gold for taking her to them. Well, I won't turn my niece over to the likes of you! Claw you both, and beasts take you!"

Dorict bristled. "The king might arrest you for helping her. It would mean a chain gang or worse."

Garet held up his hand, and Dorict stopped.

"I won't threaten you, Shinock. We're banes, not spies or kidnappers."

The bound man spat on the floor.

Garet picked up his shield from where he had dropped it to tie the man's hands and feet.

"I don't care how you feel about us. It doesn't matter anyway. You're not the one we want."

Dust showered them. Coughing, Garet stood back and looked up. A figure dressed in black and holding a spear crouched on the boxes in the upper gallery.

"No, it's me you want," Shirin said. She jumped down onto a bale of wool, rolled, and launched a feinting thrust at Dorict, who leaped away.

Garet jumped between Shirin and his friend, shield held ready.

"Kill these clawed banes, Niece!" Shinock yelled. "They took away my wine!" He rolled back and forth until the carpet slid from its stack and fell across Dorict's back.

"Don't fret, Uncle. Our guests are going to be leaving, permanently. And as for where they'll go, well, they say most of the houses in the Maze are built over bones."

She stabbed at Garet, and he barely blocked the move. The spear glanced off his defense, leaving a bright scratch across the duller sheen of his shield.

"We aren't here to fight!" he shouted.

Dorict wriggled out from under the carpet and searched for his club. Shinock grabbed his trouser cuff in his jaws and pulled him back.

"Dorict, don't interfere, and don't hurt her," Garet said, then ducked as the butt of the spear swished over his head.

Shirin pushed the point forward again and stalked the bane around a pile of wooden crates.

"I know you're angry at me," Garet said, and blocked a thrust before stumbling back. "I deserve some of that," he continued, shield raised again to deflect a ringing blow from the side. "But we both know you don't really want to kill me."

Three more slapping strikes and a volley of thrusts kept him quiet for a moment as he used all his skill to block her spear.

Shirin grinned. "In just a little bit, you'll see how wrong you are." She came forward again, making small circles with the point of her spear while Garet moved to put more obstacles between them.

"It's you who has been shadowing me in the past days, isn't it? So why wait until now? You're a Duellist; you could have killed me at any time."

He raised the shield just in time to protect his face. The strength of the blow sent him back a few feet.

"When you followed me, how close did you get? Close enough for a knife in the back?"

He charged forward and struck the spear aside, but didn't close for a strike with his shield.

Standing to the side and hampered by both Garet's instructions and the maniac chewing on his pant leg, Dorict could only watch, his heart in his mouth at each near miss.

"Why not an arrow from the rooftop, or was that too far away to satisfy your hatred for me?" Garet asked.

The spear snaked out and cut his cheek, just below his left eye. He fell back, one hand to the fire in his face.

"See!" he yelled at her. "It would have been easy to kill me if that was all you wanted. But it isn't. What is it, Shirin? What do you want of me?"

Blood trickled through his fingers.

The woman stared at him, trembling with some strong emotion while Garet held his breath. Then she drove the point of her spear into the floor planks and left it there to wobble between them.

"What do I want?" Shirin asked. "I'll tell you, bane. I

want you to see me! I want you to see that someone else is as worthy as a Heaven-blessed bane. I want you to stop looking down on me as some play-actor waving a spear while you attend to all the important business of the city!"

She fell to her knees and pounded her fists on the floor. "I want you to say that we matter, to know that we want to protect Shirath too. That is what we want, bane, yet you despise us. Is it any wonder we hate you?"

Garet knelt where he was and looked at the sobbing woman. The planted spear still swayed.

"No," he said. "It's no wonder at all. Shirin, I once felt as you, that I mattered to no one in this world. That changed for me when I came to Shirath. It changed because I killed a demon. You've done the same."

He took a deep breath and edged closer. He reached one hand out to touch the fist still clenched on the floor.

"I honour what you have done, Shirin. By Heaven's dome, I swear it! I see you now as I should have seen you then, had I been wiser. I would be your friend, and your ally in protecting Shirath."

"No," she wept, "you are my enemy. You have to be!"

There was a rustling and creaking around the building. Shadows moved across the narrow windows set with scraped parchment instead of glass.

Shinock spat out Dorict's cuff and yelled at his niece, "They've brought the guard, Shirin. Run! Save yourself!"

The door shuddered, cracked, and fell open. A squad of ward guards filled the room, and all within found blades at their throats.

"Let those two be," someone said, and Garet looked sideways to see Lord Sacourat enter behind her guards. The sword was removed, and he stood to face her. Shirin and

Shinock were being secured. In Shinock's case, that just meant keeping out of the way of his teeth. Shirin was bound in chains at both wrist and ankle. She kept her head low, refusing to look at either Garet or the ward lord.

"Well, banes," Sacourat said, "it seems you've found a wanted criminal, and I've found you, so I will take charge of them. This is my ward, after all."

She smiled, and the guards dragged Shirin and her uncle out into the alleys of the Maze. The Mask resisted only once, pausing at the door to shoot Garet a look he couldn't interpret.

"How did you find us, Lord Sacourat?" Dorict asked. He had recovered his club and disposed of his hat.

"Oh, I know all that goes on in this ward, bane. And you, aren't you the Midlander? Yes, you were at that confusion near my house the other night, weren't you?"

"Yes, my lord," Garet replied. He sketched a short bow, and Dorict copied him.

"I wish you had been quicker to stop, well, to save my house," she said. "I'm sure the Masks were at fault, weren't they?"

"No, I think that the demon was more to blame."

Sacourat flinched at the word and narrowed her eyes. "Perhaps. Well, I must go now and deliver these two to the king."

"A show of loyalty, Lord Sacourat?" Garet asked, and Dorict drew in breath at the rudeness of the question, but Sacourat merely laughed.

"Loyalty must be displayed to have value, bane. Tell Branet that the Fifth Ward keeps faith with the banehall. Goodbye."

Garet and Dorict were left alone in the storeroom. The Green pulled the spear out of the floor, needing both hands and several attempts to do this. He shouldered the weapon and looked at Dorict.

"Where's your hat?" he asked.

His companion scratched his blond hair and smiled. "I had to shove it in Shinock's mouth. The guards were afraid to come near him."

CHAPTER 17
DEALING WITH POWER

Although it was still mid-afternoon, the clouds had stolen most of the light from the sky. In a tower near the lord's house in the Thirteenth Ward, Gost lit a lamp and looked his question to the largest man in the room.

"No, sir," the giant in a ward guard's uniform said. "They took her straight to the king, and he's locked her up. The proclamation was posted in the Palace Plaza. I brought a copy."

Tarock, who had been reading the notice of Shirin's arrest, handed it to Gost.

The older man crumpled it up and threw it across the room before rounding on the guard captain.

"Maroster, you are the captain of my ward's guards. Your job was to control Shirin until she was no longer useful. You failed."

The big man flinched at his tone and shook his head. Though he towered over the older man, his face was covered with a sheen of sweat.

"Please, sir! I told you she was crazed when you

suggested this plan. She cares for nothing but killing demons and spiting the banehall. We would have had to remove her sooner or later, why not let the king do it for us?"

Gost looked up from his untidy desk. Bills of lading, letters, promissory notes, and pleas for mercy lay scattered across it. He fixed Maroster with a mocking gaze.

"Why? Because she will talk, you fool! She knows who I am; she knows Tarock here, and Trader Chirat, and you. Do you relish the thought of having a collar around your neck and digging ditches for the next ten years? Or what about exile? Fancy a trip through the demon-haunted wilderness in hopes of finding another city that will take us in?"

He slammed a palm down on his desk. "You should have killed her rather than bid her hide! She's a threat to both me and my ward."

There was a swish of fabric, and a soft, feminine voice drifted into the room. "*Your* ward, Uncle Gost? I'm sure you meant to say Lord Kirel's ward. My husband is under the impression that he rules, and you only advise."

Maroster stepped aside to let Lady Kaela into Gost's audience room. Tarock stood, and with a bow a bit too deep and a smile a bit too broad, he pulled up his chair for her.

With a sigh of relief, she sat down. "Thank you, Tarock. We see so much of you these days, and it is always such a pleasure. I do, however, need to speak to my uncle. Perhaps you and the captain could leave us alone for a moment?"

Tarock glanced at Gost, who nodded, and he left the room with Maroster at his heels.

Kaela fanned herself, though the day was cloudy and cool. "Oh dear! This child had better come soon or I'll perish from exhaustion. Even coming the short distance from our house and climbing the stairs to your charming lair tires me."

Gost poured her a glass of wine then took it for himself when she refused. He sat across from her.

"Then why make the trip at all? Is there some particular reason you want to talk to me?" He regarded his nephew's wife over the crystal rim of his goblet.

She smiled and continued fanning. "Really, Gost, can't I just want to visit you? Though, to tell the truth, there was a small matter I wish settled."

Gost waited.

"I would like you to sever all ties with the Masks," Kaela said. "For now, at least."

There was a silence in the room for many moments until Gost put his glass down on a small table and rested the tips of his fingers together.

"What an extraordinary thing to say, Kaela! I have no connection to these renegades. Perhaps I should summon Lord Kirel. He should know if your *condition* is creating such fantasies in your mind."

Kaela snapped her fan shut. She leaned forward, and her gaze was anything but delicate. "Do you look down on all women in my *condition*, Uncle, or is it just all women? No, I really think you look down on everyone. It is a foolish habit to disparage one's allies. It turns them into enemies."

"I know how to deal with enemies," Gost replied. He picked up the glass again and studied the blood-red wine within. Outside the door, Maroster could be heard telling a steward to come back later.

Kaela began fanning herself again. "That's good, since you are making so many new enemies for our ward. And all because you moved too quickly. The banehall, the king, the other ward lords – well, all except Tiralsh of the Twelfth.

Yes, don't look so surprised! I know of your dealings with her son and Chirat's trading group. These Masks are becoming a liability, and your plans are not so hidden as you might think, Gost."

Her host put his glass down again, and the wine sloshed over the side. He stood up and loomed over the woman. "Tell me what you know. I demand it!"

Kaela's reply was pure ice. "Sit down, Uncle. You'll burst your heart, and I need you alive to clean this mess up before we are all cast out into the wilderness."

When Gost stepped back in surprise and resumed his seat, she continued.

"The Masks were never meant to replace the banes in this city! Only a mad fool like Shirin would believe that. No, but they might serve another purpose, especially if you have more silkstone than you've told them."

"I deny all of this," Gost growled. He spilled more wine when he grabbed the glass again.

"Tut, tut, Uncle. You'll ruin that fine coat if you aren't careful. Now, where were we? Ah yes, silkstone. With more of that magical rock, you could build up a good number of Masks. Still not enough to replace all the banes, but enough to protect a new smaller town. The king has been planning to expand the city, hasn't he, but I believe he favours a new wall set out from the present one, not a new settlement. It would be hard to rule another town from a distance, so he would never agree to it – unless he had to."

She closed the fan and tapped it against the arm of her chair.

"These Masks are your plan to make the king grant your wish, the creation of a new town, no, a new *city* ruled by you. You created a crisis whose only solution is a mass exile of the Masks. Half the city praises them for killing demons –

oh, don't look so surprised, I'm no market girl to shrink at the word. The other half condemns them for attacking those banes. You'll let this pot boil to the point of civil war, and, when enough people have died, you'll go to the king and nobly offer yourself as a sacrifice to lead the Masks and as many others as you can trick into following you to this new kingdom, the Kingdom of Gost!"

"Maroster!" Gost called out, and the captain of the guards stepped quickly within.

"Kaela, you are really wasted as a consort! You should have been a lord in your own right. Does Kirel know about this?"

Kaela seemed unconcerned by the two men, both armed with daggers, standing near her.

"Kirel? No, my gentle uncle. He knows sewers and building plans and the number of fields we have in turnips, but not about this."

"And do you mean to tell him?" Gost asked.

Maroster closed the door.

"You are so tiresome at times, Gost," Kaela said. She held out her hand, and her uncle helped her to her feet.

"I've said that you turn allies to enemies too easily," she said, frowning. "Don't presume to do that with me. I want you to leave. I would praise Heaven's mercy if you got your new city and sat on its throne."

"Why?" Gost asked. One hand drifted down to the blade hanging from his belt.

Kaela looked up into his eyes, and his hand stayed.

"Because, Uncle, until then neither Kirel nor I, and perhaps not even our child, would be safe from your ambition. I am quite content with the ruling of the Thirteenth Ward. So you see, we are allies after all."

Gost escorted her to the door. Maroster stood aside and opened it.

"Have no fear, Niece, I shall, how did you put it? Oh yes, clean up this mess."

Kaela smiled and managed an awkward curtsy.

"I know you will. Now, Captain, can you help me down these stairs? I am really too fragile to be out in my condition."

CHAPTER 18

A FALLING OUT

"Sacourat is a snake," Tarix said across Kesla as she helped support the unsteady body of the injured Gold.

Garet nodded in full agreement. The ward lord had seemed to slither in her eagerness to gain favour with the king.

They were helping Kesla walk around the bottom floor of the hall so that she could regain her balance and get some exercise. In consideration of Tarix's leg, Kesla was putting most of her weight on Garet's shoulder. He didn't exactly mind, but felt he was the one getting the exercise.

They turned a corner, and Tarix continued. "If she weren't so anxious to help the king, I'd think she was behind the Masks."

They passed the front doors and saw team after team going out into the plaza. The patrols were almost constant now, with banes getting but a few hours' sleep before going out again. There was talk of changing the patrols in hopes of catching the demons before they could do any damage. It was Tarix's opinion that they had been lucky so far. Only a few banes like Kesla had been injured, and there had been no deaths since the horrifying attack in the Fifth Ward.

Garet had no hope that such luck would continue. The Masks had gone to ground, and that made things harder, for the number of attacks had not decreased. The best Blue Sashes were being added to teams to make up the difference, but Garet feared that might lead to more injuries as the inexperienced banes were thrust into battle. These were the things they talked of while they walked.

"I wish I could patrol again, when so many are needed," Kesla said. "But the way my eyes are, I'd likely hit Ratal instead of a demon."

"You'd likely hit him anyway," Garet said.

Kesla smiled at him, then turned suddenly pale.

"Master, I think I must sit down or throw up. Either one and quickly!"

They steered her into the empty dining hall and lowered her gently to a bench. There was a commotion in the hallway, and three banes raced past in a mirror image of their own recent progress: two helping a third to walk. The one they supported had his vest in tatters and blood dripping down to the back of his knees.

"Banerict will be busy again today. I hope the poor man doesn't lose his mind over this 'foolishness,' as he sees it," Tarix said. She looked at Kesla.

The Gold's head drooped, and she seemed oblivious to her surroundings.

"I suppose you didn't tell him that cut on your cheek was from a Mask's spear," Tarix said to Garet. "That would have added a whole new verse to his song!"

Garet smiled, then regretted it, for it pulled at the stitches in his cheek. "I lied, to my shame, and told him it was a practice injury and blamed Forlinect. As for Shirin, I just wish Sacourat had held back for a while. I think she was ready to talk."

"Hmmm." Tarix looked doubtfully at the bandaged cheek. "From what you told me, she was more than ready to kill! Perhaps she would have come around, but it's too late now. If she doesn't lead the king's guard to the other Masks, our hallmaster has demanded she be banished. He's added that cut to the list of her crimes against the banehall."

Garet sighed, and Kesla groaned back in anguished harmony. Tarix patted both their shoulders.

"Courage, you two. The masters have stopped shouting and are finally talking. We will have a more effective patrol schedule soon, and they are even considering Garet's mad idea of tiny scattered halls, though I'm afraid I had to present it as my plan so they wouldn't dismiss it out of hand."

Garet shrugged. He would be happy enough if the Reds just listened to reason. And he didn't need the recognition. He'd had enough of being the centre of attention last winter. It had rubbed on him like a rough shirt until this new threat took people's notice away.

"Master, thank you for listening to my 'mad ideas.' It means a lot that I have a friend in the banehall."

"You have many, Green! My husband among them. There are others who see these increased attacks as the final argument for some grand change. Branet will come around, I hope. He can be a sensible man when left no choice."

Kesla added her support with a weak wave of one hand.

There was a clatter, and they turned to see a young woman run into the dining hall.

"Hello, Dalesta," Tarix said as the Green skidded to a

stop. "You're running better today! Forced to play the messenger again?"

The Green smiled and nodded. "And with the same message, Master. Garet, the hallmaster would like to see you in the records room at once. Oh, and same time tomorrow, Master Tarix?"

"Tomorrow? Of course! Dalesta, I think I must go with Garet this time." She pointed at the splayed body of Kesla. "Would you please help Kesla back to the infirmary? It will be good exercise for you!"

The young woman's eyes widened at the burden she was about to receive, and Garet gave her an encouraging pat on the shoulder as he and Tarix left the dining hall.

"Master, don't you think there's such a thing as too much exercise?"

Tarix looked shocked. "Never!"

Branet had commandeered the records room so often that many now called it the hallmaster's room. His presence was expected, but when the two entered, Arict, the usual master of this room, was nowhere to be seen. Instead, the first person Garet laid eyes on was Salick. She was sitting at an abnormally clean table, to the right of Branet and across from a single empty chair.

"Tarix?" Branet said in his bull voice. "I didn't call for you, but no matter. Salick, pull up another chair for Garet's . . . master."

Salick stood and lifted a basket of scrolls off the nearest chair and moved it beside the other.

Why is she here, and why won't she look at me?

"Sit down, both of you," Branet said. "I asked Salick to take down what is said at this questioning. Master Arict is somewhat unreliable these days."

Tarix smiled and turned her head. "Salick," she said in

greeting, and the Gold nodded, still looking at the paper, ink bowl, and brush laid out neatly before her. She dipped the brush in the ink and held it ready.

Branet leaned forward to examine Garet. He tapped a broad finger on the table.

"Did you seek out Shirin in the Maze, forsaking your bane's uniform and acting against the wishes of this hall?"

The brush flew over the page.

Before Garet could answer with a self-damning "yes," Tarix spoke up.

"What do you mean, 'against the wishes of this hall?' Do the stones in these walls now rule us? Do they give us orders with granite tongues? Garet has a master. Me. He proposed this plan, and I agreed."

The brush paused in Salick's hand, then finished the line.

"That was pure foolishness on your part, Tarix," Branet growled.

Tarix growled back. "The foolishness is believing that what started last winter is over and done with. The Duellists were never defeated. They just came back as these Masks! And probably for the same reasons. Shall we repeat that feud endlessly, until none are left to fight and the beasts rule all? Mandarack knew better. He wished to fight demons, who, in case you haven't noticed, have no trouble changing their ways in this war."

Branet waited while Salick caught up with Tarix's passionate argument. He leaned back and said, "You cannot win a war against Heaven, Tarix. This talk of someone throwing demons against us like a spear is all over the hall now. What is such a fantasy compared to six hundred years of facts? Just words, yet here you repeat them. Are these

Garet's words or yours, and who is the master? You or him?"

Tarix glared at the hallmaster but said nothing. Garet could not believe Branet would be so dismissive of Tarix, who had given so much of her life and health to her duties. He made to speak, but Tarix forestalled him.

"If we wish to make comparisons," she told Branet in an icy tone, "you might be well-matched with Adrix, our old and unlamented hallmaster. Has he snuck back here to whisper idiocy in your ear? Remember how he fell when arrogance drove away all his followers? There will be a masters meeting tomorrow, Branet, and all these questions will be put out in the open for us to decide. We will come to an agreement no matter how long it takes – even if every other bane in the hall must be turned out to patrol while we argue!"

Branet stood. He did not wait for Salick to finish writing before he replied, "Then we have nothing further to say."

Garet stood as well, and spoke when the hallmaster made to leave. "Sir, a moment, if you will. I beg you not to ask the king to exile Shirin," he said as humbly as possible.

Branet laughed. "Ask him? I've demanded it, as is quite within my powers, Garet, and it is not up for debate with a mere Green."

Salick glared at the page before her, the pen in her clenched hand dripping ink onto the table.

Garet pressed ahead. "Please, Hallmaster, do not do this! She is confused, but in her heart, Shirin is like us. She wants to defeat the demons."

Branet held out his hand, and Salick gave him her notes. He tore them in half, then in half again.

"Then she'll get her fill of fighting them when she's driven beyond the walls. I intend to preserve this hall,

Garet, like the hallmasters before me. You could help me do that. You are intelligent and diligent in your duties, if not in your allegiances. You could be a Gold in a year and a master in seven, if you learn to obey like a true bane."

"That would be my decision," Tarix said. "Not yours." She stood beside Garet and put a hand on his shoulder.

Branet smiled at her and left the room.

The Red shook her head and cursed under her breath. She turned to Garet. "Claws! I spoke more angrily than I intended. Don't worry about this. He can't do anything to you, just to me. And don't worry about that either. If a Basher demon mangling my leg couldn't stop me, neither can a charging hallmaster!"

She noticed that Garet was looking at Salick, who was staring at her clenched fists on the table.

"Hmm, I'll go and help organize the new patrols, Garet. Why don't you stay here and talk?"

She left the room as fast as her braced leg allowed.

"Salick?" Garet said.

When he got no answer, he tried again. "Why did the hallmaster want you here? Did he tell you?"

Salick finally met his eyes. "You heard him, didn't you? He wanted me to take notes." She picked up a scrap of paper from the floor and began wiping clean the brush.

"Really?" Garet asked. He was tired. His cheek hurt, and he had little patience left for Salick's moods.

"Why not borrow a steward or a free Green or even a Blue?" he asked. "Don't you think you're overqualified to sit here and scribble down Branet's wisdom?"

Salick stood up and faced him, eyes narrowed. "Perhaps he wanted a bane he could trust in the room," she said. Her braids trembled as she picked up the rest of the paper and almost threw it onto a shelf below the counter.

Garet followed her, anger building up at yet another accusation, this time from someone he loved. "So, do you think I'm a traitor?" he asked, shouting the question and immediately regretting it, both the tone and the words. He was terribly afraid she would answer him, and that her reply would cut him deeper than Shirin's spear.

Salick stopped, hands on the counter. She spoke without turning. "Why do you choose Shirin over the hall, over me?" she asked.

"I don't!" he yelled. "But I won't choose the hall over the safety of the city, either. Branet is wrong. Exiling Shirin or any other Mask just shows we care more for our own position than we do about protecting the people!"

He slammed a fist on the counter. He was angrier than he had ever been before. He couldn't help seeing what was happening around him. Heaven knew he wanted to, sometimes. If he could just ignore the foolishness around him, then he might fit in, be a seamless part of this city, but his hair, his skin, and now even his thoughts prevented it.

Tired of being challenged, tired of being forced into a corner, he exploded in anger. "Why can't you see this? The demons are different! That's undeniable. I can't change that. You can't change that. And Branet can't change that! We need the Masks on our side. *We* have to change!"

"No!" Salick shouted. "We don't! *You* have to change. You have to change back into being a proper bane. Until you do, don't come near me!"

She ran out of the room, leaving Garet there alone until Records Master Arict stuck her head out of the back room where she slept.

"Sorry dear, were you calling for me?"

CHAPTER 19
THE BEAST AT THE GATE

"I don't understand," Ratal said, knitting his brows.

"Then I will explain it," Tarix said. "Again."

She looked up at the sky. It was brightening in the east, and the flowers in the plaza gardens now had colour. Above them, the last of the night birds and the first of the morning fliers fought each other in song.

Garet and Riga looked at each other and grinned. With Kesla limited to the easy duty of sitting by the banehall doors to record the coming and going of patrols, it fell to Tarix to manage Ratal.

"The masters decided to increase patrols and change the patterns. Each ward will have two teams, one led by a Red and the other by a Gold. We are also adding dependable Blues" – and here she pointed to Dorict as visual support – "to round out the teams. Clear so far?"

Ratal nodded, and Tarix continued.

"We are assigned the Sixteenth Ward until nightfall, when another two teams take over. One team will start from the outer gate, and the other from the inner gate. Kitoroth leads that team. We will cross the ward, meeting in the middle," she said, walking the fingers of each hand towards each other.

Riga covered her mouth, and Garet had to swallow hard to keep from laughing. Dorict shook his head and looked to the binding of his weapon.

The fingers met, crossed and kept going until Tarix seemed to hug herself. Ratal stared hard before answering.

"Got it," he said, "but why are they here?" He pointed at Allifur and Corfin, who stood nervously beside Garet.

A voice yelled from above. "Ratal! Just shut up and do as you're told!"

They all looked up the banehall steps to where Kesla waved a fist from her stool beside the door. She had a sheaf of papers in her hand and an unpleasant expression on her face.

That set Ratal moving, and the rest followed. At a safe distance he stopped and pointed at the Black Sashes again.

Tarix sighed. The big Gold was persistent, if not very bright. "We might need messages sent to the other team or perhaps the hall, if something happens. These two are messengers . . . Wait, what are you two hiding?"

Allifur and Corfin had their hands behind their backs and only reluctantly presented them for Tarix's inspection. Garet squatted to get a better look.

"Is that a shield?" he asked, tapping the oval of metal on the girl's arm. "It's so small . . . and it's on your left arm!"

Tarix knelt on one knee and examined the weapon. The socket of Allifur's wrist fit snugly into a metal and leather cup near the end of the shield. Leather loops held the length of it tight against her arm, and a strange arrangement of strapping disappeared through a slit in her sleeve.

"Goes around," Allifur whispered, and traced a line

from her shoulder to under her right arm. "Can't fall off that way, Dasanat says."

Tarix looked at Corfin, who had a braced dagger in his belt – not a blunt training weapon but a well-sharpened blade.

"Master Forlinect let us take them," he said, staring down at his toes. "He don't want nobody to go out without a weapon." He looked up and smiled proudly. "The others got only staffs!"

Allifur nodded.

Tarix stood up again and looked at the two. The red light of the morning cast her face in sharp shadows so that she seemed cut from stone. So did her voice. "Understand this, you are not to use those toys unless you are attacked and your lives are in danger. And you two will do what I say, or I'll order Ratal to eat up the both of you!"

Allifur and Corfin both nodded vigorously, Allifur with the hint of a smile and Corfin with a wary eye on Ratal.

Tarix seemed in no mood for further conversation, so Garet talked with fellow Greens Riga and Aralon as they walked to the gates of the Sixteenth Ward.

"They're going to kick out that Mask, I hear," Aralon said. He twirled the head of his axe as they walked. "Good riddance, I say."

Riga glared at him. She stuck her spear out to stop the rotation of the axe. "I wouldn't wish that on anyone, no matter what they've done! When I was a child, my mother used to scare me witless with that threat. 'Stop fighting with your brother or it's exile for you, and the beasts will eat you up!' Nobody's been exiled for centuries, so why do it now? She could be put on a chain gang and made to work, or even locked in a cell beneath the palace. That's enough, as far as I'm concerned."

Aralon snorted. "You're so bossy, I bet your whole family wanted you exiled."

Garet didn't listen to the ensuing insults, but looked to where Tarix trudged ahead of him. The Red looked as if more than a bad knee slowed her pace.

When they came to the gate, the guard told them that Kitoroth's team had already gone through and made their way to the outer gate.

"Heaven guard you this day, banes," he told them, and closed the gate when they were all through.

The day was monotonous. The back and forth hurt their feet and wore on their patience. At last, Tarix called a break, first for Kitoroth's team, then her own. They found a place by the outer gate where they could eat lunch, and the children and ancients of the nearby buildings brought out enough that even Ratal was satisfied.

Tarix seemed to have walked off her grim mood, for she elbowed Garet as he tried to finish a bowl of chicken and greens that could have graced a palace table.

"Perhaps this is the work of our unknown adversaries too. If the demons can't kill us, they'll feed us to death!"

Garet laughed up some of his lunch, and Ratal pounded him on the back until he could choke it down again.

The shadows were lengthening when Tarix held up her hand. They were in the stockyards, and the noise from the barns had taken on an urgent quality. In a flash of memory, Garet saw the animals on his father's farm panicking as a hidden demon approached his family's home. He took the rope-hammer off its hook and looked to the others. They were readying their weapons as well. Ratal swung his new iron-bound staff, one that was even heavier than his last, and grunted. "At last," he said, and Aralon hefted his axe and smiled.

Riga and Garet looked at each other. Neither felt any joy at an approaching demon. Tarix looked around and shuddered.

"A bad place," she said. "Too much open ground. A really big beast can build up great speed in a charge."

Her left hand drifted down to her braced knee, and Garet remembered that it was in a similar stockyard that she had been run over by a Basher demon and put in a wheeled chair for five years before Banerict and Dasanat helped her walk again.

"Spread out," she said. "Don't give it more than one person as a target. It will charge any group. You two hang back and separate," she added, looking at the Black Sashes.

They could feel it now, the fear that had set the cows and horses to running about in their enclosures, tossing their heads and biting at their stable mates.

The guards from the outer gate came running past them, followed by herders and fieldworkers, with a chain gang of manure shovellers shuffling awkwardly behind them. Last came a ward guard, weaponless and stumbling away from terror. If he could still run, Garet knew, the beast was yet outside the wall.

"Let's get to the gate," Tarix said.

That last guard had lingered to close the barrier and throw the iron bar into its locking brackets.

"That's luck," Tarix said. "And with a little bit more, the beast will be something smaller than that monster we fought in the Fifth Ward. Ratal on my left, Garet, stay on my right. Riga and Dorict stand past Ratal, and Aralon, get beside Garet."

She turned her head and called to the Black Sashes. "Corfin, you go running back and get Kitoroth up here. Go now. Allifur, make sure the stockyard gate is shut behind him and see if there is anyone else left inside the barns."

The fear was heightened, and Garet felt that the only thing between them and the demon was the outer wall, and that had never been a barrier to the kind of danger that approached. The gate creaked, pushing out the iron bar until it bent a little in the middle. There was a pause as the pressure eased, then, as if the wooden panels breathed, they stretched in again, then back. Each flexing of the gate brought a screech of metal as the bar buckled and the hinges worked their way out of the stone.

"It's big!" Tarix shouted. "Ratal, move back to that side. You two with me on this side, we'll strike as it comes past us."

Garet let out enough rope to strike from a distance and moved away from the other Green to make space for his throw.

The first of the hinges gave way, then another, and the door leaned inward. In the space between the arched stone and the top of the door, they could see the massive head of a Basher demon, its horns swept up and out, its black eyes fixed on splintering wood. It drew back and howled its rage. Then it charged.

The door burst into fragments, showering the banes with sharp splinters and jagged boards. Aralon was down, bleeding from hand and head, but Garet couldn't go to him, for the Basher was continuing on, past Tarix, who didn't move, though she seemed uninjured. Ratal whacked at it with his staff, and the beast veered, giving Garet a clear enough view of its longer front legs to launch his own attack.

The missile at the end of the line swung around one set of claws but not the other. Garet wedged the pick end of the line between two flagstones and held on, trying to stop it, for only then could the others attack in some safety.

One traps, and the others attack, just like Mandarack taught us.

The Basher turned, wrenching at the rope, but it held, and Ratal, Dorict, and Riga came at it from behind, trying to take the back legs out from under it. The Basher ignored them, even when Riga jammed her spear against its side and pushed as hard as she could to try and pierce its natural armour. The beast's attention was firmly on its tangled paw, and, when it finally discerned that it could not pull away, it came towards Garet, head down and snapping its great beak.

Tarix was nowhere to be seen, and Aralon was still on the ground. The rope-bound foot came down on the flagstones beside Garet's leg. The other fell beside his head. He wrenched at the pick, trying to free it so that he could at least hack at the creature's eyes, but the Basher's weight on the line had forced it too tightly into the crack. The nightmare head came down, and Garet could only kick at it.

"Tarix!" he cried, but the Red did not appear.

Allifur did. She came in a swirl of motion, turning in a full, whipping circle to bring the sharp edge of the shield right into the demon's mouth. It hit where the top and bottom of the beak joined, breaking rows of needle teeth and cutting into the muscles of the jaw.

The Basher demon reared, spreading its mouth lopsidedly wide, and then Tarix was beside him, screaming at the beast and shoving her trident as far down its throat as it would go. The shaft was ripped from her hands, but then Ratal came in swinging his weighted staff in a blow that Garet could scarce believe. The strength of it would have taken the head right off a lesser demon, but it did almost as well for the Basher, crushing its throat and knocking it backwards to lay thrashing on the ground.

Riga ran to Aralon and lifted him up. There were long splinters sticking out of his arm and scalp, giving him the appearance of a dazed hedgehog. Allifur held out her hand to help Garet to his feet. He smiled at her and clapped her on the shoulder.

"Well killed, bane," he said, and she smiled back, a fierce grin that changed everything about her.

Tarix stood, staring down at the Basher. Her trident was still sticking out of the monster's mouth.

"Were you hurt by the broken door, Master?" Garet asked. He looked at her but saw no blood upon her clothes.

"No," she said. "I froze." She turned to him, distraught. "Garet, I froze when that beast came in! It was like before. I dream about it so often, the gate breaking and the Basher stomping over me. The pain of it . . ." She stopped and knelt on her good knee, holding the other in both hands. There, with Garet's arm around her, she wept.

Allifur, Riga, and Aralon looked on, unsure what to do, but Ratal came over and lifted his master to her feet.

"You did not freeze," he said in a magisterial voice. Coming from that height, it had the ring of Heaven's truth.

Tarix scowled and wiped her eyes. "But I did freeze, Ratal. I . . . failed you all."

Ratal shook his head. "You did not freeze, Master, and if anyone says you did, I will have a talk with them," he said, and tapped his staff gently on the paving stones, breaking only two of them.

Tarix looked to Garet, who smiled, and to Allifur, who nodded in agreement and raised her shield. The Red looked back at Ratal, glared, and reached up to grab his ears and pull him down so that she could kiss him on the forehead.

"Ratal, you are an irritating, frustrating, stubborn treasure of a bane, and I would not trade you to another team for rubies and silk! And I promise that if we ever face another Basher, I'll let you take the lead again."

Ratal grinned and went over to Aralon. He took the shaky Green's arm and led him over to the demon.

"Come on, you. Rest time is over. Pull out those splinters, and let's split this beast's skull open so we can remove the jewel and get back on patrol."

Garet's back shivered. Something was wrong. The fear wasn't stable, it was increasing. He looked at Allifur. The child was shaking like a leaf.

"Heaven shield us," said Riga. "Look up there."

They looked to where she pointed. Atop a nearby warehouse was a Shrieker demon, leaning over the gutter edge as if it could hardly wait to descend and attack them.

Allifur screeched, and they turned to see her backing away from a Rat demon that emerged from the alley between two barns. Garet ran up beside her, still weaponless, but ready to kick the thing to death if need be.

Ratal wrenched the trident out of the Basher's mouth and tossed it to Tarix.

Aralon stumbled over to Garet and handed him his axe. "Here, I can't use this thing one-handed," he said.

Garet hefted the double-bladed weapon, but before he could advance on the chittering creature, he felt the ground shift under his feet. Alarmed, he recognized the threat.

"There's a demon under us, get back!" he yelled, and he pulled Allifur away as the paving stones shivered and fell into a sudden and growing pit.

Garet, Allifur, and Aralon were on one side of the hole. Tarix, Ratal, and Riga were on the other. And something moved in the soft earth at the bottom of the pit.

Tarix shouted out orders. "Ratal, you and Riga take the Shrieker. Aralon and Allifur, deal with that Rat. Garet, you and I will kill anything that comes out of that hole. Understood?"

The Shrieker was halfway down the warehouse wall, and the Rat demon was twisting back and forth, looking for a way past Allifur's darting shield. Aralon had pried up a small paver and was circling around behind it.

Garet raised the axe as a heavily clawed hand emerged from the mess of dirt and broken stone. Then something changed.

There was a shift in the air, a quick ripple in the blanket of terror covering the ward. The Shrieker lifted its beak and sniffed. Suddenly, it cried out, its telltale scream splitting the air and causing the youngest bane to cover her ears. It moved like lightning, but away from them, back up the warehouse wall and across the roof. The Rat demon did the same, fleeing into the alley and disappearing in a heartbeat. There was a rumbling in the ground, and the dirt in the bottom of the pit was still.

"What just happened?" Riga asked. She pointed her spear this way and that, but no demon remained. Fear was still there, re-established after that odd gap, for the corpse of the Basher still lay beside them. Ratal stroked his moustache and looked at the mound of still flesh in puzzlement, as if he couldn't fathom why this one was still here when all its friends had left.

Tarix looked to where the Shrieker had fled. She bit her lip and then turned to the others. "Garet and Riga, try to track that Digger if you can. Ratal, you have the Shrieker. Go, now!" she said, and ran up the alley where the Rat demon had fled. After a moment's hesitation, Allifur ran after her.

Garet pulled his rope-hammer off the Basher's clawed foot, dropped the axe at Aralon's feet, and raced after Riga. She was following a humped line of stones that led towards the outer wall, a faint but possible clue to the Digger's retreat – if it was using the same route to leave that it had to enter. There was nothing else to do, so they went to the wall, then through the gate to find more disturbed earth outside. It led into the fields and away from the city. They ran beside it until they reached a drainage ditch and saw no trace on the other side. Nor were there fieldworkers to point them in the right direction, for they had all fled at the Basher's approach.

"How do we follow now?" Riga asked. She drove her spear down as far as she could into the ground and found nothing but mud and clay when she brought it up.

There was a shout behind them, and they looked up to see Ratal waving at them from the ruined gate.

"Let's go back," Garet said. "Maybe the others ran away from us too."

Riga paused in wiping the mud off her spear with a handful of plucked grass. "If so, it must be because of Ratal, for neither you nor I are so frightening."

"Heaven shield us," Garet said, and walked back with her to the city.

Kitoroth was there, alone of his team, when they met near the Basher's corpse. He was sweating profusely and apologized for his late arrival.

"I'm sorry, Master Tarix, but the strangest thing happened. We had just brought down a Glider demon – Salar can throw his club like one of your stones, Garet – and I was about to send a messenger to you when young Corfin arrived. Then, there were two other demons, Shriekers, but they bolted instead of attacking. The Glider tried to get

216

away too, but we killed it, of course. We were able to track one of the others right over the wall and into the fields. Don't know what happened to the other one. What about here?"

Tarix rubbed her chin. "Much the same, Kitoroth, so don't apologize. Do we have a silkstone box for this Basher's jewel?"

The Gold looked over the corpse of the Basher and shook his head. With the jewel still broadcasting fear, the people of the ward would be trapped and suffering in their homes.

"I sent Corfin to the hall for one. He should be back soon."

He was, with Relict in tow, though the Red was supposed to be resting until the night patrol began. He presented his wife with a silkstone box and gave her a quick embrace.

"I'm glad to find you in one piece with all these strange events. This isn't the only ward where multiple demons showed up only to leave again. By the way, Kitoroth, your Glider's jewel is already in there, plus a Rat demon's from the Fifteenth Ward."

Tarix passed the box to Ratal, who took up Aralon's axe and went to work. The fear cut off as he closed the lid. There were faint echoes from the north and west, but they were too weak to represent an imminent threat.

The shadows were growing longer now, and people stuck their heads out of doors and windows to watch as they took on the butchery of reducing the Basher to pieces small enough to fit in a cart. Riga and Ratal then took the body parts away with a promise to Tarix not to stray too far from the city gates.

"Drop it in the shambles on the other side of the

orchards," she told them, "and return right away to the hall."

The rest of Relict's team arrived, sent for hastily an hour before their time but anxious to hear the news of these odd attacks. There was much talking before they could get away, and by the time Garet, Tarix, Dorict, Aralon, Corfin, and Allifur returned to the hall, the lamps on the doorposts were already lit.

Kesla's replacement, the stores master, an older man with but one leg, made a mark on his lists and waved them inside. Tarix sent the others to the dining hall to eat before resting but signalled Garet to stay.

"I'm afraid there's bad news, Garet," she said, lowering her voice when more returning teams came in the hall. "Relict told me that the hallmaster has set a deadline for the exile. She must be out of the city by this time tomorrow. The king had no choice but to agree, since the city is even more dependent on the hall right now. I wish I could give you better news."

She frowned. "Garet, I know that look! You have to accept this now! You did all you could for her, and after all, you are only one young man with a single job. Do you know what that job is?"

Garet took a deep breath. "To protect the city of Shirath, Master," he said. "I hope I've always known that."

He ran a hand over his brow. He was tired and heartsick. The events of the day had distracted him from his argument with Salick, but with a return to the hall, the memory of it came flooding back.

"Good. Go eat and then bed," Tarix said. With a huge yawn, the Red went off in the direction of the masters' quarters, leaving Garet alone.

He did not go to the dining hall, but up to where the

Golds had rooms on the second floor. He knocked on the door of one such room and waited for an answer.

Salick opened it a crack and then closed it again. She was just back from her own patrol, and Garet had hoped to talk to her more calmly than he had before.

He laid his head on the door and knocked again.

"Go away," she said, her voice muffled by both a thin plank of wood and what seemed like a great distance between them.

"Salick," he said. "I'm sorry I was so angry in the records room. Can't we just talk, like we used to?"

There was no answer.

He sighed and raised a hand to knock again but let it fall. "Salick, I love you. You know that. I . . . I want to be with you for the rest of my life, but I can't change the world for you. I can't unmake what has happened and what is going to happen. If you believe me, if you believe that I love you, please answer!"

There was no answer, not for a long time, and when it finally came, it was too late, for when Salick opened the door to speak, Garet had already gone – but not to bed.

CHAPTER 20

THE ENEMIES OF SLEEP

Darkness fell, a night bird sang, and Garet paced the roof of the banehall, trying to understand what he must do. He looked over the city, counting the lights still visible over the inner walls. Only a few lamps lit the roofs of the larger buildings, for after so many dry days, the rain now threatened. Between that and the many attacks, most citizens of Shirath had decided that it was not yet time to return to their rooftops to gossip and play the evenings away.

The bird sang again, and Garet stopped to peer over the parapet. He saw a nest built into a crack in the wall just below where he stood. People called those brown birds "sleep singers," and many parents hung hollowed ox horns outside their windows for them to nest in – if they were lucky enough to have windows – so that the liquid trills would soothe their babes to sleep.

Garet wished he might be so easily calmed. He had left Salick's door to come up here and try to think of a way to save Shirin. Salick's company would have been a comfort, but he knew now that she would never understand his concern for the Mask. To her, Shirin was an enemy of the hall and the palace, one who had also tried to kill banes, three times now, counting last winter.

The bird sang again its dark nest.

Garet sighed. He knew Shirin was angry and desperate enough to still cause all sorts of harm, but like Riga, he couldn't bear to think of anyone cast out, wandering in the wilderness until a demon found them. And as for her being filled with rage, he knew that his actions had poured some of that anger into her.

More lights appeared in the wards, each one repre-senting someone holding off the dark. *That is what the city is,* he thought. *People preserving what light they have.* He thought of the cart driver apologizing for making him step aside, the lords at that dinner in the palace, Torfor in the marketplace with its thousand colours and tastes for sale, and all the banes asleep below him. Every one of them was the city, and the city was all of them. That included Shirin and her Masks. If there was an enemy out there sending demons towards them like an archer sends arrows – and even now he must say "if," for he had no definite proof – then the city should be united in its defence. The banehall and the Masks would have to work together, and lords like Sacourat would have to give up their ambitions until the real enemy was found and defeated. Then let everyone be at each other's throats!

Garet struck the top of the parapet, momentarily silencing the bird.

"I must do something," he said to the night. "If Shirin is exiled, then Branet wins, and his vision of the city will be the only one allowed. He will wrap us in tradition and custom until he's no better than Adrix. In a year's time, the palace and hall will be at war again, and the demons will kill us all."

Silently, he continued in his thoughts. This night's retreat of the demons felt like a feint, such as Tarix used to lure him off balance and strike before he could recover. There must be a human mind at work here, and it wasn't finished with Shirath. Heaven alone knew what the next move would be.

Garet resumed his pacing and the sleep singer resumed its unhelpful song.

In a room shared by two Golds, the lamp was lit, a night bird's song came through the open window, and Salick paced back and forth trying to understand what she must do.

"Do you have to stomp all over our room?" Vinir asked.

Salick's roommate sat cross-legged on her bed, a papered board balanced on her knees and a drawing reed in one hand.

"Yes," said Salick. "I must." She glared at her friend and pointed at the reed. "You're dripping ink on the blanket again. Just what is it you're doing, anyway?"

Vinir smiled, letting Salick's moods breeze by her as she usually did.

"I'm drawing that Tunneller demon, since we have no record of it. Relict let me do some rough sketches when we moved the carcass. It seems he told the records master of my amazing talents, so she requested a good copy personally."

Salick picked up a finished drawing from the table. It

showed the demon lying on the ground amid the rubble of its attack, head cleft and dead.

Salick shuddered at the thought of Garet facing that monster.

"What's wrong with this one?" she asked.

"Well," Vinir said, frowning, "the hallmaster also wanted a copy, and the two training Reds each wanted one more, and Lord Andarack sent a note pleading for another."

Salick laughed. "So, your 'amazing talents' have finally forced you to work!"

Vinir ignored her, adding a line to the plates covering the demon's face. The drawing was quite good, lending the creature a tragic nobility in death that it certainly lacked in life.

"If you stop pacing, I'll draw you next. Garet might like a portrait of you."

Salick batted away the idea away with one hand and continued her circular route.

Vinir carefully put the drawing and her materials on the table and stood up. She intercepted Salick and put two strong hands on her shoulders. Vinir was a shade taller and wider in the shoulders, so Salick was forced to stop.

"What is it, Salick? Is it all this fuss with the Masks, or is something wrong between you and Garet?"

"Why would you say that?"

Salick tried to move, but Vinir steered her over to her own bed and sat down across from her.

"Because I've watched you turn hot and cold on the poor man until he must think you're as mad as a moon-born calf! Which you are, of course."

"Poor *man*?" Salick said, and shook her head.

"Yes," Vinir said with simple conviction. "You may add

'young,' 'newly made,' even 'barely' if you want, but you must call him a man. Now, what is wrong?"

"He goes too far," Salick said, almost shouting. "He pries and pulls at things until they're ready to fall apart!"

"I had no idea he was so powerful," Vinir said, smiling. She leaned forward and put her hands on Salick's knees to stop them bouncing.

"He loves you. You know that. I know that. The hall knows that. Well, maybe Records Master Arict is unaware, but still, she's sharper than she seems. And he's sharper than a claw, but what's wrong with that? What is he pulling at that you fear will come unravelled?"

The strong hands on her knees looked so calm compared to her own twisting in her lap. Vinir had been her best friend for most of her life. She took a deep breath. "He's pulling at the banehall. He thinks we should welcome the Masks into it, ally with them because he's got this insane idea that the demons are weapons in a war, being used by some imaginary enemy we've never seen!"

Vinir pulled back one hand to run it through her long hair, unbraided for the night. "Well, that's a lot to think on! But Salick, I don't think he's trying to destroy the banehall, though he might like to change it."

Salick looked up at her friend, tears blurring her vision. She reached out to take Vinir's hand.

"But changing it will destroy it. Nothing will be the same, and we've all worked so hard to recover from the Duellists' attack and Mandarack's . . ."

Vinir patted her shoulder and nodded. "I know. I miss him too. Branet wouldn't get away with half the clawed mistakes he makes if the master were still here. And it's cruel to send that Shirin out into the wilds to die! I don't care if it was done two centuries ago or if Banfreat himself thought it was a good idea! No, don't say anything! I know you love tradition, and it can be a shield against what hurts you, but you sometimes forget we can't really stop change, only fight like fools against it. You know that, don't you? Remember when we were young? You were a lord's daughter, and I was in my wretched uncle's care. I saw you riding by with your father – Heavens, he was a hard man – and I thought, 'She'll be a lord one day, and I'll be a washer woman, or dead from my uncle's . . . '"

She stopped and started to shake, but Salick grabbed her shoulders and brought her close for an embrace.

"You're safe now! He's dead and gone, same as my father, and you're surrounded by people who will protect you, Vinir. Stop crying, please!"

After some time, Vinir's shaking stopped. Each bane had a fear at their centre of their being. Fighting against it allowed them to battle real demons as well as the demons of their memories. Most waged that double war all their lives, and it was always a narrow thing between being crippled by fear or being able to use it as a true bane. Like everyone else in the banehall, Vinir lived within that terrible, narrow space.

"I'm all right. I just haven't thought of him for a while, that's all. Now let me go so I can dry my eyes."

She got up to open the window a bit more. "It's so close in here, isn't it? Well, tears come before a storm, as we used to say in the ward. Do you remember? But we were talking about you and Garet! What I was trying to say is that once we thought our future was carved deep into the stones of the city, a lord and a weaver, you high and I low. But look at us now, both the same, friends and banes, fighting to save our city. It's wonderful! So why are you afraid of change?"

"But the banehall, Vinir! If it changes, we may all die."

"And we may not. I think I like this idea of a war, because it means we might win, instead of fighting and dying for another six hundred years. Listen, you. Garet wants what's best for the city, of that I'm sure, and I'm even more certain that he would never want to hurt you."

Salick stood again, tears running down her face. "Then why is he trying to destroy what I love?"

She resumed her pacing, and Vinir could only shake her head at all the foolishness in the world.

IN AN EMPTY TRAINING room on the first floor, Hallmaster Branet struck again and again with his iron-bound staff, hitting the biggest bag in the room until it bled sand onto the floor. He was not wondering what he should do. With each echoing attack, he was trying to stop wondering.

And so went the night.

CHAPTER 21

CHANGE

Garet came down to his room when the rain started and slept fitfully until dawn. When he woke, Dorict was gone, and since Marick was still splinted in the infirmary, he was alone. He tried to remember his dreams, hoping to find some guidance in them, but when they bubbled up in his memory, he shuddered and opened the dusty curtain to let in some light. Images of the game board came again, with moving figures of children being pursued by the demon-like hunter piece. Across from him, the challenger changed with each move. First it was Branet, then the king, then Tarix, and Marick, and even Salick glaring at him. The last was Dorict, who shook his head and in a voice like a Shrieker's said, "This is no good, you Midland crow. You must learn to play the game!"

He stared out the window into the near-empty plaza, relieved to find a real, if cold, floor under his bare feet. He washed and dressed before going down to the dining hall. The place was quiet, as half the banes were still out on the new patrols, and the other half were trying to get a last hour of sleep before they must go out again.

Garet had a feeling the day would bring no new demon attacks. The monsters had been called away for some purpose last night. Until that purpose was fulfilled, they would not return.

The dining hall had but a few banes sitting together at the tables nearest the kitchen. Garet joined one where Dalesta and Chetorth, who also had day patrols, sat eating an early breakfast. It appeared others were also finding sleep difficult. Chetorth's face still bore an angry red scar from the Snake demon that cut him only seven nights ago. He was chewing his stew carefully, favouring the uninjured side of his mouth.

"Hello, Garet," Dalesta said. She pushed a clean bowl and spoon across to him and pointed at the pot in the centre of the table. "It's really good today, lamb stew and sweet buns. Yesterday it was beef and wild greens in a mushroom sauce! I think the ward lords want us to keep up our strength with all these attacks, but we'll get too fat to chase demons if we keep eating like this."

Garet spooned some of the stew into his bowl and stirred it around. His appetite must still be asleep, he decided, though it did smell very good. He tried a bite, and then another. "It is tasty. Tell me, Dalesta, what have you heard about last night?"

Chetorth broke into the conversation. "I hear that the temple priests prayed the demons away," he said.

Dalesta sniffed. "Six hundred years of praying and it only works now? No, I think the masters are as puzzled as we are. Our team saw a Shrieker coming across the rooftops and followed it from below. It passed up every opportunity to attack people in the courtyards and streets! By the time we caught up to it, the beast was climbing up and over the wall. Master Taron led us out the gate, but we saw nothing, only felt the fear fading away as it ran."

"The temple," Chetorth said, and stuffed his mouth again.

One of the kitchen help came out to clear the plates and stared pointedly at Garet's half full bowl. Garet started in on it again, only asking his next question when the server had returned laden to the washing tubs in the kitchen.

"What did you hear about Shirin, the Mask caught in the Fifth Ward?"

Dalesta cocked her head to one side. "You would know more than I, if the rumours are true. Didn't you fight with her and turn her over to the king?"

Garet dropped his spoon into the bowl. He'd had enough, no matter what the cooks might think. "No, Dalesta, I didn't. Well, I did fight with her, but only to try and talk our way out of this mad feud! Then Lord Sacourat brought her guards into the Maze and took her away. I only wanted to convince her to help us."

Dalesta considered this and did not seem to notice Chetorth frown then take his bowl and go sit elsewhere. She ran her finger through a spill of water on the table, tracing circles while she thought.

"All right, I see your point. It's too hard to fight both the demons and the Masks. Didn't we find that out last winter with those Duellists and the king? But why must it be you? Shouldn't Branet be doing this talking rather than a simple Green like you or me?"

She waited for his answer, her finger hovering over a drying circle.

Garet stood. "He should, but he won't," he told her, and smiled to take some of the bitterness out of his tone. "Be safe, Dalesta, and keep up with those exercises. Tarix is right; they are helping you."

"Sure, but Garet, where are you going?" Dalesta said. "And you, Chetorth, why did you move? Get back over here before I box your ears!"

Garet did not stay to see Chetorth's surrender. He left the dining hall and walked slowly to the records room. As he expected, the hallmaster was inside. Two other Reds, Relict and Taron, were there, and both men were speaking to Branet in raised voices.

"You can't restart a tradition of exile," Taron said. He was an older man with a precise moustache and beard. "It will be used to end political feuds, for revenge, personal gain, and all manner of idiotic reasons before it's done. Have you no sense of the history of the hall? Our fifty-first hallmaster, Chalan, convinced King Balin the Wise not to exile the rebel leaders two hundred years ago. Since then, no one has been cast from the city gates."

Relict nodded. "The chain gang is a harsh enough punishment. It was good enough for the Duellists, and you made no protest then! Branet, the city is torn over this. I heard the priests came from the temple this morning to plead for mercy, yet you wouldn't even see them. Why in Heaven's name do you need to see this woman dead?"

Branet looked up to see Garet waiting. "Green? What are you doing here? This is not for your ears. Leave immediately," he said.

"I intend to, Hallmaster," Garet replied.

He took off his sash. The green silk lay over his hands like a skein of spring growth. Relict's eyes widened, and he held out his own hand, as if willing him to stop, but Garet walked forward and laid the sash on the counter.

"After last winter, I made a promise to myself not to

harm anyone unless it was to save my life or the lives of others. Shirin's death does neither, Hallmaster. Goodbye, Master Relict, Master Taron. It seems I can no longer be a bane."

"Garet, no!" Relict said. "You must think about this."

He turned at the door. "My respects, Master Relict. Lately, I have thought of nothing else."

Dalesta, coming out of the dining hall, stared at him, puzzled, until she realized his sash was gone. Her mouth dropped open, and she watched him go up the stairs.

He returned to his room – well, not his room anymore, he realized – and searched until he found the bag of clothes he had borrowed from Torfor in the market. He had not had the time to return them and now must go beg the loan of them a little while longer. After changing out of his uniform, which he left folded on the bed, he pulled a wooden box out from under the desk and examined its contents: tattered pants and shoes that no longer fitted him, a wool tunic that he stuffed into the clothes bag, and a few coins that went into his pocket. There was also a small knife he hung on his belt, and nothing else. These few things were all he had from his life before the banehall.

He left the old pants and shoes in the box and sat down to write Dorict and Marick a note. He briefly considered writing another for Salick, but guessed she would probably tear it up unread. Thinking of her cutting silence, he needed a moment to find his strength again so that he might continue.

DORICT AND MARICK,

I am leaving the banehall. I cannot stay, and I think you know the reasons why. Please take care of Allifur for me. She will need friends in the hall, and you are two of the best she could ever hope to find.

    Farewell,

    Garet

HE PUT the note on Dorict's bed and hefted the bag to his shoulder. He was not surprised to find Tarix waiting for him at the front door.

"Relict told you?" Garet asked. He settled the bag more firmly on his shoulder.

The Red nodded. She looked him up and down, taking in the rough clothes and wool cap.

"He woke me up, and I nearly clouted him for it. Then he told me what you did, and I wanted to clout you, or probably Branet – yes, definitely Branet!"

The rain drummed on the steps just outside the open doors. The bane who recorded comings and goings had fled to a spot across the entrance hall where he could keep his notes dry.

Garet smiled. "I deserve a beating, I'm sure, for putting you through so much trouble over these past months. I couldn't have—"

Tarix held up a hand, then placed it on his shoulder. "Don't say it. I did what I did, and you're doing what you're doing. We all have our reasons, and I don't take this as a final parting. Keep heart, Garet, most troubles pass. I feel we will work together again when we've all come to our senses."

She watched him walk down the steps and into the Banehall Plaza. The number of people walking about was growing now, even this early and even in the rain. Word of the demons' retreat had spread, and people came out to share in the wonder of it. Garet was lost in those crowds soon enough.

"He's gone?" Relict asked. He had been hanging back to let his wife say goodbye to her student.

"Yes, for now," she said. "Come, my dear husband, I need to talk to the hallmaster."

Relict shook his head. "Maybe it should wait, or we'll both need new clothes."

But Tarix was already halfway to the records room.

At the Stewards School, Barick was still in his dressing gown. Standing barefooted at the door to his rooms, he blinked down at Garet and yawned.

"Garet! I did not expect you today, especially so early. Has the king called you? Is that why you are dressed so . . . peculiarly?"

Garet put down the bag at his feet and pulled the cap off his hair. He stood in a small puddle and was soaked to the skin.

"No, the king hasn't called me, not yet. Master Historian, you said you needed a researcher, and I find myself in need of a job."

Barick blinked again.

CHAPTER 22
PARTINGS AND A NEW PURPOSE

Salick ran up the steps to the banehall, wet and furious. It was mid-morning, and once Bandat had told her of Garet's leaving, she had been unable to think of anything else. Her master, to the Gold's frustration, had no further information, and the image of Garet laying down his sash went round and round in her head until she could barely think of her surroundings.

"Heaven's shield, Salick," the Red told her. "You're little use here, especially if we keep tripping over you. I give you my permission to go back to the hall, ask your questions, and then come back with a clear head!"

She did so, splashing off at a dead run and giving fright to many who wondered from what calamity might a bane flee so fast. She was breathless when she arrived at the hall, and paused at the top of the steps to shake the water from her eyes. Kesla was back on her stool, huddled under a tarp and staring at the new arrival.

"Salick! Is there some danger? Have the demons returned?" She rose carefully and pulled the other Gold out of the rain to stand within the entrance hall.

"Claw's sake, tell me! What is it?"

"Garet," Salick gasped out. She wiped more water from her face and looked up into the taller woman's eyes. "Have you seen him?" she asked.

Kesla shook her head. "No, I haven't, though I've heard, as you obviously have, what he did. I've never heard of such a thing! And Garet is such a good bane. Do you think he went mad or is ill in some other way?"

Salick shook her head. "I don't know. I think I might have . . . never mind. Where is Tarix?"

"On patrol," Kesla answered. "We still have half the banes out there, though no demon has been seen or felt since yesterday. Some think we've beaten them."

Salick looked out into the rain. She could barely see the riverside wall in this downpour.

"Why is he out there?" she asked the grey sky.

Kesla, having no answer, shook her head. A practical young woman, she knew that the secret of another's heart was something only Heaven could reveal. She went back to her stool, braving the rain so she would not shame Salick by being a witness to her tears.

"A STORM like this they call Heaven's tears," Torfor said. He tied down the last lashing of the tarp protecting his bakery stand. The palace market had been busy earlier with daily shopping and the gossip of the night, but now few braved the downpour. The baker turned back to his guest. They had spoken much while the rain fell.

"What do they call such a drenching in the Midlands?"

Garet thought for a moment. "Just rain, I think. Perhaps we aren't as poetic in the east. Now, what about the clothes? I have some coins here to buy them, but I was hoping you could help me get a better set than these. Barick sniffed at them like I pulled them from a sewer!"

Torfor laughed and poured another small cup of tea for them both. "They'll be clean enough now. Let's see those coins."

He took the Northern coppers in his hand and poked at them. "Hmmm, never seen such before. I'll take them over to Agar's place. He trades in foreign things and might take them for real money. Stay here and try to sell these buns to anyone foolish enough to be out in this weather."

He threw his jacket over his head and ran off down the alley of tents and stalls. Garet waited nervously, for he had little grasp of Shirath's money – banes rarely had to use it – and feared serving a customer would only show his ignorance. Luckily, Torfor returned before anyone else came by.

"You're in luck, Heaven be praised, for Agar says these are rare in the South. Here you are, my friend, a silver piece and two bronze. That will get you a fine used suit and a coat to stave off this rain, plus money in your pocket. Keep the cap if you want," he said, and hunched on his stool, hands held over the tiny brazier that had boiled the tea.

The kettle had the symbol for "luck" raised on one side. So did the cups, and there were such tokens all over the stall and even cut into the crusts of the loaves ready to be sold.

"Thank you, Torfor. You've been very kind to me, especially since I'm not a bane anymore."

Torfor laughed. "Well, you've done much for this city already, and from what you've told me, you were right to leave the banehall. Imagine, sending out someone to their death when we all work so hard just to stay alive."

"You don't think Shirin should be exiled?" Garet asked. He sipped his tea and let the warmth seep into his bones.

"Course not!" Torfor said. "You're right about talking with those Masks. That's how we settle things in the wards. Talk, don't fight, just like all our mothers said. Makes sense, crowded as we are. If we took up swords and sticks at every problem, we'd be a town of corpses. No, you can't live within these walls and raise your hand against your neighbour. Nor should the banehall raise its hand against anything but dem . . . ahhh! Sorry, I've lived so long not saying the word. Against anything but those beasts."

Garet nodded. He sipped more tea.

The old man leaned forward. "Now, can I ask you a question?"

"Of course," Garet said. He owed this man much for his kindness, and liked him besides.

"Do you think the beasts have retreated? Have we won, as the gossips say?"

Garet wished he had asked a different question. He put down his empty cup on the table beside the kettle. "No. I wish I did, but I don't. I think this is a trick, perhaps to make us let down our guard, but I don't really know. There are pieces of the puzzle missing."

Torfor sighed and filled up their cups again. "Well, I hope the hall, or the palace, or you figure it out soon. These times are wearying for an old man. But come what may, you have a friend here, Garet."

His guest smiled. "I think I need one, Torfor. There is something I must do before nightfall, something that will take some time to accomplish. If you could direct me to places in the market that sell certain items?"

"What items?" Torfor asked, his brows pulled down.

Garet told him, and the old man whistled.

"Well, well. No need to ask what you want them for, and I agree, of course, though don't tell anyone I said so. I'd better take you myself. There's one or two we can trust. Wait here, and I'll get Salan's daughter to watch the stall."

∾

"I MUST LEAVE the hall to get supplies," Banerict said to Salick.

They stood just outside the infirmary.

"Since we have more injured every day, I need more of everything! Don't worry, the older banes are here to keep an eye on things, and as for Marick, I've left his friend to watch him."

She had come down to check on Marick in the evening, long after most of the day patrols had found their beds. Now, at Banerict's words, she ran into the big room, hoping to find Garet, but stopped when she saw Dorict was the friend sitting and nodding beside the injured Blue.

Marick was asleep on his cot, the splint on his leg a sharp line under the blanket. Three other banes were abed in various stages of injury, and all asleep as well, so that the Gold felt she was the only one awake in the hall. Four banes, too old for active duty, sat at the other end of the room, nodding over cups of tea.

Salick came up beside Dorict and touched his arm.

"Oh, it's you, Salick. Are you all right? You-you've heard about Garet, I suppose?" he said, rubbing at his eyes.

She nodded and pulled up a chair beside him. "Did he talk to you before he left?" she asked, keeping her voice low so as not to wake Marick.

Dorict shook his head. He reached into his vest pocket

238

and pulled out a folded sheet of paper. He handed it to her and shrugged.

"This is all he left, besides his uniform and rope-hammer," he replied softly.

Salick read the note, then read it again. Her anger rose once more, only to be knocked down by worry and guilt. She handed the paper back to the Blue. "Was there anything else, anything for me?"

Dorict looked at her for a moment before answering. "No, I'm sorry, just this. Did he leave something in your room, or perhaps with Vinir?"

She shook her head. "No, he didn't say anything . . ." she began, then her sense of duty, which she realized had probably caused this clawed mess, forced her to add, "not after last night, and then I wouldn't talk to him."

"You're a fool then," Marick said.

They looked to see his bright eyes staring at them over the top of his blanket. The young bane checked that Banerict was indeed gone from the main room of the infirmary. With a sigh, he pushed the splint out from under the blanket and let it fall to the floor.

"There! That is a most uncomfortable thing to wear, and I know he only did it to keep me in bed! Now, Salick, tell me all the news!"

She bristled. "You call me a fool then want a favour? Claws take you!"

"They'll take you first," Marick said, "if you don't use your brains. Why did you fight with Garet? No, don't deny it, Vinir told us all about it! You're not mad at him because he thinks you have a horrible nature – which you do – or that you can't be trusted – which you can't! He's mad because you treat him like he's a Black Sash!"

Salick started to protest, but Marick ignored her and

continued, "You think you're the only one who cares about morals and duty in this hall, but you forget that Garet is just as bad. The two of you deserve each other, as far as I can tell."

Salick made to stand, but Dorict pulled her back down to her chair. "Listen, Salick. For once, he's making sense."

Salick, stunned by a glare from the usually placid Blue, did as she was told.

Marick sat up, still holding the blanket to his chin, and finished his ranting. "Yes, deserve each other! Yet you get your nose pinched by him going on about change? I know he can be boring sometimes, but he wasn't the first to talk that way. Mandarack was, and you thought he was Heaven's gift to the city – which, come to think of it, he was!"

"Enough," Salick hissed, but Dorict kept her firmly in her seat with a strength she had not known he possessed.

One hand on her wrist, he hissed right back at her. "He's right. Master Mandarack would be changing this hall, had he lived. Do you think he would have let things get this bad without taking action? The patrols would have been changed weeks ago, and you can't tell me he'd have sent that poor mad woman out to her death. I won't believe it! The master would have talked to her, found a place for her in the defence of the city. He would have done everything you hate Garet for suggesting!"

And with that, he let her go. Turning to Marick, he said, "Are you ready?"

The supposedly injured bane threw off the covers to reveal he was fully dressed in his bane's uniform. He swung his legs down, grimaced, and said, "If you really want to help the hall and your true love, talk to Tarix."

They left her there. Salick stared at the empty bed, her shoulders and head slowly dropping and detested, unbidden tears falling onto her limp hands. After some time, an old man, one of the retired banes who helped Banerict, came over and sat beside her. He put a gentle arm around her shaking shoulders and waited while she cried out all her tears.

It took a long time, but he had trained many young banes, and was patient with their sudden storms.

ACCORDING TO THE KING, Shirin had not said a word since her capture. She certainly had nothing to say to Garet, though he had tried several times to get a response to his questions. Neither pleading nor threats had worked so far, according to Trax.

"Look," Garet said, considering the approaching hour of exile, "I don't want this, nor does the king. He let me come down here to talk to you, after all. So if you won't say anything, then please just listen."

They sat on stools in a low-ceilinged cellar of the palace. Shirin, of course, was chained to the wall. She looked at him, or rather through him, her hair matted and tangled and her clothes filthy from her violent passage to the palace. There were bruises all over her face and arms. Sacourat's guards had not been gentle.

Garet held out a hand, palm up. If he was to help her, even in the small way he hoped, he had to get her attention. "Shirin, you don't have to die out there," he said. "The king has promised that you will be spared exile if you name those who command the Masks. It is the best deal he can make, for he must have something to hold off the bane-hall's demand for your death."

Her focus shifted to acknowledge his presence.

"The best deal?" she said, her voice rough and scornful. "You sound just like a Trader, and I've had more than enough of that kind of talk. Tell the king he can take back his clawed deal. It's a lie, anyway. The banehall won't relent, will they, Garet? And I know that I'm dead when I walk out those walls."

"You won't be just walking, you'll be pushed out in front of all the lords and guild masters," he said and lowered his voice. "The only people who protested – besides the king and me – were the temple priests, and they have little power to prevent your death, but there might be a way, Shirin."

She looked at him, her face as still as the mask she once wore. At least he had her attention now.

"You can get to another city, Old Torrick, perhaps, or even to the Midlands. There's work there and a life for you, if you want it."

She laughed, a hollow sound in that cellar.

"And how will I get there, bane? Alone, without food or gear of any kind? No horse, no mask, and prey for the first demon to find me?"

Garet leaned forward. They were alone and she was a trained killer, but he had things to say he dared not let be overheard by the guards outside the door.

"To the north-east, past the orchards and at the end of the wood lots, is an old logging station, like the one you Masks used to train. It will be empty now until the fall. Follow the creek that leads into the orchards directly across the fields from the Third Ward. Keep going, and you will find the station on its banks. In the tower is a bag of food, a good knife, and a bow with some arrows, not many, but some. I couldn't get the mask you had. Sacourat sent it to the hall when she found it in your uncle's home."

"Why, bane? Why help me, and why are you dressed like an ordinary man?" Shirin asked. The chains clinked as she shifted forward to study him in the light of the single candle.

Garet had explained himself to others enough lately, so he just said "Because I must" as an answer to both questions.

Her eyes darted around the room. She lifted her hands and looked at the manacles around her wrists. Her fingers curled into fists. "So, even now you want to leave me in your debt."

Garet shook his head and laid a hand on hers. "Live, Shirin. Live and leave your hate of me at the city gates. Then we'll be even."

The guards let him out, and he went up the many stairs to find the king waiting for him in the guard's storeroom. It was stacked with swords, spears, shields, and sundry pieces of armour.

"What did she say?" Trax asked. He wore a simple grey tunic and pants, lacking even the poorest gems. There were shadows under his eyes, and his voice had none of its usual bantering tone.

"Nothing of the Masks, Your Majesty. Will the exile go ahead?"

Trax signalled Garet to sit then settled himself on a stool beside a pile of gauntlets. "It must, though I loathe the idea. Your hallmaster has me chained like Shirin. If I refuse, half the people might rise against the palace to demand her exile."

Garet shook his head. "It isn't my hall anymore, and Branet is not my master. I've laid down my sash, Trax."

The king's eyes widened. He tapped a finger to his lips. "Well, I had heard that, though I could scarce believe it. I thought you a bane to your bones, Garet. Did you do this because of Shirin's fate, or were there other reasons?"

"I did it because I . . . must be useful," Garet said. He stood up and started pacing. His anger at the forces pushing him this way and that could not be contained on a stool.

"Why did Heaven bring me here from the Midlands? Why did it make me a bane if not to be of use? I want to . . . fix things, since the world is so broken, and I can't do that in the hall anymore. What other reasons could I have?"

"I can't imagine Salick is happy with this," Trax observed.

"We are . . . no longer together," Garet said. He stopped at a table holding scraps of leather, punches, and thick curved needles. He slammed his fists down so hard that it all danced on the wood.

Trax stood up and came over to him. He laid a careful hand on Garet's shoulder.

"Having felt her wrath – justifiably, of course, unlike you – I have some sympathy for your plight. Now, Barick says you need a job. He wants to give you one, but I need you more. Will you be my agent, Garet? Help me find out who is behind the Masks so that we can bring this to an end."

Garet turned to face the king. There was granite in his tone when he replied, "So Branet can exile them as well?"

Trax shook his head. "No. It pains me, but I must let Branet have this blood, but only this once. I know the people better than he does. Once it's done, they will forget they wanted it and be horrified by her fate. The next time the hallmaster demands such cruelty, I'll have all of the city on my side and we'll need not repeat this farce. The chain gangs will suffice for the rest of them."

Garet considered this, thinking of how Torfor had reacted to the sentence. He smiled wryly at the king. "I think you might be right. Some are already horrified, but are you sure you want to hire me? You know my nature, Trax. I speak my mind, for all the trouble it gets me! Do you think I'll last long in the job?"

Trax smiled. "Oh, I hope so. I need at least one honest man to frighten all the scoundrels."

"And what about you?" Garet asked. He cocked his head to one side and put his hands on his hips.

Trax feigned innocent outrage. "Me? Why, as the biggest scoundrel, at least in your eyes, I will probably need the most frightening."

He stopped his playacting and looked at the ex-bane. Garet could see how lack of sleep and worry had aged the usually buoyant man. "Garet, I'm asking you to be useful. Please help me fix my broken city."

He held out his hand, and Garet grasped it.

"I will, Your Majesty."

"Good," Trax said, beaming again. "You'll need to dress the part. We can get you a good coat, at least, and a sword. You have to bear a sword to be in the king's service! Find one here, and then see my chief of guards. She will set you up with what you need."

"How do I find the Masks?" Garet called after the retreating king.

Trax's voice drifted back. "Use your brains, King's Agent. Use your brains!"

Picking through the various swords hanging from pegs on the wall or sticking, hilt up, out of baskets, Garet picked a practical-looking weapon with a wide, sturdy blade sharpened on one side and coming to a strong, slightly curved point. He swung it a few times. The balance was not bad, and the metal rung true when tapped with a hammer.

Holding it, he felt the enormity of the change he had brought upon himself. Events may have pushed him to leave the hall, but working for the king was his choice. He swung the sword several times, until it felt more natural to his hand. This was nothing like the big double-edged swords the king's guard carried, but he thought it still might cut a demon's throat.

The sheath was intact, the guard and pommel were strong, but the strapping around the grip was loose. Garet picked up what he needed from the table and sat down to fix it. While his hands worked, he took the king's advice and used his brain to think of a way, any way, to trace the Masks.

CHAPTER 23
GOING TO THE TEMPLE

T he lord's house of the Thirteenth Ward was a fine
structure of stone and glass, as light and airy as a
crystal chandelier set on the dull ground. The four
grey towers that guarded it, joined by walls and oaken
gates, were not as cheerful. They housed the lord's relatives,
his retainers, and various hangers-on. In years past, they
were said to have held dungeons and armouries, but Gost
had assured Kaela that this was but a rumour.

She waited just outside the tall doors, wishing she
could sit down while a cart was brought around to take her
to the temple. Just now, however, she didn't want to seem
weak, no matter how much the future lord of the Thirteenth Ward kicked and wriggled inside her.

"With my dear husband and his uncle making so many
demands on the guards' time, I'm grateful that you could
be spared to accompany me," she said to the dour woman
standing at her side.

"They don't use women guards much, m'lady," the
guard said, and adjusted her sword to better fit sitting in

the cart, which now rumbled around the corner of the house, pulled by a patient pony.

The guard helped Kaela up and then joined her, taking the reins from the groom. Their passage through the ward was slowed by the number of people in the streets. It seemed commerce and community had cautiously reappeared after a week of fear.

"Do you think them Masks drove the beasts away, m'lady?" the guard asked. She had a broad face, a squat nose, and looked, Kaela decided, as if she had been born as a bear and then mostly shaved.

"I'm not sure, Cruster, isn't it? What is your opinion on the matter?"

"Mine?" the guard asked. "Well, I think it's a trick, m'lady. Can't trust them things."

"Well said! Well said, Cruster! You are a most perceptive woman. I think you are right; it is a trick. And the Masks have done nothing but stir up the city against themselves. Why, look what happened to that woman but two days past! Were you there with my lord husband at her exile? I could not go. His uncle felt it was too sad a spectacle for one in my condition."

The guard shook her head. "No, m'lady. There weren't many that did go, some say. Most lords didn't, nor the priests of the temple, nor some of the guilds. Lord Kirel and your uncle were there and had a guard, though you needn't worry 'bout that."

"Yes, it seems we can hardly separate Maroster from my uncle," Kaela said.

"Not him, m'lady. None has seen him for days. It was Shaverl who took the duty."

Kaela matched the name to a male guard with half of

Maroster's size and probably half of his limited wit. She waved her fan at the flies.

"Well, it was a sad sight, no doubt."

Cruster spat over the side of the cart. "Bad way to go," she said.

Kaela smiled. "I agree. But I'm sure the banehall and the king will exile anyone involved in the Masks' crimes, no matter how high . . . or low."

Cruster looked alarmed at this and slapped the reins to make the pony move faster. Blameless pedestrians had to scramble out of the way.

"Easy, Cruster!" Kaela said. "I'm afraid I do not like speed in my condition."

When the guard had reined in the pony, Kaela continued. "Yes, it's better to be cautious and to know who to trust to take the reins in a bad time, don't you agree?"

Not used to talking in riddles, or talking at all, Cruster thought about this for the length of the Banehall Plaza before finally nodding, though they had crossed the bridge and entered the Palace Plaza before she spoke. "Problem is, m'lady, your uncle's got those reins tight in his hands, if I take your meaning. And he has that Tarock and Chirat of the Twelfth Ward to help hold them, if I don't give offence by saying."

Kaela put a gentle hand on the rather impressive biceps of her driver. "Cruster, there will come a time when my uncle reaches too far and falls to his own destruction. That is when another hand will take the reins, and she will need loyal guards to protect her. Do you agree?"

Cruster looked sidelong at her passenger, and nodded.

Kaela removed her hand and rubbed the large bump under her gown. "So tell me, my dear Cruster, how many women guards are there who have your good sense?"

She was pleased to see the woman soon ran out of fingers and needed to borrow some of hers.

It was a lucky day to visit the temple.

FROM THE SHADOWS under the temple's central dome, Salick looked down the stairs at the very pregnant lady and her stocky guard dismounting from their cart.

That's Kaela, a simpering, conniving woman and Kirel's wife. I'd best avoid her, for she mustn't know why I'm here.

She backed further into the shadows until she bumped against something, not a pillar but a person who grunted in surprise.

Salick turned and saw the chief priest she had been sent to see, Chabost. The older woman tottered, and Salick supported her with a hand under her elbow.

"Thank you, bane," the priest said, and smoothed out the disarray in her sky-blue vestments. "Did you wish to speak with me, or are you here to speak with Heaven?"

"I have a message, Your Grace," the Gold said and produced an envelope from within her vest. "Hallmaster Branet wishes you to read and respond to this letter as soon as possible."

"As soon as possible?" the old woman said, arching an eyebrow. She took the letter over to a bench just outside the ring of pillars that marked off the sacred from the ordinary. She sat down and looked up at the younger woman.

"Living as we priests do under Heaven, the 'soonest' we know of is a full night's watching of the stars, or perhaps the turn of a single season."

She unfolded the paper slowly with arthritic hands.

After reading a few lines, she asked, "Do you know what is in here, child?"

Salick nodded.

"Then perhaps you might wait a while, in here or perhaps under the dome, while I finish this and consider your hallmaster's demands."

Salick stood a minute, watching the old woman read. As the time passed, she walked over to a pillar and leaned against it to remove her boots. After placing them behind the stone support, Salick walked forward into the shadows and under the jewelled representation of the night sky that lined the ceiling. It was cool and dark. The only light was reflected upwards from the polished floor, outlining diamond and ruby constellations when the sun broke through the remnants of the morning's clouds.

A tremor went through Salick. She had not been here for months, not since the ceremonies for Master Mandarack. She had wanted to help prepare his body for the funeral fires – a final act of love and respect – but had panicked at first, unable to do her duty. Garet had been with her then, and gave her the strength she needed. She wished he were here now as those memories came back. She saw again the long procession carrying Mandarack's body, Trax at its head, and the entire population of the city turning out to honour the man. She felt once more the despair in her heart as they made the long walk to the burning grounds that lay beyond the wall.

Why aren't you here now, when I need you?

There was a cough behind her, and she turned to see the priest holding out the letter in her hand. There was compassion in the old woman's eyes, but none in her tone. "Please tell Hallmaster Branet that we cannot deny proper ceremonies to any who need them. A Mask who dies will be honoured and burned just as a lord, a bane, or a beggar would. The hall and the king may presume to judge them in life, but we would not dare to do so in death, Salick, lest the final judgment be against us all."

"How did you . . ."

The old woman held up a hand. "How did I know your name? Your father was my cousin's boy, though you were born long after I came here. His death was the tragedy of a life wasted. By all accounts, your life has been one well spent – so far. Make sure that you keep on Heaven's path, Salick. Farewell."

Salick bowed and left, knowing that the answer she carried would enrage the hallmaster. On the way out, Kaela caught sight of her and smiled in a knowing way.

Salick shoved the letter inside her vest and cursed.

Claws, this was an unlucky day to come to the temple!

CHAPTER 24
KING'S AGENT

"**A**re you sure about this?" Captain Bixa asked. She was looking pointedly at Garet's sword. Her own was in her hands, a longsword with a hand-and-a-half grip and a blade three-fingers wide at the hilts. He had to admit his own weapon looked pitiful by comparison.

"I'm ready," he said, and shifted his weight to the balls of his feet.

Bixa shrugged and lunged forward, aiming low to frighten him into a hasty off-balance retreat. There was a wicked grin on the guard captain's face.

Instead of jumping back at such an intimate attack, Garet shifted to his right, bringing the point of the sword down and forcing the captain's blade to his left. He continued twisting, turning along the attacking weapon until he completed a full circle with his sword at the side of the captain's neck.

"Claws, you're fast!" Bixa snarled, and jumped away, only to leap forward again with a two-handed downward slash.

Since there was no way his short sword could stop the weight and force of it, Garet chose to be elsewhere, a short step to his left this time. Bixa's blade stopped when she felt the curved point of his blade pressing against her leather practice armour.

The captain raised her hands in mock surrender.

"You're better than I expected. I've never seen a bane fight before, for obvious reasons, and to be honest, you don't look like much. But if every bane is so skilled, you must do nothing but train in that hall of yours!" She sheathed her sword.

The others looking on gave muted applause, one hand lightly slapping the back of the other. It was too good a match to ignore, but a wise guard did not enthusiastically celebrate the defeat of their commander.

Garet nodded to acknowledge their approval before answering. "That's true enough, Captain. We, I mean they, train continuously. That is what banes do; they train, they sleep and eat, and they kill demons."

Bixa flinched a bit at that, but inclined her head to Garet, showing the beginnings of respect. The captain of the palace guards had not been so courteous that morning when she had summoned him for testing with his new blade. He had met her here, in a small courtyard of the Palace Ward with the half moon, waning now, still bright in the sky.

"Breakfast then," the captain said, "but not for you slugs! Have at each other again, else you'll be meat for those Masks when we catch them."

At a table in the guards' dining hall, Garet brought that topic up again. "Captain, are we any closer to finding out where they are hiding?"

Bixa finished a spoonful of her porridge. She then lifted her cup and regarded Garet over the rim. "No, and that's not for saying to anyone but a king's agent. Or the king, but he already knows it. We think the rot is in the Twelfth and Thirteenth Ward, and maybe the Fifth, but we have no proof. However, the people we suspect are being watched."

"Can I help with that?" Garet asked. He had been a king's agent for four days now but had done nothing but train with his sword and help Barick organize his history notes.

Bixa laughed and pointed at his hair. "You're not exactly one to fade into a crowd, are you?" she said. "No, boy, you're not much use out in the wards."

Garet felt the respect he had earned on the training ground slipping away. "I want to be useful, Captain. Can't you suggest something else then?"

Bixa looked annoyed, but appeared to think about it. Several spoonfuls later, she had something to say. "You're good with books and such, the king says. So why don't you stick your nose in the records of those wards and see if there's anything 'useful' in them?"

She got up and left him there, taking her cup with her out into the ward.

He heard her shouting at someone, her voice cutting into the quiet morning air. Once more, it seemed, he would have to fight to prove himself, and with more than a sword. Mechanically, he finished his breakfast and walked slowly back to the Stewards School. He had a room there, or more likely a cleared-out closet of some kind, for there were boxes of old deed titles under his cot. It was right across the hall from Barick's rooms, and the historian had monopolized Garet's time, using him as a researcher and secretary.

The stone façade of the Stewards School too soon rose before him, and he paused on the steps to brace himself for more dusty work. It wasn't that he minded Barick's company so much, it was more that he missed certain company so much more that it sometimes hurt to breathe. The nights were the worst. Then he remembered everything about Salick, from the lightness of her laugh to the curve of the sword scar on her cheek. He replayed everything that led up to their separation, searching for some fault, some mistake he could make right with her.

Several stewards passed him on the stairs while he stood there like a moody statue. He shook himself and continued upwards. It was not such a bad job that lay before him. Though Barick would rattle on all day like rain against the window, he had no real harm in him.

Garet was not so sure of his fellow agents. Captain Bixa, for example, struck him as a woman who would do anything if ordered by the king.

He went through the centre door and climbed the stairs to Barick's rooms. At least all his worries could be temporarily buried by work, and the historian could no doubt provide the records Bixa spoke of. Whether or not she was sending him on a fool's journey just to keep him out from under her feet, well, nothing but time and work would tell.

"If it's not Garet dragging me out of the hall on a fool's journey, it's you," Dorict complained. Marick ignored his complaints and pulled his friend into a narrow alley between two buildings.

"Don't say that name so loud!" he whispered in Dorict's annoyed ear. "At least not in the Twelfth Ward. After going over to the king, he's too famous to be mentioned – and so am I, come to think of it. Now, straighten that old coat. Torfor really is a friend to banes, isn't he?"

"I noticed you weren't afraid to mention . . . you-know-who, when you were badgering Torfor for these clothes. And these are worse than the last set. I look like a rag pile with legs!"

Marick chuckled. "Why, you've never looked better! There's a tragic beauty about you that near makes me faint. Now, we promised Tarix and Relict to be careful, and these disguises are fulfilling that promise, which of course leaves us free to take any other risk we want."

Dorict looked alarmed. "The last time I was in disguise, Shirin almost killed me! What kind of risk are you talking about?"

Marick, however, was no longer listening. He sauntered out into the street, winding his way among the carts and labourers. Dorict followed him until they came to the first row of Traders' houses, large, three-storey structures, each with a fortified storage room on the bottom floor and living space above. The small bane began to wind his way among them, whistling tunelessly as he walked.

"What are you doing?" Dorict asked, sidling up beside him.

"Keeping my eyes open, as you should be," Marick replied out of the corner of his mouth. "We're looking for the Masks!"

"I doubt we'll spot a large group of men and women dressed in black and with covered faces," Dorict hissed. "So what do you suggest I look for?"

"You'll know when you see it," Marick said, and continued his leisurely progress.

After a morning of looking and walking, and seeing nothing, the two found a tea stall set up in the shade of the ward wall and rested their feet.

"Brilliant," Dorict declared. He had his shoes off and was rubbing his aching toes. "We've walked this ward back and forth and back again with nothing to show for it! What now, oh Master Spy?"

"Keep looking, of course," Marick said. He sipped his tea and watched the colourful play of commerce stretching around them.

A whip cracked nearby and a horse screamed, causing the owner of the stall to drop a cup to the flagstones. He ran out into the street and out of sight. The two banes could hear him shouting at someone just around a corner.

"Easy with that whip, you clawed fool! I bet that the horse is more valuable than you, and of better nature! Your master should give it the whip and strap you in the traces."

Another voice shouted, and the whip cracked again. This time the cry was human, and the tea stall owner came scuttling back, holding one hand to his cheek.

"Heaven strike him down!" he moaned and bent over to pick up the shards of his broken cup.

Marick left a scattering of coins on the table, more than enough for their tea, and pulled Dorict towards the corner where the argument had occurred.

"I'm an idiot!" he said.

Dorict nodded. "I know that! But where are we going now? Did you see something?"

Marick knelt and looked around the corner. After a glance, he stood again and grinned. "I should have used my ears instead of my eyes. I know that voice, and the sound of that whip! The man over there with the stubborn horse, he's the one who took the Masks to the forest station. He did me an injury before, but this time he's going to do us both a favour."

They followed the man once he got the cart moving again under his ready whip. He drove the horse south, towards the outer wall, but this time did not leave the ward. Instead, he turned left into a passage between the warehouses owned, and sometimes uneasily shared, by the Trader clans of the ward. The man stopped at the farthest one and waited while wooden crates were loaded onto his cart, then he drove back the way he had come, passing by Marick and Dorict without noticing them standing in the shadows.

"Shall we go after him?" Dorict asked, but Marick had plucked the sleeve of a passing labourer.

"Excuse me, but I'm looking for Dorict's warehouse. Is it that one over there?" he asked the woman, pointing to where the cart had stopped.

The woman snorted and shook her head. "Dorict's warehouse? Never heard of it. That's Chirat's over there. Now leave off, I've got work to do."

"A friendly sort," Marick said when the woman had left them. "Should we go inside for a look?"

Dorict grabbed his friend by the shoulder. "No," he said. "No, no, no, no, no. Do you want to give them another chance to kill you? They might have improved with practice! We are going back to the hall, and you get to live and tell everyone how brilliant you are."

Marick frowned. "But this would be much more fun. We might not die, and besides, everyone already knows I'm brilliant."

He tried to wriggle out of Dorict's grasp, but he might as well have tried to slip the embrace of a Crusher demon.

"And yet you never get tired of telling us," Dorict said, and steered his protesting friend towards the safety of the hall.

CHAPTER 25
THE SHOUTING ROOM

Salick stopped on the stairs. More banes were in the hall today, and their sashes added a dash of colour to the grey stone halls. Just now, one shade, red, was predominant, and those wearing it were all moving towards the dining hall.

"Are you a bane or a piece of furniture?" Vinir asked, and gave her a friendly push. The two of them were not due to patrol until nightfall, circling outside the wall to make sure the demons were not returning after days of blessed absence.

"What are the Reds up to?" Salick asked.

Vinir looked over her shoulder to see the last of them go through the entrance of the big room and shut the seldom-used doors. Several lesser banes noticed this and looked at each other much as Salick and Vinir did now.

"Another meeting?" Vinir suggested. "Perhaps figuring out what we'll all do if the demons never return – Heaven will it!"

"Heaven will it," Salick echoed. "What would you do?"

Under Vinir's gentle pressure, they reached the bottom of the stairs and turned towards the training halls.

"Back to weaving, I suppose. I must remember something of it. What about you?"

Salick didn't answer, and her friend wisely stopped talking. She was spared the burden of further silence by the sight of Marick racing down the corridor towards them.

"Hey, stop there, you rascal!" Vinir called out, and the Blue skidded to a stop, pointedly avoiding Salick's gaze.

"What is it?" he asked. "I have duties to complete!"

Vinir laughed. "Well, there's a first time for all things, I suppose. Go on, you diligent bane! But stop by later and tell me the news."

Marick grinned as she tousled his hair. "I'll find *you* later," he said, and dashed off again.

The two Golds went into the smaller training room and took off their vests and sashes before warming up.

"Still on the outs with Marick and Dorict?" Vinir asked. She threw the end of a rope to Salick and the two tried to wrest it from each other's grip.

"I don't care," Salick grunted. Vinir was stronger than she was, but Salick refused to give up.

"You could apologize. To Garet, I mean," Vinir said. With a heave, she collected both Salick's end of the rope and Salick, who stumbled forward into her arms. "That would fix everything, wouldn't it?" she asked her captured friend.

Salick pushed away. She went over to the weapons rack and chose a heavy club. Slowly at first, then with some speed, she struck imaginary attackers with a fierceness that made Vinir step back.

When Salick paused to pant, the taller Gold chose a rope-hammer from a peg and stood in front of her.

"Maybe you should spar against this," she said, swinging the missile end of the weapon in small circles at her side. "Since you seem to be fighting an invisible Garet!"

"And a too-visible Vinir," Salick muttered. She put the club back in its spot and left the room.

Vinir took no note of this but kept swinging the heavy weight on its rope, watching it accelerate into a blur before letting it slow to a stop.

"How in Heaven's name does Garet use this thing without killing himself?" she asked, then found she was talking to an invisible friend.

⁓

"I DON'T SEE IT," Taron said. The Red stood across from Hallmaster Branet, his face as red as his sash. "Six hundred years and they just stop? We need to patrol farther, leagues out if need be, to find out what happened to them."

Branet shook his head. He frowned at Taron and pointed to the ground at his feet. "And what if we are all out chasing shadows and the demons return to ravage the city? Have you thought of that, Master Taron?"

Relict stood up, anger in his voice as he spoke. "Attack from where, Hallmaster? Will they drop from the sky? They have gone somewhere, and Taron's right. We must find out where they are!"

There was a murmur of support at that, until Branet glared it into silence. Tarix stood up, one hand raised for the room's attention.

"It is only wise, Hallmaster, to investigate all possibilities. For example, has Lord Andarack perfected the spark device he used to broadcast emotions using a demon jewel? As I recall, you felt its power last winter and praised his efforts. Perhaps he found a way to drive the demons off? Have you spoken to him?"

"No," Branet said. "Would he not have told us if he had?"

"One speaks," Taron said through gritted teeth, "only when there are ears willing to hear."

Before Branet could protest, Bandat jumped up and spoke, waving an arm to include all the masters in the room. "Why didn't you tell us that the silkstone had been stolen from Andarack's house?" she demanded. "Had we known, the appearance of the Masks would not have been so unexpected, and we might have been ready for them!"

"I will tell you what you need to know!" the hallmaster shouted, and a surprised and resentful silence filled the room.

Some of the Reds looked at each other. An older woman with a crooked back said, "That sounds much like how Adrix used to talk, Hallmaster."

"Chovan, it is my duty—" began Branet, but Relict cut him off.

"Yes, yes, we all have a duty to protect Shirath. Have you told the king about Trader Chirat's connection to the Masks? I informed you of Marick and Dorict's report days ago! Yet Taron patrolled in the Twelfth Ward yesterday and saw no evidence of arrests or searches by the king's guard."

Branet's only answer was a glower. As the noise rose again, he turned and left the room, slamming the door behind him.

"What I don't understand," Taron said, "is why he hasn't told the king. Surely he wants all the Masks locked up. Or worse!"

Chovan limped over to him and laid a hand on his arm. "Look deeper! He's set himself between a Basher and

264

a Bull demon, our hallmaster has. If the Masks are arrested, he must ask for their exile, or else he'll seem weak."

"Not to me!" Tarix said, and the others nodded in agreement.

"Nor to me," Chovan said, "but maybe to himself, and a man who lives in fear fears that most of all. The king will surely by Heaven refuse this time, and the people will back him. You know what's been said to us on patrol! Branet is wary of starting something he knows is beyond his control, and that's why he has not told the king."

"Yet the king must be informed," Relict said, and the assembled masters began to discuss this in groups of two and three around the masters' dais in the hall. Argument turned to discussion, and then to agreement. Chovan looked around the room, catching each master's nod.

"Well, that's settled. Now who will we send?"

Relict and Tarix looked at each other, and Tarix sighed in surrender.

"I hate to reward that scamp for worrying me half to death," she said.

"As you used to worry me," Chovan said, eyebrows raised. "Though, if I think back, it was much more than half!"

Two days after being sent to dig through the records of the Fifth, Twelfth, and Thirteenth Wards, Garet arrived at the palace to meet with other agents and Captain Bixa. He was directed to the Shouting Room, a large study furnished with a great, round table and many uncomfortable chairs. Barick told him this would be the likeliest place for his meeting, and Garet had not escaped the historian without first hearing a story about it.

The Shouting Room was actually called the Room of Harmonious Discussion, but no one referred to it as that, not even the king, or so Barick claimed. It was the room where Shirath's king met delegations from the wards, the guilds, schools, and the other cities. Any such meeting was bound to end in argument, hence the unofficial name.

Garet checked the sheaf of papers in his hands one last time before entering the room. He had no intention of shouting at anyone, but he feared that the others might not be so quiet when he presented his theory. The captain was already inside, tracing one finger over a map of the wards worked into the table's marble surface with gold and silver inlays. Beside her were Garet's fellow agents, or at least the only ones he had so far met.

"All right, here's Garet, and Shula behind him," Bixa said. "Let us start."

She pulled a list from a stack of papers beside her and scanned it while the others took seats around the table. "Two days of watching seven places, and what do we have? Nothing! Shula, what is your thinking on the Fifth Ward and Sacourat?"

The round woman who had come in after Garet shrugged. "She's too busy currying favour. She'd have given me tea and cake if she'd known I was a king's agent. No, it's not her."

The other two agents nodded, and Garet belatedly did the same. There had been nothing in the recent records of that ward to suggest Sacourat was behind the Masks.

Bixa grunted. She dipped a pen and crossed a name off her list. "Well then, Cheza, what do you say of Kirel and Gost?"

A rangy man with one vacant eye stood up and looked around the table. "We all know Gost is capable of this. He runs that ward like he was the lord, and Kirel doesn't even notice. His wife might be in on it though. Lady Kaela is nobody's fool. Problem is, nothing odd is going on there. The only difference of late is that big chief of guards – Maroster, his name is. He hasn't been around for a few days."

"Could be sick or out of favour with Gost," Bixa said. "All right, Salorex, what have your subordinates found in the Twelfth Ward?"

An older man stood and smiled at the captain. He looked like a shopkeeper in his last years, but his eyes were as sharp as a bird's. "We have three names you were concerned with: Lord Tiralsh's son, Tarock; Chirat; and Toovad. The last two are the heads of major trading families. I'm afraid we found nothing out of the ordinary."

He turned to Garet and smiled at him, a smile that did not touch his eyes. "Perhaps our new agent can find something odd for us to investigate."

Bixa snorted. "Unlikely. He's been looking through ward records with Barick."

Cheza laughed and rubbed at his blind eye. "That fat fool? One lucky strike with a sword and he thinks he's a hero! Mark my words, boy, there's no sense in listening to old Barick."

Garet found himself raising his voice, though he had promised himself not to. "Barick is no fool! And it is with his help that I found something."

Shula looked up from fanning herself with a sheaf of papers. Her eyes were no less sharp than the others, but she had no malice in her voice. "What is it? Did you find something interesting? Something out of the ordinary in all those scrolls and ledgers?"

Garet pushed forward the papers stacked before him. They represented two full days and evenings of research by both himself and Barick. "Not out of the ordinary, but interesting all the same. Chirat has been buying large amounts of building material. He started last year, just after the death of Master Mandarack and the Caller demon."

These men and women looked wary at the word, but Salorex laughed, a flinty sound from such a kind looking old man.

"Rubbish, boy. The word is that Chirat's warehouse needed repairs. That's why he bought timber and such."

Bixa smiled and began to speak, but Garet held up his hand.

"Perhaps that is what he said, but the amount of material he bought is enough to rebuild the entire warehouse twice over, and he owns only half of it, according to the deeds. What is interesting is that the Fifteenth Ward has delivered wagon after wagon of ten-foot timbers to Chirat's warehouse, and it has all disappeared inside."

"To what purpose?" Shula asked, and glanced at an astounded Salorex and Cheza.

Garet shrugged. "I don't know," he said. "I only know that it doesn't make sense. If I were forced to guess, I'd say he was building something big, either within the building or below it, perhaps a place for the Masks to hide and train."

Bixa sat down. After a moment she circled a name on her list.

"The Masks were using that forest station to train," Cheza said. His one eye was fixed on Garet as if they faced each other with swords on the training grounds.

Garet took a deep breath. The memory of a dream and Dorict's altered voice saying "You must learn to play the game!" over and over came back to him. Well, he was tired of games. Cheza and the others might see him as a threat, but he had no such ambition. He looked across at Bixa.

"That was to train with the demon's jewel, something that had to be done far away so as not to attract the attention of the banes," he said. "But they weren't out there all winter, for much cutting is done at that time of year when the logs may be skidded over the snow. Is that not true?"

Shula nodded. "It makes sense, though I'm thinking it's not a training room but a tunnel he's built!"

Garet turned to her, and she laughed at his expression of wonder.

"Hah! I'm surprised this escaped you. Consider, what if Chirat is aligned with Gost and Kirel? We've all suspected it but had no proof because they were never seen together. If a tunnel connected the lord's compound in the Thirteenth Ward . . ." She rose and pointed to that spot on the map, a collection of four towers joined by walls that protected Lord Kirel's house. ". . . and came up into Chirat's side of this warehouse" – she pointed again – "then they might conspire in secret, move people and goods, silkstone even, if they wanted."

Captain Bixa nodded. "Then we must find the end of the tunnel in the Thirteenth Ward before we raid Chirat's warehouse. How can we do so without raising Gost and his guards against us?"

"I might know of a way, Captain," Garet said. "Banehall patrols might be used to search it out since they come and go at will. You could send a message to the hallmaster asking for his help."

"I will do so," Bixa said. "Cheza and Salorex, concentrate on the area around Kirel's house. Look for any signs of digging." She almost ran from the room, probably to tell Trax of this development.

The two agents nodded to Shula and left the room, passing by Garet without acknowledgement.

"Those two hold grudges," Shula said, pausing to help him gather up his papers. "I'd watch my back if I were you. They make bad enemies."

"What about you?" Garet asked. "Are you a friend or an enemy?"

She handed him the last ledger and laughed. "Both? Neither? I'm just here to do the king's bidding and keep the human demons from the door. An unlucky word, but all too true for the likes of Gost."

Garet asked, "Do you think he is really behind this?"

Shula fanned herself again. "I wish they would open the windows. Of course, this being the Shouting Room, they're all nailed shut! If Gost is in charge, that might explain why that giant Maroster is missing."

"Do you believe him to be in this tunnel?" Garet asked.

"Or buried under it! If Gost is the one we seek, well, he's not a forgiving man, and things have gone badly for the Masks of late. They've lost their field commander, and now their very reason for existence has disappeared. Gost is the smartest person on Bixa's list, and therefore the most likely. However," she added and winked at Garet, "you're pretty smart yourself. Maybe it's you who's behind the Masks!" And she cackled all the way out into the hallway.

Garet was still in the room when a steward came in.

"Two banes to see you," she said, managing to sound both annoyed and gratified to be delivering such a message to such a man.

His breath caught, and he rushed to the anteroom

where he had once waited with Salick, hoping that she would be there again.

"Oh, it's you two," he said when he opened the doors.

"How rude! And I thought distance was supposed to bring true friends closer," Marick said.

Beside him, Dorict rolled his eyes. "Perhaps he should move back to the Midlands or to the southern deserts. He could leave us another note when he goes."

The Blue's tone was scathing, and Garet blushed. The meeting he had longed for had been replaced by the one he had dreaded.

"I'm sorry," he said, "I had no choice! Shirin's exile forced my hand, and you two weren't around. That was probably for the best, since you would have tried to talk me out of it."

He backed up and sat down in one of the spindly chairs set against the wall, a chair that was probably not meant to be sat in, since it creaked alarmingly.

Dorict's shoulders unstiffened a bit, and he shrugged. "What makes you think we would have bothered to try? You can be just as stubborn as Salick when it comes to your principles. Nobility must be such a burden!"

"I wasn't trying to be—" Garet began, but Marick interrupted.

"You're right," he said, punching Dorict in the shoulder. "He's just like her, at least that's what we told her the other day." He went over to a bowl of artful ceramic fruit to see if they were detachable.

"Did she send you?" Garet asked, allowing a little bit of hope to creep into his tone.

Dorict relented and shook his head. He put a hand on Garet's shoulder, but retracted it quickly when the chair creaked even more.

"No," Marick said, "I'm afraid she is still angry that you left. Tarix sent us to tell you what we found in the Twelfth Ward, since Branet refuses to. The masters are ready to spit fire over his handling of this, though none have put themselves forward as a replacement, even though I—"

Dorict stomped a booted foot on the polished tiles. "Quiet, you fool. Tarix told you she'd toss you from the outer wall if you tried to make her hallmaster by your tricks! And put that apple back in the bowl."

He turned to Garet. "Chirat is the one you want. He's a Trader in the Twelfth. The carter who took the Masks out to that logging station works for him."

Garet stood up, and the chair groaned in relief.

"That falls well within what we suspected. Please thank Master Tarix for me. I must go and report this."

He made to leave, but Marick stopped him. "Wait, you fool! How can we go back unless we know what's going on? Information for information, that's a fair trade, isn't it?"

Garet looked over to Dorict. The Blue nodded.

"Tarix will want to know," he said.

Garet thought for a moment. He looked to the doors of the anteroom, wondering who might be listening just outside.

"Let me talk to Captain Bixa and perhaps the king, if he will see me."

"And why would he not?" Marick said, juggling three of the bright apples. "Especially when you look so important in those new clothes. What a marvellous coat, and is that a sword I see on your belt?"

Garet blushed again. He knew his new clothes were far more costly than a bane's uniform.

"You even have a new sash?" Marick added, pointing at

the narrow baldric that ran from Garet's shoulder to his belt.

"That's to keep my sword from falling down," he said.

Marick laughed, dropping an apple and saving it from shattering by catching it on the top of his boot like a street juggler in the market.

"Put those back," Dorict said. He bent over to rescue the threatened apple and carefully put it in the bowl. He came for the other two, but Marick held one out of reach.

"Vinir wants the news later. I'll save this one for her to see if she tries to bite it!" he said.

Dorict threw up his hands. "Will you send a message to the hall?" he asked Garet.

"Stay here," Garet said, and left them arguing about artificial apples and appropriate behaviour in a palace.

When he returned, Marick was planted in a chair, which did not creak under the little bane's weight, and Dorict stood in front of him, arms crossed as if daring him to try and get up.

"I talked to the captain, and she talked to the king. Please tell Master Tarix and Hallmaster Branet that two representatives from the banehall should present themselves here tomorrow as the sun rises. They can come along when we raid Chirat's warehouse. Is that a fair trade?"

Dorict nodded, but Marick slipped around his larger friend to answer. "Only if I'm one of the two, since I'm the one who found out – ow! Dorict, let go of my ear!"

"Good luck tomorrow, Garet," Dorict said, and led his protesting partner out the door.

Garet sighed and made to sit down on Marick's chair, then thought better of it. He was tired of meetings and contentious plans. Perhaps he would go to the market and buy some of Torfor's buns and sit a while with the peace-able old man.

He went out the kitchen gate to avoid the cold stares of the door steward and the colder stares of the guards. He might be a mysterious irritation to them, but he was only a brief annoyance to the cooks.

The air had the freshness that comes after spring storms wash all the smoke and stink away. Above him, the dome of Heaven shone blue, and marriage bells rang from the temple. People were everywhere today, for the demons had disappeared and peace had come to the city for the first time in six hundred years.

CHAPTER 26
A FIGHT WITH FEAR

The woman came crashing out of the brush, face scratched, hands bloody, but she didn't stop. She tossed aside the useless bow and ran as if her life depended on it. The screeching call of a hunter told her that it did.

She slid down the banks and into the stream. Her only chance was to confuse her scent until she could get to the river. If she could swim across the Ar – and that was a big if, for it ran wild between Shirath and Old Torrick – she might live another day, and so might her city.

She kept moving, splashing as little as possible. The cold water, fresh from the high hills to the north, chilled her legs. After a league of travel, she paused to wash off the blood on her hands and face. Those hands were shaking as she scrubbed at them with the hem of her coat. The fear she had felt behind her all morning was growing, but that wasn't the only terror in her heart. An image of what she had stumbled upon rose up, and she retched as an empty stomach tried to purge itself again.

There was a hooting noise behind her, and she turned

275

to see a Shrieker demon sniffing along the bank. This close, the fear it cast joined with the cold water to freeze her in place.

The demon raised its beaked head and saw her. Its tongue extended from between its teeth, and it crept down the brushy bank towards her.

The woman threw everything she had into breaking the fear spell the beast laid upon her. Could she but move her legs, she could run. Could she but move her hands, she could take the knife from its sheath and fight. Ever since that night in the banehall when a demon had killed her lover, Draneck, she had loathed the monsters, hated them enough to create the Masks with Gost's devious support. Those silkstone faces let her kill demons, and that became the central fact of her life. She lived to kill them. To kill them all if she could. She drove that thought into her body like a red-hot spike.

The beast moved closer, and Shirin flexed her fingers.

CHAPTER 27

THE MASKS REMOVED

"Why must we go through the Sixteenth Ward?" Branet demanded. The hallmaster was in a fouler mood than normal, which explained why Relict pretended not to hear.

Garet grit his teeth. The hallmaster had been asking questions of the air instead of to him directly. Branet had barely glanced at him since Captain Bixa ordered Garet to escort them to the rallying point in the fields by the outer gates of the Twelfth Ward.

"So as not to draw attention to the number of guards and agents – and banes – who are gathering to raid the warehouse, Hallmaster," he said.

Relict caught his eye and gave him a lopsided smile. "A good plan, Garet. No need to alert this Chirat of his approaching arrest! Don't you think so, Hallmaster?"

Branet grunted and kept walking through the ward. They came to the great horse barns of the ward, but had no time to admire the fine stock bred there. Relict tried to make conversation.

"The people of this ward really know horses," he said.

"Do you ever wonder why some wards are good at one thing and not another?"

Branet said, "No, I haven't."

Relict deflated, and Garet stepped in to rescue the master. "Barick has records saying where in the river valley the people of each ward originated. The Sixteenth's citizens came from the drylands between the southern hills and the desert. They didn't farm that much, but bred the best horses even then."

"What of the ward we will be . . . searching, the Twelfth? Where did they start out?"

"In a Trader's cart, no doubt," Branet said, proving false his apparent disinterest in the conversation.

Garet smiled in spite of himself. He waited until they were past a rowdy band of horse wranglers before he answered. "You are right, Hallmaster. The Traders were scattered throughout the valley, answering to family and trade agreements rather than a particular lord. Even so, they were tolerated for their usefulness. Indeed, they became quite powerful, playing each lord against the others. When the city was built, they demanded their own ward, and were given it."

"That is a lot of influence," Relict said, as they came through the gate and turned left, following the curve of the outer wall. "And they still have their fingers in all the trade going from ward to ward and from city to city."

"Running afoul of the banehall is going to lose them that power," Branet said. He looked sidelong at Garet. "They will realize that we in the hall must remain the leaders of this city. Perhaps you will regret choosing a lesser power to serve."

Relict's eyes widened and he stepped forward as if he

would strike the larger man, a bane who had once been his good friend, but Garet restrained him.

"No, Relict, please control yourself. There is a great deal to do today, and we must hurry to join the others."

He turned to the hallmaster, whose expression hinted at regret over his words. "Sir," Garet said, "I do regret leaving the hall, but I would not change my decision. There are no lesser powers here, no more than there are lesser lives. I serve the city, not its palace nor its hall, and I pray you do too."

With that he turned and continued along the wall. Relict caught up with him by the time they passed the Twelfth Ward's outer gates.

"Well said, Garet! Don't worry, we can talk. He follows just beyond the sting of your words. Do you think the king would give you back to us so that I could tie you beside our dear hallmaster's ear? You could shout wisdom at him all day!"

Garet smiled at the picture in his mind. "I have a job, Relict, but if this raid goes badly, I might need another."

Relict shook his head. "I wish you well in it, though we miss you in the hall. I don't know if you have been informed of this, but we were kept out of the compound around Lord Kirel's house last night when we tried to have a look for that tunnel entrance. The guards gave Taron and his team some lie about unsafe walls and turned them away."

"Thank you, Master Relict. We did know that. Dalesta, one of Taron's Greens, brought a note in the night."

Relict stroked his short blond beard. "Well then, why are we still raiding one end of the tunnel if we haven't found the other?"

Garet looked around to make sure no fieldworkers were close enough to hear. Branet was still some distance behind them. "Captain Bixa fears that there might be spies within the guards. Once the plan had been made, we really had no choice."

He looked ahead and said, "Ah, there they are."

Guards were lined along the wall with more coming from the east. Bixa waved to Garet, and he led the two banes over to the captain.

"Hallmaster, Master Relict," Bixa said, sketching a brief bow. She was resplendent in a gold-washed cuirass and greaves. Her helmet had a great white plume atop it, and she held her sword ready in her hand.

"The ward lord's son, Tarock, just left the warehouse, according to our agents. They have secured the gates so they can't be sealed against us and give Chirat time to destroy the evidence of his crimes, especially that tunnel! We need to find it intact so that we can trace it to the other end and catch all the conspirators. I will lead the first group to take the warehouse. Banes, you stay behind us. We will signal you to enter when the Masks are subdued."

She waved the guards into two columns. She looked at Garet, considered, and then spoke. "I had meant to leave you with the banes, but that quick sword of yours might be useful against a band of ex-Duellists. Come in with the second group and keep out any reinforcements from the other Traders. They won't take kindly to us coming in force like this."

Garet nodded and went over to stand with Stanat, Bixa's lieutenant. He was a short man and even shorter on speech. His wide shoulders strained at the straps of his breastplate, and his helmet seemed a size too small for his head.

Stanat nodded at Garet and pulled out a broadsword. He raised it high, and the men and women behind him quieted. There was a moment of pure silence, then the gates were pulled open, revealing Cheza and Salorex but no ward guards. Bixa led her group in, the rattle of their armour sharp in the morning air. After a dozen breaths, Stanat lowered his blade and the second column followed.

As they passed through the gates, Garet saw Shula standing beside two trussed-up gate guards. She winked at him as he ran past.

The lieutenant signalled a stop at the corner of the first warehouse on the right. He peered down the lane of identical buildings and told ten guards to stay where they were and keep out anyone who tried to enter the lane. The rest, twenty more and Garet besides, followed him to Chirat's warehouse. There was a man, not one of the palace guards, on the ground outside the entrance. A whip lay by his hand. From within came the noise of sword upon sword and the harsh curses of the combatants.

"Surround this place," Stanat ordered. "Nobody escapes."

When Garet saw all corners and windows covered by the guards, he drew his sword and entered the warehouse.

He tripped and fell to the ground as soon as he got through the door. A woman lay across the entranceway, her guard's helmet dented. Someone else stumbled over him but managed to remain upright. Garet stayed on the ground and tried to get some sense of what was happening.

Bixa and a wedge of guards were pushing down an alley between large wooden crates. Several of their opponents bore the thin swords of the Duellists, and the captain already bled from a cut on one arm. As Garet scrambled up, he saw her break the weapon of the man in front of her, the weight of her sword overcoming the more fragile blade. A backslash took him down, and Bixa urged her troops forward.

"Get them in the corner now! And somebody block off that clawed tunnel!"

Garet looked around. Two guards were down near the north-east corner of the room. He ran over just in time to see a woman leap out of a trapdoor just behind the bodies. There was soot around her mouth and nose. She slashed at Garet with her rapier. His own sword had not her reach, but it was strong enough to bat aside her blade and leave her unbalanced. He stepped in and hit her shoulder with the pommel. She dropped her sword. He raised his left arm and drove an elbow into the side of her head, wincing at the way she fell onto one of the dead guards.

He had no time for regrets, however, for a man now came out of the trap, a giant of a fellow who bore a two-bladed axe in one hand. The other hand was wiping ash out of his eyes. Smoke followed him, and he slammed shut the trapdoor. One great swipe of his weapon sent Garet leaping back. Blinking at the scene in front of him, the giant shouted out, "They've set the timbers on fire! We can't get out through the tunnel. Save yourselves!"

And with that he howled out an oath and lifted his axe. Perhaps his eyes were so reddened that Garet was the only one he could see, or maybe he thought him easy prey, for he ran at him like a Bull demon, weapon raised and ready to cut him in half.

Garet might have jumped inside his swing, if he hadn't been backpedalling already. He might have dodged, if he hadn't found himself in a narrow spot between crates. The axe came down, and Garet could only drop to the ground, his very small sword raised above his head.

There was a crash, and instead of sharpened steel, it was soft dirt that struck his head. In a moment, he was buried in it. Garet fought his way free, slashing at an enemy he could not see. When he stood, his head hit something above him. Scraping the dirt from his face, he looked up to see the great axe buried to the haft in the crate he had cowered under. He looked for its owner, lest he come back for it or just tear him apart with his bare hands, but instead saw something quite unexpected.

The giant was pinioned about the throat by the arms of a man nearly as large, Hallmaster Branet. The bane was dragging him to the centre of the warehouse while his captive thrashed and squirmed.

The prisoner finally slipped the hold and turned to strike the hallmaster in the jaw, driving him back several steps. With a roar, Branet charged, punching his opponent in the stomach, then hammering the back of his head as he doubled over.

A cheer went up, and Garet saw that Bixa and the others had captured all the remaining fighters and tied their hands and legs. Now they watched as the two big men pummelled each other. From the vigour of their shouts, Garet was sure bets were being laid, though he had no idea who was the favourite.

Branet was again pushed back by a flurry of blows, but the hallmaster slipped the last punch and kicked his opponent in the thigh. The man went down howling, and Branet stilled him with a buffet to the jaw.

He stood above his foe, sash torn off, vest in tatters, gulping in air.

Bixa ran to him and slapped him on the shoulder. "Well done, Hallmaster! I'd thought to leave you out of this, but I'm glad you joined in. That's Maroster, the chief of the

Thirteenth Ward's guards. How odd to meet him here! Now, come and see what we found."

Garet came with them. He tugged on Branet's sleeve, and the man turned a bruised face to him.

"Thank you, Hallmaster," Garet said. "Were it not for you, I'd be dead."

Branet grunted and waved at the man on the floor, even now being tied up. "No matter . . . Garet. I haven't had a demon to fight for a long time now. This was a pleasant distraction."

He actually smiled then, or tried to with swollen lips.

Bixa called them over. "Look here, a trapdoor to the tunnel we guessed at, though it seems we won't find the other end so easily."

Smoke creeped around the edges of the door, and Bixa sent a messenger to the ward's stewards to warn of the fire danger.

"Those silkstone masks might be in here, but we'll have to search fast. Stanat tells me that Chirat's guards and some others are drawing near. What is that all over you, Garet?"

"Dirt. All these boxes must be full of it from digging out the tunnel. No doubt they intended to take them out into the fields at some point to dump them," he told her. He went with her from crate to crate, using a pry bar to open them up enough to make sure they held nothing but earth.

"Well, Chirat must be the best Trader of all time if he can make a profit selling dirt," Bixa said. She led them out into the lane and called Stanat.

"We're leaving now, with the wounded and the prisoners. Where's your helmet?"

"Hit Chirat with it when he tried to set his bully boys on us," Stanat said. He pointed to where the Trader hung limply between two guards.

There were several more of Chirat's workers down, but Bixa left them where they were.

"We wanted the Masks, and we have them. Back to the gate now," she ordered.

But it was easier ordered than done, for a mass of guards awaited them and would not budge until the hall-master pushed to the front and cursed them with every demon name he could think of. The fear of those words lashed them so badly that Bixa and her troop could force their way through, using the flats of their blades and the backs of their hands to overcome any remaining resistance.

Garet explained to Relict what had happened in the warehouse. The Red regarded the hallmaster with some awe at the description of his fight with Maroster.

As they went back through the outer gates of the Eleventh Ward, Garet breathed a dusty sigh of relief. Although they hadn't found the silkstone masks, they had found the people who wore them, and that was at least a partial victory.

"Were you successful?" Lady Kaela asked. She stood in the empty guardroom and watched as Cruster climbed up the cellar stairs.

"Yes, m'lady," the guard replied. She took the cloth that Kaela offered, bowing awkwardly, and wiped at the soot on her hands. "Nobody's coming back that way," she said.

"Let us go then," Kaela replied, but stopped when her husband clattered into the room. Lord Kirel was so busy pulling on a shoulder piece and trying to fix it to his cuirass that he did not notice his wife standing in the shadows.

"Guard, fetch my uncle at once!" he shouted at Cruster.

"Claws, and get someone to help me into this armour. The king's guard is at the gates, and the whole ward's in an uproar!"

Kaela stepped forward and put a gentle hand on his. "Let me help you, my lord. And I fear your uncle is gone. Cruster says he ordered the gates sealed with spikes and had wagons piled before them to keep the king out."

"What?" Kirel said, paling at her words. "I don't understand. How . . . why would the king . . ."

Kaela laid a finger across his lips for the briefest of moments then went back to fastening the other shoulder piece. "The less you know the better, my dear husband, though I fear you know too much already for our safety."

He looked from her to Cruster and saw the wisps of smoke coming up the stairs.

"What is that?" he asked, pointing a shaking finger at the stairs.

"Cruster, would you leave us for a moment? And could you please get those guards we spoke of earlier. Bring them all here, if you would," Kaela said. She lowered herself onto a bench and patted the space beside her. Kirel sat down.

"My dearest one, you should know that Chirat is arrested. A little bird in the king's service warned me when the guards left to raid his warehouse. That is why I ordered Cruster to obliterate this end of the tunnel you so cleverly had built. After it burns and collapses, there will be no direct evidence of your connection with Chirat, don't you see?"

Kirel looked at his wife as if, for the first time, he did see.

"But what of my uncle? Gost will be very angry if he finds out you did this."

Kaela laughed and then placed a hand on her belly. "I

am somewhat protected by my condition, but it is you I worry about. Why would he not give you to the king and forswear all knowledge of the Masks? Your uncle is a man of, shall we say, direct action? What I am doing, I do for you, my love."

"What are you doing?" Kirel asked, but Kaela leaned forward to kiss him. He resisted at first, but then fell into the embrace as if it were his last refuge.

"Now, my lord, find yourself somewhere else to be. Prowl the ward with your stewards and put out fires and riots. Tell all your people that they are safe. Remind them that you are their lord, not Gost."

Kirel stood up and held out his hand to help Kaela off the bench. He looked down at her and ran his tongue over his lips as if to taste her again.

"And what of my uncle?" he asked.

"Oh, I'm sure that little problem will sort itself out. Now go on, my brave lord, while I wait here for Cruster."

Kirel left, and Lady Kaela decided to wait in the court-yard, for the smell of smoke was quite offensive.

CHAPTER 28

BETWEEN CLAWS AND RUSHING WATER

"Can't you feel it from upriver?" Cernot asked. The Gold hefted his pickaxe and glanced nervously at the brush crowding the humped and cracked road.

Corix looked up from the litter they had made to carry the woman. "I feel it. And from the north as well. We are nearly surrounded," she said. If she felt any pressure from the curtain of demon fear closing around them, she didn't reveal it in her voice or actions. "Here, Falor, help me with these bandages. We'll need them tight when we cross the river."

"Yes, Hallmaster," Falor said. The young woman put down her spear and handed Corix another strip of torn blanket.

"Don't call me 'Hallmaster,' Green. I left Choan in charge at Old Torrick. He's hallmaster until we return. If we return."

Falor paled at that and said, "Yes, Master Corix. Are the wrappings tight enough?"

Corix nodded. She stood and ran a hand through her short grey hair.

Cernot looked at her, swallowed, and spoke. "Perhaps we should go forward on the road, Master. That's the only place I don't feel the fear." He was a big lad, helpful in carrying the litter but too eager to act.

"No," Corix said, and then reluctantly explained her decision at the sight of his worried face. "You heard what she said." Corix pointed at the unconscious woman on the litter. Her clothes were bloodstained, and one arm was roughly splinted. "Between what she reported and what we have seen and felt, I don't trust an easy escape. It might be a trap that closes its claws on us just as we think we're safe."

Falor stood up, gripping her spear. "So it's true then? It's the Caller demon we heard of from Shirath?"

"Or something worse," Corix said. "Something much worse, I fear. Give me your pickaxe, and you, tie your spear to the litter. We'll cross the river here, where the current slows a bit."

A very little bit, thought both Falor and Cernot, but Master Corix was not a bane to be denied. They picked up the litter, and the woman moaned.

"Will she live, Master?" Falor asked.

Corix turned back from where she stood at the bottom of the bank, one booted foot in the current.

"Ask me when we get to the other side, Green," she said.

CHAPTER 29
THE DIVIDED BOARD

"We can't win," Captain Bixa said. She was coming up from the palace cellars, Garet at her side. It was late, and they had just seen the last of the Masks, twenty-six in all, chained and locked away. Two of the ex-Duellists had died in the fight at the warehouse, and a third was under the watchful eyes of both physicians and guards in a separate room.

Bixa continued her analysis as they climbed. "If we break down the gates of those two wards, the people will despise us as invaders. But how can we ignore the actions of their lords? If we do, certain other wards will see it as an opportunity to defy the king and push for Heaven knows what powers for themselves, even if they come at the expense of the whole city."

Garet nodded. He was sure ward lords like Sacourat were watching to see how much they might gain from this defiance. They turned left at the top of the stairs and came into the palace proper. Bixa signalled to Shula and Cheza, who waited by the main doors, and the agents followed them into the Shouting Room.

King Trax looked up from the map set into the table. Pieces from a Surround game were placed here and there on the surface.

"Good, I need you to show me where our guards are, Bixa," the king said.

The captain looked over the map. She moved several harrier pieces in front of the inner gates of wards Twelve and Thirteen. The hunters she placed just beyond the outer gates.

"The ones in the fields are on horses and have bows, in case someone tries to break out," she said. "The ones inside are mainly armed with pikes and swords, for we don't have enough bows to give to both."

Shula pointed to the Sixteenth Ward and then the Sixth. "These two wards have archers among their guards. I've seen them shoot in contest with the palace guard."

Bixa nodded, and the king said, "Good! Send word to them at once. Braxa and Tortal are loyal. They'll not refuse me."

Shula bowed and left the room. Trax looked at the remaining three attendees.

"This looks too much like a stalemate in Surround. Gost controls his side of the board, and we control ours. But we can't leave this at a draw. So tell me, all of you, how will the people of these wards react if we break through the gates and take their lords and that rascal Gost by force?"

There was a silence as the others considered this.

Bixa spoke first. "You know how I feel, Your Majesty. I think it will be our downfall if we attack. The city will be as torn as it was two centuries ago. And what if the beasts return while we fight among ourselves?"

"Indeed," said Trax. He turned to Cheza, who looked back with his one eye.

"Your Majesty," the agent said. "I agree with the captain, but what else can we do? We'll never win the people over now, for who knows what lies they're being fed by Gost and Tiralsh?"

"So, tell them the truth," Garet said. "Give them all the facts, and they might open the gates themselves."

Cheza sniffed. "A clever plan, if it would work. How will you get that message through a locked gate?"

Garet looked at the king but Trax said nothing, so Garet thought of how his idea could be accomplished.

"If we get more bows, the messages could be tied to arrows with their points cut off. We could shoot them over the wall."

Bixa shook her head. "We couldn't cover a whole ward, let alone two. Their guards would only have to clear a small area to get to the arrows before your message could be read and passed around. We need a way to shoot in or sneak in messages all over the wards and all at once!"

"Impossible," Cheza said. He folded his arms and glared at Garet.

Trax smiled, chuckled, and then began to laugh. His mirth grew until he was bent over with it, shaking. After some little while, he sputtered to a stop.

"Forgive me, friends, but I know of two people who specialize in the impossible. It's only that this is the most inopportune time to ask for their help."

Bixa looked at him, understanding slowing dawning in her expression. Cheza and Garet, however, were still confused.

"It is a bad time, isn't it?" the captain said with a wicked smile. "But I fear we must insist."

Trax shook his head. "I'll pay for this offence to love. Heaven will find a way! Captain, could you send Garet on

292

this sensitive mission? A friendly face might take some of the sting from the timing of our request."

I⊤ ᴡᴀꜱ an odd time to be practising in the banehall, and Salick hesitated in the hallway, seeing someone had come before her with the same intent.

"So, yet another bane fails to find sleep this night," Tarix called out. She put down the trident she was swinging through wide circles and smiled at the Gold who stood in the training room doorway.

"I'm sorry, Master," Salick said. "I'll use the other room or perhaps the kitchen yard."

She had come down for some respite from turning and twisting in her bed. She could not sleep for thinking of Garet. With the demons still absent and patrols reduced to a minimum to allow the overstretched banes to recover, it seemed there was nothing to do but wander the hall, regretting the words she had said to him – and not said.

"No, stay, Salick," Tarix told her. "I'm sorry if I've been cross with you. It's my worries that make me so stiff-necked! Come, I'd like to see how far you've progressed in your training, if you don't mind?"

She tossed the trident to Salick, who caught it automatically. Tarix picked up two of the clawed batons and readied herself.

After a moment, Salick dropped into a crouch, trident head down and the shaft held above her head. She slid forward, keeping the points of her weapon fixed upon Tarix's legs.

"An invitation for a high attack," said Tarix, and struck at her head.

The Gold reversed the height of her hands, the left going high and the right low. She snapped her hips into the move, and the baton went flying from the Red's hand to bounce off the wall.

"Well done!" Tarix said and launched a flurry of feints and strikes against Salick with her remaining weapon. Salick blocked them all, letting the anger and frustration of the last days fuel her defence. When Tarix slowed, Salick forced her to retreat with jabs at her legs and head, then caught the baton between the trident's tines and forced it to the floor.

"Hah! Enough, Salick, You have improved this past year. How old are you now?"

"Almost nineteen years," Salick said, then added, "a year older than Garet."

Tarix smiled. "So you are. A shame you aren't older. You could be a Red with your skill level and experience. But it's always said 'never a Red before thirty' or some such nonsense."

"How old were you when you became a master?" Salick asked. She placed the trident in the weapons rack and accepted a ladle of water from Tarix.

"Twenty-eight," the Red said with a wink, "but I lied about my age."

"Maybe I should," Salick said. She sat down, weary to the bone but unwilling to go back upstairs and fail again at sleep.

"Do you want a red sash so badly?" Tarix asked. She sat down beside Salick.

"I used to," Salick admitted, "but now I don't know. The hall is my life, Master. I never thought of any other life, but what if the demons are truly gone?"

Tarix shook her head. "They're not. I know that in my

oft-broken bones! But listen, Salick, *life* is your life, not this hall, and you can live as well outside of it as in. What about those you care for? I know that you and Garet have fought, but you may yet reconcile. If not, there will be someone else for you . . ."

"I don't want anyone else!" Salick said. She stood up and clenched her fists. "I want him to come back and everything to be the same."

Abruptly, she sat again, and Tarix laid a gentle arm around her shoulders.

"You're shaking, Gold! Ahh, I know that you want him to return, but even if he came back, the hall's changing now. Maybe we all thought things were back to normal after last winter, but we were wrong. Come now, stop crying and think."

Tarix pulled off a strip of bandaging cloth from the roll hanging on a peg. She handed it to Salick to wipe her eyes.

"Change there may be, but much good remains. You are part of that good, and so is Garet. The way I see it, the both of you will always try to do what is right. You just have to find a way to do it together."

"Like you and Relict?" Salick asked. She wiped her nose and took a deep, shuddering breath.

Tarix laughed and stood up. "Well, we make our mistakes together, and that seems to be enough for us."

She pulled up the Gold and gave her a brief hug. "Now go and rest. Who knows what else this night will demand of us?"

∼

"No, we cannot stop in this dark," Corix said. "There might be more."

She stood by the corpse of a Racer demon barely visible in the light of a quarter moon.

Cernot pulled his pickaxe out of the beast's back. He looked down the trail, straining his eyes to catch any movement. It was no good tracking the fear, for it was everywhere.

Falor looked up from tending their patient. "Surely there can't be more than four, Master. Two Shriekers, a Catcher, and this one: there can't be more!"

"The master's right, Falor," the Gold said, wiping the pick's point on the mossy side of a tree. The trail was so narrow, it had forced the Racer into a straight-line charge. That had made it easier to kill. All Cernot had needed was proper timing, and Corix ran a well-trained hall.

"I wouldn't have thought that we'd be attacked by two demons, let alone four," he told her. "We have to keep going, so chin up, Green. You stuck that second Shrieker like a Gold. It was a good kill."

Falor smiled, but flinched when a distant howl sounded from the east.

"Well, at least they're not surrounding us on this side of the river," Corix said. "This old trail is too overgrown with brush to let them flank us. Falor, you take the litter again, I'll guard our backs."

"Do you want my spear, Master?" Falor asked, but Corix shook her head.

"No, in this light, or lack of it, I'll need to get close," was all she said.

Cernot took the pack off his back and handed it to Corix. She removed two metal gauntlets and slid them onto her hands. Cernot tightened the straps for her, and the Red lifted them into the weak moonlight.

Metal bands protected her arms from wrist to elbow. A

steel plate on the back of each hand stuck out beyond her knuckles as a wide and sharpened dirk.

Cernot and Falor picked up the litter and stumbled off in the direction of Shirath. Corix tapped the two blades together before following.

"If you want a feast, demons, we'll make you sing for it first," she said to the night.

"COME IN, Garet, come in out of the dark!" Andarack shouted over the singing. "I'm glad you could make it to our wedding feast. Where is my bride? Dasanat, see who is here!"

Garet had come to Lord Andarack's house in the Eighth Ward not knowing what to expect. Bixa told him that the couple had moved their wedding date up as the astrologers had declared these demon-free days very lucky indeed. The captain had no idea if a wedding feast was still planned, but ordered Garet to find Andarack even if he had to pound on the door of the lord's bedchamber.

That at least had not been necessary, to Garet's profound relief. The feast, however, was still in good riot, the musicians making a joyous noise at one end of the hall and a troupe of theatre actors doing comic pieces at the other. Dasanat was sitting atop the lord's dais looking patiently bored.

She stared at Garet for a moment, placed him, and then came down to deliver a gracious greeting, considering.

"You're here," she said and waved at the laden tables. "Eat something."

"Thank you, no," Garet said. "I must talk with both of you. Is there somewhere more private and less noisy? It is of some importance!" He had to shout the last as everyone in the great hall, Andarack included, sang the last chorus of "My Winter Love."

Dasanat grabbed her new husband by an arm and took Garet to a hallway behind the dais. It led to a small sitting room. Dasanat closed the door, and the noise dropped to a tolerable level.

"What?" Andarack said, somewhat surprised to find himself away from the feast. "Oh, Garet, of course. Did the king want something? It's a shame he couldn't attend. Affairs of the city and all that, I'm sure."

"Yes, he does want something, I'm afraid. But first, I want to congratulate you both on your wedding. I didn't know the date had been changed, though I'm afraid the events of the day would still have kept me from attending."

"Well, at least you could come to the feast," Andarack said. "What is this about?"

Garet accepted a glass of wine Andarack fetched from a sideboard. "I don't know if you have heard much of what went on today, but we raided Trader Chirat's warehouse in the Twelfth Ward. We found the Masks, well, the people who wore them, but not the silkstone masks. Those we arrested are in the palace cellars now, but Gost and Tiralsh have sealed the gates of both wards against the king."

Dasanat looked at him, but her thoughts were elsewhere. Andarack put down his own glass and gave his head a shake.

"Now I wish I had drunk less! What of Lord Kirel?" he asked.

Garet shrugged. "It is not known if he is still the lord or if Gost has taken over. It doesn't really matter. The king needs a way to speak directly to the people of those wards. We need to scatter a written message from the king into every corner of wards Twelve and Thirteen. Can you think of a way to do this?"

Dasanat's attention snapped back to the conversation.

"Kites, but we could not depend on the wind. Hmmm. Sotor was working with heated air. It can make a paper ball rise in a tube, but the wind is still a problem, and the fire, of course, if the flame must go with it."

"Of course," Andarack said, rubbing vigorously at his temples, "we could use arrows."

"Too limited in their present form. It's a problem of scale, you see," Dasanat replied, looking at Garet.

"I don't, actually," Garet said, but the two ignored him.

"We could build a giant mechanical archer!" Andarack shouted, grinning at the idea forming in his head.

Dasanat took the wine glass from his hand and looked at him. His grin faded.

"You're right. Too impractical," he said, "but a giant bow might work."

She nodded.

"Slow loading though," Andarack said. He took Dasanat's hands in his own.

"Not if you design a loading rack and an automatic release mechanism," she replied, and leaned her head against his chest.

"I believe I have a drawing somewhere of an automatic wagon-loader for logs. It could serve as a start, but the crank . . . spark powered?" he asked, and embraced her.

"Perhaps," she said, and kissed him.

After a long pause, Andarack freed his head to turn and look for Garet. The young man was waiting at the window, trying to hold his attention on a quarter moon floating in a scud of cloud.

"Sorry, Garet," he said, and laughed. Dasanat kept her head on his chest, eyes closed.

"Not at all," Garet said in a strained voice. "It is your wedding night. However, the king needs this device in the morning. Can it be done?"

"Of course," Andarack said. "Do you mind much, Dasanat?"

Her eyes opened, and she stood away from him. "We will need several mechanicals from the feast, and cold water to sober them up. I'll arrange that now," she said and left the room.

"I'm really very sorry, Andarack," Garet said. "If there is anything I can do to make it up to you?"

Andarack smiled at him, a hint of mischief in his eyes. "I have a severe punishment in mind, young man. It shall be your job to go out into that crowd and tell everyone who is not a mechanical, which means every lord, lady, and drunken lout, that they have to stop drinking and go home."

By the time Garet had pushed out the last reveller and closed the doors, he wished he were back at the hall dealing with demons. At least they never threw up on you.

CHAPTER 30
A BITTER WIND

The king had been up late, so the siege of the two rebellious wards had to wait until he had eaten his breakfast and read the reports of the night.

"Poor Andarack and his bride!" Trax exclaimed. "Pass the butter, please."

Garet pushed the plate across the table and concentrated on the eggs in front of him. He was rested, since he had gone back to bed after getting up very early and being told that the king was still asleep and likely to remain that way for a while.

When Trax did call for him, Garet was told to sit and eat again, a much better meal than the porridge he'd had at the Stewards School. Despite his guest's impatience, the king seemed content to scan the papers laid out on a silver tray and crack his hard-boiled egg with a silver spoon.

"Do relax, Garet. Andarack will probably need this extra time to perfect his ingenuity. He promised to send word when it was ready, and I've heard nothing yet. Besides, we want the people of those wards up and about to receive my letter. You've read it now? What do you think?"

Garet folded the page he had received from the steward in charge of the copyists. Twenty men and women had been working all night, writing the letter over and over again. "It should work, Your Majesty," he began.

"Call me Trax when we're alone, Garet," the king said around a mouthful of egg.

A hovering steward took Trax's plate away and replaced it with a bowl of berries and cream. Garet waved the woman away when she tried to fuss with his own plate.

"Trax then, I think it will work. It tells them what Gost and Chirat are up to and offers mercy, negotiations, even amnesty for the guards. There's one thing I don't understand. Why not offer forgiveness for the lords as well?"

Trax shook his head. "No, not for them. Gost at least must be removed from power, or his plots will resume right away! I might be more lenient with Lord Tiralsh and her scheming son."

The king took an enthusiastic mouthful of berries and licked the cream off his spoon.

"Do you know why Gost did this?" Garet asked.

"Oh well, as you must have heard by now, for it's supposed to be a great secret, the city must soon expand. It's either that or stop having babies! I prefer a second ring of walls around Shirath, but the idea of a new city, built to the north-east, is a favourite of some lords. A few of those worthies think it should be their city, and that they will warm a new throne with their noble bottoms. Gost is only the worst of that lot."

Garet put down his fork and wiped his lips with a silk napkin embroidered with flowers and birds. "Will there be a new city, Trax, or just a bigger one?"

A steward crept into the breakfast room and whispered in Trax's ear.

"That is still in Heaven's hands," the king said, and put down his own cutlery. "But if we survive the day, one of those things must happen."

He stood up, and Garet quickly joined him.

"Come along, King's Agent. We can't dawdle while the citizens await our heroic deeds, can we?"

Garet raised his eyes to a ceiling of painted swans. "No, Your Majesty, we certainly cannot dawdle!"

Bixa was waiting for them in the Banehall Plaza, her troops arrayed as they were on the map: lines of pikes and bows facing both wards and less ferociously armed guards holding back the crowds.

Trax dismounted and gave his reins to a waiting groom. "Well, Captain, is there any sign of Andarack? He sent word he was on his way before I left the palace."

Bixa pointed beyond the king to the west. A large flat cart came rumbling around the corner of the banehall, pulled by eight horses and bearing a burden that, at this distance, defied description.

"I think that is the sign," the captain said.

The cart's load soon resolved itself into a large bow, much taller than a person and set crosswise on a beam that was thick with ropes and gears. Fixed above it was a tall rack bearing spear-like arrows.

Trax smiled and went up to the tired-looking couple.

"Well, what have we here, the first child of your blessed union?" he asked, and took Andarack's hand before bestowing a kiss on the cheek of a rather confused Dasanat.

"What have you named him?" the king asked.

"Bow," Dasanat answered. She rubbed at eyes that had not been closed all night.

Andarack smothered a great yawn and signalled the

mechanicals to shuffle forward and get the copied letters from the equally tired stewards holding them.

"I thought arrows wouldn't work," Garet said. He stepped up to examine the machine.

The arrows were blunt, there wooden ends wrapped in cloth and twice as long as any normal shaft, and there were scores of them. It seemed many mechanicals had gone sleepless to ready this device. Yawning grey-clad workers were tying the letters, several at once, to each long missile and placing them in the rack above the bow. Dasanat oiled a crank that pulled back the bowstring. From what Garet could see, the crank handle also turned a large lopsided cylinder that would drop the arrows down into a slot on the beam, one at a time.

Garet shook his head in wonder. Andarack's other creations – the spark containers, the silkstone armour, and the food-lifter at the palace – were all impressive, but this was closer to the ex-bane's heart. Such a weapon, with steel points instead of letters, was something he'd like to see used against a Basher, or maybe tested against that monstrous Tunneller with its stubborn skin.

When the machine was loaded, Andarack borrowed some guards to turn the crank while he aimed the bow to fire above the inner wall.

"We'd hoped to use spark power to wind it," he told the king, "but we had little time to ready the device."

Trax nodded in royal forgiveness and gave the signal to proceed. The guards cranked away. At first, nothing happened, then the machine creaked as the bow string pulled back, clanked as a lettered arrow dropped into the groove, and twanged as the missile was sent arching on its way. The process repeated itself again and again as long as the guards laboured at the wheel and new arrows were loaded into the rack.

After each shot, Dasanat turned a wheel between the beam and the wagon. By this, the front end was made to go up and down by degrees. Garet saw that she could send the missiles nearer or farther by such adjustments. Her husband crouched behind the sweating guards, turning a handle that moved the back of the beam left or right on a small wheel set crosswise and resting on the wagon bed. This sent the missiles to one side or the other.

They shouted back and forth to each other, coordinating each shot so they could cover more of the ward. The guards cranked in shifts while the mechanicals loaded more arrows, and the machine kept up its amazing rate of fire.

The Twelfth was soon done, and the machine was pulled over near the Thirteenth to begin again.

"There, on the wall above the gates," Bixa said, and they all looked up to see Gost glaring down at them, surrounded by his ward guards.

"Try not to hit him, Andarack," the king said. "I'd rather get him alive, but if you could come close . . ."

Gost, however, did not stay to make himself a target. He disappeared from the wall, and soon the other guards followed.

"Now," said the king, and the machine started playing its discordant music once again.

A pavilion had been set up for the king and his party between the rear of the banehall and the disobedient wards. Trax ordered food and drink for the watching guards and made arrangements with Bixa for them to be relieved in sections to rest. The sun was bright and high, and it looked to be a long wait.

By mid-afternoon, the crowds saw the siege as an inconvenience rather than a spectacle and began to disperse. It was nearing dinner when a party came from the banehall. The hallmaster led them, his face a wonderfully purpled mass of swelling and scrapes.

Trax rose to greet him. "Why, Hallmaster, I heard of your deeds from Captain Bixa, but I had no idea you were so badly used by that fiend Maroster! Please take this stool and tell me that you feel better than you look," Trax said as the injured man came under the canvas.

After sitting down with a barely concealed groan, Branet answered, "I wish I could tell you that, Your Majesty, but it would be a lie. However, I didn't come here for sympathy. Is it true that Gost and Tiralsh have closed their gates to you?"

Trax poured some wine and handed him the cup.

"True it is, Hallmaster. I wish I could say that it was not. We have sent letters over the wall calling for peace and forgiveness if they surrender."

Branet sipped carefully, wincing when the liquid touched a cut on his lip. "Claws! Well, you may send another letter, if you wish, telling them that no bane will enter their wards until they surrender. That ought to rattle them. Some may think the demons are gone, but most will not trust in such luck."

Trax raised his eyebrows. "This is a very . . . useful gesture, Hallmaster. I thank you for it, but can you, in good conscience, leave off your duties to those wards?"

The hallmaster shrugged. "If the gates are closed, we cannot perform those duties anyway, so you might as well tell them we won't and end their folly."

The king nodded at the sense of telling a small lie born

of a greater truth. "Thank you. Your cooperation is most welcome!"

Branet rose. He looked to where Relict stood just outside the pavilion. "Don't bother thanking me. I've had no end of people preaching cooperation to me since, well, since I became hallmaster. It must be sinking in at last."

Trax stood and held out his hand. Branet took it.

"There's still much we disagree on, Trax," Branet said.

"Only because we are both so disagreeable," the king replied.

Branet smiled then winced again. "Claws, that brute was worse than a Basher! Come on, Relict, let's have a look at Andarack's latest toy."

The other banes followed. Garet searched their faces, but Salick was not among them.

FALOR LEANED against Cernot and looked up at the sky. The sun would soon be down.

"Master, are we there?" she asked, as she had with regularity throughout the day.

Corix didn't bother answering. She pointed ahead of them. The brush growing in from each side, almost smothering the old road, ended. Within but a dozen yards, they saw trees planted in straight lines. The Red shifted her grip on the front of the litter and pulled Cernot, who held the back, into motion. "The last race," she said.

Her bladed gauntlets lay across Shirin's legs. Both were bloody to the metal wrists. The injured woman stared up into the blue sky, her eyes empty of intelligence.

Falor grabbed one of the poles from Corix's hand. The Red shook her head.

"You're wounded in the side, Green, and you're exhausted," she told her. "Stay behind us and look for any that still follow."

Falor kept her grip. "You're exhausted too, Master, and so is Cernot! If this is the last race, we should all run it together."

Cernot raised his eyebrows at such impudence, but Corix only grunted.

"Hmm. Run then," she said. "The city walls are our only hope."

They ran, and the litter swayed between them, carrying its staring, bleeding burden.

CHAPTER 31
THE EXILE RETURNS

It was dusk when the gates of the Thirteenth Ward opened. A cart came out with two figures on the bench seat, one a squat woman in armour holding the reins, the other a heavily pregnant woman in fine dress and waving a silk fan.

The gate stayed open behind them.

Bixa looked at the king, ready to have her guards run forward to secure the gate, but Trax shook his head. He left the pavilion to meet the wagon halfway. Garet, Bixa, and Relict, who had stayed when Branet returned to the hall, went with him.

"Kaela!" Trax said, putting a hand on the horses' harness and smiling up at the young woman.

Cruster reined in the animals and set the brake. She bore no weapon other than her expression, which could have struck birds from the sky.

"Greetings, Your Majesty. I am so happy to see you," Kaela said. "Oh Cruster, don't frown so! The king means us no harm. He is a gentleman and will treat us kindly, or so his letter said. Besides, when he sees the gift we bring, I'm sure he'll know where our ward's loyalties lie."

"A gift?" Trax said. "Really, Kaela, you are full of surprises. Here, let me help you down. Captain, will you look after her escort?"

Bixa waited until Cruster stepped down then signalled two guards to flank the woman, swords drawn.

Kaela said nothing. She looked at Garet and Relict and smiled again.

Garet put a hand to his sword.

"Peace, bane, or ex-bane, I should say," Kaela told him. "Come and help me unwrap the gift I bring, and you will have no more doubts."

He stepped forward and looked into the bed of the wagon. A form wriggled under a tarp. Garet pulled back the covering with one hand and held his drawn sword with the other, for his doubts had not yet been belayed.

What he saw, however, made him sheathe the blade again and look searchingly at Kaela.

"Well, well," Trax said, peering over his shoulder. "It's what I always wanted, a Gost of my very own! And I know just where to put him."

He signalled Bixa. The bound and gagged man was lifted thrashing from the cart and carried off between a squad of guards towards the bridge gates, Bixa in the lead.

"Kaela," Trax began, leading the woman towards his pavilion, "this might be an indelicate question, but does your husband know what you've done?"

Kaela's laughter was a silver trill. "Of course he does, Your Majesty. My uncle's plots and plans only recently became clear to us, to him, I mean. Since he is a loyal lord, he arrested Gost and sends him to you. If he were not hard at work calming the citizens of his ward, I have no doubt he would have brought the man out himself."

"Kaela, you are a wonder!" Trax said. "No diplomat could match your tongue, and no soldier your tactics. I thank you for this gift, and, if you will stay here a moment, I'll have my own carriage take you back to your oh-so-fortunate husband."

"Thank you, my gracious king," she said. She sat on a padded chair and began to pick among the delicacies set beside her by a steward. "Please give my regards to Lysere. Tell her I how much I admire your handling of this . . . unpleasantness. She is a very lucky woman! Perhaps I should have pursued you more vigorously when I had the chance all those years ago."

Trax bowed and signalled Garet to follow him out from under the canvas. When they were some distance away, he shuddered.

"Claws, that woman terrifies me! I'm glad she didn't catch me back then or I would have had to give up the throne and move to Solantor. Garet, when Bixa returns tell her not to enter the Thirteenth Ward in force. She can go in with Shula, Cheza, and a few others to see what's happening. Tell her to keep that gate open and find out about Kirel. If he is ready to surrender, have him turn over any of Gost's friends. I hope the other conspirators are still alive, but with Kaela, well, you never know. I'm back to the palace. Join me there after you've talked to the captain."

He left Garet to wait for Kaela's carriage. The king's agent stood awkwardly across from her while she ate bits of pastry.

"It might be of interest to you, bane . . . ah, sorry again, ex-bane, that your old hallmaster, Adrix, has been part of this Mask business. It seems he bears a grudge against you for laming him," she said, bestowing a sweet smile upon Garet. "I'm sure when you see him brought out in chains it will chase that scowl off your face."

Garet wondered if it would indeed make him happy to see it. Once it might have, for Adrix had humiliated him when he first came to the banehall and had almost destroyed the banes with his scheming. Now those memories had faded, scarred over by the terrors of the present day.

He was composing an answer that would be both polite and dismissive when Bixa came riding back, clattering at full speed over the paving stones of the plaza.

"Garet! The king needs you at the bridge gates. There's a commotion. Something about a group of banes from Old Torrick, beasts chasing them, and . . . they've brought Shirin back."

"What?" Garet said.

Kaela stopped her fanning to listen. Garet ignored her.

"Shirin, she's back, but badly wounded," the captain said. She dismounted from her labouring horse.

Garet looked to the pavilion. Kaela was deep in conversation with Cruster.

"Captain, the king says you are to secure the gates and take a small party to look inside the ward," he said, and began to run towards the bridge gates.

"What am I looking for?" Bixa shouted after him.

Garet stopped and turned, unwilling to spend even a heartbeat on anything but what was happening at the bridge gates.

"Anyone who seems to be in charge. Kirel and any conspirators! Oh, and silkstone! Yes, take any silkstone masks to the hall and any other stone to . . . Andarack, I suppose!"

He legged it then, leaping over the small hedges of the gardens, scattering foraging birds and wandering citizens.

There was a crowd at the eastern-most gate, and Garet ran directly there. Pushing through the onlookers, he found the king and a small group of banes kneeling around a litter placed on the ground. Trax saw him and waved him closer. Garet took a deep breath and approached.

Shirin lay on the litter. Her arm was splinted, and her clothes were soaked in blood. Rough bandages covered what must have been many wounds. Her eyes opened, blinked, and focused on Garet. She tried to speak.

He knelt by her side and took one of her cold hands in his.

"Shirin, hang on! We'll get you to Banerict in the hall. He's the best physician in the city."

The wounded woman shook her head. She tried again to speak and managed a whisper. "Warning," she said.

Garet leaned closer. He felt her uncertain breath on the side of his face as she spoke again.

"Warning, Garet. From the north, demons, fifty or more. Attack," she managed to whisper, and then her eyes closed again.

A strong hand pulled him back, and he looked into the face of Corix, the hallmaster of Old Torrick. He had met her only briefly last year, but no one could forget a woman of such uncompromising will.

"She needs the physician," Corix said, and volunteers from the crowd picked up the litter and took it as gently and swiftly as possible to the hall.

Trax wiped blood from his fingers. His hands were shaking. "If she said to you what she said to me, Garet, then Gost can wait for a less frightening time. Come. We are both going to the hall."

Garet paused before following the king. He had seen many banes come running from the banehall, including two familiar Blues who had crept up close enough behind him to hear Shirin's words.

He caught Marick and Dorict's attention, and then glanced to the north. The two nodded and ran off over the bridge.

Garet bit his lip. He was putting them in mortal danger, but keeping them in the city wouldn't lessen that peril, not if Shirin was telling the truth. He took a deep breath and ran to catch up with the king.

"I can do nothing but ease her pain," Banerict said. He had re-bandaged her wounds, and Garet had been sickened to see the clawing she had suffered.

He turned to where Corix was deep in conversation with Branet, Tarix, and Relict.

"You tell me these stone masks allow anyone to kill a demon?" the Old Torrick bane said. "Yet we found no such mask near her. She was half in a stream, wounded as you see. There was a dead Shrieker under her with her knife in its throat."

"And no mask? What can that mean?" Tarix said. Both she and Relict moved aside so that Garet could join them.

"It means she was a bane, at the very end," Garet said. He did not look at Branet as he said this, for he feared he might strike the hallmaster to let out a measure of the grief and anger that threatened to burn him up from the inside.

"Agreed," Corix said, ignoring the hallmaster's discomfiture. "Do you have these masks now?"

"We will," Garet said. "The captain of the palace guard is searching for them as we speak. I told her to bring them here."

"Thank you," Branet mumbled. He was saved from

further embarrassment by the physician, who signalled them to approach the bed.

"The end is coming fast, I fear. If you would have words with her, now is the time," he said.

Trax pulled a chair up to her bed. "Shirin, I am truly sorry that you were sent into the wilds. For my city, I apologize to you with all my heart."

"Luck," the woman whispered. "My luck . . ."

Garet came up upon the other side of the bed and took her hand again. "Bad luck for me too, for I would have had us friends, Shirin," he said.

"Fool," she whispered. "I'd have killed you . . . someday."

"Perhaps, but I still wish to part friends. Please tell us what happened."

She struggled to breathe for a moment. Garet put an arm around her shoulders and lifted her slightly so that she could breathe again. After coughing up fresh blood onto the old stains, she spoke.

"Went towards Old Torrick . . . new life . . . like you said. Saw them . . . demons driven from the north. Fifty or more . . . then they found . . . my scent. Fled. Shrieker caught me."

She fell back again. Her eyes started to close, and her breath came in hoarse gulps.

Garet felt tears wetting his cheeks. He put a hand on her forehead and said, "Well killed, bane."

After one last, shuddering breath, she lay still.

As Garet stood and turned away, Branet took his place and knelt beside the bed. He repeated Garet's words.

"Well killed, bane."

Others took up the praise, and Garet looked to the door to see Salick mouthing the words as she stood behind

Bandat. He wiped his eyes and looked again, but she was gone.

"She told me the same tale about the demons, and she said she had been exiled," Corix said. "For fighting demons. I could scarce believe her."

"It is true. I forced her exile on the king," Branet said. He looked down at his big hands resting on his knees. "It was ill done, but I feared losing our place in the city to the Masks."

There was no reply from any of those present, though Relict put a hand on the hallmaster's shoulder.

Branet stood. "Perhaps we should pick a new hallmaster for Shirath Banehall. I . . . I have made many mistakes."

Trax rose, glaring at the hallmaster over the body on the bed. "And what good would that do? It won't help her," he said, pointing down to Shirin's still form. "It won't help the city, and by Heaven it won't help me!"

Branet bristled a bit but subsided. "Trax, don't you see? I've done a terrible thing."

"As I did last winter, when I sided with the Duellists," Trax said. "Until Garet and Salick snuck into the palace to talk sense to me. I've had to live with that, Branet. I've had to live with lives lost just as you will, my friend. Don't you think I wanted to crawl away and hide my shame? But I couldn't, and you can't either, not if you want to save the city. You can be a better hallmaster, Branet, if you understand that the hall, the palace, and even the stones of this city must protect those who live within it."

At that, his shoulders dropped, and the king smiled. "Well, there's a speech! But I mean every word of it. What do you say?"

Branet looked to where Tarix and Relict stood by the foot of the bed.

"Don't look at me," Relict said. "I never wanted to replace you, just to talk as we did in the old days."

Tarix smiled. "You are our hallmaster, Branet. Like the king says, you will get better. It's like being a bane; you have to learn while you're doing it."

"Harsh lessons," said Corix, and she cocked an eyebrow at her fellow hallmaster.

"Very well," Branet said. He took a deep breath. "Bring all to the dining hall," he said to the Reds crowding the infirmary room's door. He looked down at the still form of Shirin.

"From Red down to Black Sash, everyone needs to hear this news."

When they left, Banerict called his assistants to prepare the body for its last journey to the temple and the burning grounds beyond the wall.

THE TABLES WERE FILLED with every bane not on patrol and some who should have been but weren't. They strained to hear what the Old Torrick hallmaster had to say, shushing each other if someone dared to gasp.

"The last was a Catcher," Corix said. "I'd bloodied it, and the beast had knocked us about, but it stopped suddenly and turned away from us. A bad choice, since Cernot jumped on its back and drove his pick into its skull."

Ratal looked at the Old Torrick Gold and spoke in a tone bordering on awe. "I want to try that," he said.

"No," Cernot replied, with some feeling, "you do not."

Tarix shook her head. "Five demons in all, one after the

other! But you were not attacked once you reached the wood lots?"

Corix nodded. She ran a hand through her grey hair. In Old Torrick, Garet had never seen the iron-willed woman look so . . . tired.

"When the Catcher turned, did you feel anything strange?" Relict asked.

Falor answered. She stood beside Kesla, one hand pressed to her side. "The fear shifted in some way, for a moment, but that was all."

Branet nodded. "We felt, and experienced much the same several days ago. Garet here thinks the demons are someone else's weapon, one that can be unleashed and then recalled."

Corix looked at Garet a long time before speaking. "I remember you. You were a Black Sash. Why are you not in a bane's uniform?"

"He protects the city in a different way," the king said. "We thank you, Hallmaster Corix, for you may have saved us all by bringing Shirin's message. Well, Hallmaster Branet, why would so many of these beasts gather near the city but not attack?"

Branet shook his head. The other Reds did the same, for this was beyond belief.

Garet stepped forward. "I have an idea," he said.

Trax smiled. "I'm shocked! What do you think is going on?"

Garet reddened a bit. The voices in the hall stilled as every ear strained to hear him.

"I think they are gathering for a mass attack, fifty, maybe more demons, attacking all at once and over-whelming our banes so that they can destroy the city."

He stopped, for there was no chance of being heard.

Protests erupted all around him, continuing until Branet's bull voice shouted for quiet. "Enough! Let him speak."

Garet looked at Corix. "Hallmaster Corix, you felt a mass of fear from several directions at once? What did you make of it?"

Corix nodded. "I thought much as you do, that there was a gathering of demons coming together towards Shirath. I didn't believe we would survive to reach the city walls."

"Master!" squeaked Falor.

Kesla put a protective arm around her shoulders.

Tarix looked at Garet and said, "Why now? You argued that the single attacks of demons were enough to achieve their goal – locking us up within these city walls."

Garet held up a hand, and the crowd stilled. This was the moment when they would laugh at him or believe him. Part of him wanted the laughter, for silence would mean he was right.

"We are no longer locked up. Your Majesty, I must reveal your plans for the expansion to make my argument."

Trax waved a languid hand at him, which Garet took as approval.

"Shirath is crowded. We all know that, but there are plans to expand the city or build a . . . companion city nearby. By doing this, we are proving to our enemy that we no longer just survive. We prosper and grow! That is why the Caller demon was sent to us last year. That is why the attacks increased so recently. It was supposed to knock us back down, but whoever planned this did not expect the Masks to appear and help us kill them! That made our enemy change plans again. This is just their newest tactic, a mass assault."

"Could it be done?" Kesla asked. She looked fitter than

before, though Garet's words had shaken her and left her pale.

"I believe it was done at least once before," Garet said.

Into the ensuing silence, a new voice spoke. "On the road to Shirath, you asked about this."

Garet turned to see Salick step out from behind Vinir. He held his breath, not wishing to interrupt and end the moment.

Salick glanced at Branet and then back to Garet before she continued. "You asked Master Mandarack about Terrich, a big town or perhaps a city that once lay between Shirath and Old Torrick."

Branet nodded. "It was wiped out by demons many centuries ago, for they fought with the other cities and their banes abandoned them."

Tarix and many other Reds nodded at this.

Salick stepped forward, a very small step. "Garet asked the master how many demons it would take to destroy a city, and why they didn't move on to the other cities when they were done. At the time, we didn't know that the beasts might hunt together, so I . . . did not listen to him," she said, and looked at the floor. When she looked up, it was possible the corners of her lips twitched a bit.

Vinir grabbed her in a one-armed hug.

While the Reds discussed this bit of history, the cooks brought food and drink in for a very late second dinner or a very early first breakfast. Those who had bothered to learn anything about Terrich became the objects of attention at their table.

There was a commotion at the door, and Marick and Dorict came running into the dining hall. They skidded to a stop in front of Garet.

"Claws, it's true!" Marick said. He gasped for breath, and Dorict took up their tale.

"We went north on borrowed horses, though we had to leave them in the orchards. They wouldn't go any farther, and I don't blame them."

Marick recovered enough to interrupt. "There's a mountain of fear out there, beyond the wood fields."

"Lots," Dorict said. "Wood lots."

Marick grimaced. "You might as well call them fear lots now, for the feel of them. We saw no demons, but there must be a great party of them farther out in the wilds! It's as if Birat's necklace hung from every tree!"

Trax grimaced. The centuries-old tale of a necklace made of demon jewels was known by all in the city, and he himself had felt the hideous terror created by a box full of such jewels last year. It had sent him and his guards running back to the palace when they had tried to enter the banehall by force.

"What can we do?" someone in the hall shouted, and the question carried to a hundred voices and then more.

"We fight!" Branet shouted, and the banes shouted back, the noise echoing and growing until the dust shook off the rafters.

When the noise had died again, Branet called to the Reds. "We need field patrols to alert us if they begin their attack. Those who have not rested, go and try to find some sleep now. We must devise a strategy, for fifty demons climbing over Heaven knows how many spots on the walls will be impossible to stop."

"Meet them in the fields," Tarix said.

Chovan nodded. "We'll save more citizens that way, though we may lose many more banes."

The king shook his head. "You are the demon experts,

but how do you intend to convince these creatures to come to a certain place to meet your courage?"

Marick tugged the king's brocaded sleeve. His Majesty looked down into the grinning face of the Blue Sash.

"Leave that to us. Demons forget everything else when a meal is running in front of them," he said.

Trax frowned. "But it's no good if the meal gets caught and eaten up before it reaches the other banes."

Marick bowed. "But Your Majesty, I never get caught."

Trax shook his head and turned away. Marick felt a tap on his shoulder and turned to find Corix looking down at him, her expression as unyielding as he remembered from his days at Old Torrick Banehall.

"I caught you once," she said. "What makes you think those demons won't?"

Marick looked up into those steely eyes and grinned even wider. "Demons don't cheat, Corix. You didn't play fair that night. You gave me a choice."

It was the first time Marick had ever seen the Red smile. He shuddered. After that, the idea of playing catch-me with a bunch of monsters didn't seem so bad.

CHAPTER 32
ALLIES

"I wonder how long we have," Branet said. He moved aside as a heavy wagon rumbled out of the Fourth Ward gates behind him. Around the hallmaster and his companion, every available worker in the city was digging, moving stone, or cutting timber.

"A day or two more," Trax replied, "by the calculations of your two Blue Sashes. Herding the beasts can't be as easy as herding cows, after all."

Branet snorted. "And what would you know about either, Your Majesty?"

Trax shrugged. Another wagon went by, and the king grabbed the lead horse's halter when it reared at the noise of hundreds of hammers and saws. He pulled it down, and then led it on until they reached a stone bridge. When he gave control back over to the driver, she nervously mumbled her thanks.

Brushing the dust off his golden sleeves, he turned to Branet, who had followed him.

"My father was a man of practicalities, Hallmaster," he said. "When I was a child, he sent me out to work in each ward for a moon. I learned cow-herding, horse-wrangling, even pottery and baking, though I'll admit the last two tasted about the same."

Branet smiled in spite of himself. "Well, Shirath's first bane was a baker, so I'll take your word for his sake. May herding those clawed beasts pose a host of difficulties for the herders, fatal ones, by Heaven's shield!"

"HOW MUCH BLOOD WAS THERE?" Tarix asked. She and the Old Torrick master were moving down the line of Black Sashes, adjusting the height of their cut-down spears.

"Step forward and thrust low!" Corix shouted. They watched as the line moved forward to pierce an imaginary and very small enemy.

"Faster, Rat demons are quick. Now toss!" Tarix said, and the spears flipped up and the imaginary threat flew away to an invisible fate.

"A single person's stock of blood, or so I judged. No more, but no less, so it wasn't Shirin's – or at least not all of it. And not where we found her. I backtracked a bit to see where she'd come from. I found the blood, broken and spent arrows, and several demons sniffing about in the woods. But none of them seemed badly wounded."

"So, you think the blood came from one of these . . . drivers of demons?" Tarix asked. "I wonder if Shirin killed him . . . or her . . . or it?"

"With what," Corix asked, "a wavering bow? A knife? And with this demon driver surrounded by his, her, or its beasts?"

Tarix stretched out her braced leg. "Having faced her once, spear to trident, I don't think the odds would have stopped her, though too much fear might have. You know what this means. Garet was right. The demons are a weapon in someone's hand, not a curse dropped on us by Heaven."

The line reached the wall and stopped. Before Tarix had a chance to call out, a shrill voice yelled, "Turn!"

"Thank you, Allifur. Will you continue ten more times please?" Tarix said.

The girl nodded, her hair tied back in a messy ponytail, possibly by Corfin, who stood beside her. When the girl took a step forward and raised her shield to lead, Tarix saw that her friend was the only Black Sash to possess a cut-down trident rather than a spear. The Red decided she would fail to notice this.

"All right, but if the blood came from one of the drivers, and say Shirin didn't kill . . . him. Why would the demons do so?"

Corix shrugged. "People get killed herding cows some-times, and demons would be more contrary, I suppose." Her expression hardened, and she called out, "You there! Pick up your feet!"

Tarix glanced sideways at the Old Torrick bane. She knew the two of them looked much alike. They were of a similar height. Both were lean and muscular. Even their hair was the same length, though Tarix had less grey. The Shirath Red watched as Corix walked along behind the line, frightening the Black Sashes by her very presence. Only Allifur seemed unaware, yipping out commands and jabbing down with her shield, again and again, at the same imagined demon.

Tarix shuddered. When she got to Corix's age, she hoped she would still have some sense of humour left, at least for her husband's sake. A sudden image of Relict and

Corix as an aged mismatched couple was too much and she burst out in a chuckle. When the Old Torrick bane looked at her with a face that could have frozen fire, Tarix held up an apologetic hand and said, "Herding cows! Very funny, Hallmaster Corix."

MARICK CHUCKLED as he and Dorict looked over the volunteers. Most were Blues, but there were a few younger Greens mixed in the group. They were all trying to look nonchalant, as if they were out on a picnic, not preparing to face death. All of them sat outside on the banehall stairs, drinking tea the cooks brought out and sharing buns delivered by the basketful from the merchants of the Palace Plaza.

"These are good, Dorict," Marick said. "The world should end more often if it means such generosity."

His friend swallowed and stood up. "Listen, everyone," he shouted, and the young banes all fell still.

"You volunteered for this, so I don't have to explain much. Teams of three, so at least one survives to get close enough to the city to fire off a signal arrow. Protect whoever is making the signal! Flame arrow at night. Smoke arrow in the day. Understood?"

The others nodded and looked at the bows they held. They were new-made, small, and not meant to last beyond the desperate need of the day that was dawning around them. There were two bows and a set of arrows for each group.

"Make sure there's pitch and a spark striker too," Marick added. "If you come across our friends, run back until you can see the walls, then fire up, not at the demons, not at the wall. Where do you fire?"

Forty-seven index fingers, including Marick and Dorict's, pointed at the sky.

Sacks of food and skins of water were handed out to each team before they left for the fields and forests beyond their assigned ward. Dorict ticked off the last team save one on the scroll he held. "I see you've kept the most dangerous one for us," he said. There might have been the hint of a smile on his lips.

Marick clapped him on the shoulder. "Dorict, I think you are actually beginning to enjoy adventure! Think of the glory we'll have if we alert the city to the demons' approach."

"I think there must be very little glory in a Basher's belly," his friend said. "Who's our third?"

"When have we ever needed more than the two of us to save the city?" Marick asked. "Now let's get to the Fourth Ward and out into this fine day."

"A FINE DAY TO DIE, you mean," Maroster said. The big man sat uncomfortably against a stone pillar in the palace cellar. He bore more chains than any of the other Masks, and at least as many bruises as Branet.

"No," Garet replied. "As I said, this is a fine day to reconsider your loyalties."

He looked around him. Over twenty men and women lay on the stone floor, all chained, and all ignoring him. He tried again.

"We don't intend to die, but to win! If you fight against the demons that approach, the king will grant you an amnesty. The hall has already agreed to this – if you put on your masks and fight."

A small woman chained near his feet laughed out loud. "So, the Great King will send us out to the slaughter while he hides in his palace and counts his coins?"

"Quiet you!" Captain Bixa said and moved forward, her hand on her sword.

The chained woman glared up at her, then spit on the floor. "We want freedom, but not as a gift that can be snatched away," she said, and many others shouted in agreement. "When we're done, it's back to the chains for us, isn't it?"

"If you hate chains, then fight the beasts who imprison us all!" Garet shouted. Into the silence that followed, he spoke in a lower but still passionate voice. "Some of you want to leave this city for a new life. Others want to change the way the hall and the palace control everything, but you forget why they do that! They must because the demons have moulded Shirath as a potter moulds the clay. For six centuries! It is those beasts and whoever controls them that have forced us into the form you detest. Fight them, if you want to change the world!"

There was some arguing and some agreeing around the candle-lit room.

"That's like what Shirin talked about near the end," the woman said. She sat up straighter, rattling her iron chain. "All right, there's truth in that, Midlander, and we could be allies for this, and this alone," she said then spit again. "But I still hate the king."

Garet shrugged. "Despise all of us if you wish, just hate the demons more. Now, I count about twenty of you that seem fit enough to fight, twenty-one if Maroster here can manage."

The big man growled and shook his copious restraints. "I can manage, crow!" he said. "If I have my mask."

Bixa looked at Garet.

"We have twenty-five masks here," the captain said, "delivered by the hallmaster. That leaves four masks free."

"One is already spoken for," a cheerful voice called from the stairs.

Garet turned to see Trax coming down. He was dressed in padded training clothes and held a glass of wine in one hand.

"Sorry I'm late. I was counting coins upstairs. Now, do we have an agreement? Will we fight together?"

The woman sitting on the ground stared at him for many heartbeats before speaking. "Is this a trick?" she asked.

Trax smiled and drained off his wine. He leaned over to place the glass upon the plinth of the pillar that held her chains. "If it is, it's a bad one," he said, wobbling a bit as he stood. "Last drink for a while – or forever, I suppose! Now, that leaves three masks free for similar idiots."

"Two," Bixa said. "I'm for one. Now we just need two more idiots."

"Can you find them?" Garet asked. He looked from one to the other. They could have no idea of what they would face. It was probably just as well.

"In the palace guard?" Bixa asked, looking slightly stunned at the turn of events. "I'll have to fight them off with my sword when they hear about this insanity."

"Your keys, Captain," Trax said, and then knelt to unlock the woman who had spoken before. He then tossed the keys to Maroster and extended a hand to the woman, who ignored it and rolled upright like an angry cat.

"Do you think you can just put on a mask and be one of us?" she spat.

"I was rather hoping that was the case . . . but no, I suppose not," Trax said. He smiled at the angry woman glaring at him. "I guess I will have to rely on your instructions, Master," he said.

"Madness," Bixa said and shook her head. All around her, the freed prisoners were shedding their chains and standing up to stretch and stare curiously at the king.

Trax could have been at a royal dinner, for all the charm and manners he was extending to the woman who stood before him. It seemed ridiculous in the circumstances, and to be fair, it was really having no effect.

"So, you wish to fight as my apprentice?" she asked. The scorn in her voice caused a rush of nervous laughter from her fellows.

Trax stood straighter. The good cheer vanished from his eyes, and he raised his voice to include all in his reply. "Mask, do not doubt me! I will fight with you and for you. I will stand before our walls amid flame and blood and measure my life in the strokes of my sword. I will neither retreat nor surrender. If the citizens of Shirath are all to die, I will be the first," he shouted, and a reluctant cheer went up from some of the others.

He dropped his shoulders and smiled again. "And if you wish, my good Lady Mask, you can be the second."

The woman went over to talk to the others, leaving out Maroster, who glowered at everyone in the room without any particular favourites. When she came back, the Masks arranged themselves in rough ranks behind her.

"We'll fight, Trax, as we told the Midlander, but with our own weapons and not in your colours."

"Your weapons are being brought, and as for colours . . .

ah! There you are, Barick. Just like old times, eh, finding things lost in the storerooms?"

The historian was puffing down the stairs, his arms full of purple cloth. He stopped, alarmed, at the bottom of the flight when he saw the Masks freed and staring at his burden.

"Yes, Your Majesty. They were still where I put them. Should I . . ." He stopped when the woman came forward and took a purple sash from the pile in his arms.

"I didn't think . . ." she said, and turned to show it to the others. "I threw mine away when I fled to Gost's ward."

"So did I," said a man. He reached out to stroke the silk fabric, tracing the red line that ran beside the purple.

Several others agreed.

"They are yours again," Trax said. "Some we found, and some were taken from your fellow rebels last winter. You see, I really don't care if you think of yourselves as Masks or Duellists, as long as you fight for our city."

The woman slipped the sash over her dusty black clothes. There were tears in the corners of her eyes. "You fool," she said quietly, and waved the rest to come and retrieve their sashes. "That is all we ever wanted."

"Your Majesty," Barick said. He gave the last Mask all the sashes that remained and approached the king. "The captain says you intend to fight the beasts! Please reconsider. After the battle, we will need your wisdom more than ever," he said, hands clasped under his wobbly jowls. "Your royal line will die out! What would your father have said?"

"Hah!" said the king. "That would have been a scorcher of a talk! Don't worry, Barick. Think of it as more fodder for your history of the city. A true scandal to report: 'The King Who Escaped His Duty by Being Eaten Alive.' And as for my royal line, no line of kings lasts long in Shirath. So be of good cheer. Whoever is left alive on the Ward Council will choose a suitable replacement."

He stopped to examine the sweating man before him. After a moment, he clasped Barick's broad shoulders and smiled. "Why, you yourself would make an excellent king, though they might have to widen the throne for you. Yes, you're a man of ponderous dignity and wisdom, so I hope they choose you. No one knows the mistakes of past kings better."

He let the startled man go.

"Now, Garet, shall we marshal our troops and put on our armour? We leave for the Fourth Ward as soon as possible."

Garet put a hand on his arm. "Barick makes some sense, Your Majesty. Your decision was very sudden. I had not expected . . ."

"Such nobility?" Trax asked, then laughed. "Well, circumstances and your wretched example have left me little choice. No, I'm not crazed, Garet, nor as drunk as I'd like to be. I know this is going to be . . . unpleasant, but I really can't ask others to die for me when wearing one of those stone faces makes it possible for me to fight beside them. Now, let's go get that armour on. If Lysere finds out what I'm up to, it will take more than a mask to protect me from my intended's wrath!"

CHAPTER 33
THE CLAWED WALL

Garet stood at the base of the trap, amazed. On either side, walls as tall as a Basher's head angled out from the bridge behind him, which spanned a deep ditch that diverted water from the walls when it poured rain in the winter. Dry now, that ditch had been filled with stacks of oil-soaked branches. A hundred yards away, where the much wider mouth of the trap opened into the fields, more oil-soaked branches had been set in a freshly dug, tightly packed ditch, ready for the torch. The sun, dodging between puffed white clouds, glinted on metal blades sticking up from the top of the walls.

Garet smiled. The master mechanical of the palace had sent a legion of stewards from house to house in every ward, taking knives from any family that had more than one. Not even the king's household had been spared. The argument with the palace cook had been loud and profane, but the king's butler had come out of it with a very red face and an armful of blades.

Now those knives were set in mortar, ready to cut any

demon that tried to crawl over the wall and escape the trap. To help in this, sharpened wooden stakes had been attached inside the walls, pointed downward. Between those stakes, holes pierced the stone to allow long pikes to poke through and bloody any too-eager beast.

That it had taken but a day and two nights to build it all seemed impossible. The mechanicals of every ward had participated, save those of the Eighth Ward where Andarack was rumoured to be working on something special for the city's defence. What that might be, Garet had no idea. But if it came to nothing, this trap was their only hope.

The plan of it had been born after Shirin's death and the meeting in the dining hall. Branet, Corix, Garet, Bixa, and Trax had taken over the Shouting Room to think up an effective defence against fifty demons. Garet had pushed for a confrontation in the fields outside the walls, while Bixa and Corix had argued for letting the demons into a single ward before attacking them.

The king and Shirath's hallmaster had sided with Garet, pointing out that fire as well as steel would be needed to contain so many demons, and in the chaos of battle those flames could spread from a single ward to burn half the city. Branet had gone so far as to suggest giving the silkstone masks back to the ex-Duellists chained in the palace cellars, pointing out that every person capable of fighting demons would be needed to defend the city. In the end, Garet's idea of a trap that might funnel the demons into a kind of killing field was accepted, though not with any great enthusiasm by anyone, even the ex-bane.

The master mechanical was called and told what was needed. To his credit, he made no protest but went straight from the room with Garet's rough sketches. Construction began before the risen moon had shifted more than an arm's length in the sky.

The mechanical had not asked how the beasts would be brought into the trap. When Bixa asked instead and heard Branet's answer, she had the decency to shudder. Now Garet stood there, in the morning of a fine spring day, waiting to see if it would be his friends running for their lives.

"Sir?" said a voice behind him.

At first Garet wondered who the man was speaking to, then realized it must be him. He turned to see the master mechanical of the palace holding out his sword.

"The mechanical who sharpened it is a good lass. She's made it sharp enough to cut dropped silk, sir."

Garet took it and fixed it to his belt. "Thank you for bringing it to me. Your walls are magnificent! We should name it after you, Master Forlor."

The mechanical's smile stretched to its usual extent, meaning the mere suggestion of a curve. He looked at the line of stone and spikes stretching out one hundred yards on either side.

"I'd rather you didn't," he said. "The whole thing is unstable, as we had no time to dig a foundation. Any deep frost will overturn it. Besides, those who laboured on it these past two nights have named it already."

Garet laughed. "What do they call it then?"

The mechanical ran his eyes along the wooden stakes, the pikes sticking out of their embrasures and the knives bristling along the top.

"They call it the Clawed Wall."

"How do I look?" the king asked. He stood with the other city defenders on the bridge connecting the base of the trap to the outer wall gate, and turned around so that his gold-washed cuirass and assorted pieces of armour – all set off by the puffy purple silk of his tunic and trousers – could be admired.

The little woman squatting beside him snorted. She went back to sharpening the point of a pike she held steady over one knee. "You look like you're on parade. Keep the gauntlets, greaves, and cuirass, but discard all else. If you don't, you'll faint ten minutes into the battle. I'm surprised you didn't wear your crown."

Trax peered down at her. "I left it with Barick, in case you turn out to be a poor teacher."

The woman went on sharpening the pike, the whetstone in her hand making long rhythmic passes along the top spike. When she spoke again, her voice was no more gentle than the stone's. "Listen then, child! When it's time to put on the masks, you'll start to feel the fear. It creeps up on you until you dare not move. Mostly, you feel it here," she said, pausing to point the whetstone at her forehead. "That's why the masks work. They shield the worst, but you have to trust in it. When I first feel a demon, I turn my head back and forth, just a little bit so it doesn't seep in around the edges. That makes the fear . . . wobble."

"Wobble?" the king asked, raising an eyebrow.

"Yes, Your Clawed Majesty, wobble," she snapped. "Like the trill in a bird's song or a baby's cry. When you sense that, will yourself to believe the fear is coming from outside the mask. If you can believe that it's not part of you, then you can breathe and maybe fight."

Trax nodded at the sense of this. He knelt to put his head on a level with the squatting woman. "Dear teacher, if

I live today, it will be by your lessons! What is your name and ward?"

She spat onto the stones that paved the surface of the bridge. "Why, do you think you've heard of me? What a joke that would be! Did we meet at some fancy ball or state occasion? Don't fool yourself, Trax. You don't know me."

"Perhaps not, but I was thinking you might be descended from a certain vegetable seller I read about."

She paused in her work to look at him again. Her expression was one of disgust. "If a glib tongue could slay demons, the rest of us could go home. I give you some credit that you're here, but I still hate you, Trax."

"CAN WE FIRE . . . THE ARROW YET?" Dorict gasped. They paused by a first stand of cherry trees, trying to catch their breaths. The Blue looked behind them, staring into the wood lots north of the orchards.

Marick held one hand to the wound on his leg. "Claws!" he said. On the lucky side, the stitches were holding. On the unlucky side, they still had a long way to run. "Not yet, Dorict. They might not see it from here. Let's get nearer the city first."

His friend pushed himself off the trunk and checked the quiver on his back. "We might not make it that far," he said.

A howl sounded far behind them, then another in a different timbre.

Marick shivered. "Don't worry. If you fall into that Racer's mouth, I'll carry on for you."

"Many thanks," Dorict muttered and started running again.

"Stop moving around!" Vinir said. She reached up and pulled Salick down to a well rim that served as her chair.

"Let go!" Salick said, and jumped up again. She looked to where Branet stood just inside the outer gate of the Fourth Ward. He was speaking to Captain Bixa, who nodded and disappeared from sight.

Salick wished she could go with her.

"Why must we be the reserves?" she asked Vinir.

Her friend pretended she had not answered this a dozen times already. "Because the trap may not work, and the narrowness of the bridge limits the number of banes and Masks who can stand together against them."

"But why us?"

Vinir sighed. She too wished to be outside, standing with Master Relict and the others on the bridge. She feared what was coming, but even more she feared that those she cared for would face it without her help.

"Heaven alone can answer that. Perhaps you should ask those priests."

Salick snorted. The priests had been silent participants in the preparations, carrying water and food to the workers. Now they chanted their ancient songs of hope and victory.

"I'm going to talk to the hallmaster," Salick said.

Vinir sighed louder and longer than before and stood to follow.

"Because the first three times he said no might have been a mistake," she muttered.

"Now?" asked Dorict. They had reached the last trees of the orchard. He had the smoke arrow in one hand and the bow in the other.

Marick struck steel to flint and the pitch rag caught.

There were rustles uncomfortably nearby. The two banes looked at each other, one grinning, the other grim.

Dorict shot the arrow straight up into the air.

"THE SIGNAL!" Tarix shouted. She turned to look at the banes hiding behind the one of the long walls of the trap.

"Keep down, everyone. We don't want to attract the demons over here. Don't use the pikes unless one of them tries to come over, and keep your weapons near in case one makes it."

She crouched down, just behind the last half-finished section of the barrier. Ratal and Kesla were beside her. Fifty more Reds, Golds, and Greens waited nervously beyond them.

There was a tingling, then a sharp pain in the Red's knee. She grimaced. Ever since that Basher had run her over, she felt a demon's fear first in her old injury.

"Fix your masks!" the woman with the pike called out. She tied hers on first then checked the king's.

"Remember what I taught you," she said, her voice hollowed by the stone mouth.

"I will, teacher. But I have to say these masks feel very rough on the face," the king replied. "Did you never think of padding them with silk?"

His teacher cursed.

"Claws, no," said the hallmaster. "This is the plan we agreed on. If they call for help, then we go. If they fall, then we are the last defence of the city. You will stay here."

Salick ground her teeth. She had never agreed to this. After a deep breath, she spoke again. "Hallmaster, you know I am a loyal bane, but Garet is out there, and we may never . . . I mean, there are things I have to say to him. I beg you, please let me join him on the bridge."

Vinir stood back, arms folded, and watched the hallmaster shake his head.

"I would rather be out there too, Salick, but a bane serves more than a single man. She serves the whole city. Now tell me, are you a bane?"

Vinir's mouth dropped as Salick stripped off her sash and hung it on the bar of the gate.

"Not today, Hallmaster. If we get through this, you can ask me again tomorrow," she said, and slipped out through the crack.

Vinir grabbed the gold cloth from where it hung and followed, pausing only to say to the hallmaster, "Don't worry, I'll get her back, though it may take a while!"

Branet growled and pushed the door nearly shut. Two small banes slid out unnoticed as he turned to scowl at any others who might have wanted to defy orders.

"We'll get in trouble," Corfin said. He clutched his shortened trident nervously.

Allifur hit him with the flat side of her shield. "We can help," she whispered, and dragged him over to the base of a hastily erected archer's tower.

They crawled underneath the beams and watched some

of the defenders put on their silkstone masks while others looked to where the signal arrow had appeared, tracing a line of smoke against the blue sky.

"Dangerous," Corfin said, and the two smiled at each other.

TRAX FELT something brush by him and barely kept himself from turning his masked face to look. He would have to be careful about that. He watched Salick run through the line and out to where Garet stood in the middle of the trap, looking beyond the fields.

"Pardon her, Your Majesty," Vinir said, stopping beside the king.

"Does she bear a message from Branet?" Trax asked. His neck was getting stiff, but he didn't dare turn to speak to the bane. Every man or woman wearing a mask looked straight ahead.

Vinir coughed. "Well," the Gold said, "she does bear a message."

GARET HEARD RUNNING steps behind him and turned to see Salick crossing the bridge and sprinting towards him. He felt joy, then fear at her being in such a dangerous place, then confusion. Something was different about her, but it wasn't until she came to a stop by his side that he realized what had changed.

"Your sash!" he said. "It's gone."

Salick looked at him, then out into the fields.

"It's all the fashion now, I'm told," she said. "Where are Marick and Dorict?"

"Salick, what are you doing?" Garet asked. Before she had arrived, he had been looking at two dots that might have been the Blues returning, but now he couldn't take his eyes from the young woman at his side.

"I'm doing what I must, just like you did! I want to be here with you, my Midlander fool, more than anything else. Don't worry about the sash. Branet will probably let me wear it again, if your trap works!"

He took her hand, then they pulled each other into a quick embrace and kiss. There was a gust of whistles and calls from the defenders on the bridge, and the two flushed and separated.

"The trap will work, I hope. But I'm glad you are here. If . . ."

Salick put a finger on his lips. "Be quiet, my love. 'If' is always there, especially for banes and king's agents. Look, isn't that . . ."

The dots had resolved themselves into two running figures. They were not alone. A hundred yards behind, two low, quick demons followed.

"Racers," Salick said. She raised her trident, and Garet unsheathed his sword. He strove to unknot the muscles of his shoulders.

"Where's your rope-hammer?" Salick asked. The running banes were closer now, their legs pumping as the gap between them and the demons narrowed.

"No good in a crowd," Garet said. He hefted his heavy chopping sword. "This will have to do."

Garet and Salick stepped aside to let Marick and Dorict pass between them. Salick took the first Racer on the tines of her trident, bracing her feet to stop the speeding demon in mid-charge. The force of it pushed her back several feet.

Garet did not try to stop his. He slashed along its side as it passed, and watched as it tumbled over and over to fall still at Dorict's feet, nearly cut in half.

"A sharp sword," Salick said. She kicked her kill off the trident's points. "Well killed."

"And yours," Garet replied. "I wish a Basher's hide was so thin."

"Are you two going to kiss again?" Marick asked. He pressed a hand to a wet patch on his leg. "We saw you do it when we were running and nearly turned back."

"Don't worry," Dorict said. He pointed towards the orchards beyond the fields. "There's no time for such things now."

CHAPTER 34
THE BLOODY BRIDGE

The trees were bending. Even at this distance they could hear the crack of branches. Beaked heads showed above peach and apple groves. Bashers and Catchers shouldered aside the tortured trunks. A narrow monster swayed above the tallest trees, swivelling its head this way and that before following the path of destruction towards the city.

"Is that tall beast a Stalker?" Dorict asked. His voice was strained, for the fear that came now was tremendous, even at such a distance.

"Yes," Salick said. "Though I've only seen drawings before. You two go back to the bridge now. Garet and I will wait here and draw them in."

Marick bristled, but Dorict dragged him away.

"You seem awfully sure of our courage," Garet said. He worked to keep his breathing steady.

"In this clawed and changing world," Salick said, "it's the only thing I am sure of."

∾

"Wʜᴀᴛ ᴀʀᴇ ᴛʜᴇʏ ᴅᴏɪɴɢ?" the king asked. He peered through the eye slits of the mask at the two banes still standing beyond the bridge.

"They're making sure the demons come to us," his teacher said. "Claws! Are you always so stupid?" She was making small sideways movements of her stone face.

Trax was doing the same. By force of will, he kept the spear points of fear on the other side of the mask, holding them just far enough away that he could move his hands on the hilt of his great sword.

"Always?" he said. "I don't know. Vinir, what would you say?"

"This is the first time we've met, Your Majesty, but since we are all standing here waiting to fight fifty demons, I'd say you are no more foolish than the rest of us."

Vinir had taken a pike from the stack placed at the wall end of the bridge and, from the corners of his eyes, Trax could see her weighing it in her hands with a look of approval before her expression turned serious and strained against the building assault of demon fear.

He tried to laugh at her words, but it stuck in his throat. He covered his discomfort by nodding, relieved to still feel a ripple in the terror assaulting him.

It is outside, he thought, and thought it again until he could force out a poor chuckle.

"Well said, bane. It is an honour to fight beside you."

Vinir smiled. "The honour is mine, Your Majesty."

"I really do hate both of you," the woman said.

Tʜᴇ ꜱᴍᴀʟʟᴇʀ ᴅᴇᴍᴏɴꜱ were breaking out of the orchards now: Shriekers running on all fours, a Squeezer using its long arms as levers to spring forward, Rat demons skittering between the others or clinging to the larger demons.

There were plenty of those. Garet counted at least four Bashers and many others of equal size. They came, not as an army but a mob. A Catcher bowled over a Crawler in its eagerness to reach the two small figures standing within sight. Bull demons and a Tunneller thundered behind it. The Stalker brought up the rear, wavering on its ridiculous stilt-legs.

"No Gliders," Garet said. "Good. But we still have to keep the small ones from getting through the line, or the Masks will all be killed."

"And so will we if we don't move now!" Salick said, and grabbed his hand. The Shriekers were closing fast. She pulled him away and they ran back to the bridge.

The demons were almost at their heels when the first went down with a needle-tipped arrow in its chest. A cheer went up from one of the two towers, each with a masked archer, set between the bridge and the walls. The second demon tripped over the first and died under the king's sword.

Trax backed away, bloody blade held ready, until the three of them were behind the ranks of pikes.

"Shall we fire the ditches at the mouth of the trap?" he asked Garet, but the bane shook his head.

"Not until all are inside. Patience, Your Majesty. Oh, and well killed."

"Thank you," said the king, though it came out as a squeak. The small woman pulled him back into the line, reaching up to smack the back of his head when he tried to turn and face her.

"Keep forward and don't lower your sword," she said. "The rest are coming now."

"They're almost in!" Bixa shouted. She sat on Maroster's shoulders, one hand shading the eye slits of her mask.

Garet looked up to her, then to the archers' towers. A Mask in the left-hand tower waved a red cloth.

"That's it," Garet said. "They're all in now. It's up to Tarix and Corix."

THE DEMONS WERE WELL within the embrace of the walls when Tarix yelled, "Fire the ditch!" Ratal ran out, dragging a lit torch along the brush dug into the ground between the ends of the Clawed Walls. He met another Gold, Cernot, in the centre and both ran back to their respective walls. A new wall of oil-and-wood-fuelled fire barred the demons from retreat. Ratal wiped soot from his eyes and picked up his iron staff.

"Do we attack now?" he asked, shouting over the roar and crackle of the fire. Behind him, Blues brought up piles of brush to feed to the blaze lest it die too soon; others carried wide planks of wood, ready to drop across the flames to create a temporary bridge into trap that would be soon eaten by the flames once the banes had crossed.

Tarix shook her head. She stood on Kesla's thigh to stick her head up over the wall. Between the knife blades, she saw the shambling monsters approaching the bridge.

"Not yet. We need them all fighting the defenders on the bridge so that they're concentrated and a rear attack will have the most effect. We daren't split them up, lest they overwhelm us and break through these walls to get into the city. Patience, Ratal. The banes and Masks on the bridge must hold the line for a while longer."

Ratal frowned, but as soon as Tarix stepped down, Kesla hit him.

"Fool, don't go running off and trying to be a hero. The beasts are still too spread out. That Stalker would scoop you up and bite off your empty head in a second."

Tarix looked across to where Corix and Taron waited as nervously as she.

"Soon," she said, to herself, to Corix, to her husband on the bridge, and mostly to Heaven, if it was listening.

THE DEMONS WERE APPROACHING FAST.

"Unless you plan to hide up there, get your clawed backside off my neck!" Maroster shouted.

Captain Bixa slipped down to the paving of the bridge. She adjusted the mask she wore and drew her longsword, fighting continuously against the wave of fear crashing down on them. Eyeing Maroster's great double-bladed axe and the length of his arms, she stepped back several paces.

The big man stood at the front of the line, plugging a gap in the pikes as the first true wave of demons smashed against the ranks of the defenders.

BRANET STARED through the gate and paled. He turned to the thirty banes, mostly Greens and Golds, who fretted under the terror seeping through the outer wall.

"Steady," he said.

The outer ends of the Fourth, Third, and Fifth Wards had been evacuated. Black Sashes, under the command of Records Master Arict and several retired banes, stood ready to lead the citizens of Shirath out into the wilderness and to some distant city, should it come to that.

Branet prayed to Heaven that it would not come to that.

~

SALICK'S TRIDENT pinned a small Snake demon as it tried to crawl beneath a defender's legs. She pushed it back beyond the line, and Vinir's pike chopped at its armoured head. Stunned, the creature could do nothing as two more pikes jabbed down and pierced its throat and eye.

"Watch out!" Vinir cried, and Salick ducked as a Catcher's long claws swept in to knock down the Mask fighting beside her. The claws caught her trident as they pulled back with the limp body of the woman in their grasp, ripping the shaft from her fingers.

She fumbled for her dropped weapon, vulnerable, but Garet dashed in to hamstring the beast with his sword. As the creature went down, Maroster hacked off one gangly arm and Bixa cut its throat.

"Back up three steps!" the captain shouted. They all retreated, and the monsters coming against them struggled as they crowded onto the bridge. Arrows fell in quick succession, killing smaller beasts and enraging the larger ones. Garet saw the Tunneller fall sideways with an arrow through its tongue, crushing a Horned demon's leg. Maroster chopped down at the Tunneller but froze as a small wrinkled thing flashed by him. The rest of the Masks did the same, and one was immediately gutted by a Shrieker.

"Find that Rat demon!" Garet shouted, dragging back the trembling king.

Banes tried to chase it, but it evaded them, twisting and turning up the bridge on its way to the city wall.

Garet knew if it got behind the archers, all their advantages would be lost.

Two small figures ran forward, stabbing downwards at the beast. It jumped this way and that, but so did its hunters. They seemed just as quick, and soon the one with the shield decapitated it with a well-timed slash. The other picked up the head and ran forward to throw it over the top of the defender's line into the mass of demons beyond.

Maroster shook himself free of Relict's grasp and roared back into the fray. Bixa and the king did the same, though with less enthusiasm.

"Corfin, Allifur! What are you doing out here?" Garet shouted, but the two had retreated to the end of the bridge and were bent over, looking between the defenders' legs for any more demons who dared creep beyond the line.

It was doubtful they even heard him, when every demon bellowed out its rage and every defender screamed back in defiance. Garet ran back to the battle, slashing at the reaching claws of a Basher and bracing the Masks and banes who jabbed at it with their pikes. They forced it back, and the beasts crowding behind it, until they regained control of the bridge. A high-pitched shout of victory sounded in his ear, and he found Marick and Dorict beside him, adding their strength to his.

Garet grabbed them by the shoulders.

"Go now, and tell Tarix and Corix to attack. We won't hold them if more get through and paralyze the Masks again!"

The two Blues nodded and ran back to the end of the bridge and down on each side into the dry wash below. They jumped the bundles of oil-soaked wood that waited for a final fiery defence and looked at each other once before climbing up opposite sides to pass the word to the banes hiding behind the trap's walls.

The Tunneller recovered and resumed its brute passage towards the city. It kept its head low to shield its throat, the only weak spot in its frontal armour. Pike points slid off the flattened plates covering its head and shoulders and barely made a dent in the thick skin of its legs. Step by step it forced the defenders to retreat until they were back at the city end of the bridge.

Again a small demon, this time a Crawler, breached the line. It climbed up on the armoured shoulders of the Tunneller and launched itself over the pikes. Two banes, a Red and a Gold, killed it with their flails but were immediately set upon again. Garet pulled back as many Masks as he could, but the shifting line and the dead demon's jewel left them paralyzed.

"Allifur, Corfin!" he shouted, without any hope of being heard. A man's scream rose as the Stalker lifted him off the ground to rend him apart.

Garet waved his sword at the Blues waiting along the ditches. They threw down their torches and the bridge was engulfed in fire and smoke.

THE TWO YOUNG Black Sashes had seen the giant with the axe fall and ran forward to find the demon responsible. It could not be seen in the mass of bodies and the broiling smoke that now surrounded the remaining defenders.

"Get up! Get up!" Corfin yelled in Maroster's ear, but to no effect.

Allifur searched nearby, but the demon was hidden

from them somewhere in the chaos. Giving up on that, they both tried turning Maroster's head this way and that, but the man did nothing but moan.

"It's no good," Corfin shouted at Allifur. "These masks only work in one direction."

Allifur examined the bodies lying around her. She pulled Corfin closer and said something that made his mouth drop open. He tried to protest, but then saw the look in her eyes. The boy dashed off between the legs of both defenders and demons. He returned quickly, a stone mask in his hand. It was flecked with blood.

Under Allifur's directions, he tied it clumsily to the back of Maroster's head so that its curved frame overlapped with the first and all the strings were knotted together.

The big man shook himself and got groggily to his feet. He felt the new mask with his fingers and looked down at the two children. Corfin pointed to where his axe lay on the ground. Maroster picked it up, turned around in a complete circle, and gave a shout of joy. He ran at the Tunneller, bowling over smaller demons in the process. Reaching the armoured monster, he swung from below, catching the creature under the beak and wounding it so badly that it reared, giving Vinir and Forlinect a chance to set their weapons in its throat.

GARET TOOK a mask from a dead woman on the ground, looked at it, looked at the joyfully violent Maroster, and tied the stone face to the back of the king's head. While he looked for more, the king raised his sword.

"Good thinking!" Trax said, and stabbed a Basher in its side as it tried to run over Relict.

Garet fought on, trying to get the defenders back into a line that might hold. Even with the Tunneller down and many other demons killed, the beasts had scattered the banes and the few remaining Masks.

Relict and Forlinect held the right side of the bridge deck barely a third of the way in. Maroster and Taron stood by them with a knot of ragged Golds and two Masks. The king and Garet held the left side near the same level, with the other Masks and three Reds. The middle of the bridge was now held only by the dead, and down it the Stalker demon came, long-legged, into that gap, moving with a weaving single-mindedness towards the gate.

"Too many have turned to fight us!" Ratal said. He fought side by side with Cernot, knocking down demons so the Old Torrick Gold could finish the stunned creatures with his pick.

"He's right," Corix said. She punched a Shrieker with her bladed gauntlets, knocking it under Tarix's trident. "Our line's too stretched. When the fire is done and we are dead, these beasts will get into the city!"

"Then we'll adapt," Tarix said. She stepped back to see the situation. Counting the Greens and Blues who should have stayed back, at least eighty banes fought to hold that outer line, but Corix was right. Trying to stretch a line from the tip of one wall to the other left them vulnerable. There was a better way to deal with demons, and she knew what it was.

"Form teams of five and help each other!" Tarix yelled. Corix passed the order on to Ratal and the others.

Tarix noticed a Green puffing and wheezing beside her.

353

The young woman fended off a Crawler with her spear and watched it scuttle away towards the bridge.

"Dalesta! I thought you were tending the fires," Tarix said. She rested for a moment, leaning on her bloody trident. Kesla ran past, chasing down a Shrieker before it could get past Ratal.

"Sorry, Master, but the wood is all gone now, so we came in to help."

"There's a bane in you girl, and no mistake," said Tarix. She put an arm around her shoulders. "Now, let's finish off these beasts!"

Dalesta swallowed and lifted her spear. With Ratal and Kesla, they moved forward as a team, isolating and attacking demons as they went and slowly driving them towards a bridge they prayed was still defended.

FINALLY FREED of the need to face in one direction, the king fought with a certain abandon, sweeping his sword in circles that held off the attackers for at least the moment. He knocked aside one of the Stalker's long hands, then backswiped a twisted beast he had no name for. The thing went tumbling head over heels, howling out its pain like a wolf.

The Stalker hooted and swept its arms left and right, knocking back the king on one side and Relict on the other. It took a step forward, then another, and then stopped. It lifted its beak to the sky, and with the grace of a falling tree, toppled backwards, laying itself out the entire length of the bridge. Through the smoke, all could see a clawed hand gripping the shaft of a massive arrow sticking out of its chest.

Garet looked to the archers' towers but they were empty. He had not seen an archer for some time, but there was a sharp clank, and another arrow cut by him to take a Basher in the shoulder. The defenders cheered and pressed in, sealing the gap. Garet looked back to the walls. A wheeled box of great dimension sat before the gates. Branet stood beside it, pointing and yelling.

Garet ran to the hallmaster's side. The front of the box was made of silkstone stuck to a wooden frame and pierced by a single hole in the centre. The rest was covered in wooden planks and the whole thing sat on two iron wheels with a single support beam sticking out the back. As he drew near, another arrow flew through the opening and arched over the defenders. Now he knew what was in the box: the messenger machine Andarack had used to send the king's letters into the Thirteenth and Twelfth Wards. And he guessed these arrows were now tipped with steel instead of words.

"Another miss, Andarack!" Branet growled. "Can't you aim this fool thing?"

Lord Andarack's voice came muffled from within the box. "Not well, and not without sticking my head up and freezing!" he yelled. "That's why I need a bane to guide me."

"I'll stay," Garet said. "Hallmaster, we are holding, but the battle is still to be decided. I beg you to bring out your reserves, for without them, we may yet lose."

Branet looked to where the defenders hacked against demons emerging from the smoke wreathing the bridge. As each appeared, it was set upon by a diminishing number of banes and Masks.

"I will," he said. "You try to make this thing work better!"

And with that, he turned and ran back to the gates.

"Andarack!" Garet called. "Where did you find more silkstone?"

The response was loud enough to cut through the sound of battle. "In the tunnel Gost tried to destroy! Bixa had us dig it out to find any secrets they left behind, and we found this yesterday. Too late to make more masks, but easy enough to glue onto this little toy."

There was a pause in Andarack's speech, and another arrow flew out. The cheers of the banes and Masks told Garet it had found a target.

Andarack, still hidden within the box of stone and wood, continued, "Bixa says Trader Chirat was buying up all the silkstone in the five cities for months now. I fear this is all that is left!"

Garet began to climb onto the top of the box where at least he could see the arrow's flight and what it might hit, but a shout stopped him.

"Back here, lad," a rough voice called, and Garet ran to where the rear of the box gave some protection from the continuous broadcast of fear. Three ward guards huddled there. One of them was Gonect, Andarack's captain of the guard and an old ally of the hall. His arm was still strapped to his chest, but he seemed otherwise hale.

"What are you doing here?" Garet shouted. Even with the protection of the silkstone, it couldn't have been very comforting to be so close to all those demons.

Gonect clapped his good hand on Garet's shoulder. "Someone has to be back here to push this thing forward and adjust the sideways angle for firing. Here, open this hatch and you can talk more easily to the happy couple."

"Couple?" Garet asked, and pushed open the little door. He looked within the box to see Andarack on one side of the arrow-thrower turning a crank to raise it, and Dasanat on the other side tending to a strange collection of spark tubes and wires.

"Can this thing move closer and be more accurate?" Garet asked.

Andarack looked at Dasanat, who nodded.

"Closer, yes. Accurate, no," she said to both of them. "We can fire quickly but it is impossible to aim between shots. And we need a clear space to fire through."

The arrow machine clunked as the last missile fired.

"And we need more arrows," she added. "They are stacked within the gate."

One of the guards, a young man, swallowed and took off at a run, trying to keep the silkstone box between him and the demons. He almost made it, but faltered to tumble down and twitch on the ground.

Garet stood to go and help him, but had to cope with the sudden return of the fear as he left the protection of the box's shadow. While he caught his breath, two small banes ran past to grab the guard and drag him slowly through the gate. After a moment, they returned, each carrying a bundle of arrows.

They dropped them on the ground at Garet's feet.

"We'll get some more," Allifur said, and she and Corfin ran away. On the way to the gate, they passed Branet and the remaining Golds and Greens coming towards the battle. The hallmaster wielded an iron staff of prodigious proportions, and looked as if he could hardly wait to use it.

Gonect wiped his brow. "I'm glad your little banes helped my boy. He's foolish, though brave."

The young woman crouched beside him snorted. "No one's as brave as you, Captain. Or as foolish!" she said, though her voice cracked partway through her jibe.

Gonect laughed at that and said, "Since you're my daughter, there's a good chance you'll outdo me in both measures. Now, let's pass these arrows through the hatch."

Garet looked to the gate and saw Corfin, then Allifur running back with even more bundles of long shafts in their arms.

"Drop them right here, and we'll pass them through," Gonect's daughter shouted at them.

Garet looked over the silkstone covering of the automatic bow. A desperate line of Masks and banes fought off wave after wave of demon. Defenders and attackers were mixed in combat, allowing no easy shot. He swallowed. There was one trick, a desperate one, that might work.

"Andarack, reload the weapon and wait for your chance to fire again, understand?" he said into the hatch.

Dasanat's face appeared. "But we can't fire effectively without a clear target," she said, her voice no different than as if she were discussing the proper temperature of a forge.

"Leave that to me," Garet said, "and congratulations again on your wedding!"

Dasanat actually blushed. "Married life is much more interesting than I thought it would be," she said.

Garet grinned and ran to where Trax directed the remaining Masks, all of them doubly protected with masks of the fallen. A Shrieker lay at the king's feet, and he stomped down on it with a booted foot until it stopped hooting.

"One step forward, please," he shouted. "Pikes to the front! One more step. Drive them back!" he yelled, and thrust his great sword forward to bloody the snout of a Bull demon. The creature swerved and gored Bixa's shoulder.

Garet caught the falling captain and yelled at the king,

"Trax! We have to pull the middle of the line apart and let them in!"

Trax shouted without turning, though the mask tied on the back of his head made it seem he was speaking directly to Garet. "Are you mad? Without this line, they'll get to the gate and inside the city!"

"Andarack's machine needs room to fire," Garet shouted in his ear. "Draw back left and right onto the verge. All the demons are on the bridge now, so none will get behind you. Look, the other banes are joining you now."

A glance showed Trax that the demons in the field were all dead. Corix and Tarix's forces had chased down the last of them and driven the rest onto the bridge. Now those banes attacked the remaining beasts from the rear, and the raging fires below the bridge kept them from jumping over the stone walls and into the ditch to escape. From behind, Branet's reserves swelled their ranks, yet people still died under the claws and teeth of their single-minded, bloody foes.

"Agreed," he said, and swept the flat of his sword to hold back the defenders. "Captain! You take that half and line the road. I'll take the other to this side. And watch out for arrows!"

Captain Bixa held her sword in one hand; her injured arm dangled by her side. She began to force her troops back. Garet saw Trax doing the same, and stood in the cleared space for a moment before he remembered the next part of the plan. When he did, he jumped to Trax's side, waved his arms and yelled, "Now, Andarack! Let fly!"

The machine hummed, clanked, and spat out arrows again, faster than any archer could match and with far greater power. The Bull demon went down in the first two steps of its charge. Next fell the last of the Catchers with three arrows in its belly. A Snake demon reared beside it, only to tumble again, and then more, each of them impaled by the machine's arrows.

"WHAT ARE THEY DOING?" Ratal shouted. "They've opened the line!"

He forced back a Squeezer demon that had tripped Dalesta. Kesla whipped her flail down to smash in the side of the beast's face.

The Gold signalled Ratal to crouch, and she climbed onto his back. From that height, she could see the opened line at the other end of the bridge, the demons going through it, and the first of the arrows firing into their midst.

"Everybody! Get down on the ground!" she screamed and dropped, sweeping out Ratal's legs so that he lay beside her.

The other banes dropped into the mud, soot, and blood at their feet while the demons died and the odd arrow missed its target to pass through the very place they had been standing a moment before.

Tarix spit out a mouthful of red grass. She turned her head to look at Corix, who lay beside her. "I'm going to have a word with Andarack when this is over," she said.

Corix nodded. "You can have as many words as you want, and I'll hold him down while you say them, but when you're done, I want the plans to that demon-slaying machine!"

AFTER THE ARROWS had finished and the machine had ceased its noise, Trax yelled, "Now, from both sides. Let none live!"

The trap closed. Branet held the centre of the line. Trax and Bixa came from the sides, and Tarix rose up with banes of every coloured sash to strike from behind. Men and women still fell, for the creatures were as savage in defeat as they were in victory, but the demons were stopped, surrounded, and finally beaten. Salick and Vinir killed the last, a Digger that was desperately trying to tunnel its way through the rocks of the bridge so that it could attack them from below. There was a cheer from the surviving banes and Masks, a ragged one that barely covered the cries of pain from the wounded.

The wind shifted, and the smoke cleared from the bridge. Garet looked among those still standing, for he was too fearful to search among the fallen. He saw Vinir limping, one arm around a companion, a bane without a sash. Salick raised her eyes and saw him. They stood looking at each other for a long while until Bixa, who had some sense of the importance of the moment, could restrain her groans no longer and Garet had to help her to the carts brought for the wounded.

Trax stood over the body of a woman dressed in black and bearing the broken shaft of a pike. He looked up as Garet joined him.

"I still don't know her name, but it seems I spoke the truth to her. It was by her lessons that I survived."

A member of the palace guard, double-masked like the king, came and held out Trax's sword. It was bloody to the hilts.

"Found it in a big beast's belly," the guard said. His knees wobbled with exhaustion.

Trax put a hand on his broad shoulder and took the

blade from him. "It was kind of you to return it, Stanat," he said.

"Kinder of you to put it there," the guard said. "Beast was trying to tear me apart."

Trax knelt and straightened the purple sash that lay across the small woman's body. He then placed his sword on the woman's chest and folded her hands over it.

"Stanat, when the demons' jewels are removed and the priests come, please tell them that the sword must remain with her until they take her to the burning grounds, and if any relative should come to the funeral, the sword must go to them."

"Why?" asked Garet. He looked at the king and saw tears creeping out from the bottom of the mask to wet his collar.

"Because I cannot leave her a mask in honour of her deeds. Those must stay with us for the city's defence. I think she would agree with that. But I must praise her in some way, Garet, though she'd hate me even more from Heaven for doing it."

They turned to watch banes stumbling around the field and the bridge, chopping open the skulls of the fallen demons, removing their jewels and piling them upon the stones of the road.

"What will you do with them?" Trax asked and attempted to scratch at some itch hidden under the doubled mask.

"They should be taken north, to the depository in the hills," the hallmaster said, "but I fear to send any in that direction until we are sure no more demons wait there."

And so the jewels were piled into silkstone boxes while Andarack, Dasanat, and their guards made do with huddling behind the arrow machine until those boxes were sealed.

"Your trap worked," Salick said to Garet. They walked together towards the Palace Plaza, behind the machine. There was singing coming from the windows of the Fourth Ward. People did not yet dare come out into the streets, but their voices did.

"They think we've won," Garet said.

CHAPTER 35
A NEW DAY

"I thought I'd find you here," Tarix said. She leaned against the doorframe and smiled. "Of course, that was after I thought I'd find you in the dining hall, or in the training room, or perhaps in the records room."

Garet stood up from his old chair and closed the book he had been reading, his old, much-corrected copy of Moret's *Demonary*.

"How did you even know I was in the hall?" he asked.

"By Salick's smile . . . and besides, the king is here and you're his shadow these days," his former master replied. She took the book from his hand and flipped through the pages. "We'll have a lot more to add to this book, and there will be new manuals to write, I fear. Would you care to return to the hall and take up that task?"

Garet smiled. He had been thinking of such things, sitting at his old desk and looking at the notes and drawings he had made, but everything in this room seemed part of his past, not his future.

"I'm afraid you'll have to argue that with the king and the historian, for it seems they both find me indispensable."

Tarix clapped him on the shoulder, then ruffled his hair. "So young to be so important! I am humbled to have had some part in your rise to greatness. Come then, O Hero of the City, we are all meeting to make some sense of events."

They went down the main stairs and into the dining hall. The doors were closed and Ratal stood guard. He was somewhat battered by recent events: his moustache was singed, and he sported a magnificent black eye.

"Claws, what happened to you, Ratal?" Garet asked. "Did you find a demon that could punch?"

The big Gold shook his head. "No," he replied. "After the battle, I told Kesla we'd make a fine couple, and this was her reply!" He stroked the remaining half of his moustache and opened the door for them.

"So that was a no then?" Garet asked.

Tarix shook her head. "Perhaps," she replied, "but remember, it was Kesla, so it could have been an overly enthusiastic 'yes.' Ah, to be young again!"

When they went in, the grinning Gold closed the door behind them.

"At last you rooted him out, Tarix," the king said. He slouched in a chair beside Branet, a cup of wine in his hand.

"Oh, don't frown at my glass," Trax said. He raised the wine in salute and drained it off. "I've been drinking since the troubles of yesterday, and I intend to keep drinking until I can sleep."

Branet gently took the cup away. "Easy, my friend. There's many a bane that's tried that particular remedy . . . much to their sorrow. If you work and train, then sleep of some kind will come."

"And the nightmares?" Bixa asked. Dark circles lay under her eyes.

"The price of a demon's death," Corix said. "And we all pay it."

She poured Bixa and the king tea from a pot left in the centre of the table.

Trax forced himself to sit up and took the cup Bixa passed with her one working hand. He sipped it and shuddered.

"Well, I've had enough of playing bane, Hallmaster, so we had better come up with a way of defending the city that doesn't include me wearing a mask."

"Arrow throwers on the walls," Corix said. She tapped a sheaf of drawings laid out in front of her. "Lord Andarack is lending my hall a pair of mechanicals to build the first and train our smiths."

"A good start," Branet said and scratched his unshaved cheek. "But we cannot count on stopping them outside the walls, especially if they attack at night. We will, I fear, have to split the hall as Tarix suggested and place banes in each ward."

Tarix smiled. She laid a hand on the ex-bane beside her. "It was Garet's idea that I stole, Hallmaster, but I thank you for agreeing. I know this is not what you wanted."

"It is not! But I have little choice, thanks to the harsh lessons of the past weeks. Now, are there any other tactics that might save us lives? We have thirteen banes going to the temple today, and only seven Masks survived the battle."

Tarix lost her smile. She looked down at her scarred hands before she spoke. "That is likely not the final tally. Master Bandat may yet lose her arm, and Taron will be laid up for a month, Banerict says. His infirmary holds three other Reds and a depressing number of Golds and Greens. Who knows how many will return to their patrols?"

Garet spoke into the silence. "It was a dear price, but it bought us much. We know that trained Masks are as effective as banes. Yesterday also proved that the arrow-thrower works for more than messages, and what's more, we've seen masked archers kill demons. Perhaps if banes wear masks, they can use bows without fear of hitting each other."

While the others considered this, Garet turned to Trax and asked, "Are Lord Andarack and Master Mechanical Dasanat making more masks with the silkstone they found in Gost's tunnel?"

Trax laughed, a sudden gust of mirth that swept out much of the misery in the room. "Branet and I decided the newly married couple needed a measure of privacy, so we begged them to take some time away from the cares of the city," he said.

Branet grinned. "As I recall, you threatened to chain them together in your cellars if they refused."

The rest joined in the laughter, though Bixa soon stopped and held her injured shoulder.

Trax put a hand on hers. "My friend, you are wounded and should be at the Physicians School recovering. Others can take your place until you return."

The captain shook her head. "Yes, but first there is the matter of what to do beyond the defences already proposed," she said. "We cannot defend forever, especially if our enemies keep changing tactics."

"Agreed," Corix said. "We must find out more about them."

"I think we all agree on this," Branet said. "And firstly, we need to know if another attack is coming."

Garet shook his head. He looked across at the hallmaster, who nodded for him to speak.

"I think it is unlikely, since this attack failed. If our enemy could acquire demons so easily, they would launch such an assault every week until we were all dead. No, this was an act of desperation. They overstretched themselves to stop the expansion of the city."

"But how did they know of the plan?" Tarix asked. "It means they have more knowledge of us than we do of them."

"Since we have none, that would be no great feat," Corix said. "What do you suggest?"

The Red leaned back in her chair. "Well, the hallmaster, the king, and I have spoken of this. We plan to send scouts out to the north, south, and to the east beyond the Midlands. The west we must leave to Solantor and the other cities there. Our people will seek the source of the demons. Once that is determined, the five cities of the South might be able to join together and mount an attack that will end this threat."

Corix nodded. "A bold plan. We will support it, of course. Have you banes in mind?"

There was a commotion outside the door.

"But I'm guarding the door!" Ratal could be heard to say.

The doors opened and Kesla entered, dragging Ratal by his collar. Dalesta followed them. Behind her came Dorict, Marick, Vinir, and Salick.

"Banes, welcome," Trax said, and sketched a bow from his seat. "Oh! I think I need more tea, Corix, if you would be so kind? Now, Tarix, would you mind explaining their mission?"

Tarix stood and looked over the assembled banes. "You are chosen to be our eyes and ears, and I fear you must travel far from the protection of our walls to find the source of our sorrows. Kesla will take Ratal and Dalesta east, beyond the borders of the Midlands. Hallmaster Corix will take you part of the way, and I have a letter of introduction for the hallmaster of Bangt."

Kesla nodded, and Dalesta coughed, wide-eyed at the news.

Tarix smiled at her. "After yesterday, I have every faith in you, Green. Now, Vinir, Dorict, and Marick will travel to the Far South, taking a ship from Solantor past the great desert."

Dorict looked thoughtful, then nodded. Vinir smiled down at Marick, who began to twitch in anticipation of the adventure.

"We should take Allifur and Corfin with us," the little Blue said.

Dorict gave his friend a push and said, "I think not. Besides, someone has to stay here and make trouble – since you will be gone!"

"True," said Marick, "and they are the most promising of my students."

Tarix, Branet, and Corix each raised an eyebrow in masterly unison.

"And I, Master?" Salick asked, for she found herself left last in the tally.

Tarix smiled at her confusion. "You will also leave from Solantor, but in the opposite direction. You must travel on the great ships that sail to the North, for the forest is too dangerous to traverse on foot."

"Am I to travel alone?" Salick asked. She held her eyes on the Red.

"Why, is there someone with whom you wish to travel?" Tarix asked, her tone one of innocent curiosity.

"Enough!" Branet said. "Stop teasing the girl. Garet will

travel with you. You all go under false stories, so you cannot wear your uniforms, I fear."

Trax winked at Garet. "It's a shame to let you go, since you were finally becoming useful, but I feared Salick's wrath if I refused."

Salick faced him and said, "You need not, Your Majesty. Your recent actions have . . . lessened my wrath."

Trax smiled. "Well, that is more amazing than demon armies and arrow machines! Friends, I must return to the palace to prepare for the ceremonies at the temple. Garet, would you go with me please? There is much yet to say."

Salick stepped up and put a hand on Garet's shoulder. "I fear that I must steal him from you for the day, Your Majesty. We also have much to say before we go to the temple."

Trax dismissed them with a wave of his fingers, and they left the room together, hand in hand.

THE SEABIRDS CALLED to each other in harsh, unlovely voices.

They must be lovely to each other, Garet thought, looking up from the great docks of Solantor. *Or else they'd never gather in such numbers.*

Sky-covering flocks of the grey and white birds flew over the bay, escorting the small boats out to the fishing grounds. Only a few payed attention to a long, lean craft that followed them, the oars pulled by twenty Solantor banes, ready to assist the fishers if a water demon appeared. No bird bothered with the largest boat, a three-masted giant that had already turned south-west, sailing towards a more favourable current for the long voyage down the coast.

Salick lowered her arm. At this distance, it was impossible to say if Vinir, Marick, or Dorict had done the same. The parting had been emotional for Salick and Vinir, calm for Dorict, and impatient for Marick.

"Come on," he had said, almost jumping up and down in his eagerness to explore their transportation to the City of Fountains in the far south. "Adventures await!"

Garet felt a touch of fear as he watched their sails get smaller. Not demon fear, but a nagging unease that something was ending here, and that, when they met again, things wouldn't be the same.

Salick wiped at her eyes and nudged him. "Well, they're off, but our ship won't leave for two more days! Do you want to go aboard again?"

Garet shrugged. "No, thank you. The captain took our coin, but he has already made plain what he thinks of two traders from such a backward town as Shirath! You saw the bunkroom I'll be staying in?"

"It's no worse than mine!" Salick answered. "And besides, they suit the lie we travel under." She stopped to look around, but the only spies were a handful of perched seabirds. Their comments were neither musical nor comforting.

Garet sighed. It would be weeks of cramped living, and a frustrating lack of privacy, but at the end would be the North, and maybe the answer to a question that had haunted Shirath, Solantor, and all the other cities along the River Ar for six hundred years: why do the demons attack humans, and who is behind them?

"Back to the banehall?" he asked.

"Claws, no!" Salick said. "The Reds I'm with look at me as if I were scraped off the bottom of a boot, even though they know I'm both a bane and a master." She made to touch the red sash that should have been hanging across her chest, but the secret nature of their mission meant that they had to dress as ordinary traders whenever they left the Solantor banehall.

Garet smiled. "And a master well made!" he said. "It's the same for me. And there's also this . . ." Here he waved a hand at his own face with its skin darker than any in the city. "It's like when I first came to Shirath, though the name 'crow' hasn't been used yet."

Salick frowned. "Do they call you something else?"

Garet didn't answer that question. As an agent of Shirath's king, he was confident enough to fight his own battles. Besides, he had no wish to unleash Salick's fury on the Golds with whom he shared a room. They needed the goodwill of Solantor's banehall for two more days.

"I know," he said, taking Salick by the arm. "Let's go to the city centre and see the palace and temple again. We may never get another chance."

He stopped short when Salick didn't move to follow him. He came back and looked into her eyes. They were far away, maybe to the south with Vinir, or to the north where they must soon go, or perhaps back to the east where Shirath lay, beautiful with its tall white walls standing on each bank of the Ar.

Salick blinked – and discovered Garet's close examination.

"Claws!" she said and stepped back. "What do you mean we won't get another chance? We're coming through here on the trip back to Shirath, aren't we?"

Garet laughed, glad she had come back to him, and hoping that she always would.

"We may, and we may not. For all we know, the trail to our enemies may lead us back along the eastern mountains, or down to the Midlands again, or even through the forest that lies between the North and Shirath." He raised an eyebrow. "We may even meet Tarix on the way back."

Looking around one more time to make sure no unfeathered listeners were near, Salick shook her head. "I still don't see why they kept her mission to search the forest such a secret. We weren't even told until the day we left."

"Hers was the only one they could keep secret, I suppose," Garet said. He waved a hand at the departed ship, then at all the ships lining the long docks. "Too many people in Solantor's palace and hall know where we are going, though they kept us here for a whole season waiting on their approval! Hallmaster Corix can send people east, and Tarix and her team can leave quietly from Shirath. It makes sense. With the army of demons having come from that direction, somebody has to go into the trees and search. I'm just glad it wasn't us."

Salick gave him a pitying look. "Say that again after we freeze all winter in your precious North."

"It's my parents' North, not mine," Garet said. "Though I do want to see it, at least once."

Salick started walking, then abruptly stopped. "Garet, I haven't asked you about this, but aren't you worried about . . . meeting him?"

Garet grimaced. "My father? Yes, I am, though there's no saying where he really is. It was just a rumour my mother heard, that he went back North."

"Leaving both her and your sister in Bangt," Salick said, her tone clearly showing what she thought of the man. Looking at Garet's expression, she suddenly pushed him into forward movement. "Forget him! He's nothing to do with you, and our mission has nothing to do with him. Let's go to the temple then and send up a prayer for a safe journey south for those three, though it may take more than one prayer since Marick's with them."

The two linked arms again and walked towards the temple complex. There, under the high blue domes, they could wish their comrades well. If they decided to add pleas for their own safe return, Garet knew that Heaven was grand enough to hear all their requests, though it was fickle about which ones it granted.

Without even the smallest hope of food, the handful of birds perched on the dock scattered, some south, some east, and some north, for the larger flock to the west was far away now, and these few had been left behind to survive on their own.

LIST OF NAMES

Adrix: A hallmaster of Shirath Banehall.

Alanick: A seer and astrologer of the Fifth Ward.

Allifur: A Black Sash of Shirath Banehall.

Andarack: A mechanical, lord of the Eighth Ward, and Master Mandarack's brother.

Aralon: A Green Sash of Shirath Banehall who looks to Master Tarix.

Arict: The old records master of Shirath Banehall.

Bandat: A master of Shirath Banehall. Salick looks to her.

Banerict: A skilled physician who serves in the banehall infirmary.

Banfreat: A baker who became the first Shirath hallmaster six hundred years ago.

Barick: Once the king's butler and now the historian.

Birat: An early, cruel king who used a necklace of demon jewels as a punishment.

Birsal: Lord of the Eleventh Ward.

Bixa: Captain of the king's guard.

Boronict: A bane of Old Torrick Banehall who is now the hallmaster in Bangt Banehall.

Branet: A master of Shirath Banehall and ally of Mandarack. He took his place as hallmaster. Known for his temper.

Braxa: Lord of the Sixteenth Ward.

Cernot: A Gold Sash of Old Torrick Banehall. He looks to Hallmaster Corix.

Chabost: The chief priest of the Shirath temples.

Chetorth: A Green Sash of Shirath Banehall who looks to Master Taron.

Cheza: A king's agent.

Chirat: The wealthy head of a Trader family in the Twelfth Ward.

Choan: A bane of Old Torrick Banehall.

Chovan: A master of Shirath Banehall who once taught Tarix.

Corfin: A Black Sash of Shirath Banehall and friend of Allifur.

Corix: Hallmaster of Old Torick Banehall.

Cruster: A guard of the Thirteenth Ward.

Dalesta: A Green Sash of Shirath Banehall who looks to Master Taron but sometimes trains with Master Tarix.

Dasanat: The master of all the mechanicals in Shirath. She works with Lord Andarack and helped develop the silkstone suit of armour.

Dorict: A Blue Sash of Shirath Banehall. He is friend to Garet, Salick, and Marick.

Draneck: Salick's cousin and a Duellist who was demon-killed while trying to murder Garet.

Falor: A Green Sash of Old Torrick Banehall who looks to Hallmaster Corix.

Forlinect: The training master of Shirath Banehall. Garet works with him to train the Black Sashes of the hall.

Forlor: The master mechanical of the palace.

Garet: A young man born in the Midlands and taken to Shirath Banehall by Master Mandarack to be a bane. He is now a Green Sash who looks to Master Tarix.

Gonect: Lord Andarack's chief of guards in the Eighth Ward.

Gost: Uncle to Lord Kirel of the Thirteenth Ward.

Hoster: A guard of the Sixth Ward.

Kaela: Wife of Lord Kirel of the Thirteenth Ward.

Kesla: A Gold Sash of Shirath Banehall. She looks to Tarix.

Kirel: Lord of the Thirteenth Ward, husband of Kaela, and nephew to Gost.

Kitoroth: A Gold Sash of Shirath Banehall. He looks to Taron.

Lysere: The intended of King Trax of Shirath.

Mandarack: A master, and then hallmaster, of Shirath Banehall who trained Salick, Marick, Dorict, and Garet. He died killing the Caller demon, a fearsome beast who could control others of its kind. Lord Andarack is his brother.

Marick: A Blue Sash of Shirath Banehall. Known for his tricks, he is friend to Garet, Salick, and Dorict.

Maroster: The chief of guards for the Thirteenth Ward and henchman to Gost.

Ratal: A Gold Sash of Shirath Banehall. He looks to Tarix.

Reebat: A disagreeable old woman who runs a second-hand shop in the Fifteenth Ward.

Relict: A master of Shirath Banehall and husband to Tarix. Salick's friend, Vinir, looks to him.

Riga: A Green Sash of Shirath. She looks to Tarix.

Sacourat: Lord of the Fifth Ward.

Salar: A Gold Sash of Shirath. He looks to Relict.

Salick: A Gold Sash of Shirath Banehall. She looks to Bandat, though she once looked to Mandarack. Friend to Marick, Dorict, and Vinir. She and Garet are very close.

Salorex: A king's agent.
Sata: A Black Sash of Shirath Banehall.
Shinock: Shirin's uncle who lives by thievery in the Maze of the Fifth Ward.
Shirat: The first king of Shirath, and a man of strange humours.
Shirin: An ex-Duellist who blames Garet for the death of her love, Draneck.
Shula: A king's agent.
Stanat: Lieutenant of the king's guard.
Tarix: A master in Shirath Banehall and wife to Relict. Garet looks to her. She was once restricted to a wheeled chair or crutches by a demon-caused injury but has lately returned to regular patrols.
Tarock: The son of Lord Tiralsh of the Twelfth Ward. An ally of Gost.
Taron: A master of Shirath Banehall. He is a friend to Relict and Tarix.
Tiralsh: Lord of the Twelfth Ward.
Toovad: A Trader of the Twelfth Ward.
Torfor: A baker in the Palace Plaza market.
Tortal: Lord of the Sixth Ward.
Trax: The king of Shirath. An ally of the banehall, although in the past he has opposed it.
Vinir: A bane of Shirath Banehall and good friend to Salick, Garet, Marick, and Dorict. She looks to Master Relict.

About the Author

Kevin Harkness is a Canadian author who, at a late age, began writing the books he wanted to read. He lives in Vancouver, walks a lot, and occasionally mutters.

https://kevinharkness.ca

Ingram Content Group UK Ltd.
Milton Keynes UK
UKHW040824030723
424469UK00004B/240